THE ROSE AND THE VINE

THE ROSE AND THE VINE

Unity Hall

This edition specially produced for
The Leisure Circle Limited
by HEADLINE BOOK PUBLISHING PLC

Typeset by Alacrity Phototypesetters,
Banwell Castle, Weston-super-Mare.
Printed in Great Britain

For my dear Philip Wrack,
for all his help and support,
and the quite remarkable dedication
he showed in assisting the
research into champagne.

Acknowledgements

I would like to give my most sincere and grateful thanks to the many people who have helped me with this book.

In particular to the marvellous and enthusiastic Philippe le Tixerant, the Délégué Éxterieur d'Affaire of the Comité Interprofessionnel du Vin de Champagne who gave so freely of his time to answer questions and open Champenois doors.

And to another enthusiast, the champagne historian Colonel François Bonal, who was also so generous with his time and with invaluable information. As a collector of praise to champagne, I hope he will approve the words that begin the cover story on this book.

To Monsieur Christian Bizot and his charming wife, Hélène, of Bollinger, who were generous enough not only to inform, but to entertain with style and great courtesy in their own home.

Also to Malcolm McIntyre of the C.I.V.C. in London, who kindly made so many helpful arrangements for me.

And last, but not least, to the people of Champagne who grow the grapes and create the wine. Those I had the good fortune to meet were always ready to explain their art. I thank them for that, and for their wine that never fails to create a celebration.

BOOK ONE

Chapter One

"And what do you want?"

The perpetual note of belligerence was in her father's voice. She could hear him quite clearly from the kitchen where she was scrubbing down the deal table. She had already registered the strange footsteps on the wooden verandah that ran along the front of the house; a man's footsteps, but definitely not those of her brother. The screen door had rattled and with a muttered curse her father had gone to see who was outside.

"I said what do you want?" he repeated.

"Work ..."

The answering voice was lighter than her father's, but it was not an American voice. The sound of Europe came through in the one word.

Curious, she put down her scrubbing brush and moved from the shady kitchen into the hallway where she could glimpse through to the front door.

"I haf no work to give you." Her father's own accent became more defined when he was irritated. His stance showed impatience and bad temper as he stood silhouetted in the doorway, the brilliant late-summer sun drawing his outlines square; his hairless head a round cannon-ball above.

"I think perhaps you do." She could not see the other man, her father's bulk blocked him, but his voice sounded young and self-assured. The accent was not German though. Something else that held a trace of familiarity.

"Oh yeah!" her father snarled, and as she hovered in the shadows she gave a quick little smile and her shoulders hunched upwards in a sharp movement of pleasure. Few people stood up to Hans Brunner. Like all bullies he was disconcerted when they did so. She enjoyed these rare moments of his discomfiture.

"Yes," the stranger said, his voice confident. "I have been regarding your vines. They have need of attention."

It was true. The twelve acres of vines were too much for her brother Peter, her father and herself to cultivate properly. There was blight in another field, and the weeds were taking over on the hillside. The dreaded phylloxera bug had decimated one field which they had burned. The twisted remains lay blackened and grim under the hot California sun. Her father feared it would spread to the healthy vines.

"And what do you know about vines?" Her father had stepped forwards onto the verandah, clearing her view so she could see the stranger. He was tall, perhaps six feet, and muscularly lean. He wore workaday dungarees and the faded cotton shirt of a farm labourer. But the face was at odds with the clothing. He had a satyr's mass of curly black hair springing from a high forehead, long dark eyes set wide of a slender, thin bridged nose. His chin was short and square and his mouth almost too red, but full in the lower lip. It was a face drawn in the careful strokes of an artist creating a handsome man. He had the looks, she thought, of a gentleman.

"I am a *vigneron*." He sounded proud, and his shoulders straightened, straining through the rough cotton fabric that covered them.

"A *vigneron*?" Her father seemed to be thinking about the word. "From where?"

"Champagne."

It was fitting, Rosie thought. They said champagne was the supreme wine, so it must produce the supreme man, like the one who stood on their weather-worn verandah, unimpressed by her father's scowls and threatening posture. She stepped forward and trying to keep the eagerness from her voice said:

"Pa, ask the gentleman in out of the heat."

Her father turned to face her, his features blacked out by the flooding sun behind. She could not read his expression, but she felt that the single word champagne had impressed him. Her father loved the grapes and his wines a deal more than he loved his children. He laboured and sweated in the heat of the wooded and rocky valley where they had settled, trying to reproduce the golden scented harvest of his native Rheingau. He had not yet achieved his objective, any more than he had achieved any of his golden dreams in the New World.

The stranger had moved to stand level with her father, his eyes narrowed to peer into the hallway where she stood. With a spurt of pain and embarrassment she was aware of her plain gown, the stained apron, her roughened hands and untidy hair. She quickly moved back into the shadows, postponing the moment when his eyes, clear of glare, would see her properly: a too thin girl of eighteen who had never found a man that attracted her. Not that there had not been offers aplenty in this community where women, and particularly pretty women, who could work, were scarce and sought after.

4

"Madame," he was saying, bowing slightly, his eyes still sun blind.

"Come on in," she said quickly. "You'll get yourself a dose of sunstroke out there in that heat."

He laughed.

"I am used to the sun," he said, and she had a passing vision of a place of ordered hillsides where man had conquered the land and the land did what it was bid. Perhaps not unlike her father's native hillsides which he would describe when whisky had mellowed him for that eggshell moment before the one too many tot coarsened him.

The stranger had taken her at her word and was coming into the cool of the hallway. Once he was inside, she said impulsively: "Champagne country? Is it hot?"

"In the winter Le Champagne –" he pronounced it differently this time, with a nasal accent on the end of the word – "is very cold. It has snow and much rain. But when the sun shines it is hot and it is beautiful."

"Where is it?" she asked abruptly. "In Germany?"

"Indeed no," he said, his pointed eyebrows rising. "In France."

That was it. That was the trace of something remembered in his voice. "My mother was from France," she told him. "Paris."

"A fine city," he said and sounded sad. She could see that his eyes were appraising her and she quickly bunched her apron, to hide the stains.

"You want work?" she asked.

He nodded.

"Now, Pa, we sure need help." She heard the hectoring tone come into her voice, the tone she had adopted with him from the time she had grown too big to be beaten and since his continuing defeats from the siren call of the New World had quietened his natural bellicosity. "How many folks around these parts know about the vines? If this gentleman here is from France he'll be a heap of help to you and Peter." Her natural confidence was returning. She turned to face the Frenchman, hands on hips. "Pa's not rich, but we can give you a bed and your keep and maybe a few dollars besides, eh, Pa?"

The brief silence seemed to quiver and for the rest of her life she would be able to conjure up that moment. She would recall the dark shapes of the men in front of her, the open door and beyond it golden light dappled by shadows thrown by the oak set square in the scrub of dusty grass in front of the house. The light wavered as her father stood thinking.

"You can prune?" he asked gruffly.

"Of course, and weed and layer and pick – it is nearly time you were picking. I can make all that is necessary." His voice was impatient as if the question was superfluous. "In Champagne my brother

5

and I ran our vineyard together, *les deux* ...”

“Must have been small,” her father grunted.

“Less maybe than yours. Not sufficient, *hélas*, to serve us both. And with the coming of the phylloxera ...” He shrugged.

Her father was softening, his shoulders beginning to loosen.

“We got it here, too,” he said. “All over California.”

“I saw you had burned a field. But it is no use to burn. It is bad?”

“Bad enough. That field you saw was a first planting of slips from European stock. Thought they might resist it, but it got them too.” He cleared his throat noisily as he always did when he had a change of heart or mind against his better judgement. “Like a drop of whisky?” he asked. “Or you can try the wine that came from that field. It isn’t bad. I come from a family of vine-growers myself. In Germany. Rheingau ...” He waited and received the reaction he required when the Frenchman made a murmur of respectful approval. The murmur clinched it. Her father was stomping into the kitchen, beckoning the younger man to follow him, and shouting: “Get us food, Rosie, and bring the whisky and wine.”

She moved back to the kitchen herself, her tread measured, careful not to let her father see she was pleased. She and he conducted a war of attrition, but one which wore down only her younger brother, Peter. Nature had been confused when she and Peter were born. His looks were soft, his build slight and girlish, and the features that they shared were too delicate for a man, while on her they were almost too strong for a woman. At a time when the fashion was for delicate blondes, she had the black hair of her mother and her mother’s wide mobile mouth.

And she was the fighter. Peter the peacemaker.

Had Peter been at home, her father might have been less antagonistic when the Frenchman first arrived. Rosie was aware that her father could never really relax before her. She was too strong for his comfort. He needed to be the dominant, masculine figure. But for all her competent housewifery, and her buried yearnings for a fulfilled life with a man, she was the man of the family. It was her strength that kept their existence tolerable in the isolation her father had chosen for them.

Now, with the Frenchman sitting at her newly scrubbed table, thoughtfully sipping at her father’s wine and listening to his stories of life back in Rheingau where the finest wines in the world were produced, she felt a rising warmth inside her. She was acutely aware of her breasts and her breathing. She could feel the soles of her feet and the pads of her fingers as if they were a series of small, hot particles and each one blazed with a warm, orange fire.

She knew that her body was responding to the man who sat before her with the sunshine full on his face as it streamed in through the kitchen window. The sun seemed to find him as if he were a sliver of glass, a mirror or a magnet that attracted only the light. And when he nodded his head in agreement, or maybe simply to defer to her father's statements, she found herself fearing that such brightness must ignite itself and blaze away into nothing.

And if she was aware of him, he was aware of her. Her intelligence told her that, though her lack of vanity decided this could not be for any reason other than natural curiosity. The dark lashes, long as a child's, that curtained his eyes, were raised when she neared. Raised just sufficiently to show how blue the whites of his eyes were around the deep blue iris.

"I came here for the gold rush," her father was telling as he slurped more wine into the Frenchman's glass. "Ach! Like all my life, I was too late. I should have stayed home. But it was much the same as for you. Too many family, too little land to support us. I was going to make my fortune, come home with a sack of gold." He snorted. "And I'm still here. And there's no gold in the grapes."

"It was a long time ago, the gold rush," the Frenchman said in his careful English.

"Forty-nine," her father said. "I got here in 1851 – too late. It was pretty much over. And now we're heading for a new century. Where did the years go, eh? That's what I ask. I was a young man then. Just twenty. Same hopes, same dreams a fellow like you must have. But it never worked out."

"For me it will work out." The Frenchman said the words as a flat statement of fact.

Her father grunted, sighed and poured himself another whisky. "That's what I thought once, mister." He shook his head and then asked: "What's your name and how old are you?"

"I have twenty-three years and my name is Jean Paul Dupuis. And you, monsieur? And your daughter?"

"I'm Hans Brunner. She there's Rosie. My son is Peter. He'll be in soon."

Rosie had found a clean linen tablecloth and was setting the table, placing the knives and forks her mother had brought from France in front of the men and making two other places for herself and for Peter.

"Rosie," the young man said thoughtfully, and she had never heard her name sound so pretty as he spoke it with the last 'e' longer and lingering. "*Enchantée*, Rosie," he said, and rose to half-bow to her.

She felt the blood run up into her cheeks, as she stood, the knives and forks in her hand, a complication of emotions seething under her stoic face. She wanted to tell him she was really Rosanne, not common-or-garden Rosie. She always thought of herself as Rosanne, but her confidence had gone again.

7

"Glad to know you, Jean," she said, trying to duplicate his pronunciation of his name.

"Jean Paul," he corrected her gently. "In France we use both names."

She wanted to be cool and sophisticated like the French women that he must have known back in Europe; women with whom he drank champagne. What was champagne? She knew it sparkled and she knew it was expensive, but she couldn't imagine how it would taste or look. It would be like liquid honey, she decided, but heard her deep throaty voice say: "Jean Paul? That sure is a mouthful."

He laughed.

"No, not at all. It runs from the tongue."

Silenced, she turned on her heel and went back to the wood-burning stove where a meat stew bubbled in a blackened pot. She dropped in some peeled potatoes, leaning over the hot steam that swirled up, to give some reason for her burning cheeks.

She was certain he was still watching her even though her back was turned to him, and it pleased her, but she busied herself with the stew, checking it for salt, stirring and watching the bubbles form on its thick surface.

At moments like these when her father talked and she worked, Rosie would retreat to her private world of fantasies, but today it was not possible. Normally she could switch off her surroundings and would daydream of how her life might have been had the Brunners' circumstances not changed so dramatically when she was nine years old.

Her father was relating the old disaster now to Jean Paul, and he seemed to be listening with interest, leaning on the table, all his attention directed to the old man.

"I thought it would all work out, too, and for a while there it nearly did," her father was saying. "Things were good. After the gold rush ended, back in fifty-seven, there was an experiment to produce fine Californian wines at Anaheim. It's well south of here. Hotter country. Everyone involved in the project was German. I was twenty-four years old and hanging around San Francisco. I'd got a stake I'd stashed away from the gold-mining days, so I made my way south, and they let me join. They even welcomed me with open arms. I was German, and I knew about wine. I was one of the few who did."

"It was a success?" the Frenchman asked. Her father shook his head slowly and outside in the yard she could hear Peter working the handle of the pump, sluicing away the morning's dust before coming in for his food. He would be surprised to see the stranger. Surprised and pleased, she thought.

"Yah. For a while there it was great. We had our ups and downs and come fifty-nine, fifty of us Germans bought the stock. I got my share of

8

it, and I was doing great. We were one of the leading wine areas in the whole Goddamn country. We had the acreage and we had the production. But we were using the old mission vines and hardly anyone involved knew anything about wine-making. Basically it was a mess. What we turned out tasted like foxes' piss, but it sold. Nobody knew any better.

"The place flooded in sixty-two, but we got over that until the vines took disease in the eighties and destroyed the project for good. It went bust." He was back in time, talking of the might-have-beens. "Lost practically every cent I had," he was saying. "So I came back up here where the climate's more like home, to have a try at producing something better. My wine ain't great, but it don't taste like fox piss."

Peter came into the kitchen and she was standing waiting with a towel for him to rub his face and hair dry. He looked questioningly at her as he wiped his fingers, one by one.

"Just about to tell this young fellow about the good old days when we had a mite of money," Hans turned to say to his son. "He's a vine-grower himself. From France. Come to give us a hand."

Rosie always knew what her brother was thinking. Coming through the door and seeing the stranger sitting at the table had produced first suspicion, then anger that her father was drinking, followed by boredom that he was telling the old tale again. And then she felt his lightning change of mood to relief at the idea of help around the vinery. The bulk of the work always fell to him.

"Pleased to meet you, mister," he said, smiling.

"And I you," the Frenchman said, rising to his feet.

"The kids don't remember too much about those early days," her father went on as Peter settled himself at the table and she began to ladle out the food. "But they were good days, even if the wine was lousy."

"Which grape did you grow?" The Frenchman was attacking his food as if he had not eaten in a long time, but carefully so as not to spill any, and she recognised the table manners their mother had taught her and Peter.

"Mission grapes. Vines the Spanish priests brought through California when they set up missions in the area. That was before California was part of the United States. Every mission had its own vineyard to make the sacramental wine. That's all those vines are good for. But they are tough. They still use them a lot in these parts. By the time our project in Anaheim went bust we were doing better, using European root stock. That's what I've been trying here." He was pushing his food down his throat as he talked, the whisky getting to him.

Jean Paul laughed shortly.

"And in France, to combat the phylloxera, we are grafting onto

9

American root stocks. Will our wine taste like the piss of the fox?"

"God knows," her father said, his voice doubtful. "They say that when the grafts take, the wine is like that from back home. It could be as good. Better, one day."

"You are right," Jean Paul agreed. "It is true that it can be a success."

As she sat down to eat her own food, mentally rejecting her father's dreams, Rosie was aware of the Frenchman still watching her from under his dark lashes as she watched him from under hers. He was leaning back so that the sun was out of his eyes, and his face in the shadow looked finer drawn and the skin darker. He was like someone from the stories she had read when she and Peter had been little, when they lived at Anaheim with their mother to look after them and teach them about the world outside.

The Frenchman was eating slowly and carefully now, his first hunger relieved. She liked his table manners, and consciously she improved her own. They had lived too long in this outback. Peter and her father had, in self-defence, taken to the speech, the habits and customs of the small farmers who made up their few neighbours. It made for more comfort. But she had stubbornly refused to change, and she had suffered for her refined manners at the school. Mockingly the boys would sweep the boardwalk in front of her feet with their caps as she walked along and, in retaliation, she accepted it as her due.

"The kids' ma was French," her father said, putting down his fork. "She was teaching 'em the lingo. Say something in French, Rosie."

She had a memory of her mother, merry eyes in an olive-skinned face, saying, '*Répétez après moi ... ma chérie.*'

"*Répétez après moi, ma chérie,*" she said, and laughed.

The Frenchman laughed too, his head thrown back, his mouth open, so she could see the soft red of his palate.

"And what did you repeat, mademoiselle?" he asked.

Her mother's face was clear in her mind again, the black hair looped back, the full, naturally red lips, mouthing the lesson, encouraging, loving ... gone.

Automatically she said: "*J'ai, tu as, il a, elle a, nous avons, vous avez, ils ont, elles ont.*"

"Ah, you know the verb to have," and added, "and you have an accent *formidable*, mademoiselle. But can you *tell* me something in French?"

She looked at the sun on his face, and it was as if her mother were there, prodding at her memory.

"*Il faut beau, monsieur,*" she said.

"It is indeed a beautiful day," he said, his eyes on her mouth. "A most beautiful day."

"How long you been here?" her father asked, shovelling the last of the gravy on his plate onto a chunk of the bread she had baked that morning.

"Two years," the stranger said. "I came in by ship to New Orleans. I worked my way here."

"You come by the train?"

"Yes. In stages, you know. When I needed money I stopped a while. Found work. Then came on."

"I hear they're growing vines back in New York state," her father said. "Would have been nearer."

"Too cold," the Frenchman said positively. "I wanted to find the sun. And a new life, far from Europe. Here is very far fom Europe."

"You can say that again," her father said. "I came across the Isthmus. At Panama. It was a choice of that or round the Horn. Chagres, where we took the boats up to 'Frisco, has to be the worst place on this God's earth. Jesus! The filth, the people – all coming from all over the world for the gold. Chinks, Irish, Japs. You heard every tongue, and my God you needed to watch your back."

The tale of his journey would occupy him for a little while yet. Rosie got to her feet and removed the plates, putting them in the bowl ready to wash when she had boiled some water. Peter got up to help her, throwing the scraps from the plates into the yard for the chickens.

"The Frenchman seems OK," he whispered.

She just nodded, lips pursed, as she moved to take some apples and grapes from the big larder, ready to put on the table.

"It'll be fine to have some help," he said, still whispering.

She turned and smiled at him, a smile that widened her full mouth to show neat teeth and lit the flecks in her amber eyes.

"It's time," she said, "He expects too much of you."

"And you, as well," he said.

"Just put the fruit on the table," she told him.

She could hear her father's voice still telling the old, old story as she slipped through the kitchen door having filled her apron with some corn for the chickens. She stood outside in the strength of the afternoon sun, throwing handfuls while she walked down the path and towards the trees. It was not the time she normally fed the birds, but she needed to think. She felt as if her life had turned upside down. What was the word her mother used to use? *'Bouleversé'*, that was it. She felt as if something she had long been waiting for had finally happened.

Over to her left lay the main buildings of the winery. Roughly constructed out of planks, their deeply angled roofs shingled with redwood, the buildings looked tumbled-down and neglected. Beyond them, still to the left, began the small vineyard, rising gently on a

11

sunbathed hill until first came round green blobs of trees, like a child's drawing, then the grey stone of the mountains that overlooked the part of the valley where her father had chosen to settle.

Perhaps by now he'd be telling how he won the land, the house and the winery in a poker game. She sometimes wondered if this were true. Perhaps he had acquired the stone home in which they lived by even less reputable means. When she had gone to school in Calistoga she had heard tales from other pupils of their gold-miner parents taking the land from the older settlers by force and trickery.

She chided herself for always thinking the worst of him. When the forty-niners were rampaging in the Napa Valley, her father had been further south, with the Germans at Anaheim. He had brought his family to Calistoga not long before her mother had died. She had loved the little town more for its school for her children than for the hot springs and spa that brought the fashionable people from San Francisco there. The town had a general air of prosperity and civilisation, there were fine houses in Calistoga. But after her mother's death they had moved into this house in the valley. They rarely went to Calistoga now schooldays were over.

Remembering her mother made Rosie think of the Frenchman again as she turned to the right and moved towards the wooded area at the side of the property. This was land her father had always intended to clear and replant with vines. It had never happened and now, at seventy, he was too old, and his son, at sixteen, too young and too physically small to do the work.

Perhaps now the Frenchman had come it would be suggested again, she thought, while hoping it would never happen. Away into the trees there was a gentle pool where small fish darted. Fed by a mountain stream, it never dried even in the heat of the summer. The pool, almost a small lake, was on their land and she swam there. Once across on the other side she was free to lie on the shale bank in just her spencer and drawers, shaded by the great oaks, with a sharp, rocky hill rising behind. She had to watch out for poison ivy and the adders, but other than that it was the most beautiful place in the world.

Now was the best time of day at the pool; the water green where the shadows of the trees reflected and left the sunlit patches a brilliant blue.

She was debating whether to go so far when she heard her father's bellow from the house.

"Rosie! Where's the Goddamn coffee?"

Without replying, she turned back, not hurrying. The tin coffee pot would be bubbling on the range. Why didn't they serve themselves? Men! she thought as she moved inside to where the three of them sat. She snatched a cloth to take the pot by the handle without burning her hand, filled three mugs and put them down in front of the men.

12

"None for you, sis?" Peter asked. He had picked up her irritation.

"No, thanks," she said shortly, uncertain as to why she felt so scratchy.

"Have some coffee with us," Jean Paul said.

He had twisted his face into a quirky little half-smile, as if he, too, understood she was cross. "Please," he added.

She noticed how her father gave him a quick, uncertain look as she nodded and settled back down in her place, filling herself a mug.

"Now," her father said, his voice hearty. "Where we gonna put this young fellow, eh? Where we gonna sleep him?"

She opened her mouth to suggest the small guest bedroom which was tucked under the shingled roof of their roomy stone-built house, but her father did not wait for an answer.

"I reckon you can turn that loft over the barn into a fair old comfortable room, Rosie," he said. "And then Jean Paul will be ready and rarin' to get on with his work come the morning. You join us in here for breakfast, eh. Rosie here is up real early. Yah, real early," he repeated, adding: "You got a timepiece?"

"I have," Jean Paul said, patting under his overall. "And I have a bedroll. I left my things on your verandah. I shall be fine."

"But Pa –"

"That's it, Rosie," her father said, his voice authoritative in the way that meant no more argument. "Now you just go show Jean Paul here his place."

She burned at the slight to the Frenchman in the way her father said 'his place'. She put down the coffee she had not touched, then rose to her feet with a swirl of her skirt.

"When Jean Paul has finished his coffee," she said coldly, knowing even her father would not be that rude to a guest at their table.

She liked the way the young man finished his drink at just the right speed. Not so fast as to show subservience, not so slowly as to appear insolent. Then he followed her back through the hallway and onto the porch where, at the side of the doorway, he had left a large, carefully rolled bundle.

"They your things?" she asked, aware they could belong to no one else.

"Yes," he said, his voice rueful. "Not too many things. For now."

They walked down the steps side by side. He had shouldered the bundle easily, and she saw now that he was of average height, but half a foot taller than her.

"This way," she said, leading him to the left and back behind the house to where the winery littered the landscape. "It's there." She pointed to the structure which they called the barn, but which housed the pressing equipment and some barrels. "There's a good-sized room

13

above. It's sort of furnished with the things we couldn't get into this house when we moved here."

"From Anaheim?" he asked.

"Yes," she said. "We had a really big house there."

"And your mother?"

"She died. Having another baby."

"What age had you then?"

"Nine. Peter was seven. I kind of brought him up."

"You miss her?"

"Every day of my life," Rosie said slowly. "Every single day."

"That's because she loved you," he said, staring towards the mountains. "In this country the battle is too strong to leave much room for love."

She understood exactly what he was saying.

"My ma always used to say that love was the most important thing in the world and that I must love my father, and Peter, and my husband when I had one," she told him.

"Your mother was French," he said, laughing. "We French believe in love. Many kinds of love," he added, but this time she was not sure if she entirely understood his meaning.

They had reached the barn and were climbing the inside ladder up to the chamber above. There was a strong, heady smell of wine from the barrels. Upstairs the sun beat on the shingles, and the room was hot, the smell of the wine all-pervading. Here and there a shingle had been lost and the golden sun flooded through in neat square patches, illuminating the drifting dust that their arrival had stirred.

He would not need his bedroll, there was a broken-down but large bed on a rusting brass bedstead. An oak chest of drawers and a buttoned chair, man-sized but with the horsehair stuffing spilling from the bottom, stood by the one small window. There were rag rugs on the floor that her mother had made, and a speckled and spotted mirror with a gilt frame that was turning rusty red.

"It is a *château*," he said.

She looked at him suspiciously, certain he was laughing at her.

He caught her expression. "No, no, it is true. You have not seen where I have lived to get here. I promise you, it is a *château*."

He was already putting his things on the bed, and then he turned and sniffed, drinking in the yeasty hot smell from the barrels below.

"It is only red grapes here?" he asked.

"Most," she said. "This part of the valley is hot."

"There are white grapes in other places?"

Why was he wanting white grapes? Would he be moving on for them?

"Some," she said, deliberately unhelpful.

14

"Then some day I shall make champagne here. I have studied the terrain and the climate and I see no reason why not."

He had thrown himself into the old chair, one leg flung over the worn arm. A square of sunlight hit his shoulder, but his face, serious with intent, was half-shadowed.

"Champagne?" she asked. "What is it like, champagne?"

"Ah, such a question! It is gold, it sparkles as the sun sparkles and dances in your golden eyes. It caresses the lips and the tongue with its life and it is full of the tiniest, most persistent little bubbles that most delightfully tickle the nose and the palate. It is the most seductive of wines. Seductive as a woman. The wine for celebration and for love."

The last words were said slowly, his eyes watching her face. She felt heat rise from the pit of her stomach, and she prayed her cheeks were not scarlet.

"It sounds delicious," she said, making her voice composed. "I'd better be getting back. Pa'll wonder where I am."

He rose from the chair and walked towards her, slowly, still watching her face. He stopped a pace from her, and she stood transfixed. She could no more have turned and gone than she could have flown through the shingled roof.

He took her chin between his two hands, and she felt the roughness of skin that had known much labour. He stood looking down at her, his dark eyes seeming melancholy.

"Thank you, *petite* Rosie, for speaking for me. I am grateful."

He then leaned forward and kissed her lightly on the forehead. She caught the summer scent of her father's wine on his breath; felt just a touch of the shadow of his beard.

No one had kissed her since her mother's death and she knew her pa would have good reason to beat her had he seen what had just happened.

Finding her legs would move, she turned as if nothing had happened, and walked down the ladder into the comparative cool of the barn. Her insides were a mass of warm, wonderful feeling, but with the same composure she had shown when schoolboys swept the ground before her she walked back across the dusty yard and into the house.

Chapter Two

On the day after the Frenchman arrived, Hans Brunner announced that they would begin to gather the grapes the next morning. He made it a pronouncement after the evening meal when Rosie and the three men were still sitting at the kitchen table, in the pale, yellow light of the oil lamps. The room was too warm with the heat from the range. Outside, moths battered on the screens which covered the windows.

"Breakfast at five thirty, Rosie," he ordered.

"OK, Pa," she said, getting up to wash the dishes.

They were all back in their same places the next morning before the sun was up, white-faced in the pale light, yawning and silent.

She served the coffee with thick slices of warm bread and butter spread with sharp-flavoured grape jelly she made from the wild vines that sprawled in indecent profusion over the valley. There was milk, too, from the one cow they kept in the old stables beside the winery where their two horses also spent the nights.

"Today it begins," her father said, gulping at his coffee. "You will gather, too," he added, and stabbed a thick finger at Rosie where she stood by the range.

The Frenchman – she still could not think of him as Jean Paul – nodded.

"It is time," he said, his voice authoritative.

Her father gave him a brief, momentary glance of resentment, and then nodded himself.

"Eight hands will be better than six," he said.

"I like the gathering," Rosie said thoughtfully. "It's kind of an achievement. It feels good. Like – like –" she hesitated. "Like getting somewhere."

"It's hard work. Hard on the back when you're my age," her father said, glaring at Rosie as if she had said something infinitely stupid. His ill-humour stopped the conversation. The kitchen sank into silence.

But then, thought Rosie, he always stopped any conversation until he had had the whisky which seemed to wind him up like a clock. Then, tick-tock, tick-tock, he talked in a monologue as monotonous as the swing of the pendulum itself. He was a bore and a pig, she decided.

Under her lashes she looked at the Frenchman as she settled down to eat her own bread and drink her coffee. Taking no notice of her father, he grinned at her.

"*Bonjour, petite* Rosie," he said.

"Good morning," she said, looking straight at him and taking in that the rough shirt he was wearing was a clean one. His hair glistened and stood in sharp little spikes, still wet from where he must have thrust his head under the pump in the yard. His dark blue eyes glinted at her, and bread in hand he turned to her father and asked the question he had asked her the night before last.

"Tell me, Monsieur Brunner, are there white grapes here?"

"Where?" her father asked, his voice as sour as the remains of last night's whisky.

"In this valley. Chardonnay, maybe? Pinot Blanc? Grapes that would make champagne?"

Her father grunted.

"They already make it over in Sonoma Valley. Don't know what grapes they use. Old man Schram – he's from the Rheingau, too – has tried it. His place is lower down the valley. We made it for a while there at Anaheim."

"It is possible then?"

"In this country, anything's possible," her father said. "And equally impossible," he added.

"I think to say possible is better," Jean Paul said. He looked at Rosie and smiled and the smile seemed to have some special meaning.

He and she worked together side by side in the cold, pervasive fog of the dawn as they cut the grapes from the vines, making their way along the regimented rows, settling the tightly packed bunches of the violet-coloured Zinfandels into the straw baskets that her father always used for the gathering. She liked watching the way Jean Paul cradled the bunches carefully along his slender, fine-boned hands until the grapes were clear from the wood, the knife flashed and the bunch was free.

The first thing he had done before they began gathering was to pick one grape and squeeze it gently, almost lovingly, between his fingers. A star pattern of juice sprang from the purple skin.

"See," he said triumphantly. "As I said – ready for crushing."

And then, his eyes on her, he licked the juice from the round, smooth ball of the fruit and added: "Perfect."

She felt herself shiver.

The sun rose gradually in the sky, sweeping away the morning chill,

17

and the small birds of the valley began to dart above. Somewhere a flicker was pecking at a tree, or maybe even at the old wood of the winery, and the sound echoed, mocking itself. By nine the mountains stood out clear against the blue of the sky.

The Frenchman had rolled up his sleeves to work, and the sight of the dark hair on his arms sent another small shiver through Rosie. His high forehead was beaded with sweat and she knew hers must be too. She was hot in her black blouse and, daringly, had opened the high buttons at the neck and rolled up her own sleeves, revealing plump, freckled arms. Her long black skirt clung to the back of her legs, and her feet felt twice their normal size.

"When I was little," she said on impulse, "my ma would let Pa take me to help with the gathering. She let me go barefoot in my cotton shift. Is that the way they do it in France?"

"Sometimes," he said, standing to stretch his back. "But it is not so hard in France. In the villages everyone comes to assist with the *vendange*. It is a festival. An occasion. When the hard work of the picking is done, much wine is drunk, and we sing."

He stood silent for a moment, as if remembering, and she put her hand on his bare arm.

"Perhaps Pa will give us some wine tonight," she said.

"*Peut-être*," he said, as if speaking to himself.

She remembered the word. "Perhaps," she said, and grinned.

The four of them had stripped the field of Zinfandel by lunchtime and they rested under the shade of one of the big oaks that bordered the vines. Rosie had packed a picnic of cold salt pork and chicken in one of the grape baskets, and she shared out the food between the three men. She had little appetite, but they ate fast and hungrily. She sat dreaming, looking at the wagon now loaded with a tumble of purple grapes. Castor and Pollux, the two carthorses that her mother had named as young foals, now heavy and solemn with maturity, stood patient, ears twitching, waiting to move on.

Her hands and face were dusty from the vines and she was aware of the indefinable smell of grapes, rich soil, dry late-summer leaves and the scents of wild flowers and grasses. The sight of the valley and the smell of the gathering were the same as ever, but Jean Paul's presence had added something. It was his faintly musky body smell, almost like the grapes themselves, that troubled her. She stole quick, darting glances at him. The blue shirt was clinging in damp patches, outlining the muscles of his back, and there were rings of wet under his arms. He had opened his shirt almost to the waist and his chest had the same mass of dark hair that covered his arms. She could see the disapproval on her father's face at this boldness, but she let her thoughts dwell on how the Frenchman's waist was narrow, narrow as her own, and how

18

even the thick studded belt that held up his working denims made him more attractive; more desirable.

It was at that moment she decided she would marry him.

Peter was engaging his attention, talking too quickly, telling of their lives, Calistoga, and San Francisco where he had once been. His small hand rested on the Frenchman's shoulder and Jean Paul was listening, smiling faintly, but his eyes watched her. Her father did not miss this, his own glance darting between his daughter and the Frenchman.

"Right," he said abruptly, getting to his feet. "Now for the Cabernet Sauvignon."

"You have the Cabernet?" Jean Paul asked, his voice respectful. "Are they ready so early?"

Her father nodded.

"One field – the sunniest, on the hillside. They're ready. The summer's been good and they grow well there. There's a fellow called Crabb who lives further down the valley. He imports cuttings. I bought them from him one year when the harvest had been poor. Wine was fetching nearly two dollars a barrel. I was lucky for once. The cuttings grew well. But," he added gloomily, shaking his head, "I guess the Goddamn phylloxera will get them eventually."

They rode on the back of the wagon to where the Cabernet grew in lush, deep purple profusion, lighter on the bough than the Zinfandel, the fruit less tightly packed, but dusted with the bloom of black. As they began to work Rosie asked Jean Paul: "You like these grapes?"

"The great clarets of Bordeaux are made from them," he said, laying a bunch with care into the basket on the ground between them. "Yes, I like this grape. Who is this man Crabb who brought them here?"

"I don't know that he's about any more." Rosie said. "He had many, many different cuttings from Europe. Hundreds, I believe. But I guess the phylloxera killed them all."

"*Quel dommage*," he muttered to himself.

"I don't remember that," she said, anxious not to lose his attention. "What does it mean?"

"It means what a pity," he said. "Shall I teach you French, *petite* Rosie?"

"I'd like that," she said gravely. "I know a lot already from my mother."

They worked in silence for a while. She could hear her father's heavy breathing two rows of vines away, and her brother's light whistle as he moved cat-footed through the greenery.

A mist was creeping into the valley from the mountains and the sun was red. Soon, it would slip like a burning disc behind the horizon. Unconsciously all four of them had begun to work faster and her father and brother became more separated from where she and

19

Jean Paul cut the bunches from the bough.

"Why did you come here?" she asked suddenly. "If you know about wines, if you're from Champagne, you could have gone to one of the big successful wineries. They'd have taken you on. Why pick on us?"

"Perhaps I did not want to go to one of the big successful wineries," he said. "Perhaps I wanted to work somewhere like this."

"Now why should you want to do that?" she asked.

"You cannot guess?" he asked teasingly, turning his face to look at her. He was very close, so close she could see the beginning of the evening growth of beard on his cheeks and upper lip. He was, she realised, one of the few clean-shaven men she had ever met. Her brother had a small and not luxuriant moustache that drooped in blond fronds over his upper lip. Her father's beard was thick and white.

"You want to buy our winery?"

"How could I? I have no money."

"You couldn't just want to help." Her voice was dubious. In her experience, people did not do things for altruistic reasons.

"Perhaps I had heard that there was a pretty daughter."

She felt the unwelcome blush rise from above her breasts. "You're teasing," she said, "but you're wasting your time, here, mister. Pa wouldn't sell. But he'll never make anything of the place. He's mean. Real stingy. This place wants money spent on it. It could be fine and the valley is so beautiful . . ." She was silent for a moment and then said flatly: "Pa's a loser. He lost my mama. He'll lose this place. I guess the phylloxera will get it all eventually, if the birds and the wild deer and the bees don't. It's all a fight. And he'll lose Pete and me as soon as we can find some place else to go. Because I'm not going to be a loser too."

"Does he have the money to make it right?" Jean Paul asked, casually.

"Sure –" she began, and then stopped. "Well," she said carefully, "I guess he maybe does. He never spends any. Pete and I are no better than those Southern slaves I heard about."

"What do you want to do with your life, *petite* Rosie?"

"Oh, a lot," she said.

He turned to look at her, before placing a cluster of grapes into the basket.

"You look like a woman with dreams," he told her.

His dark eyes were compelling her to look at him again and she stood upright, her hand at the small of her back. She had the sensation that if she were to look into his eyes she would be lost.

"Look at me," he said softly.

Reluctantly she turned her head. The dark eyes encouraged; she could not look away.

"I want to go away from here. Well, not here so much," she heard herself telling him. "Away from Pa. Maybe get wed. Maybe have kids. But live. See places. Pete was telling you about San Francisco, I've never even been there. I want to do something; be someone. I don't want to be ignorant all my life. I tell you, if this place were mine, if I had the chance . . ." her voice trailed away. These were not the things that girls were meant to want and she knew it. "Fine clothes, I guess," she added not entirely truthfully, "and maybe to drink champagne one day."

"I will make it for you and we shall drink it together," he said, and she felt again that separate tingling of breasts, stomach and a tightening of the throat that was pleasurable and exciting, but leaving a sense of loss and something like rejection when she could grasp the feeling no longer.

It was suddenly chill as the soft rolling mist came in from the Pacific somewhere behind the mountains. The sun was about to drop from sight and her father's loud voice was calling.

"Come on," he shouted. "What are you doing there. We gotta get these grapes back. And quick."

"*En avant, petite*," he said. "Your papa is calling."

The men crushed the grapes that night. Rosie, back in the house, could hear them labouring by the light of oil lamps in the winery. They would be tipping the fruit into the hopper which stripped off the stems, leaving the fruit to fall through into the crusher. They would come back to the house dirty, sticky and smelling of the yeasty scent of the ripe grape. In readiness she dragged buckets of water from the pump and heated them on the range. She took down the big tin tub from the hook on the wall outside the kitchen. Gradually she would start to fill it, judging the time when they would come into the house, hungry and dirty, wanting both bath and food.

In the past she had always stayed in the kitchen busying herself with her tasks while her father and brother had bathed. It wouldn't be right to stay while the Frenchman cleaned himself, but would she look stupid if she left? Her mind was occupied with the problem as she prepared food and started on the bread for the next morning. She realised she wanted to stay. She wanted to see how he looked without his clothes, though she would avert her eyes as he climbed in and out of the water.

As it happened, she had no say in the matter. When she heard the men crossing the yard from the winery, she hurriedly poured the rest of the water into the tub and gathered the clean towels.

"Out of here," her father said gruffly. "We'll call you when we're ready to eat."

He set the lamp he was carrying down on the kitchen table and the soft, gold glow lit Jean Paul's face where he stood behind. Peter was standing close to him and all three looked hollow-eyed and exhausted, their hair glued to their heads with sweat and juice, their shirts and hands stained red from the skins of the grapes.

She nodded and left the room, wandering down towards the front door and out onto the verandah. The moon, ringed with mist, sailed high above the mountains. The air was still. Somewhere in the eaves a bird stirred and chirruped in sleep and the gentle buzz of night insects broke the breathless calm.

The lamps still burned in the winery. Her father must have been tired to have left them. She went behind the house and crossed the yard to lower the wicks, one by one, enjoying the pools of fresh darkness after the sharp disappearance of each separate glow.

The winery buildings turned black and silver. The juice of the grapes would soon begin to bubble and live in the casks, and she felt she too was just beginning to live.

Contented she sat on the back step of the house and waited for her father to call her back in, smiling to herself in the darkness.

By mid September the gathering was finished. The vineyard was stripped of its fruit, the new wines filling their fermentation casks. The hard work of the fields was over and her father declared himself well satisfied with the *vendange*.

There had been little time for Rosie to become better acquainted with Jean Paul since the morning that the cutting of the grapes had begun. For one thing her brother had attached himself to the young man, working at his side, asking him questions about the world beyond the valley. Rosie, from where she worked with her father, could hear their voices but catch little of what was said and was filled with impatience for the grapes to be gathered in.

Her life was always one of relentless work, but this time of the year was the hardest – up before dawn every day to begin the gathering which went on until deep dusk and the chill of the autumn night air called a natural halt to the work. The long day left her and the men exhausted. And each night the crush had to be done before the grapes spoiled. The men laboured in the cool of the winery while Rosie made their food and baked the next day's batch of bread. For the three weeks it took to denude the vines and press the fruit, they had all gone straight to their beds after eating.

The larger wineries in the valley would still be working, but Hans Brunner had his harvest in, without hindrance from wind, rain or hail. The fermentation had taken place with each new batch of grapes exactly as it should in a perfect world. Nothing had been spoilt. In Rosie's fancy all the good fortune of this 1899 gathering came from the presence of the Frenchman.

In the cellar the new wines were rolling and boiling in their casks and the heavy scent of the fermentation hung over the winery and the house, pervading every room. Watching the must tossing in the cask, the pulped fruit forming a cap on the surface, her father said solemnly: "Man does not make wine. Wine makes itself. With God's help."

"I had not understood that you were a man of religion," Jean Paul remarked.

Her father stared at him suspiciously, looking for mockery.

"Only at the *vendange*," he said. "Only then. A man needs to pray then. A man needs all the help he can get."

"You should perhaps also pray that the phylloxera does not attack your vines when the spring comes," Jean Paul suggested.

Her father grunted and said bitterly, "That Goddamn insect is the devil's beast. No prayer works against the son of a bitch. It's as well this is a good harvest. It may be our last." Then he added, returning the mockery: "Guess we won't be having too much work for you then, mister."

Rosie had been scrubbing out one of the small oak barrels that would hold the wine when it had settled. She felt herself go cold.

"I thought perhaps it would be possible to replant the field you have never cleared," Jean Paul said. "How long has it been without cultivation?"

"Never been cultivated," her father said. "But what you going to plant it with, eh? There's no money for new cuttings. Not until the wine is ready and maybe not then."

"You have no need to buy root stock," the Frenchman said. "I shall graft your Cabernet Sauvignon onto the wild vines that grow here and make new stock for you. Stock that will resist the phylloxera."

Rosie looked up, surprised, pushing the hair from her face. Her brother who had been standing with the men said: "The wild vines? Them there that Rosie makes her jelly from?"

"The very same," Jean Paul said, smiling at her. "They have more to offer than jelly, Rosie. Have you not noticed? They do not die. It is because their roots fight the phylloxera. So they exist while the finer species wither. Therefore the noble Chardonnay will live with their humble roots."

Her father was interested.

"You reckon it will work?" he asked.

"I know it will work. Remember – you spoke of it yourself." It was said with a touch of confident arrogance that usually darkened her father's face. But now he looked thoughtful. "It is how the vineyards are being replanted in France," Jean Paul explained. "And here, too."

"You can graft?" Hans asked.

"Of course."

"Sounds good, Pa," Peter said. She noticed that his hand was on the Frenchman's arm, and for a moment felt a touch of blinding, idiotic jealousy.

Her father sighed. "Well, there ain't no harm in trying. But we can't plant until late March. The frost would get 'em."

He was thinking of having to pay wages for so long, Rosie realised. And from his demeanour it was a prospect he did not relish.

"There is plenty to do," Jean Paul said. "You have had a good harvest. You need help with the work in the winery. The field must be cleared and terraced, and given much . . ." he hunted for the word, gave up and said: "*fumier*."

"Guess you mean manure," Hans said. "OK, then – so we try your grafts in the spring. It will still be four years before a gathering. I should live so long!"

Jean Paul shrugged. "You will live so long," he said.

"Happen you'll be right. For once," her father said.

The concentrated work of the past three weeks had left them low on stores. The chicken population of the back yard had been decimated and flour, sugar and other staples were almost exhausted. Hans announced the day after the crushing was complete that he was going into Calistoga to stock up, and taking Peter with him.

"Look out for yourself," he said gruffly to his daughter as he left. "We'll be back near after noon."

Watching Castor and Pollux trundling down the rough path that led to the road into town, Rosie felt her spirits lift. She knew exactly what she was going to do, and finding Jean Paul was her first priority. In her sparse bedroom she looked at herself anxiously in the mirror. She brushed her dark hair vigorously, in too much of a hurry for the hundred strokes her mother had taught her. She then looped it back into wings around her face, securing the heavy mass into a knot at the nape of her neck. She looked at her brown face despairingly. If only Pa would allow a little powder to hide where the sun had made her unfashionably dark. Her eyes were bright amber in the deep smooth bronze of her skin – a bronze that appeared regardless of how careful she was to shade her face while working in the fields. The men were brown, too, but on them, she thought, it looked good. She looked like a farmhand. She bit her full lower lip to redden it and debated whether to change into her best gingham gown. It would look too obvious, she decided, and settled for the workaday black skirt, but with a white, soft lacy blouse.

She had few clothes to choose from and she wondered again what the French women that Jean Paul must have known would wear. Her mother had always said that French women were different – chic, she had said, and then laughed and added that France had her peasants, too.

The sun was warm on her head when she came out into the yard and the remaining chickens ran to cluck around her feet. Absently she shooed them away and stood motionless, wondering where Jean Paul could be. Then she purposefully crossed towards the winery and into the barn.

"You there, Jean Paul?" she called up the ladderway. Silence. She peeped back outside again to make sure he was not in view and then lightly ran up the ladder and pulled herself into the room. It was neat and tidy; the bed made, the water bowl and pitcher emptied. His few clothes were folded, and rising above the heavy smell of the wine from below was another scent – a man's smell, she realised, recognising it from the morning smell in both her father's and her brother's rooms.

She sniffed deeply, pulling it through her nostrils and into her lungs, and the excited, warm feeling began. A sensation so pleasurable that she tried to keep it and contain it by gulping in more of the air that his clothes, his body, his breath had scented. Then, afraid he would catch her in his room, she hurried back down into the barn, and darted out, past the barrels into the winery.

The air was very still and nothing stirred in the yard. But she herself was in a turmoil of impatience. She felt as tossed and churned as the must on the wine.

Then she heard a light, sweet whistling that seemed to hang in the stillness. The tune she did not recognise, but the sound itself she knew from the music that Jean Paul and her brother had made whistling together as they picked the grapes. The Frenchman had the deeper tone; her brother's tone was breathy and light.

The sound was coming from the right where the field they were to replant lay, and where her swimming hole rested beside the oaks. She set off from the winery buildings. She did not know exactly what she intended, but something, somehow had to happen. She had the conviction that it was a time of decision. The sense of impatience that had been driving her since the wagon left hastened her footsteps and she was nearly running as she came to the pool.

And there she stopped dead.

He was in the water, standing in what she knew was the deepest part. When she stood there she was covered almost to her shoulders, but he was standing free from the small glittering ripples, his chest and shoulders running with small streams as he threw more water over his hair which had curled tight to his head in flat, carved tendrils. He had not yet seen her, and he jumped and then ducked himself, coming up spluttering and pasting his hair flat again with brown hands.

He stood, the sunlight turning the water that streamed from his body iridescent. He was white except for a long V of brown where he had worn his shirt open to the waist throughout the picking. Then he suddenly saw her.

"*Bonjour, petite* Rosie," he called. "*Viens ici.*"

"I don't know what that means," she called back untruthfully.

"Come here. That is what it means," he said and began to stride in towards the shore. "The water is very good."

"I know it," she said, transfixed where she stood, uncertain as to what she should do if he strode naked from the pool like Pan or some other woodland god. God forbid that he should be naked, she thought feverishly.

As he rose from the water with each step, it became clear that he was not without cover. He was wearing his long johns, and as he came closer she could see first his flat stomach, then the broad column of his thighs covered in greyish white wool. Yet wet as a fish as he was, he might as well have been unclothed. Resolutely Rosie kept her eyes somewhere around his shoulder level.

He was out now, and flinging himself on the small strand of light shale, panting a little with pleasure rather than exertion.

"I was hot," he said by way of explanation. "I have been working, *ma petite* Rosie, for you and your family."

"That sure didn't look like working," she said, staring down at his face.

"Before swimming," he said. "Look around and you will see."

She looked across the pond, at the trees and at the mountain.

"No, no," he said impatiently. "*Regards.*"

He sprang to his feet, bent and pulled up a never-ending length of red-stemmed vine that still held a few tired grapes and wrinkled leaves. Then she saw he had cut a small pile of them.

"This," he said and, laughing, began to run round her, wrapping her in the long springy shoot which swayed and quivered in his hands like some monstrously long snake.

"You wanted to know why I picked your winery to rest?" he said. "Because of these. The wood there is full of them, but my *petite* Rosie has not noticed because she does not look down. The wild vines grow to the ground as nature intended. Without man's help they grow *en foule* – like a crowd – and –" he searched for the word and could not find it. "They do not stand up," he finally said.

"I *have* noticed them," Rosie said indignantly. "I pick the grapes and I use them. Of course I know they are there."

"Ah, now she is *fâchée*. Angry. But with even just this one length of vine that holds you enslaved at this moment, I shall produce at least thirty new vines. It does not take much, you see. I shall teach you how."

"You said you would teach me French," she said, still cross, standing within the circle of red, thick stem in which he had twisted her. "And now you'll teach me how to make new vines from old. Is there anything else you can teach me?"

His expression suddenly changed; the scampering satyr disappeared.

"Oh, yes," he said softly. "A great deal. There is much that I shall teach you, *petite* Rosie."

She was vividly aware of her pulse. She shook herself and the vine round her whiplashed away, springing into trailing coils on the ground.

"Ah, you are free," he said reproachfully. "I had thought to bind you."

"I'm not free." She still felt irritated. "But I shall be. One day," she said.

"To be free is something you must teach yourself," he said, and moved a pace closer to her. "I can help, *peut-être*, a little by teaching you to be a woman."

"I *am* a woman," she said.

"Not yet," he said, "and that, my *petite* Rosie," he added, his voice gentle, "is *pas encore* in *Français*."

As he spoke his face was coming nearer to her, and his long eyes were more binding than the vine. He took her face between his hands as he had done on the night he arrived and moved forward to kiss her. But this time his mouth was not for her forehead, but for her own mouth.

At first he kissed her soft-lipped, and she stood in mute acceptance. Then she felt his arms go round her and was aware that he was still wet from the pool as he pulled her tight towards him. His mouth became harder on hers, and his tongue was pushing her lips apart, and she found herself clinging to him, fiercely responding.

It was the most extraordinary sensation; the most exciting thing that had ever happened to her. Her body seemed to have become liquid heat, a solar power; she had the sensation that if he held her one fraction tighter, she would burst into flame. She pushed herself closer, aware of a hard ridge pressing against her as he kissed her, deeply and slowly.

"Lie down," he whispered. "Here, where it is soft."

Without letting her loose, he was edging her towards the soft shale at the side of the pool. A momentary flash of panic that they might be seen struck her, and then she dismissed the thought. Pa and Peter were in Calistoga. There was no one else to see. She knew what Jean Paul was about to do and she knew she wanted him to do it. She understood her impatience of the day and she planned on no resistance. It was not in her after the weeks of his proximity. She slid to the ground, and lay on her back, watching the dark shadow of him settle beside her as he blotted out the sun.

His hands were no longer round her back. One had slipped inside the white cotton of her blouse, and was searching for her breast, but her tight spencer, held by criss-crossed lace cord, was in the way.

"Will you help me?" he whispered.

She heard herself chuckle, full of anticipation.

"But *you* are teaching *me*," she reminded him.

He leaned above her, unbuttoned her blouse, and pulled it back off her shoulder, grimacing when the challenge of the spencer met him. She lay there, smiling up at him, deliberately provocative. It seemed the natural way to behave.

"Now what will you do?" she asked.

His work denims were within reach on the sand where he had shed them to swim. He leaned away from her and she saw he had taken a heavy curved knife from the pocket.

"This," he said, lowering the point to her breast. She felt the sting of it cold on her flesh and it was a chilling moment. She had the urge to run from him, but lay, still smiling into his intent face. She would not show fear. Never.

"I shall do this," he said, hesitated, then with a sharp movement ran the knife beneath and along the length of the lacing that held her spencer in place. The garment sprang apart, freeing her full breasts and she arched her body towards him. "It was fast that way," he said, his dark head descending to find her exposed red nipple that waited, already erect.

The sensation was more exciting than the kissing. She heard herself moaning gently as his teeth and tongue teased at her breast. She knew in a sudden revelation why cats howled at night, why hares danced their wild gavotte in March and why some of the girls at school in Calistoga had been in trouble. She understood at last why those more mature girls had been so sharply and predatorily aware of the boys. Now she, too, was entering the world of this special knowledge; she would not let go of the soul-stirring pleasure that came from a man and a woman making love.

He had lifted his head, and she whimpered at the cessation of the pleasure.

"Let down your hair," he ordered. Obediently, without sitting up she busied herself with the pins. While she did so, he got to his feet and with a few impatient movements peeled off the wet underwear from his body.

She stared up at him, surprised at what happened so dramatically to a man at a time like this. She felt the urge to reach and touch, but he dropped onto his knees before stretching out beside her again, roughly running his hands through her hair. Then, while she felt his naked shoulder and smoothed her hands down the length of his back, he began to kiss her again.

"You have too many clothes on," he whispered in her ear, his breath warm against her skin. "Do you not agree?"

She nodded and, moving away from him, stood and pulled off her skirt, then her petticoat, drawers and shoes. She had worn no stockings under the long skirt. Then naked, feeling the light breeze on her skin, she stood with her head high, her back straight, while one hand covered the patch of dark pubic hair, the other cupping her breast.

"Beautiful," he said. "*Belle. Très belle.*" He put out his hand. "*Viens ici.* You remember?"

She nodded again. Words seemed superfluous as she lay down beside him. First he stroked her cheeks, muttering to himself in French, and then he took her hand and guided it down to the firm column below. His flesh felt very smooth, velvet-like, as she touched him a little tentatively. The skin seemed too soft for the strength beneath.

"What'll I do?" she whispered. "Teach me."

"Take me in your hand and stroke me." His face was buried in her shoulder. "But not too gently."

"And then will you make me a woman?" she asked, her hand hovering above him, teasing.

He ran the flat of his palm over the round of her belly, and slid his fingers deliberately slow between her legs. Involuntarily she felt her knees open.

"I think you are ready to be a woman," he said, as he gently probed until the pleasure became insupportable.

"I am. I am," she urged.

"Then it must be now," he said. "I can wait no longer."

At school they had whispered that it hurt, but she felt no pain. Perhaps just one sharp second, but the memory was lost in the joy of him thrusting, holding, panting while she clung to him, and as they were joined, instinctively she wrapped her legs around him.

Afterwards he dozed for a moment, while she lay still beside him, one arm thrown over his chest. She wanted to think about what had happened to her, and the careful replay of memory was almost as good as the real thing. By remembering, she could recreate again the waves of excitement.

Jean Paul and his lovemaking had been what she had been waiting for throughout all her adolescent daydreaming. She had known exactly what to do when he lifted himself over her. And when he collapsed on her with a long drawn-out groan, pushing the breath from her own lungs, she, too, had experienced a crescendo of feeling so violent that she felt herself crying: "Oh, God! Oh, God! Oh, God!"

She shifted a little as the grittiness of the shale began to trouble her, and the movement woke him. He stared at her for a moment as if he was not sure who she was, then he turned to kiss her.

"It was good?" he asked.

"I guess it was the most wonderful thing that has ever happened to me," she said. "It was so beautiful I reckon I could cry."

"The *tristesse* of love," he said. "There is always sadness when it is good. And you have the appetite."

"What do you mean?" she asked.

"You will want it again. And again."

"Oh, I will," she said cheerfully. "Real soon."

He laughed.

"Now is too soon. We must swim and we must dress before your father and brother come home."

She gasped.

"I'd forgotten them. What time is it?"

"Not late. We have time. Come into the water with me."

He was on his feet, boldly naked. Now he looked as Peter looked and she tried not to stare at the transformation to normal as he bent to take her hand and pull her up.

"Come. We must wash and swim," he said.

"OK," she said happily.

Relishing the freedom of her nudity she ran into the water slightly ahead of him and turned to splash him as he joined her. Laughing, he swam quickly towards her and grabbing her legs pulled her under the water. As she came up, spluttering, he held her close to him and his chest felt very hard. Then he pushed her back a little so his hands could stroke her full breasts.

"See the pointed, pretty pink nipples," he said. "Do they point for me, *peut-être*, or for the cold or for the water?"

"Pointed?" she asked, and pushed his hands away so she could touch herself. "They're still all hard," she said. "Like when I'm cold or when ..." she stopped, not wanting to explain the nights when she explored her own body for pleasure; a pleasure that could never rival what they had just shared.

"When you are cold, and when you are hot in the throes of love and I shall give you more lessons, little virgin," he said, adding tenderly, "eager little virgin. *My* little virgin."

"Is there more to learn?" she asked.

He laughed. "A great deal more."

She leaned to kiss his wet face.

"We will have another lesson soon, won't we?" she said.

Chapter Three

She was dressed in her working apron and back in the kitchen by the time she saw from the rising dust along the dirt road that her father and Peter were nearly home. As she hastily made the dough for the next day's bread, she told herself to be composed; she must give nothing away. If her father were even remotely suspicious he would send the Frenchman away.

But the excitement of the encounter still lingered with her. She also felt supremely confident that Jean Paul was the man for her and she the woman for him. They would assuredly marry, she thought, as she put a cloth over the bowl and settled it near the range. They would marry in the spring, after the planting of the new vines. They would go to San Francisco for a honeymoon, and they would start a baby right away.

She felt a faint, momentary anxiety at the thought of a baby, but then consoled herself by remembering that everyone said it couldn't happen the first time. And besides, she thought, as she began to peel the potatoes, if she should be pregnant, then he would marry her. He was a gentleman. A French gentleman.

Jean Paul did not show any signs that anything had passed between them as he sat with her father and brother eating boiled ham and potatoes. As usual Peter irritated her by taking all Jean Paul's attention, chatting inanely, asking stupid questions. Her father interrupted his prattle.

"Been thinking what you said about the wild vines," he said to Jean Paul. "I've had word of it myself, of course, but you seem mighty confident."

"I have confidence," Jean Paul said, "because I have the knowledge."

Rosie looked warily at her father. She was always afraid that these periodic bursts of arrogance would one day provoke an explosion that would have Jean Paul sent on his way.

"How do you have the knowledge?" her father asked, his attention seemingly all on his plate.

"Because in France the phylloxera has done much damage – more than here," Jean Paul said. "We knew it would come to Champagne, but because we are far north in the world of vines, it arrived more slowly and spread more slowly. It came to us seven years ago. There were five vineyards affected at first in the valley of the Marne, but it was spreading to the mountain of Reims where my family's vineyards are. I knew that soon it would cause the same devastation as it already had in the south.

"We tried to keep it away in Champagne. Monsieur Chandon, the son of a great and famous family of the region, paid for and burned the first of the fields to be affected in the region of Ay.

"But as you have found, it is no good to burn. It avails nothing. The whole of France, from the south to the north, has been attacked by this *effrayant* beast. The so-called cures were expensive and did not truly work. Many, many people have been ruined. Many starved."

He was silent for a moment and then his voice lightened.

"But not all was lost. In the south, since as long before as 1869, they were experimenting with graftings from the American wild vines. Indeed, some vineyards had already been replanted, but the *vignerons* could not believe that these roots could produce grapes of the same quality. They persisted in trying to find methods to kill the insect. They only killed the vines.

"For my family, it was a question of money. We believed the grafting would work, but if our vines died, we had not the resources to wait for the new to grow. Perhaps we would not be able to afford the root stock that we needed. When I left my home, just one of our fields was dying. By now the rest will almost surely be dead, too. I left what there was for my brother and made the decision to come here – where the resistant vines grow. But first ..." he stopped speaking and looked challengingly at Hans.

"First what?" her father asked, pushing away his plate.

"First I went to the south where the *vignes-mères* – I do not know your word for the men who cultivate the plants – were experimenting with American wild vines. Growing them and grafting them, with success.

"I went to a town near Nîmes, not far from the Mediterranean, and I learned the work. Then, from Marseilles, I came here."

"You learned the work?" Peter asked.

"Yes."

"Is it difficult?"

"It needs skill."

"Will you teach me?" Peter asked eagerly, and Rosie felt the same idiotic jealousy that her brother's friendship with Jean Paul always seemed to bring.

"He'll be teaching me," she said, getting up with a whirl of her skirt.

"Oh, sis! It ain't woman's work!"

"Strangely, it is," Jean Paul said. "In France the selection and the cutting of the vines is done by the women. The men are more skilful at the grafting."

"Any fool can graft," Hans said. He was irritated and it showed. "I learned when I was twelve. But there's a hell of a lot of different wild vines out there, mister. Which one were you planning on using?"

"The one that grows on the land you mean to replant," Jean Paul said. "I do not know its name, but I recognise it as the one that I worked with at Nîmes."

"And that, I suppose, is why you picked here to come and work. On my vineyard," Hans said, his voice sour.

"Perhaps," Jean Paul said, but he gave Rosie a swift and secret look as he spoke and she remembered him saying: "Perhaps I heard that there was a pretty daughter."

"Well," her father said, "we can give it a try. But if the other vines die, four years is a long wait until we get a grape or two."

"You have no choice," Jean Paul said. "No one in the world of wine has any choice. I do not believe there is a cure for the phylloxera. Only a resistant root."

"Maybe you're right," her father said. "I've heard folk tell that grafting's the only answer. But since you've the experience — well, we'll give it a try."

And give it a try they did. Rosie was conscripted from the kitchen and the house into the fields. The three of them sweated in the shortening days, cutting the profusion of dark red wild vines that carpeted the woodland and stony areas. Jean Paul would not permit the long shoots to be cut unless all the leaves had fallen, and they would pile the new cuttings in fifteen-foot lengths until the sun began to sink. Then, with Castor and Pollux's assistance, the bundles were taken back to the winery.

In the wavering light of the winery buildings, Jean Paul, Peter and her father cut the shoots into the three-foot lengths, and stocked them in the coolest and most draught-free place in the buildings. Jean Paul sprinkled each pile as it was made with fine damp soil, complaining that it should be sand. But Hans was too mean to buy sand.

"It should have been that we selected the best of the Cabernet Sauvignon to be grafted," Jean Paul said regretfully. "Those vines bearing the best fruit should have been marked. Now we shall have to use our judgement and our instinct when we come to the grafting in February."

Hans Brunner snorted.

"All my vines grow fine grapes," he said. "There'll be no problem there."

Jean Paul looked as if he would have liked to argue, but was silent.

The two weeks that they worked cutting the vines were a time of frustration for Rosie. Jean Paul was so near – and yet as removed from her as the mountain that loomed over the valley. They worked together, she could smell his special smell, she could hear his breath, but she could not touch him. And he took little notice of her, except for the odd shy glance or quick reference to their encounter when her father and brother were not close by. He seemed to pay more attention to Peter than to her, and Peter was excited, almost girlish in the pleasure he showed in his new friend. She and her brother had always been close, but now Rosie felt a tiresome and childish sense of resentment towards him. And it seemed that he, too, was wary of her. Their old comradeship and the united front they presented against their father was lost. And their father watched all three young people with a worldly and cynical eye.

It was not until her father again announced that he was going to Calistoga and taking Peter for supplies that she and Jean Paul were left alone. He was not to be found when Peter and Hans harnessed up the wagon and Hans made some grumbling remark that perhaps the man had good reason for not being seen in town.

No, a better reason, thought Rosie, a bubble of excitement beginning to grow as Castor and Pollux trundled off down the dirty road.

She waved them off and then ran light-footed up the ladder to his bedroom above the barn, hoping that he would be there. He was stretched out on the bed, wearing just his denims. His bare chest still showed the long V of dark brown and the room was faintly chill in the damp of October. He smiled as he saw her come through the door, turning his head on the pillow to watch her.

"Come here," he said quietly. "Quickly."

"Wait," she said, and slowly, deliberately provocative, began to undress. She turned her back on him when she knew the movement of taking off her white drawers would not be graceful, but turned again to face him as she unlaced the bodice she wore under her blouse.

"Won't let you cut the strings off this time," she said. "Ruined a perfectly good garment, that knife of yours did."

"Just come here," he repeated. "It is time for your lesson."

He taught her a great deal that afternoon on the rickety bed where they both lay naked. He showed her how to please him with her mouth, and pleased her in turn with his. He made her explore his body as he explored hers. Their love-play lasted a long, long time as they turned, twisted and sweated, Rosie light-headed with the new tremulous

34

sensations that her violin bow of a body played as she waited for the crescendo.

And after it was over, she slept briefly, her head on his shoulder, his arm under her neck.

When she woke, she sat up, pulling the tips of her nipples across his sleeping mouth in a butterfly movement, and then leaning down to kiss him.

"I should go," she said.

"Not yet," he said, dark eyes watching her. "There is time."

"Can we do it again?" she asked happily, and he laughed.

"It must be true you had a Frenchwoman for a mother. You know about love. You were born knowing about love."

"Seems funny Ma and Pa did this," she said thoughtfully. "Can't imagine Pa at all."

"No one ever can imagine their parents," he said. "It is the unthinkable." But she had already forgotten the thought. Her hand was sliding over his flat stomach and down to the thick curly black hair below. She scratched there impatiently.

"Can't we do it again?"

"If you can make me live again, as I showed you."

"Pleasure, sir," she said, her head going down to follow her hand.

She wanted to sleep again afterwards, but this time he insisted that they both dressed.

"You must be composed, and sitting in the kitchen when they come back," he said. "And you must never come to this room again. It is too dangerous for you. Suppose someone should see?"

"Who's to see?" she said.

"I mean it," he said. "Never here again. We will find other places."

"What sort of places? Bed's nice."

"You will see. And now, I have a present for you."

"A present? For me?" She could not keep the note of surprise out of her voice. She could not begin to remember when someone had last bought her present. Her father hardly remembered her birthday, and apart from going to church at Christmas, the celebration was not observed in their home. Her father always said that no Christmas could touch a German one, and that it meant nothing in this polyglot country full of Jews, Chinese and God knew what.

"Yes, for you," Jean Paul said. He was buttoning his shirt as he crossed the room towards the big bag that he had been carrying the day he arrived.

"What is it?"

"A book."

"What sort of book?"

"A special one."

35

He had it in his hand, and she saw it had a dark brown cover with some gold lettering.

"Is it a story book?"

"No. Look."

She took it from him. The cover read: *La Pratique de l'Anglais.*

"What is it?" she asked, puzzled.

"A book to help you learn French. It will not be easy for you because it was designed for French students to speak English. I bought it in Marseilles when I left France, and from it I have learned my basic English. Perhaps it will help you to speak a little French. Maybe, who knows, you may go there one day to see your mother's birthplace."

She held the book in her hand and stared at him, wondering if he meant that maybe they would go there together, but she merely said: "I shall study it every day."

"And I shall help you. You father cannot object to that. Perhaps teaching you French is what we should be doing when they come home — which will be very soon now."

She looked out of the tiny window at the darkening sky.

"Oh, Jesus!" she said, frantically struggling into her blouse. "You're right. We must be quick."

The supper was on the range and she and he were sitting on opposite sides of the kitchen table when her father and Peter came home. She was reading: "*Je trouvais ma jolie cousine, dans la cour de l'écurie.*"

Her father threw her a suspicious look as he shrugged off his jacket.

"What you doing?" he asked

"Learning French, Pa," she said. "I just said I found my pretty cousin in the stableyard."

"You haven't got a pretty cousin," he said. "Load of nonsense. Where's supper?"

"It's ready, Pa," she said, pushing the book aside and getting to her feet.

He moved to pick the book up.

"What you want to do this for?" he asked belligerently.

"Because of Mama."

He nodded and stumped towards the door, his shoulders heavy and drooping.

"Going to get washed up," he said. "You'd better too, Peter."

Peter's expression was suspicious, and as the two of them went out into the yard he gave Rosie and Jean Paul a quick backward glance. Rosie heard the handle of the pump work and turned to look just once again at Jean Paul. His face was thoughtful.

"I think your father loved your mother," he said. "He will not mind you learning her tongue."

"I would like to think he loved her," she said. "But why does he never say?"

"Because some men do not," he said, which left her remembering he had never mentioned love to her.

As winter approached, the chances to make love and to be alone with him became rarer. He still insisted that they could not go to his room, and she could not ask him to hers, sleeping as she did in the room next to her father's.

The work of the winery went on. Jean Paul was sent to terrace the neglected rock hillside where the new vines were to be planted. Hans and Peter worked in the winery itself, rebottling, scrubbing casks, disinfecting, catching up with all the work of the wine producer. The vines themselves slept, simulating death, their branches black, bare and twisted.

Jean Paul was the one who was made to work really hard and sometimes at night around the kitchen table his face would be white with dark circles of shadow under his eyes.

Hans relentlessly whipped him on to clear more and more ground and when Peter, suddenly brave, protested, Hans said: "Hard work will keep the son of a bitch out of mischief."

"But it ain't fair," Peter said, voicing the things that Rosie dared not say. "You ask too much of him. You've not even given him his money. You're just an old slave-driver, Pa."

"I got my reasons," her father said. "He'll not be here long, you just mark my words. We'll get from him what we can."

The words frightened Rosie. She, too, had a sense of impermanence about the situation. A foreboding that something bad was going to happen, but her nature was optimistic and she tried to bury the thought. Her father's confident statement that Jean Paul would move on brought all her fears to the fore. The book he had given her became the most important of her few possessions. She studied it while she worked around the house, mouthing phrases, wondering when she would ever need to use sentences that instructed: "Every man should have three doctors, carefully selected, to consult with discretion."

But she learned it all, nonsense and sense, and in the evenings, if Jean Paul was not dropping with tiredness, she would try out her day's learning on him. He said she had a natural accent, and indeed much of what she learned was familiar or remembered. As she managed a conversation, her father would eat his food in noncommittal silence while Peter sulked at the amount of attention she was receiving from Jean Paul.

At other times he taught her different words that were most certainly not in the book. This was on the rare occasions when they managed to be alone. She was always hungry for him. And the places that he found

37

for them to make love were exciting, as he had said they would be, adding a piquancy to the act. Once he took her in the back of the wagon – both of them naked, their clothes a thin and unsuccessful mattress. Once they managed, quickly and furtively, while both were still dressed, she with her skirts bunched around her middle behind the biggest of the barrels in the winery, her back pressed against the cool slates and the warmer wood. Another time when her father and Peter had gone early to bed, they had succeeded with the kitchen table as their couch.

"Anywhere can be a bed if the appetite is there," he told her.

"The bed was the best, though," she informed him. They had just enjoyed each other in the stable where Castor and Pollux munched, snorted and stamped their feet as a background to her rasping breath and pleading for more. She had straw in her hair and clothes.

"Help me get this off, or Pa will guess." She could hear the petulant note in her voice. "You know, if you told Pa about us, it would make it a whole lot easier."

"Oh no it would not," he said. "If your Papa thought we were in love, he would watch us without ever for one moment letting us be alone. And then what would you do, my greedy little one?"

"Get married, I suppose," she said, and waited, breathless, for his response.

"With what?" he asked. "Your father has not paid me a sou. Perhaps you can persuade him. Without money, how can I do anything? How can I go anywhere? How can I have a wife?"

She shut her eyes at the thought of being his wife. She imagined night after night in a big bed with him, with all her needs and wants satisfied. He would be hers for ever – and she would be safe, fulfilled. That was what she wanted. That and his babies. In her nightly fantasising, when she lay in her own narrow bed, wanting him, she wondered if it would be no bad thing to be pregnant. Then marriage would be imperative. And their baby would be beautiful.

"If you had some money, would you marry?" she asked cautiously.

"I might." The words weren't quite what she wanted to hear, but he had said them, eyes twinkling, mouth curved, to show perhaps that he was teasing her. "But your father is not generous," he reminded her.

"My pa's just plain mean. I've never had a cent from him either, except for a new dress or underclothes or something he's just got to pay for. Nothing ever to spend on myself." She looked to the sky. "That's what I want. Money for myself one day. Never to have to ask for it, ever."

"Exactly," he said. "Never to have to ask for it. How can I ask your father for myself? To do so has no dignity. It requires someone else to tell him of my needs."

She looked at him calculatingly. "I'll tell him," she said. "But if I get you your money – then what?"

"Wait and see." His eyes twinkled, his expression was droll. His words said nothing, but his face told her that all would be well. She stifled a sigh. It would have been better if he had said outright that they would be together for always – if it were possible – though perhaps that was not his way. Men did not always say what they meant. Yet a chill stayed with her – like the sudden cold when they dug into the hot ground in high summer only to find the cool, hard earth beneath.

Her mind still on marriage, she asked: "Has your brother a wife?"

"He hadn't when I left."

"Does he live on his own?"

"With our mother."

It occurred to her then that though he would talk of France endlessly if encouraged, she had never heard him speak of his family. She was suddenly curious.

"What are they like?"

"Like?" He shrugged his shoulders. "Like people anywhere."

"But don't you miss them?"

"Never," he said flatly and moved to stroke Castor's rump. The horse grumbled throatily and Jean Paul made soothing noises.

He was making it plain that there was to be no conversation about his family, but she wanted to know more.

"Where do you live exactly?" she pressed, moving to stand beside him.

"We do not live in a village. We live on the property."

"But it must be near somewhere?"

"A very small village called Chigny les Roses."

"Roses!" she said, delighted. "That's easy to remember for me."

"Indeed."

"And what's your brother's name?"

He sighed. "He is called Clovis."

"I've never heard that name," she said, repeating it to herself. He did not reply, and she went on hurriedly to break the silence. "Anyway, I think I can get my father to pay you. I'll think of a way."

"You will?" He was beguiling again and gave her a quick hug and a kiss on the tip of the nose. "Ah, but you are a clever girl, my *petite* Rosie."

She accepted the kiss and the compliment and then told him fiercely: "I love you." It was the first time she had said it.

"And I you." He said it without hesitation. "But it is time to get back to work before your father suspects us."

She was a shade resentful as she stood in the back yard, the chickens clucking around her feet as she absent-mindedly threw them corn. If he

39

loved her and she loved him, why shouldn't they tell everyone and be courting like other people? Not that she would want to give up the loving until they were married. She could not imagine living without the loving now. It would be like doing without food. But they had managed secret ways to do that before and they could again. And anyway, if Pa did guess it would be all right if they were to be wed.

But a niggling feeling of uneasiness persisted. She decided to ignore it and concentrate on finding a way to persuade her father to pay Jean Paul some money. That might be the answer to the entire problem.

The essence of a plan came to her over supper that night when her father was asking Jean Paul more questions about the grafting he had learned in France. Listening, it dawned on her that Jean Paul had become very important in her father's life. If Hans Brunner used the Frenchman's knowledge he might just beat the phylloxera, and that might be the key to a new start, a new fortune.

Could it be that he had not paid Jean Paul because he believed that lack of money kept him working at their winery?

If she could make Hans think that Jean Paul would go because he had *no* money and had *not* been paid, that might make the difference. But her father would have to believe that he was actually losing his hired help before he would pay out a red cent.

Her chance to try out the plan came after her father and brother had been into San Francisco for the day to see wine buyers. For the first time she and Jean Paul spent the day in her own bed and she felt that the bed itself was transformed by what had occurred there. She knew she would feel his outline, his flesh, and want him there with her every night of her life from now on. She felt a fleeting regret for the loss of the many childhood dreams of love and being loved. She knew the loss of innocence and she would never be the same again.

She did not tell Jean Paul her plan, in case it did not work. Also she wanted to keep him a little on edge, needing her and dependent on her. He wanted her to tell him what she planned. He stroked, kissed, teased her body until she was butter melting in the sun, a grape about to burst its juices, but she would not tell him. Eventually he sulked and still she did not tell him, enjoying her first taste of power over a man.

She caught her father on his own in the winery that evening. He was tasting from a barrel, a frown on his face.

"Reckon I should've got more for this barrel," he grumbled. "It's good."

"Never mind that, Pa," she said. "Just listen to me. Do you want to keep Jean Paul about the place here?"

"Don't want to. Guess I have to," her father said.

"Then you're going to have to pay him or he'll go."

Her father put down his wine.

"What do you mean?"

"Well, today he was asking me about old man Schram and his champagne, and old man Crabb and his imported vines. He reckoned that if he went to see them they'd pay him for his idea about the wild vines. He wanted to know where in the valley they both lived. I told him I didn't know. I said he'd have to ask you and he said he didn't think he'd do that. So I guess he's planning on taking off without telling you. He said he couldn't be without money, not one minute longer."

She waited to see the effect of her words. Her father was standing, his bull head lowered, thinking.

"I reckon old man Schram would be pleased to see him," he said finally. "As for Crabb, I think he's gone away. Just fancy that young pup remembering me talking of those two. He's smart, I'll give him that."

"What will you do, Pa?"

"Pay him something, I guess. And tell him there's more to come. Eventually. When I sell the wine."

She held back her sigh of relief.

"Makes sense," she said. "If you want him to stay."

"Only till February when the grafting's done," he said. "There's something about him I just don't care for. Maybe because he's French. Funny folk, the French."

"Mama was French," she said, angry.

"Your mama was different," he told her.

It was over supper that night, the only time throughout the short, late autumn day when they were all together, that he handed Jean Paul a roll of notes.

"'Bout time I paid you something," he said. "There's thirty dollars there and more to come when I get the money for the wine we sold today. That keep you happy?"

Jean Paul put the notes on the table and looked at them. He did not speak, and then he looked quickly towards Rosie who half nodded. She did not want her father to think there had been any collusion between the two of them, but she did want Jean Paul to know that it was she who had worked the trick.

Peter had gone quite pink, she saw.

"That's great, Jean Paul," he said. "You won't be going away now, will you?"

"Not if your father wishes me to stay."

"And no visiting old man Schram." Hans made it an order. "I don't want him or nobody else knowing my business. Understand?"

"Of course," Jean Paul said, his pointed eyebrows rising.

"Right then." Her father was getting up from the table. "You'd best

41

give Rosie her lesson. I'm going in the parlour to have me a glass of whisky."

Peter had taken to trying to learn French along with Rosie, but he had no ear for it and his mind was not as quick. He complained it wasn't fair, and that he had been too young when Mama died to have absorbed as much as his sister.

"I remember she used to talk French all the time to you," he said, "and I never knew what she was saying. I hated it."

"So you just used to whine," Rosie said sharply.

"You must not fight," Jean Paul told them. "You must both be good. For me." And his expression for just a moment was so smugly full of buried meaning that she felt a return of the uneasiness that often troubled her.

None of them was long up. The old man went to bed first and they all sat and listened to his stumbling, whisky-marred tread on the stair. Then Peter went to the privy, followed by Jean Paul, who came back to take his thirty dollars, stuff them in his back pocket, and say goodnight to them both.

"I'm glad Pa paid you," Peter said. "It would have been terrible if you'd had to go."

Rosie meant to say nothing, but found herself wondering if perhaps Jean Paul had also lobbied Peter to get him money. Well, if he had, Peter had not managed it. She was the one and Jean Paul should know it for certain.

"I told Pa you'd been asking about seeing old man Schram and old man Crabb," she said. "Told him you thought they'd pay you for your ideas about the wild vines. That's why you got your money."

"I see," Jean Paul said softly. "My clever *petite* Rosie."

Peter's face was crimson in the soft light from the oil lamps.

"But I've been asking him all the time," he said indignant.

"But you didn't think of a good enough reason for Pa to pay," Rosie said, smiling at him. "I did."

At that moment she was fully aware of the rivalry between them, and realised how Jean Paul had managed to part her from her brother. It was ridiculous, she thought. Men could, and should, be friends and men and women could, and should, be lovers. They were two separate things. It was absurd for Peter and her to be rivals for the one man when they both needed something so different from him. Jean Paul was smiling at them and the feeling persisted that he enjoyed his effect on their relationship.

"I'm going to bed," she said abruptly. "See you all in the morning."

She made her call to the privy and then hurried upstairs. In her room, which still seemed full of Jean Paul, she let down her hair and splashed her face and hands in the cold water that filled the big, blue china basin. Then she quickly undressed, and climbed into bed, not bothering to put on her nightgown. Pa would have a fit, but she savoured the feel of her own flesh against the linen of the bedsheets and she liked reliving what she and Jean Paul had done there that very afternoon. She went over every move he had made in the love game, remembering, recreating the feeling, wanting it again. And now he had thirty dollars. It was a really good sum. Would he marry her?

She had a strong suspicion that it wasn't going to be that simple.

She slept fitfully and woke suddenly in the middle of the night. She could hear her father snoring in the next room. Peter's room, as always, was silent. She lay staring at the etched outline of the oak tree outside her bedroom window, thinking about Jean Paul. The matter had to be settled, she decided, before, God forbid, he did go or February came around and her father sent him on his way.

She felt feverish with impatience, and resolved that something must be done and that now, while he had money, was the time to do it. She got out of bed and stood listening. The house was calm, her father still snored. She put on her slippers and her nightgown, then she wrapped herself in a dark cloak that hung on a peg on the door and very quietly went into the hallway. The stairs stretched ahead to be negotiated in the darkness, but she knew every one; where they would creak and groan and where they were silent. Carefully she made her way down and then through to the kitchen where she took an oil lamp and lit the wick, turning it as low as it would go before letting herself out of the kitchen and into the yard. The house still slept, yet gave soft, familiar cracks and creaks of the night.

There was a moon which turned the yard black and silver, a chicken clucked in its sleep, making her jump, but on light feet she sped towards the winery and the barn where Jean Paul would be sleeping.

The door was open and inside she drew breath in the darkness. He would be angry. He had said she must never, never visit his room, but now she was doing so. How could she defuse his anger? She thought how and chuckled softly to herself. She put down the lamp, took off her cloak, her nightgown and slippers, folded them and laid them in the cleanest spot she could find. She then stood for a moment, stretching and smoothing herself before starting to tiptoe up the ladder to the room where he slept. The smell of wine from the barrels below was heavy, and intoxicating, adding to her fever. She would not knock, she decided. She would open the door quietly, creep across the room and climb into bed with him. When he felt her pressed against him, he would not be angry.

She had the oil lamp in her hand and it was difficult for her to swing herself into the loft. Carefully she put it down on the floor of the room above her and then lifted herself up. When she stood, she bent again

43

for the lamp, and then turned towards the bed.

In the wavering, swinging light she saw that Jean Paul was not alone. Sitting up in his bed and staring at her nakedness, an expression of horror on his face, was her brother.

Chapter Four

Retreat seemed the only answer. Devastated, she almost fell back down the ladder into the warm, fetid atmosphere of the wine casks below. Safe on the ground reason stopped her dashing naked into the night. She frenziedly put on her nightgown and slippers, wrapping the cloak round her with trembling hands. Somehow she had managed to keep hold of the lamp, and quickly blew it out. There was complete silence upstairs. The two men must be listening to see what she would do – a thought that filled her with anger. Now she was dressed again, she was tempted to confront them, but decided to get back to her own bed.

She was almost in control of herself by the time she slid in through the kitchen door and crept back up the stairs. Her father still slept. She could hear the snores and for once she blessed the whisky he had drunk before going to bed.

In her own room she flung the cloak down on the floor in a fury, kicked off her slippers and climbed into the high bed, sitting, her knees up under her chin, thinking chaotically.

Her only thought when she saw the scene in Jean Paul's room had been that she had made a fool of herself in front of both her brother and her lover. Now, with breath drawn, she was asking herself what the hell Peter had been doing there – and in Jean Paul's bed. She had heard whispers of unnatural things that went on between men, but had no real knowledge. Surely that could not be? It would explain all the warning feelings she had experienced about her brother over the past few weeks. It would explain her instinctive jealousy. Her brother was girlish and sometimes silly. Maybe he was one of those strange men who were not men. The thought was abhorrent.

But Jean Paul? Surely not. She thought of the ardour with which he had made love to her. What could he do with another man that would compare? She could not believe anything perverted of him.

Yet if he was making love to them both, what was happening in the room above the wine barrels? Was her brother demanding explanations that she herself would like to hear?

In spite of her confusion, she could not resist a quick little snort of satisfaction at the memory of his horrified face as he sat there, naked himself, staring at her. Jean Paul had just been an indistinct figure in the bed. Now Peter would be whining at him as he used to whine as a child when things did not go well for him.

But she was wrong. She could hear the faintest of rustles; the same furtive night-time noises she must have made herself ten minutes earlier. Her brother was coming back. She heard the soft pad of his tread hesitate outside her bedroom door. She held her breath wondering what they would say to each other if he came in. What *could* they say to each other? But the footsteps crept on again and she heard the whisper of his bedroom door open and close.

She lay awake for some time afterwards and, having logically gone through all the possibilities of the night's happenings, began to feel angry. Had Jean Paul made the rule that she must never come to his room because Peter was there? If so, *why* was Peter there? How was she going to face them both in the morning? That seemed the biggest hurdle, but underneath the questions, the embarrassment, the general uneasiness, there was still an ache for Jean Paul. Whatever it was all about, she wanted and needed him. He was the most civilised, charming, intelligent, clever man she had ever met – and possibly the only man of such quality she would ever meet, stuck as she was in these backwoods. He was hers. Her brother stood no chance of separating them.

She made a promise to herself then that she would win this curious conflict. In fact, she vowed that she would never be a loser in life in any way at all. Losing was not a word she would allow into her vocabulary.

And comforted by the thought, she fell asleep.

She was up at her usual time in the morning, down in the kitchen before anyone else, brewing up the coffee, readying eggs and bacon for everyone's breakfast.

She went through the everyday motions automatically, her mind in turmoil. She was impatient for Jean Paul's explanation. She was anxious about the first face-to-fact encounter with her brother, uncertain how to behave.

Just act normal, she kept telling herself as she waited for them all to appear at the breakfast table.

Her father was first. She recognised his heavy step on the stairs and he came into the kitchen with a scowl on his face, his head lowered like a bull about to charge.

"Jesus, I need a cup of coffee," he said. "Didn't get a wink of sleep

46

all night. What were you and Peter up to?"

Rosie had the heart-stopping sensation that she had read about in the cheap novels and magazines that she used to borrow from the Calistoga library.

"I don't know what Peter was up to, Pa," she said pertly. "I wasn't up to anything."

Her father threw her a hard glance, full of knowledge, and then grunted.

"Then give me some coffee," he said. "And don't crash the pot about while you're doing it."

"You shouldn't drink so much whisky, Pa," she said, her voice deliberately sanctimonious. "It always makes you feel bad."

She was longing to say that she had heard his snores; that he could not possibly have thought that she and Peter were up to anything. But it would not be tactical.

Besides, Peter was coming down the stairs. She could hear his light-footed run, but it seemed slower and more reluctant today – and not surprising! No doubt he was as uncomfortable about facing her as she was about facing him. They probably both had something to hide, she thought grimly as she poured coffee from the blackened pot into her father's big cup.

"Morning, Pa." Peter was at the door and she was not certain whether or not he had a light dusting of perspiration on his forehead. She did not want to look too closely.

He did not look at her, either, but settled himself at the table and waited for her to pour him his coffee.

"Where is the Frenchman?" their father asked. He rarely used Jean Paul's name.

Rosie was asking herself the same thing. He was generally at the table ahead of Peter, but perhaps he too was unenthusiastic about the enforced meeting.

"Don't know," Peter mumbled. "Shall I go call him?"

"No. If he can't be on time for breakfast, too bad," Hans said. "Get cooking, Rosie."

As she cracked the eggs into the pan, trying to take the rigid lines of anxiety from her back, inside she was screaming: "Where are you? Where are you?" But after she had served both her father and her brother there was still no sign of Jean Paul. Reluctantly she set about cooking her own breakfast, carefully putting aside his share.

When she, too, was seated, the silence at the table was oppressive. She and Peter avoided looking at each other. Her father seemed miles away.

"Well," he said finally. "Guess you were wrong, Rosie. He just wanted the money to get away from here."

47

The same awful thought had been troubling her and presumably Peter, too. He looked up and, his voice wobbling, said, "Pa, you don't really think ..."

"Yes," Hans said. "That's exactly what I think."

"I'm going to look." Peter sprang from the table and banged open the back door, clattering frantically down the steps. She wanted to follow him, but held herself in check, telling herself to keep calm as her father impassively finished his breakfast, mopping up the egg yolks with a chunk of bread.

"He fooled you, Rosie," he said, "and you fooled me. Pity. Still, I could graft vines when I was twelve years old. Reckon I can do it again. We'll manage without him."

She was silent. How could she say that *she* could not manage without him?

Neither spoke as she tried stoically to eat, forcing each mouthful down, determined to show no emotion.

And then Peter came back, still running.

"He has gone. None of his things . . . and this –"

He flung a piece of paper onto the table.

It was Rosie who picked it up and read out loud: "*I am returning home.*" And his signature.

Rosie stared at the paper in the sudden silence. Each word was a bullet. Peter collapsed, sobbing, his head in his hands. Hans Brunner looked at him.

"Guess I'll never make a man of you, son," he said, pushing his plate away. "You're the man of this family, Rosie."

Slowly he stood up and walked heavily towards the kitchen door.

"Get on clearing that field, Peter," he ordered. "Give you a few muscles if nothing else."

He closed the door behind him with exaggerated care.

Alone, the two of them stared at each other, Peter brushing tears away from his cheeks.

"What were you doing there last night?" she asked fiercely.

"What were you doing?" He was on the defensive.

"What I was doing was natural. What were you doing?"

He had gone scarlet and his voice went up an octave.

"Rosie, you don't think ..."

"I don't know what to think."

"You're wrong. You're wrong," he said hysterically. "I'd just gone there to talk a while and keep some company. It got late and I just fell asleep. Didn't seem worth coming back. But you – you were disgusting. No clothes. Pa would kill you."

"You mention a word to Pa and I'll kill *you*, do you hear."

"I shan't tell Pa nothing. Never have," he said. "Rosie, if he's gone,

48

we've only got each other. We have to be friends again."

She sat looking out through the kitchen door and into the yard. She felt totally exhausted. While she did not know if she could believe Peter, she wanted desperately to accept his explanation. If he were telling the truth, then her lover remained hers – wherever he had gone. Until he found another woman, she thought bleakly.

"Guess you're right," she said slowly. "It was all silly anyway between you and me."

His face lightened, and drooped again.

"Do you think he really will go back to France?"

"I expect so. He liked it better than here. He talked about it all the time."

"It's awful," he whispered, almost to himself.

"Let's go look at his room," Rosie said. She hoped that maybe there would be some clue left behind of where and how he had gone. Calmer now, she was contemplating following him. But first she had to know which way to go.

"How would he get home?" she asked Peter as they crossed the yard towards the barn.

"Train, I guess, these days. He'd start from Calistoga. Maybe he'd take a boat from 'Frisco, but when we went there to sell the wine, Pa was saying they don't go that way much these days."

A train. She had never been on a train, nor a boat come to that. How far was France? How long would it take? How much would it cost? The idea was impossible. She pushed it from her head.

It was she who spotted in the barn that one pile of their painfully gathered wild vine cuttings had disappeared. Just about as many as a man could carry.

"See what he's taken," she said, pointing to the lowered pile.

He stared.

"That's it," he said. "He'll be taking them back to start his own vineyard again. But will they live till he gets 'em there?"

"He said they would dry out if you travelled with them," she recalled, understanding now what might have been in his mind as he gave her the information. "He said that if that happened, all you had to do was soak 'em in water and they'd be right as rain again. But he hasn't anywhere near enough for a whole vineyard. Just a start."

Peter stood looking at the ground as if it might tell him something.

"It's hard to think we'll never see him again," he said sadly. "It was nice to have a friend."

She put her arms round him, suddenly loving him again, and hugged him tightly. "I know," she said. "I know."

But she could not bring herself to say to him that, for her it had been something much stronger than just nice to have a friend.

49

As November rained on, the consequences of having had a lover became apparent.

Rosie realised that she was pregnant.

It must have been the last encounter in the company of Castor and Pollux or maybe the one in her room that had caused this quite dreadful problem and she knew she had only herself to blame. She had almost hoped to be carrying his baby. But that was before he went away.

The ten days since he had left had been a nightmare, she missed his presence so badly. She yearned for him physically, her body ached with longing for love. All the while she had to pretend everything was normal, but she felt her father knew. The looks he gave her were quizzical, but sometimes she felt he understood her loss and would have liked to help – had he known how.

Peter was a bigger problem. He kept asking prurient questions, slyly put, about her relationship with Jean Paul. It was as if he wanted to feed on the details she would not give and she began to believe that he had been telling the truth about his presence there that last, desperate night. If something wrong had been happening, how could he bear to hear of her happiness with Jean Paul?

If she had felt despair at the loss of her lover, the thought that she would have to carry his child alone brought an even greater misery. For two nights running she sobbed herself to sleep, face buried in her pillows so her father would not hear. She ought to kill herself, she thought at first, but she knew she did not wish to die and that there must be some way round the problem. She thought briefly of getting rid of the baby. They said some girls did this, but she did not know how and something in her screamed "No" at the thought. Whatever dreadful unhappiness her pregnancy might bring, she wanted the baby just in case it proved as beautiful as he had been. But she knew that her father would never forgive her. The disgrace to the family would never be forgotten with the child as a living reminder.

For a week she felt desperate and even returned to the thought of killing herself, but Rosie's optimism and spirit were never buried for long. She had to get herself out of this terrible predicament and she would, she promised herself one morning. The sun was shining, just a feeble yellow glow through her bedroom window, when she woke. The rain had stopped and it was time her silent tears stopped also. Some action must be taken instead of this endless round of grieving and worrying.

She lay looking up at the ceiling, thinking the problem through logically. What did girls do when they got pregnant with no husband?

They got rid of the baby.

She did not know how.

What else did they do?

They married, preferably the father, or were forced to live a life of shame.

And that, she decided, was what she must do. Marry, preferably the father. She had no intention of living a life of shame.

But first to find the father. If he had gone back to France, he must have made it under his own steam, and if he could get there, so could she. It was a question of time and money.

But what if, when she arrived at wherever it was of the Roses, he would not marry her?

She would have to have such a tempting dowry that he could not resist.

Money was the obvious answer, but money was going to be problem enough. She had no idea how much it would cost to get herself to Europe; she had a very good idea of where she would get the money for the journey, but it was unlikely there would be much left over once all the fares were paid.

What would tempt him? The answer was blindingly simple. The vines. Those added to the ones he had already stolen from her father would help his vineyard grow again.

And time was of the essence. If she were to travel all those thousands of miles, she would need to start as soon as possible – before she grew too large and her condition was obvious to the world.

Full of resolution, she made her plans.

That night she said to Peter in the short time they were alone after supper: "How long do you think it will take Jean Paul to get back to France, Peter?"

He pondered.

"They say you can cross the United States in as little as seven days now on the railroads. I guess he'd go to New York to get a boat, but how long it would take from there, I don't know. A month, maybe."

"I think it would be quicker," she said. "I don't believe it took Pa that long all those years ago."

"Then I don't know," he said, and added wistfully, "I guess he might even be home by now."

"I guess," she agreed, echoing his wistfulness, and at the same time wishing she'd paid more attention to geography at school.

She solved the problem by talking her father into letting her go to Calistoga. It was ages since she had been and as she jogged in on the old wagon, Castor and Pollux finding their way without help from her, she saw that the little town, a favourite spa resort with San Franciscans, seemed to have grown enormously. It was a fine, bright place with shops and hotels, bustling with tourists. She could have lost her way in the changes, but the railroad station was still where it had always been, and she made her way there after leaving Castor and Pollux

51

and the wagon on one of the many hitching rails

The stationmaster seemed to have changed, too, and for that she thanked the Almighty. He was a string bean of a man with a long, lugubrious face and teeth that pointed east and south, but smart in his heavy dark uniform, self-importantly presiding over the wood-frame, sloping roofed building that had been there since she was born. She was sure she had never seen him before and he would not know her from a calico petticoat.

"Can you help me, please?" she asked him. "If I needed to get to New York, how should I go, and how much would it cost?"

He pursed his lips.

"Long way, New York, for a bit of a girl like you."

"Well, maybe it is," she said, managing to smile. "But how much and how long?"

He sucked his teeth and said: "Take you about a week, lady. Maybe more. Weather's not so good at this time of the year and there's a deal of snow over the plains. From here you can either go down to San Francisco on the Napa Railroad and take the ferry to Oakland and pick up the Union Pacific from there, or you can git yourself to Sacramento and go direct."

"All the way?"

"No, ma'am," he shook his head. "As far as Chicago and there you git yourself another railroad. Where'd you want to finish up?"

"New York City."

"Right in the city?"

"Yes."

"OK, then, you take the Lake Shore and Michigan Southern and New York Central from Chicago. Takes you right to Grand Central Station in the north of New York City. Just about as near the centre as you're likely to find."

"How much will it cost?" she asked him.

"Depends how you travel." His expression, looking at her dark, dull dress and old bonnet, said he figured that she'd be needing the cheapest. "It's real cheap – about thirty dollars coast to coast on a freight with a passenger compartment or two. But that takes a while longer. Lot of shunting goes on. Normal train with just a seat, you can reckon on around fifty dollars."

She was thinking.

"It takes a week?"

"Like I said, maybe more."

"How about sleeping and washing and eating?"

"You want a sleeping car?" he laughed. "Reckon you can more than double the fifty dollars for that."

She asked him to write down the times of the trains and the

connections at both Oakland and Sacramento. He baulked at giving her precise information for the change at Chicago.

"Listen, ma'am," he said, "in this country every state works on different times. When you make your mind up, I'll find out for you then."

There was a brightly coloured map on the wall of the Pacific Union's route across the country to Chicago. She looked at it and shook her head.

"It's a long way," she said.

"More'n two thousand miles," he said. "Sure you want to go?"

"Sure, I'm sure," she told him. "I'll be back."

"Hey," he called after her as she turned to go. "Ain't you old Brunner's daughter?"

She showed him a puzzled face.

"Who?" she asked.

"No, I guess you ain't," he said.

From the railroad station she went to the library and found a map of France and a book about the country, and she discovered that there were steamship sailings from New York to Le Havre. It was three thousand miles and it took another week or ten days. On the map Le Havre didn't seem too far from the area known as Champagne. But whether there would be another railroad at Le Havre to take her where she wanted to go she had no idea. She believed that nowhere could be as modern as the United States, and California in particular. Perhaps the French hadn't even got trains. As for the place with Roses in the name, it was not to be found on the map. It must be too small, she realised.

She quickly made the necessary purchases to cover the reason for her trip and then jogged gently back on the wagon to the winery, thinking hard. It was damp, but the sun shone in small valiant bursts, and her spirits were higher than for a long time.

It seemed to her that the best plan would be to cope with the problem in stages. Get to New York first. That shouldn't be too bad; at least folk along the way would speak American. In New York, she'd just have to sort herself out with the ship and then, when she got to France, rely on her wits and her determination to get to where Jean Paul lived. She'd find him. She had to find him. The French lesson book would now have to be studied in even greater earnest.

She pulled her cloak round her more tightly against the damp of the late afternoon and thought that soon she'd be saying goodbye to this place – maybe for ever. She did not feel sad. She felt an inevitability; one long anticipated. She was not afraid, though the thought of the journey, alone and in mid-winter, should have been daunting. If anything, she was excited. She had a feeling that her life was just about to begin.

Money was the next step. And a lot of money. A woman alone and pregnant could travel thousands of miles the cheapest way, but for the sake of her own health and the baby's, it would be better to take what the stationmaster had called a sleeping car. More than double fifty dollars, he'd said. She thought to reckon on about a hundred and fifty, and that was without food, the price of the boat, plus the price of the rest of the journey in France. She was going to need a fair sum, and it was the thought of the money and the only way she could get it that troubled her. If she couldn't get enough, if things had changed, then she'd just have to go by the freight train.

She began to put her plans in motion the next morning at breakfast.

"Guess I'll give the house a good clean through today, Pa," she told him as he drank his last mouthful of coffee.

He grunted. "No place for menfolk, then," he said. "I'll be working in the winery. Peter, you get on with that field."

Peter looked frail and tired, but he was making progress with the field, carrying on where Jean Paul had left. She wondered if he were taking out his disappointment and loneliness on the stones and weeds, just as she was trying to bury hers in plotting and planning.

Neither man hurried over his meal, and her impatience grew. She had decided to allow herself no more than a month from now to get to Jean Paul. She didn't want her condition to be too obvious to his brother and his mother when she arrived.

It worried her that French people might be even more strict about that sort of thing than Californians, and in California, God knew, it was bad enough. Hypocritical with it. Didn't matter how early the baby came as long as the girl was married at the time of the birth. Folks whispered a bit and added up the months on their fingers, but once the wedding band was in place, no one minded too much. Would France be the same?

After Peter and her father went their separate ways, she began a flurry of activity to prove she was going to give the house a 'good clean through'. But it was her father's bedroom that really interested her. She needed an excuse to move the bed. She had moved the bed once before when she was about fourteen and having a real 'good clean through'. Washing the wooden floor beneath, she had leaned on a loose plank which had moved upwards as if it were meant to. She lifted the wood and beneath was a little cache of photographs of her mother, with old letters and papers, most of which were in German and which she could not understand. Her birth certificate and Peter's were both there. But the most fascinating thing that was hidden was the money. Quite a lot of money. Panicking that her father might catch her at this secret hiding place, she had pushed the plank back down and pulled the bed into place without investigating any further. Her father, she knew, would have half-killed her had he found her rummaging among his private possessions.

She had never lifted the plank again – until now, and she felt a great reluctance to snoop into his secrets. But there was no choice, other than staying here and facing his wrath. She thought that he might prefer to lose his money than to live with his daughter's disgrace.

Slowly she pressed on the wood. It looked much the same as it had those years before, except that the money pile had grown. She looked at it, wide-eyed and suddenly so angry that she had to stop to draw breath. All those years she and Peter had been labouring away without a penny of reward. Jean Paul's labour too must have helped to produce this treasure trove under the floorboards. As she lifted the cash in handfuls she no longer felt dishonest and mean about what she was doing. It was her father who had always been mean. Mean and miserly. Keeping them all thinking that poverty hovered like a hawk in the sky when in fact he was stashing away more money than she had ever seen in her life.

Still angry, she took out the money and counted it. It came to $3,425, and beneath it was a bag of about fifty gold dollars and also a small chamois leather pouch of gold dust. That she remembered from her last look in the cache, but she had been too scared to open it to see what was inside.

The gold was entirely his, she reasoned – left over no doubt from his forty-niner days, and he had kept it as an insurance against whatever the future held.

That she would never touch. Nor the gold dollars which might well have come from the same labour.

But as for the rest of it – she and Peter had helped to build up that money with no reward. She leaned back on her heels, fingertips lightly touching the floor in front of her. There was no doubt in her mind how much she was going to take. She was going to take exactly one third, leaving one third for Peter and one third for her father. But not now. Not until she was absolutely ready, just in case every night Hans Brunner counted his money in the privacy of his room like some miser. She thought it unlikely as she had never heard him move the bed, but rather than find that tonight of all nights he wanted to gloat over his wealth, she put everything back just as she had found it.

Throughout the day as she frenziedly cleaned the house, beating rugs on the washing line, polishing the furniture in the parlour with the beeswax, shining china and glass, her mind was obsessed with the thought of $1,141 – her share. That much money must be enough to get her to whatever it was of the Roses in Champagne. And there might even be enough left over to tempt Jean Paul to marry her for her money. But the vine cuttings were still necessary. A combination of

55

those and cash should prove irresistible to him.

That night, before she slept, she felt an unexpected deep sadness that all this should have to be. She grieved that circumstances were forcing her to follow a man she did not entirely trust, with whom she would have to bargain for marriage. But even recognising the hollowness of the victory, she knew that she loved him, she wanted him and, most important of all, she was carrying his child – a child who must have a father.

When her father and brother were out of the house again the next day she took herself up to the attic. Under the eaves was a trunk that her mother had brought with her from France, and Rosie had decided that she would take it home again – full of wild vine cuttings.

It would be appropriate. Her mother, who had missed France to her dying day, would have approved. There was also a battered old carpet bag, the pile worn thin, and a tired valise – both of which her father had used on his travels.

Neither would do. She made up her mind that with over a thousand dollars, she could travel like a lady. Before she took the train to Chicago she would buy new clothes and baggage in San Francisco. She intended to leave her father's roof with no more than her mother's trunk full of vine cuttings, the clothes she wore and her birth certificate. In San Francisco she would buy all that was needed to give fellow travellers the impression that she was a woman of means, travelling alone.

But the trunk would be a problem. It was heavy in itself, as she found when she manoeuvred it down the stairs from the attic and into her bedroom as a first step to getting it out of the house. She had no fear of her father finding she had moved it to her room. The problem of concealment would begin when she had the opportunity to get it into the winery and fill it with cuttings.

She looked at the big black box with its metal supports standing solid in the corner of her room and tried to imagine how she would manage to carry it halfway round the world. Yet if her mother had, so could she.

Her mother's name was still painted in white on the lid. "Anne Marie Cremont – Paris/Le Havre/San Francisco." Her mother had sailed from Le Havre and now her daughter would sail back. What sort of journey had it been for Anne Marie Cremont? How long had it taken? Which way had she come and why? She would now never know the answers.

Her mother had brought the trunk here in less sophisticated times, alone, and survived. Rosie would do the same, taking it back full of something special from the United States for France. The vines.

But then she realised she would be taking back something much

56

more important. She would be taking home her mother's grandchild.

That night she dreamed of Jean Paul. She was lying in his arms and they were making love surrounded by roses and the scent of roses. It was beautiful, and in her dream she could not understand why the roses had no thorns.

Somewhere a child was crying, and she knew it was her responsibility to go to comfort it, but she could not leave Jean Paul's side. It was as if she were chained to him and could not pull away.

Suddenly his face changed to that of her father who shouted: "The child! The child!"

Terrified, she ran from the rose bower, naked, fearful of meeting someone, and began to search for the baby. She ran looking through a huge, dark house that she did not know, and in a room at the very top she found the source of the crying. In the bare room a cradle rocked on boards and the slap of the rockers on the uncarpeted floor half-drowned the sound of the cries. She ran to the cradle and stilled it with her hand, then reached inside to bring out the child and put it to her swollen breast.

But the cradle was empty and she herself was falling, falling, falling, until, mercifully, she woke.

Chapter Five

"On madame it is charming!" The saleswoman, round, grey, and sharp of eye, stood with her fat little hands clasped in front of her, her head to one side, like an inquisitive bird. "If I may say, madame, it was made for you. Only you could wear it."

Rosie nodded absently, looking at herself in the cheval mirror of Madame Claudine's Paris Modes, a store she had happened upon in San Francisco's Union Street. She had arrived at Oakland across the bay that morning and left her trunk and one small parcel in the station baggage room. Then for an extra twenty-five dollars she had reserved herself a Pullman Palace sleeper car on the train that left for the East the next morning. Everything organised, she had then taken the ferry boat across to San Francisco.

As she managed each new step for herself her confidence grew. The quest for Jean Paul was still of the utmost importance, but the journey itself was proving to be an exhilarating adventure. So far, trains, boats and big cities had not frightened her.

She felt capable of coping with anything, and money, as she had suspected, oiled the wheels of life in a very satisfactory fashion. She still felt guilty about having removed what she considered her share of her father's cache, as well as her birth lines and a drawing of her mother, but reassured herself that none of it was truly theft.

She had chosen to start her journey from San Francisco because she wanted to buy clothes. Calistoga had some fine dressmakers, but it would have been dangerous to shop there. Folk might have recognised her and wondered where the money for her purchases came from. But even in Calistoga, a little town with big ideas, they admitted that San Francisco had the very latest fashions and that the stores were as good as, if not better than, those in New York.

Rosie was determined to be in the mode before she set off on her journey. She had already purchased two pairs of soft leather boots, plus a pair of house slippers. It gave her pleasure to leave her old boots in the store, suggesting grandly that the assistant dispose of them.

Now she intended to buy two frocks, two hats and one coat. No more, as her shape would soon begin to change and to purchase more would be a waste of money.

She had packed her own underwear, reasoning that as no one would see it, it could not spoil the image she wished to present. Nevertheless, she spent some minutes looking enviously at the prettiest black lace-trimmed corset with a few diamantés scattered over the right breast which Madame Claudine discreetly displayed. That, too, would be a waste of money, she told herself. Her breasts were proud without any aid.

Madame Claudine was waiting as Rosie considered herself from every angle, and when she nodded and said: "Yes, it's fine," Madame clucked with delight.

As the woman was French, Rosie had told her that she was buying clothes for a journey to France. They had exchanged a few words in the language, and Rosie had been encouraged to find that she could cope easily with the pleasantries and understood what was said in return. Now, looking at herself in the mirror, she thought she might even hold her own among Frenchwomen. She would not have believed she could look so elegant. The dress that Madame Claudine's knowledgeable eye had selected was of pale amber wool which complemented Rosie's dark amber eyes and skin. It had full, bell-like sleeves, narrowing to fit tightly over the forearm. At the wrist, a delicate cuff of pale cream lace lay languidly over her hand. The same cream lace peeped from a panel in the skirt and made a deep false collar that framed a bib, buttoned with tiny jet buttons.

With Madame's help, Rosie had already chosen another dress in a dusty pink which had copious embroidery around the hem and at the neckline.

Madame, who was enjoying the metamorphosis of the cloak-wrapped Rosie who had arrived at her establishment, had picked out a charming wide-brimmed velvet hat. In dark amber, it exactly picked up the colour of the coat she was urging Rosie to buy. This, too, had leg o'mutton sleeves, and was trimmed with a panel of the softest fur. The hat was trimmed with the same fur.

"*Ravissante, ravissante,*" Madame Claudine breathed, urging a brown fur muff on her. "The perfect finishing touch, madame."

Rosie stroked the skins voluptuously and slid her hands into the silk lining. She wanted it.

"Oh, very well," she said, as casually as she could manage.

Madame Claudine's eyes opened wide when she was asked for the name of a store that sold luggage. The little black eyes snapped from

Rosie's old cloak, wool skirt and blouse which lay discarded on the dressing room floor to the elegant young woman who stood before her.

"It is an elopement?" she whispered, looking around her shop as if the clothes themselves might give away the secret.

"Yes," Rosie whispered back, enjoying herself. "You have not seen me, remember."

"Ah, *l'amour, l'amour*," Madame sighed, clapping her hands to her breast. "*Chère madame*, depend on me."

The clothes packed, Rosie looked again at the black corselet. It was saying "Buy me", loud and clear. It was wicked and decadent and she coveted it.

"And I'll take that," she said firmly.

Madame Claudine looked to the heavens.

"Ah, the lucky monsieur!" she said.

Rosie paid the not inconsiderable bill from her purse, which she kept on a belt round her waist and under her clothes. As she counted out the cash, she realised with a touch of alarm that she had made quite a dent in her money. But since the moment she had left Castor and Pollux unhitched outside Calistoga railroad station (knowing they would make their own way home) she had come more and more to the conclusion that she must travel as a wealthy woman.

Wealthy people, she knew from the novels she devoured when she was at school in Calistoga, met other wealthy people. Wealthy people did not have to fight so hard. Her mother had always said that money talked. The right impression could be vital.

But so far, so good. The little train from Calistoga to Vallejo had been fun, though the engine had made her jump by letting off steam with a great roar just as she was boarding. Trundling down the Napa Valley, she was astonished by the speed and kept a tight grip on the windowsill. A miasma of December mist was her last sight of the mountains that had surrounded her for most of her life. She found she was leaving without regret. The excitement grew when at the end of the railroad line she changed for a ferry for Oakland. Travelling on water was different again, but she had no fear. Measuring with her eye, she reckoned that even if the great overloaded thing did sink she could swim back to safety. And as the steamer made its way down the upper reaches of San Francisco Bay she had held on to her stomach and sat demurely waiting for the journey to end.

Leaving Madame Claudine breathing words of cheer and good luck, she went to buy her baggage at a store of the Frenchwoman's recommendation. Then, a little too laden for comfort, she wandered a while on the steep streets of the town until the winter chill became too much. In the cold sea wind she rode a cable car up to Nob Hill and back down again to Fisherman's Pier, dizzy as it plunged downwards, bells ringing. She did not remember ever having seen the sea before and she enjoyed the sudden, unexpected glimpse of blue in the distance, sparked by pale winter sunshine. The town seemed to be ringed with water and hills, with little islands bobbing in the bay. She had never seen anywhere so large and with as many houses, wooden and brightly painted, the taller buildings downtown silhouetted on the skyline.

Tired, she hailed a hansom cab and asked to be taken to an hotel.

"Which one, lady?" the cabbie asked.

"The best," she told him.

"The Palace?"

She had no idea, but said "Yes."

As he turned his horse in through the carriage entrance of the Palace she was overwhelmed. The hotel was beautiful; a graceful, five-storey building, built on four sides of an open courtyard. The balconies of each floor were constructed of white painted wood and fretwork. The entrance was through an elegant arch, and in the perfect circle of the courtyard, shiny black hansoms waited.

For a moment she felt lost, but headed for the entrance trying to appear as if she had been acquainted with smart hotels all her life. Inside, she hesitated. The lobby was as opulent as outside. It even had electric light. She wanted to stop and stare. As she hesitated, uncertain what to do next, a small bellboy, perky in his red and black uniform, came to the rescue.

"This way, ma'am," he said, leading her to the reception desk.

She could not help but notice that the reception clerk's eyes were definitely full of admiration as she registered into the hotel. She stood quietly while he fussed for a key and then smartly banged the bell on his desk for the boy to come to take her and her baggage upstairs. He was showing off a little. For her.

The guests, mostly male and dressed in black, lounging around the lobby, surreptitiously watched her progress to the open iron-grilled elevator, and continued to watch until, creaking, it had borne her from their sight. Rosie tilted her head higher, her back straighter, and inwardly giggled, wondering how much notice they would have afforded her in her old cloak and worn boots.

Alone in her room with its high, brass bed, the bellboy gone with a ten cent tip, she let the exhilaration bubble out, and sat rocking backwards and forwards, hugging herself, wanting to laugh out loud. Gradually she became composed and began to explore the room which was to be hers for just one night.

It was twice the size of her bedroom at home and amazingly it had a bathroom — the first she had ever seen. Cautiously she discovered how to use the brass taps over the sink and then tried those on the bath. They worked. And the water was hot. Awestruck by such luxury,

61

she decided to take her first ever real bath.

As the water ran, she went back into the bedroom and looked at herself again in the mirror. The amber of her new dress had tamed her olive skin, excitement had made her eyes gleam and her cheeks were high with colour. She hardly recognised herself, but she understood why the men in the lobby had watched her.

Carefully removing her hat, brushing an anxious hand over the velvet, she let down her hair and stripped to her drawers and spencer. Suddenly she was Rosie again. But only temporarily. She stroked the fur of her muff, eyes closed, enjoying its sensuous softness. Then she took the corselet from its tissue paper wrapping, and put it round her, hooking the front so tight that her breasts spilled out over the black lace edging. The diamanté over the right nipple twinkled bawdily at her in the mirror, and she winked back at her reflection, hands on hips, and then giggled. This was going to be the new Rosie, sophisticated; a woman of the world.

It was early the next morning when she left on *Eureka*, the big white paddlesteamer, in order to be in good time for her train. She was hungry; her new-found sophistication had deserted her when she funked a visit to the hotel dining room for both dinner and breakfast. She bought an apple from a street vendor and ate it while she watched the ferry buildings and the tall tower of the Embarcadero receding, feeling a little sad. San Francisco was a fine city. She had a sense of saying goodbye as she watched the curling fog roll in from the bay, masking the painted ladies of houses that lined the hills, and blotting out the downtown buildings. She put her hand on her stomach, queasy with the plodding movement of the huge paddlesteamer and thought of the life that was growing there.

It would be a boy. A son for Jean Paul. And what would they call him? Jean Paul would have to choose. She did not know enough French names.

As the city faded away, ghostlike and wavering in the fog, she brought out the one thing – apart from the baby – she had from him. Her French book.

She was well in time for her train. She redeemed her trunk from the left luggage office and stowed it, with a porter's help, in the baggage car on the train. The vaulted Southern Pacific station was bustling with noise and people and she found the size of the engine that waited, puffing impatient dragon clouds of steam, a little frightening.

But, head up, she followed the porter towards the Pullman carriages. They looked elegant, and she was pleased that her new carpet bag and valise had the sheen of money, enough sheen to make the porter deferential as he led her to the black Pullman porter who checked her reservation, his smile bright in the ebony.

"Come right this way, ma'am," he said.

She nodded and took a pace forward, working out the most graceful way to climb the stairs. She was filled with triumph. She had done it. She had escaped. The new Rosie was on her way to a new life.

At that moment, someone roughly grabbed her arm from behind.

She spun round, alarmed. "What are –" she started to say, and stopped, alarmed. It was her brother, wild-eyed, wearing his old dungarees and looking as if he had not slept, clinging with vicious fingers to her arm.

"I didn't believe it was you. Not at first," he said, breathlessly. "Who'd recognise you in that finery? What you doing, Rosie? Why you here? Pa says you're to come home straightaway. He sent me to get you."

She could not believe this was happening, just when departure was so close. She was filled with blazing anger.

"Peter, just let go of me," she said, her voice steely, trying to pull away from his grip.

"You're running away, ain't you?" he said. "You're going to Jean Paul. I know it." His voice was anguished. "They told us at Calistoga you'd booked to here. Pa said you'd be going East. But you're not going any place, Rosie. Not while I'm here to stop you."

"I am going East," she hissed, aware of the porter's fascinated face, "and you just let me be."

"No, you're coming home. Pa wants to see you. He's mad. I've never seen him so mad. He's fit to be tied."

His fingers were digging into her flesh and he was pulling her slowly back from the train door as she tried to release herself.

"I'm never going back." She was trying not to let anyone hear, though she felt like screaming. "I'm through with all of you. I'm leaving, you understand?"

She was thinking of the money. Pa must know she had taken it; that was why he was so angry, but most likely he had not told her brother. Peter, seeing her clothes and luggage, would be imagining God knows what.

"Better get on that train, ma'am." The porter looked perplexed, uncertain of how to help; a black man with a job to do but no right to interfere with white folk.

"Let me go," she almost shouted at Peter. "I'll miss the train."

"You ain't getting on that train. You ain't going no place."

She could have burst into tears of frustration but stood still for the moment, trying to think what to do. He still hung on to her. She had

63

not realised he was so strong. Breaking stones in that damn field must have done it.

"Ma'am –" It was the porter again, now anxious. Then his face cleared and he sighed with relief as a tall man in an elegant black suit and striped cravat, wearing a tall hat, strode up to them.

"Let go of that young woman's arm immediately," the man said to Peter. "Or I shall have you arrested."

Peter glared at him.

"Ain't none of your business," he said. "You leave us be."

"It is indeed my business." The man ran a well-manicured finger over his large black moustache. "I am a director of this railroad, and we do not permit our lady passengers to be molested. Let go, I say."

The last four words were delivered with such authority that Rosie felt Peter's hand drop from her arm.

"Please get into the train, madam," the man said, nodding at the porter, "and if you," he said, turning Peter, "are not out of this railroad station in thirty seconds, you will be finding yourself with some very serious questions to answer."

Rosie did not wait for the rest of the exchange. With a leap that lacked dignity, she was aboard, rubbing her arm and breathing hard with the relief of it.

"Sit down. Sit down and compose yourself," a light, pretty female voice was saying. "My, it was so lucky that my husband was by. What did that ruffian want?"

Gradually Rosie was taking in the scene – a carriage full of red plush buttoned chairs, deep and comfortable, each arm trimmed with bobbles, velvet curtains held back with silk ties, thick carpets and a splendour of gilt paint and small crystal chandeliers. Most of the seats were occupied, but the woman speaking to her was standing. She was maybe thirty and dressed in a crimson coat and dress, cut not unlike the outfit Rosie wore. Her hat was large and befeathered, a mass of small gold curls peeping from beneath, and her face was bright and friendly.

"What did he want?" she repeated, helping Rosie to a chair.

"I don't know." In spite of her confusion, she was aware of the need to speak slowly and carefully. "I think perhaps money."

"Jim should have had him arrested," the woman said indignantly. "That's just terrible."

"Oh no." Rosie almost panicked and, feeling a pang of pity for her unfortunate brother, said quickly: "That isn't necessary. Perhaps he was hungry."

The woman's face saddened.

"Oh poor thing, perhaps he was," she said. "I never thought of that. Shall I tell Jim to give him some money?"

"I think he's gone." A quick look out of the window showed no sign of Peter, and Jim was standing looking as if he were on guard, his timepiece in his hand, one foot poised on the step of the carriage.

"Well, you just sit down and rest." Her helper was still standing. "Would you like a glass of water maybe or my smelling salts? You look a little pale."

"No really – I'm fine." She was indeed now the train was beginning to move. She had escaped and Jim was aboard coming towards them, his face satisfied.

"Well, we dealt with that, did we not?" he said. "This railroad believes in looking after its passengers, particularly its Pullman passengers and most particularly young ladies travelling on their own. Let me introduce myself. I'm James Webster and this lady is Elizabeth Webster, my wife."

"How can I thank you, Mr Webster," Rosie said. "And your wife. She has been so kind."

"She is a kind lady," he said, smiling indulgently. "Now sit down, my dear, while I find out which car belongs to ..." he waited.

"I'm Rosanne Brunner," Rosie said quickly. "I'm going to New York and then to France."

"My," Mrs Webster said. "What a long, long way. Are you going to travel so far alone?"

Rosie nodded.

"Imagine! Mr Webster and I went to Paris for our honeymoon, but I think I'd have been real scared to have gone by myself."

"I have no choice." Oakland station was left behind. The train was puffing through seedy buildings that lined the track, shutting out the light. Peter would be wondering how he could face their father. Perhaps he would say he did not find her.

Mrs Webster's face was all sympathy and curiosity.

"Why is that?" she asked and then added hurriedly, "If you don't mind my asking, of course."

It seemed wrong and unkind to tell lies to this pleasant woman, but how could she tell the truth?

"My parents are dead –" that much at least was half true. "I'm alone in the world. My mother was French and I am going to France to find my family there."

Mrs Webster's blue eyes were round.

"Do you know where they live?"

"In Champagne somewhere. A village with the word Roses in its name."

"Is that why they called you Rosanne?"

"Exactly. How did you guess?"

They both laughed.

"How will you ever manage! I do think you're brave. Isn't she just, Jim?"

He must have been about fifteen years older than his girlish wife, and he nodded ponderously. "You must let us give our protection as far as New York, my dear. You will be company for Elizabeth on this long journey."

"I should appreciate that, Mr Webster," Rosie told him.

"Oh, and so should I," Elizabeth said, clapping her hands.

It was indeed fortuitous for them all. As the train rolled on through scarred mountains, deep in snow, and finally down to the endless blinding white expanse of the plains, Rosie and Mrs Webster sat together while her husband headed for the club car and the bar and the company of men. He would return with heightened colour, his conviviality increased as he led the two women into the dining car. And there, he gallantly insisted on paying the dollar for Rosie's meal each time they sat down.

Alone in her sleeping car every night, relaxed on the comfortable bed sweet with fresh linen, Rosie pondered her changing fortunes. She and Elizabeth Webster had become friends. She was Rosie now and Elizabeth "Lizzie". Lizzie was kind, gentle, a little immature, and mother of two little children, boy and girl, whom she missed painfully on her travels around the United States with her prosperous husband.

"He just likes to have me along," she confided in Rosie. "But to tell you the honest truth, I'd far rather stay at home with the children. I guess he thinks I might get into mischief if he left me behind because I'm so much younger than he is. But mischief!" She rolled her blue eyes. "If another man never laid hands on me again, it would be too soon."

Lizzie was from a well-connected but impoverished New England family who could trace ancestors back to the *Mayflower*. Her husband was first generation American. He had made his own way, and so successfully that he needed a wife with class as the finishing touch.

"He picked me," Lizzie said. "My parents encouraged it. He does have an awful lot of money, and he is kind to me. I feel he cares for me a lot. But I guess I just never did love him like I should. I feel bad about it sometimes."

Rosie listened and said little. She was fascinated by the way her new friend spoke, moved and behaved. She felt she must learn all Lizzie's mannerisms. Everything the older woman did echoed what Rosie had been aiming for when she refused to fall into the careless speech and ways of her schoolmates and had borne their mockery for her pains. She recognised Lizzie as the kind of person she herself wanted to be.

Yet while using Lizzie Webster as a model, she nonetheless felt warm and happy in her company. Rosie had never had a proper friend before. Now, having found someone with whom confidences were possible, she felt cosy and relaxed, as if she was at home.

Even so, in the long hours when they sat chatting in the Pullman car while endless America slid past the train windows, she could not bring herself to tell Lizzie the truth of her own circumstances. And doubted if she ever could.

Chapter Six

Dusk was falling as Peter deliberately let Castor and Pollux amble up the dusty roadway back to the winery at their own leisurely pace. He did not relish seeing his father. His toes clenched in his boots at the thought of the violent anger he would have to face.

He had made up his mind that he would not tell his father that he had been so near to bringing Rosie home again. He determined to say that he had never seen her, that the stationmaster at Calistoga must have been mistaken and that if Rosie had gone East she must have left from Sacramento. It was logical that she would have done. Sacramento was the more direct route across the country. In fact he couldn't understand why she had gone to San Francisco at all.

He couldn't shake the picture of her from his mind's eye. So elegant; dressed like a lady in her fur-trimmed coat and the big fur muff. He had never seen such an extraordinary change in his whole life, and he felt a spasm of envy, fiercely wanting for himself grand clothes, elegance and the self-assurance that Rosie had shown. The sight of her, suddenly so different, had made him discontent with the coarse dungarees and sweatshirts that were the uniform of his labour among the vines and that typified the low quality of his life. If he'd been dressed differently, he could have handled it all better. He could have stood up to that arrogant man on the track. The man wouldn't have threatened him if he hadn't been dressed like a peasant straight from some muddy middle-European field.

It wasn't fair, he thought, nearly ready to cry. With Rosie gone and Jean Paul gone, he'd always be a peasant; he'd never get away. Not now there was no one to help and encourage him. He'd just have to waste his youth fighting the phylloxera and his father – and for what? There were no rewards. Not now Jean Paul and Rosie had deserted him.

But where had Rosie got money for the clothes and the Pullman

68

ticket and the expensive luggage that the black porter had been carrying? That was the puzzle, and he would have liked his father's opinion on the matter. But there was no way he could broach the subject without his father realising he had seen his sister. It was all the fault of that arrogant man, he decided resentfully. A man who had threatened him with trouble just for trying to bring his sister back home again.

But maybe the man had his reasons. Maybe the man had paid for the clothes. Maybe Rosie had gone whoring. She had acted the whore with Jean Paul; why not with the moustachioed man? That was it, he thought, full of self-righteousness. She was whoring and he could never tell their father that; it would kill him.

And so Peter had found the way to square his conscience with the lie he was about to tell. Without difficulty he convinced himself that the falsehood was kinder than the truth.

The house was just a few slow hoof-paces away now and only one light burned in the kitchen, sending a flickering glow through to the front porch. Still postponing the encounter with his father, Peter stabled Castor and Pollux and then went to wash himself slowly and noisily at the pump before pushing the screen through to the kitchen door.

His father was sitting in the half-dark at the kitchen table, slumped over a glass, the whisky bottle at his elbow. The light gleamed on the stretched skin of his bald head, but his face was in shadow.

"So where is she?" he asked.

Peter went to take the warm towel from the rail on the range to rub his face and hair dry.

"I don't know, Pa,' he said, his voice muffled by the towelling. He held his breath and waited for the bellow of rage.

"You didn't find her?"

"No, Pa. The stationmaster must have got it all wrong. She must have gone to Sacramento all the time. Or maybe she plans to stay in San Francisco. She wasn't on the train East."

His father groaned and poured himself another whisky. He drank it down before saying, as if speaking to himself: "Well, she won't come back now."

"I guess she will," Peter said eagerly. "What else would she do? Where else could she go? I mean, she ain't got any money ..."

Hans Brunner made a noise that sounded like a snort of derision.

"She'll go East," he said. "She won't be back. It's like her mother all over again."

"Ma didn't run away from us," Peter said indignantly.

"Not from us. From her folks. Rosie's like her. Wants too much from life. Won't accept the way things are. Never gives in. God, when

69

you were children she'd fight me all the way. And when your ma died, it was her who told me to mind my manners and watch my drinking, just like your ma did. And if I gave her the back of my hand, or told her to do as she was told or to shut her mouth, she'd look at me with that Frenchified haughty look, her nose in the air, and her eyes hot and brown and so like her ma's that it hurt."

Peter had never heard his father speak in such a way, and he was embarrassed. He shuffled his feet, uncertain what to do or say as Hans took another gulp of the whisky before looking up, his narrow eyes glinting in the lamplight. "But you," he said contemptuously, "you look more like your German relations. Not that there's much of the Hun about you." He pushed the bottle across the table to where Peter stood. "Have a man's drink. You'll need it now your sister's gone. Who's gonna fight your battles now, son?" he asked. "You'll have to learn to stand up for yourself now, won't you? You'll even have to stand up to me. She always did that for you, too, didn't she?"

Peter knew with dismay that he was going to cry, and that once he started, what with all the tension of the journey home, he wouldn't be able to stop. His father's words had brought back the memory of the nine-year-old Rosie during his first weeks at school. Hair flying, fists flailing, she would rush to his rescue when the bigger, rougher boys in Calistoga had pushed him around and called him names he didn't understand until they'd reduced hm to tears. Then they would jeer at him, until Rosie's whirlwind intervention scattered them as a shotgun scattered crows.

Nobody ever messed with Rosie, but they tormented the life out of him until they found that Rosie's wrath always caught up with them. He remembered it all and felt the loss of Rosie for the first time as the tears streamed down his face.

"Crying?" said his father. "Crying for Rosie, or your French boyfriend? You didn't have to stand up to him, did you? You just had to bend over."

Peter gasped as if he had been punched. He felt the tears dry and his face burn. He wanted to strike his father but was afraid of the big fists, the broad shoulders and bullet head. He fought in the only way he could.

"OK, Pa," he said, years of spite heightening his voice. "I wasn't going to tell you. I did find Rosie, dressed in rich clothes and on the arm of a rich dude. She was getting on the train East, and she was travelling Pullman. You should have seen her luggage. I told her you wanted her back, and she just laughed at me. She said she'd rather go whoring than spend another day with you and your meanness and your drinking and your tempers. She said she hated you, and she always had, and she couldn't understand why Ma had married you in a

70

million years. She said Ma must have been mad. What she was saying, Pa, was that you're the biggest son of a bitch unhung and that a life of shame was better than a life under your roof."

He had been taking backward paces as he spoke, ready to run the moment his father leapt from the chair towards him. But Hans Brunner did no such thing. He had stared at his son as the words of hate poured out, and when he saw that Peter had finished, he gave a long, slow groan and his head dropped down to the table to rest on his thick arms. Horrified at what he had done, Peter saw that his father was sobbing, the thick shoulders moving up and down in grief.

For a moment he wanted to comfort his father; tell him it wasn't true. His hand was almost on his father's shoulder, and then he remembered the filthy thing the old man had said about him and Jean Paul. He burned with both shame and anger as he turned and went up to his room.

It was on the morning of the third day of the train journey that Rosie woke feeling sick to her stomach. She found herself quite incapable of eating the breakfast the porter brought. She made an attempt to get out of bed, but abandoned it, and with every roll of the wheels the waves of sickness came and went.

Lizzie came by to the sleeping car, anxious-faced, to see what was the matter. She made Rosie drink a little water and told her to go back to sleep. She managed to doze, and amazingly by lunch time the awful feeling had gone. But each morning the nausea persisted.

"I just don't understand it," she said to Lizzie. "I'm never ill."

Lizzie looked thoughtful.

They changed trains at La Salle station in Chicago. Again Mr Webster took over, very much the man in charge, but his eyebrows rose at the sight and the size of Rosie's trunk.

"It was my mother's," she explained hastily. "I wanted to take it back to France. It's full of my clothes."

The black porter who was attempting to load it rolled his eyes.

The sickness stayed with Rosie all the way from Chicago through Indiana, Ohio, and into New York state. On the last morning of the journey, as the train steamed down the Hudson River Valley, Lizzie, her face very pink, said: "Rosie, dear, forgive me, but could you be pregnant?"

Rosie could see Lizzie was finding it hard to look at her as she sat up in bed, wearing her cotton nightgown, her face green and her hands clutched over her heaving stomach.

She looked at her friend's concerned and embarrassed face and, to her dismay, burst into tears.

"Oh yes. Oh, yes –" she sobbed.

71

Lizzie's eyes instantly filled with tears of sympathy and her warm plump arms slid round Rosie to give a spontaneous and loving hug.

"I thought you must be," she said. "It's exactly how I was with my Emma. Oh poor you. What are you to do?"

"Find the father," Rosie said painfully. "Oh, Lizzie, when I feel just a little better I'll tell you all about it."

Later, when the sickness had subsided, they sat together while Mr Webster drank with his cronies. Rosie, with an enormous feeling of relief, did tell Lizzie all about it. Every last detail, and Lizzie held her hand tightly as the truth poured out.

"But you're so brave," Lizzie said at the end. "I can't imagine myself ever having such courage."

"Aren't you shocked?" Rosie asked her. "You don't have to go on being kind to me, you know. I shall be perfectly all right."

Lizzie pursed her pretty mouth, and shook her head.

"It must be wonderful to love someone as you did Jean Paul," she said. "I can't imagine it. I can only envy it. I should not tell Mr Webster what you have told me, of course, because I fear he would be . . . He might feel –" she hesitated.

"That I was not a suitable companion for you?"

"Well, perhaps. It shall be our secret, and I shall help you all I can. But, oh, Rosie –" she gave another of her impulsive hugs. "How shall you manage on your own after I am left behind in New York?"

"Like I did before, I guess," Rosie said. "The trunk was the hardest thing." Never one to be down long, she let a small giggle escape. "It was difficult enough to get it out of the house. Then I had to hide it, real good, while I got all the vine cuttings together. I snuck them from different piles so that my pa wouldn't notice.

"It took a while to work out how I was going to move it. And then I had this brainwave. My baby carriage was still in the attic. It wasn't in good shape, but the wheels were OK. I took two of them from the body and with a couple of slats of wood I hammered them on to the front of the trunk. Two more slats on the back made handles and I had a sort of wheelbarrow.

"I used two thick planks of wood to wheel the trunk onto the wagon, and got it off the same way at Calistoga. I wasn't sure how I'd manage, but Pa always said anyone would do anything for money, and he was right. I just showed that porter at the station a quarter and he was real keen to help. And so was everyone else."

The moment's elation faded.

"But, Lizzie. I feel bad I told you so many lies," she said miserably. "I hope you understand. I just had to. And all of this –" she looked round at the opulence of the Pullman carriage, "it's all new to me. I've never seen anything like it in my life before, nor ever met anyone like you. But it's funny –" she shook her head. "It all feels right. I'm not uncomfortable. It feels like it's how my life ought to have been."

"To the manner born," Lizzie twinkled. "Maybe your mama was a titled lady?" Her hands were clasped with the romance of it all.

"Don't know anything about my mama except that she taught us good manners, wanted me to speak French, and wouldn't let any of us say ain't. I suppose my mama was a lady. And I guess back home in Germany, my pa's parents were well-educated folk. Pa used to say that they'd both have done a darn sight better staying back home than coming here, to the promised land. But Mama used to laugh and say that then they'd never have met each other. She'd still be a governess in Paris, and Pa would be growing wine in the Rheingau, and what about Peter and me?" She stopped, surprised. "That's funny," she said. "I'd forgotten about her being a governess. Just talking to you made me remember it. I wish I'd asked my pa more about her."

"Well, you know her name. It's on her trunk. Maybe you really can find some relatives when you get there," Lizzie suggested.

"First I have to find Jean Paul and make him marry me," Rosie said, her spirits diving again. "Oh, Lizzie – imagine if he won't. What shall I do, so far from home and maybe with all my money gone?"

"Save enough to come back to New York," Lizzie said promptly, "and I will look after you."

"I believe you would." She laid her head on Lizzie's shoulder and sighed. "Oh, it's so good to have a friend. Maybe that's why I fell so hard for Jean Paul. Maybe I'd been lonely."

They were mopping each other's tears and half laughing when James Webster arrived to take them to the dining car for luncheon.

"Now, now," he said indulgently, "what is troubling you two lovely ladies?"

"We're just sad the journey is nearly over," Lizzie said quickly, "and that we have to part."

"If that's the only problem," Jim Webster said, "we can delay Rosie's departure. Stay with us for a while, Rosie. See New York. Keep Lizzie company. We'd be glad to put you up. God knows we have the space. When is your sailing?"

"I don't know," Rosie said doubtfully, thinking that she must continue her journey without delay.

"You have no reservation?"

"I didn't think I'd need one."

"My dear child," he sighed the sigh of a man of enormous efficiency surrounded by idiots. "You will have to stay with us. I shall take the matter in hand, arrange a berth and see you have all the necessary documents." As Rosie opened her mouth to make the polite protestation, he raised an imperious hand: "No more conversation about

73

the matter. We shall go in and eat, and you can stop worrying your pretty little head. It will all be taken care of."

And it was. From the moment the train pulled into the astonishng soaring edifice of Grand Central Station Rosie was taken over by the Websters. Their carriage waited at the station – they were bowed off the train into it. It seemed that Jim Webster was a director of the New York Central and Hudson River Railway as well.

"It's not that he actually works for them," Lizzie whispered as she graciously handed her umbrella to a porter. "They just borrow his money."

The Webster's dwelling on Park Avenue was not so much a home, more a mansion. If Rosie had been impressed by the luxury of the Palace Hotel and the pullman carriage, the house left her breathless.

The butler waited at the head of the stone staircase that led to the front door as their carriage drew up, and the driver helped them into the paved street. Rosie looked down the windy length of Park Avenue, surprised by its dignity in spite of the cold sleet that blew in the December air. Lizzie hurried her up the steps.

"I'm so longing for you to meet our children," she said, laughing. "And I'm so longing to see them myself."

Two little children, one fair as his father and one a girlish replica of Lizzie, bounced into the hallway, a stiffly starched nurse standing behind. Both flew into their mother's arms, and Lizzie, on her knees hugging them, turned to Rosie.

"This is how adorable children are," she said, her words full of meaning.

Later, after Rosie had been settled into her elegant bedroom and they were alone taking tea in Lizzie's own little parlour, Rosie, trying not to sound naive, said how much the house impressed her.

"It is so full of beautiful things, Lizzie. And so big. Don't you get lost sometimes? The drawing room would take all of Pa's house and the back yard, too."

Lizzie sighed.

"I often wish it was cosier and smaller – like my home in Boston. That was a much older house. We overlooked the Common. I was so happy there. Can you believe that Jim has another house in Connecticut? It is our summer home, and it is bigger than this. To tell you the truth, I hate it. But the men in the railroads are all making so much money that they are all out to beat each other with possessions and mansions and travel abroad." She sniffed. "My mama and papa find it all very vulgar, but they are pleased I shall never want for anything. And Mr Webster is very kind."

Rosie was silent. As Lizzie poured more tea and handed a plate of creamy cakes, she was wondering if marriage without love could be made tolerable by great wealth.

"But we must show you New York, Rosie, in case you become completely French and leave us for ever. It is the most marvellous city in the world. I must concede that Paris is beautiful, but not in the least modern, like here."

And indeed, Lizzie showed her New York. Rosie was spellbound at the opera, watchful at gracious tea parties in other wealthy homes, and marvelled at the Wall Street district where the tallest buildings were. She was taken to the Plaza for lunch, and introduced to the marvels of shopping at Macy's. She felt as if she were a sponge, soaking up every new experience, learning all the time.

She stayed with Lizzie while Mr Webster fussed with her reservation and various documents she was required to sign.

"He likes to have something different to do," Lizzie said placidly as she sat embroidering. "It makes a change from making money."

"I'd give anything for the opportunity to make money," Rosie said, from the other side of the fire. "You can't imagine how horrible life can be without it."

"Sometimes it is horrible to have too much," Lizzie said sadly. "Too much can be too little."

In the spacious bedroom that her hosts had chosen for her from the dozen or so in the house, Rosie lay each night, watching the dancing shadows from the open fire. The maid lit it early every evening to augment the steam heat against the chill of the nights, and because, Lizzie said, a real fire was so much cosier. Drowsy and warm, Rosie reflected on her good fortune, and thought how in her wildest dreams she could never have imagined that her instincts to appear moneyed could have been so astonishingly successful.

But what gave her the greatest satisfaction was that Lizzie and Mr Webster seemed to like her for herself. She reasoned that even he, by now, must realise she was not quite what she had appeared that morning on the station platform.

When she repeated the thought to Lizzie, her friend said: "My dear Rosie, Jim is no snob. How could he be? You would understand if you met his mama and papa. They came here from Estonia, and Jim's real name is quite unpronounceable. His parents are simply not grand, but Jim insists they are here for every Christmas and they come to the country house for at least two weeks in the summer. I like that about Jim. So many first generations here are such snobs. If they are successful they try to hide their parents from their friends. Can you imagine – they are embarrassed by their own folk. I guess it is understandable, but Jim isn't like that.

"And besides," she added quickly, "why indeed should he or

anyone else be a snob with you? You are charming, courteous, brave and very pretty indeed. If things were not as they were, I think he would insist that you stayed here with us until he had made a good match for you."

"But I love Jean Paul," Rosie said. "And there is – " she placed her hands on her stomach.

"I know." Lizzie looked sad. "Oh, but Rosie, I do fear for your future."

"I'm not scared. Think how fortunate I have been this far," Rosie said cheerfully. "You're just about the best thing that has ever happened in my life. I've learned so much from you, seen so much, had such kindness. Honestly, Lizzie, you're my lucky star."

"We will keep in touch?" Lizzie said. "You will write and tell me what happens? I shall be desperate to know."

"Of course I'll write," Rosie promised her.

Her good fortune continued the following day, when Mr Webster came home with both her passport and her boat tickets.

"You have a first-class cabin on the *Acquitaine*," he announced. "She is the finest and newest of the ships on the Atlantic run, and I can assure you, Rosie, that you will be well looked after during the crossing. I have had one of the directors speak to the Captain."

"First class?" Rosie said, thinking of her shrinking money. "But – "

"It is," Jim Webster said, back to the fireplace, fingers in his vest pockets, "a gift from Lizzie and myself. Well," he coughed, "half is from me, and the other half from Lizzie. She has insisted that it should be a return ticket."

"Just in case, Rosie," Lizzie said from her seat by the fire. "Jim says the return lasts for a whole year, which should give you lots of time to make up your mind."

"Don't worry," Jim Webster said, seeing Rosie's bewildered face. "If you don't use it I get my money back." He gave a huge guffaw of laughter to show it was a joke. Rosie stood staring at them both and then, overcome by their generosity, laughed too and flung her arms round Jim Webster, surprising herself by kissing him smack on the mouth before turning to give Lizzie a hug that knocked the breath from her.

"You're the two most wonderful people in the world," she said, and then, equally surprisingly, burst into tears and fled from the room.

Chapter Seven

My dear Lizzie,

Well, thanks to you I am truly on my way. What would I have done without you and Mr Webster! How can I ever thank you? One day I will find a way to show you how grateful I am for everything you have done for me.

I think of you every time I look around this beautiful cabin, and Lizzie dear, as I get nearer to France, I can hardly contain my excitement. I just pray that I will find Jean Paul and that he will be pleased to see me. He must have loved me while we were together, but then, why did he go?

Her pen faltered. Why *did* he go? Rosie did not care to dwell too much on the reason. She sat and stared at the porthole where grey Atlantic light filtered through. She was picturing Jean Paul in her bed, remembering how his hands felt and the warm dampness of his mouth and how it was when they were joined in musky closeness. A rolling wave of desire at the memory made her gasp. She shook the picture away, wondering how she could be pregnant and yet still burn for love, missing it more as each day passed. But then he had said she had the appetite; that she would crave it always. She turned her mind back to the letter.

I must stop thinking about negative things. I must be positive. And yet I cannot tell you what a feeling of security it gives me to have my return ticket. But as much as I long to see you again, I hope that it will not have to be used.

Lizzie, tell Mr Webster that the farewell party in the cabin for the three of us was perfect. I have both the cork and the bottle of that champagne in my baggage and I shall keep them for good luck. The bottle came from Ay, one of the places that Jean Paul told me about.

And when I heard that pop I remembered what he had said. He told me champagne was like gold and it sparkled like the sun. He said it was for celebrations and for love. He was right.

It was the perfect choice for our farewell, for I do love you both so much. Oh, Lizzie, we shall keep in touch, shall we not? Always.

I must tell you now what is happening to me. I felt so strange as I watched the Statue of Liberty disappear into grey haze. She is so big she made even this ship feel small. I kept thinking how Mr Webster had told me that she came from where I am going, and that she was the last sight I would have of America. I am sure he feels I am crazy to go, but perhaps one day you can explain. After the baby is born and all is well.

I have not been feeling so sick to my stomach as I was on the train. Maybe the excitement has something to do with that. And I am truly grateful for the gowns you gave me, for everyone here is so smart. My two frocks would have been looking sad by now against all the finery.

Everything is grander and more luxurious than even it was on the Pullman car. I am amazed all the time, but I have to try and look as if it is the way I am accustomed to live. Sometimes it is not easy. Thank goodness for the time I spent at your home and all you let me learn from you. I have even managed the array of knives and forks and dishes that come with every meal without making myself look foolish.

So much has changed for me. When I think how I funked the restaurant at the hotel in San Francisco! And I might well have starved on the train if I had not had you and Mr Webster for companions. I swear I would never have found the courage to go to the dining car alone!

Here on the boat I have a table to myself in a quiet corner and the waiters are kind to me, yet when I first walked into that huge dining room, I tell you, Lizzie, I was petrified. But I kept my head up like you, and my shoulders back, with my nose in the air and looked at no one until I got to my seat.

Now, thank goodness, I do not have to eat alone. I have met the most charming man called André Lefevre. He is old, but so courteous and has taken me under his wing. We met in such a curious way ...

Rosie paused to think exactly what she would say about André, when there was a discreet tap on the door of her cabin. The steward was outside, waiting to hand her an envelope.

"I have to wait for a reply, madame," he said.

Rosie slit open the envelope with the paper knife that lay on the small desk where she was writing. She read, nodded and said: "Tell Monsieur Lefevre that I shall be delighted to join him."

André wished her to come to a small party in his cabin before dinner and would be charmed if she would dine at his table afterwards. She smiled. Though she had joined him for meals for the past two days, he still never presumed. He always invited her. And she always accepted.

She had been writing wearing her dressing gown to help conserve her still meagre wardrobe. Leaving the letter unfinished she put on the soft pink embroidered dress she had bought from Madame Claudine. There was plenty of time to arrange her hair and pinch her cheeks to pinken them. She had settled to write to Lizzie in the hour or so before the dinner gong would summon passengers to the restaurant. Sebastian was abed and she was alone.

Sebastian was the reason that Rosie had come to know André Lefevre. Sebastian was five years old, a bright, active child who never sat still and who never stopped asking questions. André was his grandfather.

It was on the second day out that Rosie saw the little boy for the first time. The Atlantic, spitting white and none too good-tempered, was rolling the *Acquitaine*, causing most of the passengers to take to their cabins. The dining room was nearly deserted, but surprisingly the tossing of the boat had not troubled Rosie. She took her morning promenade around the wet deck, enjoying the wind tugging at her hair and clothing. As she came back into the shelter, her cheeks red and smarting from the cold and spray, she heard feet running behind her and turned to see a small child, crying piteously, fists dug into brown eyes. He had black curly wind-tousled hair and was shivering in a white frilly shirt. He wore no coat.

"Oh madame, madame," he said, clutching at Rosie's skirts before bursting into a babble of words. It was a second before Rosie realised the little boy was speaking French. She then bent to hear more clearly.

"Slowly, slowly," she told him.

Gradually Rosie understood through the tears and the snuffles that the child's nanny was in bed, suffering *mal de mer*. Quite simply, he was lost. He could find neither his grandfather with whom he was travelling, nor his cabin.

Rosie took the child by the hand and, with the help of her own cabin steward, in a few minutes was knocking on the door of a suite of rooms belonging to Sebastian's grandfather.

As André Lefevre opened the door, the boy flew towards him. The man, very tall, lean and elegantly attired in a black velvet jacket, cravat and dark trousers, bent to pick him up when he saw the small, tear-stained face.

"What is it, *mon petit*?" he said in French, and Rosie's heart turned

79

over at both the accent and the endearment. "Why have you no coat? You are cold."

"It's all right," she said quickly. "He was only lost."

The man looked at her, and so searchingly she had the uncomfortable feeling he had seen through her as though she were glass.

"You speak French?" he asked. He was over sixty, Rosie decided, but he was still handsome. His features were finer than Jean Paul's, the nose long and narrow, the eyes blue. He had thick white hair swept back from his forehead, deep bushy sideburns, and a narrow, white moustache. He stood straight, broad shoulders held back. He was nothing like Jean Paul in reality, but there was something ... just something that reminded her. Maybe the accent. Maybe simply that he, too, was French.

"You speak French?" The man asked her again, this time in English.

"Just a little." Rosie was confused by the sudden shyness she felt. "My mother was French."

"And you have rescued my *petit* Sebastian for me. You are very kind."

"Grandpapa, Grandpapa," the child was saying, "Nou-Nou is sick. She has the *mal de mer*."

The elderly man looked concerned.

"You have been alone this morning?"

"*Oui*, but it was good until I was lost."

"Is there no one to look after him?" Rosie asked. She had understood the conversation quite easily.

"Well, there is me," the man said. "But Sebastian finds me poor company, I am afraid."

On impulse, Rosie said: "Would you like me to look after him for you?" She laughed. "He can help me to practise my French."

"You would not mind?" he asked. "Children can be very tiring. Sebastian, I fear, exhausts me."

"I would not mind," Rosie said, and half-smiled at the look of relief on his face as he first thanked her and then introduced himself.

"I'm Rosie Brunner. I'm going to France." She was still shy in his presence and blurted out the information.

His blue-grey eyes twinkled at her.

"I had assumed so," he said dryly. "But where in France?"

"Somewhere in Champagne," she said.

"Somewhere?"

"Somewhere with Roses in the name."

He tapped his upper lip with a long, thin finger.

"That is all the address you have?"

She nodded.

"You are travelling alone?"

She nodded again.

He shook his head, and tutted gently.

"Perhaps you should sit at my table for luncheon and tell me about it," he said. "You will find that Sebastian's table manners are good for such an active little boy, and from the way he is holding on to your hand, I believe he will be pleased with your company."

"I will be pleased with his," Rosie said. "I have been a little lonely."

Afterwards she asked herself why she had said that. It was not in her character to make such admissions, but there was something so warm and, in spite of his age, so masculine about Monsieur Lefevre that she wanted to appear feminine and not her usual independent self.

She walked Sebastian around the deck, trying to tire him, but the child was unquenchable. His brown eyes would regard her slyly and sidelong before he attempted some act of mischief. She had to cling to his hand, and controlled him in a *mélange* of French and English. Eventually she discovered that her expression was sufficient to make him behave. And when he was good he was full of charm, stretching his arms to be picked up and cuddled, hugging and kissing her in an almost frenzied manner.

"He had no mother," André explained over lunch. "My daughter-in-law died when he was born. I try, but he lacks love. Philippe my son can sometimes hardly bear to look at him. He looks so like his mother, and Philippe feels her loss deeply. And the boy can be wilful and bad-humoured. He is difficult, but I myself am convinced it is the lack of a mother. His nurse is old. He is drawn to you because you are young and beautiful, and he is already enough of a Frenchman to appreciate that."

Rosie felt herself blush. Sebastian, sitting on a thick cushion, good as gold, was eating his soup silently, watching them both with questioning eyes. As Rosie sought for a reply, he suddenly gave his grandfather that sly sideways look and then banged his spoon down into the bowl. A cascade of hot liquid showered the table, mostly splashing the olive-green velvet dress that Lizzie had given Rosie.

Startled, Rosie leapt to her feet and Sebastian opened his mouth and let out a roar of dismay, anticipating punishment. A waiter appeared magically with a cloth, and Sebastian sat grizzling while her dress was sponged. André Lefevre had risen to his feet, towering over his grandson.

"Apologise!" he thundered.

"*Excusez-moi*," Sebastian whimpered.

His small head tipped back to look at her, and the round brown eyes, brimming with tears, melted Rosie. She bent to snatch him up, thinking perhaps her child would look like this.

"You are a naughty boy," she said in English. "A real bad boy, but you're adorable, too." And she planted a kiss on his nose.

Sebastian's face broke into a smile; the quiver of his lips stilled.

"Me good boy," he said, in French. "I like you."

André Lefevre shook his head.

"You see. What am I to do?"

"He'll be good now," Rosie said. "See."

Sebastian was not ready to chance his luck again. With a little help from Rosie, he ate his meal like a small adult, his behaviour exaggeratedly perfect.

"He is too precocious for such a small boy," André Lefevre said. "If my wife were alive it would have been better. But she has been dead six years now. She never saw her grandson." He shook his head as if to shake away the subject and added: "What are we to do about your dress? Is it spoilt?"

"I don't think so." Rosie was secure in the knowledge that she now had others. "And if it is, well, I guess it's not the end of the world."

"You are a very nice young woman," André said, and there was a note in his voice that was not paternal, and that caused her to lower her lashes. To her astonishment, she felt a touch of the same quickening feeling that the thought and the sight of Jean Paul had always been able to induce. "But this man is old," she told herself, while appreciating he was also elegant, charming, and somehow beautiful. He had, she realised, the same air of class that had attracted her to Lizzie. More class than Jean Paul could ever claim, and she found the elusiveness of the quality appealing. Again, she wanted it for herself, but she was beginning to realise that it came in the bone, and she would never grasp it completely.

"And why are you going to Chigny les Roses?" he asked.

She felt herself beam as she recognised the name.

"That's it! How did you know?"

"It is part of the Champagne," he said. "And there are not too many villages with 'roses' in their names. I thought it must be."

"It is."

"And why are you going?"

She drew in her breath.

"To find someone."

"A man?"

She nodded.

"A lover?"

She was nearly shocked at his casual use of the word, but felt herself nod again.

"He left you?"

A lump grew in her throat and she could only nod again.

82

"The man must be an imbecile," André Lefevre said, and patted her hand.

His touch gave the same kind of shuddering little shock that she had only experienced before with Jean Paul. Scarlet-cheeked, she jumped in her seat and said to cover her confusion, "Do you know Champagne?"

"The countryside, a little, my son used to have a house on the River Marne. The wine, well. I have drunk a great deal of it in my time."

"Oh." She was still ill-at-ease. "Is it your work?"

"No, just a pleasurable occupation," he said. "I have no work. I was in the army and I could call myself colonel if I wished, but military titles in times of peace are stupid. I was a military man because my parents wished me to occupy myself and it seemed as good a way as any – until I found myself fighting the Boche. I did not care for that."

She was not sure who or what the Boche were, but said: "Were you in New York on vacation?"

"Not exactly. My son is there. He is in the wine business. Not just for champagne. Every type of French wine. I thought it a better, more civilised occupation for a young man than fighting wars and masquerading in uniforms. Sebastian has been to visit his father, and now we are both returning to Paris."

"His father lives in New York?"

"For the time being. French wines are popular with your country-men. My son is the representative of a Paris wine-shipper. They move him around the world, though next year he is to return to Paris."

"American wine is good," she said defensively. "My Pa is a *vigneron*."

"Indeed?" His strongly-marked eyebrows rose. "In New York state?"

"In California."

"California! You have travelled so far alone?"

"It wasn't difficult. There's a train, and there were folk who were kind to me and helped me."

"I'm not in the least surprised," he said.

In the afternoon she played with Sebastian in the sitting room of the suite which André Lefevre occupied. Later she bathed the little boy and put him to bed. It took a long while before he went to sleep, clutching her hand.

The next morning the sea had calmed a little and a thin, watery sunshine brightened the grey, rolling expanse. Sebastian's nanny appeared, a plump pudding of a woman with a downward turn to her mouth. She was still green and shaky, but even so Sebastian seemed cowed by her.

André Lefevre insisted that Rosie take her lunch with him again, without the boy.

"So we may protect your pretty dresses," he said. "And besides, it is stupid for us both to eat alone. Eating is one of the great pleasures in life – particularly at my age. It is a pleasure that should be shared. There are few others to share these days."

He was looking straight at her, his tone conversational, but she knew exactly what he meant and felt there was a message there for her. She found herself curious. Did men of his age still want love? Surely not. He must be as old as her father, and her father had never looked at a woman after her mother died. Yet could it be possible to waken men of his age? She wondered.

André and Sebastian became her constant companions. She realised there would be whispers among the other passengers, but she did not care. She was happy and André treated her like a daughter. And he insisted they speak French.

"In Chigny les Roses no one will speak English," he said. "If you do not learn, you will be isolated there."

Their conversations were therefore slow as she stumbled, trying to speak to him.

"But it's impossible," she said crossly once. "I want to amuse you. How can I amuse you when I don't know the words?"

"Learn them," he said, "or you will never be able to amuse anyone at all in France."

At least some of the people at his party might speak English, she thought as she walked down the stuffy corridors to his suite, her toilette complete. She had barely been permitted to speak English for four days. But a babble of French greeted her as André himself let her into the cabin.

Eyes twinkling, he introduced her to the four other people who stood holding champagne glasses in their hands. The Purser and the Captain, both Frenchmen, and an elderly couple – the man short, fat and not unlike a toad, with an elegant, classically beautiful wife who seemed to be ablaze with diamonds.

The Purser, young, dark and with beseeching eyes, attached himself to Rosie. But her eye was on André. He seemed captivated by the diamond-studded lady, and Rosie found herself oddly irritated. "She may be better looking than me," Rosie was thinking rebelliously, while trying to concentrate on the Purser's platitudes, "but I'm younger."

She had a glass of champagne in her hand and found that she had drunk it rather quickly. It was immediately refilled. By the time the Purser and Captain returned to their duties, and the other couple, speaking too fast for Rosie to understand what they were saying, had also left, she had drunk three full glasses of the delicious bubbling wine.

"You didn't speak to me," she accused André, as he came back into the cabin after giving the steward his tip. He was pouring himself a glass of champagne.

"Of course not. The party was practice for you."

"It was really difficult."

"You did very well. I was proud of my pupil."

What very blue eyes he had, she thought dreamily. Even though they were wrinkled all round, like some nocturnal animal, the eyes themselves were still young, and blue and shining at her.

"That is just the second time I've had champagne," she whispered, not sure why she was whispering. "And I had three glasses. I feel quite funny."

"Not ill?"

"No funny. Floating. As if I hadn't any feet. Who was that woman?"

"Which woman?"

"The one you were ignoring me for."

"But the Purser had quite fallen in love with you."

"Had he? I didn't notice." She giggled. "What a pity. I should have noticed. You didn't answer. Who was she?"

"A viscountess. An adventuress. Her husband is very rich."

"Are you very rich?"

"Very. But he is richer." He moved to take both her hands in his and looked down at her, still smiling.

"Tomorrow is the last night at sea, Rosie."

She sighed. "I know. All the problems will begin again."

He pursed his lips. "No. At least not until you get to Chigny les Roses. I shall see to that. No, tomorrow is the Captain's ball. May I escort you?"

"Oh, yes. How marvellous." Suddenly she snapped back to near normal, dropping both his hands. "A ball! Oh no, that won't be possible."

"Why?" He had imprisoned her hands again.

She stared at him. Then she laughed.

"Oh, André, dear André, Cinderella cannot go to the ball because she cannot dance and she has no ball gown. André, I'm not a viscountess. I'm an ordinary girl straight from the farm. I had never before dreamed it possible that anyone would even ask me to a ball. I am an imposter. I am not rich or properly educated or anything. My clothes ..."

"But of course. That is obvious," he said calmly. "You do very well, *ma petite* Rosie, and you learn fast. Soon you will be exactly the person you wish to be. And nothing matters a – " he clicked his fingers – "because you have charm, beauty, taste and you are *gentille*. You cannot fail. I hope your lover appreciates you."

She let out her breath in a huge sigh.

"It's good you realise," she said. "It's hard pretending all the time. And there's so much to learn ..."

"You really cannot waltz?"

"I really cannot waltz."

"You will learn that in two minutes. Come here ..."

He pulled her towards him. His arm went round her back, and he held her right hand firmly. She felt herself against him, and she could smell the wool scent of his evening clothes. He was showing her the steps and counting, "One-two-three, one-two-three." She let him guide her and did her best to follow until she landed heavily on his foot.

"Ouch!" he said, involuntarily.

"Oh, I'm so sorry!" Without thinking she wrapped her arms round him and hugged him tight. "Did I hurt you?"

"No." His voice seemed rather strange. She looked up, and then saw in his eyes what she had seen so many times in Jean Paul's. She gasped, and felt her head tipping back and her lips parting as he bent to fold her into him and cover her mouth with his. He kissed differently from Jean Paul. His mouth was gentler, and he made little murmuring noises of pleasure. She pressed herself closer to him, and then realised with a sense of triumph that it was possible to wake a man of his age.

Instantly he stepped back.

"I think we should go into dinner," he said, still smiling.

She now felt as if her legs had joined her feet in some other place as she moved to cling to him again.

"Not yet," she said, tipping her face to be kissed again.

He sighed, ran his finger gently over her closed eyes and said: "Rosie, I am old. I should not please you."

"Then I will please you," she told him, full of confidence that she could.

He laughed.

"Oh, you would please me, of that there is no doubt. The sight of you pleases me, your eager listening eyes, your soft smiling mouth. Dark lady, beautiful girl. You please me. You are kind and loving. And you are brave. Rosie, I think I love you, so I shall try to forget you."

He was holding her face between his hands, and he bent to kiss her again, but lightly as if she was Sebastian's age.

"And besides," he added, "if we do not go into the dinner, the Viscountess and the worldly-wise Purser and his Captain will know exactly what we are doing. You were watching me with far too much attention and I admit it made me happy. But then I am an old fool."

She moved away from him and sat down on a leather chair. She did not want to move away from him. She wanted to be kissed again and more, but she also needed a moment to think. She was still bewildered by her intensity of feeling for this man who could even be old enough to be her grandfather. He had made Jean Paul recede in her mind – not completely, but the burning need had gone. What harm would it do, she asked herself, to give pleasure to André who had been so kind and so caring? She felt love from him in a way she never had from Jean Paul. There was a true affection; she felt safe when he was there. Jean Paul, she realised, had really only given her physical love and uncertainty.

"André," she said hesitantly, speaking in English as it was so important to say the words right, "I know you are old, but it doesn't matter because you are, well, special. You made me understand what the word gentleman means. We will go into dinner now because you know those people and it might embarrass you if we did not. I shall never see them again after tomorrow and so I don't care what they think. But tomorrow, I cannot go to the ball. You could teach me to dance, but you can't make me a ball gown. So tomorrow night – the last night – we will be together alone. No one will miss us and I want to give you pleasure, and I believe you will make me happy, too."

He was still and very grave, watching her. Then he bent to pull her from the chair.

"Rosie, Rosie, so tempting, so young and, I think, so full of champagne," he said, but his voice was tender. "Shall we see what happens tomorrow? And if nothing happens, my dear one, I shall remember always what you have said."

At dinner in the chandelier-lit dining room, he watched her every move as she ate. He watched her hands particularly, staring as she stroked the stem of her wine glass. His hands were much larger than Jean Paul's, she noted, but then he was a bigger man altogether. Taller, broader – and yet so much more refined. He managed to turn their meal together into a ballet of unspoken messages; his hands cupping a champagne glass were cupping her breasts; his eyes watching her mouth were watching them kissing. It was all delicate and understated, and yet he was able to heighten the desire she had felt in his cabin. And she, in turn, quickly learned the meaning of his messages, and sent him back her own.

He kissed her forehead when they said goodnight, and added 'until tomorrow' with special meaning. Alone in her cabin, she sat down to finish her letter to Lizzie, the pen spluttering over the pages as she wrote quickly. Writing would keep her mind off the lovemaking that she craved.

She told briefly of her encounter with Sebastian, and some of what had happened since. Should she tell Lizzie about what had happened that evening? She hesitated, pen dipped in ink, decided against it and sighed. Was she always going to have to have secrets from people she

87

loved? Life was becoming more and more complicated.

"He makes me speak French all the time," she finally wrote, "and I am really getting quite good at it. He is careful to speak slowly so I can understand, and to correct my pronunciation. I believe I shall manage when I get to Chigny les Roses. He has promised to see that I get there safely, though I fear he has not yet seen my trunk. Remember Mr Webster's face! Lizzie, I have been so lucky. I have received such care. It must be meant for me to arrive safely."

She added loving messages, and then sealed the letter in an envelope to give to the steward before undressing and getting into her bed.

The sea was reasonably calm, and she lay flat on her back, her hands over her breasts, staring at the dark ceiling. The engines of the ship throbbed insistently in the background, as they did all the time. It was as if the ship had a heartbeat like a person. A person. André had said that soon she would be the person she wanted to be. Her only problem was that she was not yet certain who that person was.

There was a different atmosphere on the ship the next morning, as people readied themselves for the last day. Rosie ventured onto the other decks where the second- and third-class passengers were, to see how she would have travelled had it not been for the kindness of Lizzie and her husband. She was allowed there, but they were not allowed where she had come from. It was not fair, she thought. The quarters she saw were cramped and not too clean, the noise from the engines louder, and the smell quite different, particularly in the third and steerage classes. Again Rosie told herself that somehow she would never be poor again.

Later she walked with Sebastian, the nanny, sour-faced, walking behind. Nou-Nou, as Sebastian called the woman, had made her dislike and distrust of Rosie obvious. She was jealous perhaps, and she watched Rosie constantly, her manner sullen. She was also stern with the boy and while she was near there were none of the sly, sideways looks and naughtiness from Sebastian. But she ruled by fear and Rosie wondered if she should say so to André.

As it was the last day, Sebastian was permitted to join Rosie and his grandfather for luncheon, having promised passionately to be good.

As they waited for the entrée to be served, André said suddenly: "I have been thinking about what you told me last night."

Expecting criticism, Rosie felt her chin go up.

"Don't look so defensive," he said, smiling at her. "I was merely wondering if you had let your family know that you are safe."

The question puzzled her.

"But they won't care," she said. "Not a bit. I expect my father will miss the work I do, but I don't think he'll miss me."

"Ah, thoughtless youth!" André sighed. "Your father is probably frantic with worry. Any father would be, I assure you, my dear, however uncaring he might appear. Will you do something for me?"

"Of course," Rosie said, wondering if he could be right. Her father, she was sure, would still be very angry indeed about the loss of his money. His money would be the only thing he wanted back.

"I want you to write to him, explain why you took his money, and why you felt justified in doing so. You owe that to yourself as well. And you must tell him you are safe. Will you do that?"

Rosie thought about it.

"Do you think it was wrong of me to take the money?" she asked.

"Under the circumstances, no. But it would be more honourable, and kinder, to explain. You might feel less guilty about it yourself even," he said with a smile.

She realised he was right, and nodded.

"I'll do it this afternoon," she promised.

It was as the pudding, an exotic concoction of nuts and cream and sponge, was being served that Sebastian said: "Grandpapa, why can't Rosie stay with us in Paris? Why does she have to go to Champagne?"

André and she looked at each other, and she was startled by the momentary naked longing in his eyes.

"I have to go, Sebastian," she said, and André's eyes were asking 'Why?'

"Perhaps Rosie would spend a day with us?" he suggested. "You could show her Paris, Sebastian, and she could leave for Reims the next morning."

Now he was not looking at her, but at his plate, and he had spoken carefully and noncommittally.

She hesitated before she replied, thinking that it would be one more day before she had to face Jean Paul, tell him the news of the baby and wait, in fear, for his reaction. It would be one more day in the safety of André and his care for her.

"I think that would be very good," she said, and Sebastian's squeals of delight went unheard as she and André smiled at each other. Then he said: "I shall take you to dinner at Maxim's."

"Maxim's? Is it special?" she asked.

"It is special. And we shall waltz."

"I have no gown."

"You will have a Paris gown. Ah, Rosie – let us drink champagne. If I could have my way, you would drink nothing else."

He came to her cabin that night. The corridors were silent; even the room stewards were on duty at the Captain's ball. Only the throbbing of the engines disturbed the quiet and stillness.

She waited for him in the robe and black corselet she had bought

89

from Madame Claudine, agonising as to whether this was the right thing to do. It seemed wrong to be fully dressed and the corselet was the kind of garment that men liked, though she only had a pair of white frilly drawers to go beneath it. She remembered Jean Paul's problems with her spencer and smiled at the idea of André, gentle André, dealing with the matter in the same violent manner. She knew instinctively that he would release each hook, slowly and gently, until she was freed. For a moment, she felt ashamed at what she was doing, but the need was too great. All the time she could hear Jean Paul's voice saying: "You have the appetite. You will want it again. And again."

André was dressed when he arrived. He kissed and caressed her without speaking and then urgently slid off her robe. When he saw the corselet and the frilly white drawers, a smile curved under his white moustache.

"And where did you get that?" he asked her, and she could see he was trying to control the smile.

"In San Francisco," she said. "Is it all right?"

"It's very pretty," he said, "but you are prettier."

As she had thought, he deftly unhooked the garment, and then half-carried her to the bed and covered her with a sheet. He then removed his own clothes neatly and quickly. She had put on only one light in the cabin, and he left this as he moved towards the bed where she lay, only then sliding the frilly white cotton drawers down to her feet. His body was still firm and had thick grey hair over the chest and stomach. He was not yet proud, she saw, but he lay down beside her and held her close to him, muttering endearments, stroking her hair, pulling it back from her face and kissing her eyelids and cheeks with light butterfly kisses. He examined her body, exclaiming over the beauty of her breasts and their hard, red nipples. He stroked her belly and the luxuriant hair below. "So soft, so soft," he sighed. And then he kissed her, searching her mouth with his tongue, before turning his attention to her breasts, gently biting and teasing at them until she felt weak with the delight of it. He was surprisingly agile for a man of his age, and turned easily in the narrow bed to kneel and inspect, fold by fold, what lay below the rounding orb of her stomach. "So beautiful," he said in English. "So lovely." And then he was kissing her, probing, and she wanted more.

But her hands sliding over him discovered that though his love-making had a tenderness and sensuality that she had never known with Jean Paul, he was not young and nor was he strong and erect.

He whispered in her ear. "I told you. I am old. I shall disappoint you."

"No. It's already too late for you to disappoint me," she whispered. "And besides ..."

She was remembering her lessons with Jean Paul. If you can make me live again, as I showed you, he had said when he, too, had been as André was now.

She laughed at the challenge, straddling him and leaning over. "I shall enjoy my work," she informed him as she stroked, kissed, rolled, drank, thinking of improvisations that had not been necessary with Jean Paul.

"Now," she eventually said, lifting her head and turning swiftly to lie beside him.

He turned on his side, and she guided him in. They clung together, while his hands still played with her body, hurting her a little, until quite suddenly it was over for them both. There was a long silence. Then: "There," she said contentedly, "I told you."

"You are a marvel," he said. "An old goat like me – "

"No, no – not a goat," she said. "Just slower. That's good. It lasts longer."

"Rosie, dear Rosie. What are we to do with you," he said despairingly. "You must be careful with your life. I should not have let this happen. If I could have you for always . . . but I am too old and you are too young . . ."

"And I have to go to Champagne," she said, her face buried in his shoulder.

"Why do you have to go to Champagne?"

She took a long breath and let her instinct for honesty take over.

"Because I am pregnant."

His arms tightened round her.

"I see." He got out of bed and turned out the light. Then he came back, and held her close. "Tell me."

She told him, slowly, but missing out nothing. "I have to find him," she said eventually. "I do love him, and the baby – the baby needs a father."

"Then why me tonight?" he asked in the darkness.

"I don't know exactly. It's hard to explain. I *like* you better than I ever liked Jean Paul. You're nicer – a gentleman." She had to revert to English. "I think Jean Paul had more class than all those farmers and grape-growers I grew up with, but he wasn't like you. There's something about you. Lizzie had it too. Something I want. And apart from all that – you are beautiful."

He laughed out loud.

"You are looking for a father, maybe?"

"Well, maybe. You must have been a wonderful father to have. But I wanted you – in the way we've just been."

She heard the faint breath of a sigh.

"Rosie, the appetites of the young are strong. Your Jean Paul woke

91

you up and left you. I'm the first man you've been close to since. I know in your country women aren't supposed to have desires. In mine it's allowed, and women do. Men do, too. But as we get older, they lessen. I had no thought of making love for years. I thought it was over for me. Now you've aroused the man I thought was gone. Rosie, I would like to say that I will marry you and give your child a father, but I must think about it. My instincts are to imprison you with me. How could I let you go? You've made me young again. But there are difficulties. My family ..."

"Would not approve," she said. "But André, it isn't even in question. I want my baby to have his real father."

"I could give him a better life," he said defensively.

"No. It would be wrong. Let's not talk about it any more. Let's sleep."

"You sleep, I must get back to my own bed before the ball ends," he said. "I would like to stay, but you need protecting from yourself."

He was out of the bed and dressing swiftly, the light back on.

"Sleep well," he said, kissing her forehead. "Tomorrow you travel with Sebastian and me, and you stay as a guest at my home. Remember, we dine at Maxim's before you leave. And I love you."

The door opened and closed quietly and he was gone. Rosie sighed a deep sigh of contentment, and slept.

The only snag in the exodus from the ship and from Le Havre the next morning came when André saw Rosie's trunk, along with the other luggage, inside the harbour buildings.

"I meant to tell you," Rosie began nervously when she saw André's face. "It's full of vine cuttings. It's not as heavy as it looks."

"You managed to get this far with that?" André was shaking his head. "I can't believe it."

"I did have help," she told him.

She was impatient to be away from the harbour and into France properly. All morning she had stood by the ship's rails, watching the startlingly green coast of France and the white and rust villages on the clifftops slip by in the distance. She kept thinking of her mother. Her mother had sailed this way, so long ago now. And now she was coming back from what her mother believed was the promised land, hoping to find a promised land of her own.

"You'll need more help," André said dryly, giving the trunk a light kick with the toe of his well-polished boot. "Don't move away from where you are. I'll be back soon." He strode away leaving Sebastian clinging to her hand as they stood with Nou-Nou watching the activity while people flooded from the ship to claim their baggage.

André arranged everything. Nou-Nou went in a separate cart with all their baggage, including Rosie's trunk, to the railroad station. Then she was with him and Sebastian in a hansom cab, clip-clopping along the cobbled streets through rows of small narrow houses, heading towards the station.

"Paris is better," he assured her, waving a hand at the view.

"This is nice," she said. "It seems silly now, but I wondered if there would be streets or trains here. I believed America was the most modern place in the world."

"It is," André said, "but the rest of us are not savages. In fact, in some ways ... but you will learn for yourself."

The first-class carriage of the train was clean and comfortable. It had none of the luxury of the Pullman, but then, the journey was so much shorter. In less than two hours they were pulling into a station where André's own carriage and pair were waiting with a coachman and manservant. It was a sharp, clear afternoon with a cold sun shining. The smoky station was full of chattering, shouting people; porters in blue, urchins in caps, fine ladies in furs, and solemn self-important men in frock coats and top hats. Rosie drank it all in as once again the baggage was sorted, trying to tune her ears to the language. Even the smells were strange and different, and the buildings around the station looked more solid and heavy than those at home.

"Thank heavens I am with you," she said. "I should have been so lost."

"Rosie," he said, "if it were not me, someone else would be looking after you. You will never be alone." He patted her hand. "And now we shall take you the long way so you can see a little of Paris. I live on the Île de la Cité, but we must show you some of the glories of Paris as we go."

They drove up and then down the length of the Champs Élysées and through the grandeur of the Place de la Concorde. The fountains played frostily, surrounded by the splendour and dignity of buildings that seemed to Rosie very old. She was deeply impressed as they drove along the border to the Seine, crossing the river at the Pont Neuf and then past the vast brooding mass of Notre Dame.

"It's like Lizzie said," she told André. "It's not modern, but it is so beautiful. And cold," she added, shivering in her wool coat, her hands tucked into her muff.

His house was tall and thin with many dark rooms and spiky-leaved plants in pots. Family pictures covered the walls, and the furniture was unlike any she had seen before, formal yet elegant. She felt she would be afraid to sit on the chairs with their damask coverings and delicately carved pale grey woodwork. And yet the house was welcoming. A warm smell of cooking came from the kitchens below, a manservant had opened the door and shown not a flicker of surprise at the sight of Rosie. He merely called a smiling maid to show her to her room, where a fire burned as if they must have known of her arrival.

"Dinner will be at seven, madame," the maid said in rapid French. To her relief, Rosie understood, nor, after her stay at Lizzie's did she demur as the girl began to unpack her clothes from the luggage which had already been brought up.

There seemed to be a great many servants to look after one man and a small boy. Two served at dinner in the quiet, heavy-curtained dining room. She was nervous over the meal, wondering if he would want to stay with her under his own roof. But the bed in her room was small, and there were so many people about she hoped he would not. She felt as warm towards him as before, but the fire in her was quenched. She did not need him in that way. Her thoughts had returned to Jean Paul.

She had no cause to be anxious. André walked her to her bedroom at ten. He took her hand and kissed it.

"I shall say goodnight now," he said. "But tomorrow we will go shopping, eh? Sebastian, I fear, will insist on coming with us. Do you mind?"

"But certainly he must come," she said. "I am here at his invitation. Remember?"

She slept fitfully. Alone in the room where the shadows lengthened and the light changed from orange to grey as the fire died down, it was dawning on her that her journey was almost at an end. One more day and then Chigny les Roses, and Jean Paul. The reluctance to face him had changed to a feverish impatience for the meeting to be over and her fate to be decided. What if he did not want to know her? At least, she thought, optimism rising as usual, there was Lizzie's return ticket and now André. If the worst came to the worst, André would see she came to no harm. But the fever of impatience kept her awake until dawn's grey light slid under the heavy velvet curtains of her room.

André had risen early, absurdly full of excitement. He had slept soundly, happy with the thought of Rosie under his roof. It was enough that she was near; she did not have to be in his bed. He lay awake, planning the day and not wanting to disturb his valet, Marius, so early. But at 7.30 he rang and almost instantly Marius knocked and came into the dark bedroom carrying a large cup of coffee on a small silver tray.

"It's a fine day, monsieur," he said. Marius, a small, quiet man who had been with André since his army days, always gave his forecast of the weather before he drew back the curtains. Having let in the pale winter sunlight he brought a silk dressing gown to the bed, and said: "I took the liberty of preparing a bath, monsieur."

"Ah, good," said André, "and I think the new coat for today."

Marius merely bowed gravely, but André understood perfectly well

94

why he had prepared the bath and Marius understood perfectly well why the new coat. Marius in his own way was a man of the world.

Before dressing and going downstairs to breakfast, André stood looking at himself in his long cheval mirror. He tightened his biceps, disliking the flagging skin on his upper arms, and pulled in his stomach muscles, which were still flatter than those of many a young man. Having regard for his age, he was not entirely displeased with what he saw. Then, remembering Rosie's youth and ardour, he would have wished himself twenty years younger had he been a man to indulge in futile wishes.

"You," he said, addressing his reflection, "are an old fool."

Nevertheless, she had still let him make love to her, and maybe would again, in her own time. The consolation of age was that the fires burned more slowly; he could wait. But what foolishness to fall in love with such a child. And yet there was a maturity about her that women of twice her age lacked. And with the maturity, a sudden, touching vulnerability that tore at the heartstrings and made him want to cocoon her from the world.

His experience told him that this headstrong venture she had launched herself upon must be doomed. If the young man had had the wit to see what a treasure he had won, he would never have left. But André admired her bravery in setting forth to right the wrong and to give her child a father. If the lad rejected her, would she return to Paris? And would he himself marry her? Chance would be a fine thing!

He was waiting for her in his own small sitting room, an empty cup of coffee before him, already attired for the street except for his cape and top hat, when he heard her footsteps hurrying down the passage.

She came into the room with a clatter, her colour high and her hair dishevelled.

"André," she was speaking in English and almost whispering, looking around as if afraid of being overheard. "If we buy a gown, will I have to try it on?"

"But, of course," he said.

"Then we can't."

"Can't what?"

"Buy a gown." She sounded exasperated.

"Why not?"

"Because my under-things will show. They are not good enough. I made them myself."

He laughed.

"I see. Then we shall have to buy some under-things first, shall we not, and perhaps something black to go with that other pretty garment of yours?" He was teasing her, but he was pleased that the memory of her in the provocative, spangled garment tightened his loins.

Her cheeks reddened.

"I didn't mean that. You can't buy me those things. It's not right."

There was something in her voice that made him stop teasing. She was distressed.

"Is something the matter?" he asked.

"No, I'm just fine," she said, but palpably was not. He looked at her anxious face, debating whether to question her, but then decided that she would tell him all in her own good time.

Her anxiety and apprehension shot through the morning. She refused coffee. She was distracted in the carriage, and almost abrupt with Sebastian when he chattered to her, and then his watchful eye saw her remorse at the anxiety in the child's face, and noted her sudden hugs and kisses in atonement. She was not concentrating; her mind was elsewhere. With her Jean Paul, he thought, and sighed.

At the corsetière's Sebastian babbled happily that in her new gown she would be his Queen while André sat on a gilt chair, far too small for him, and picked out a selection of silk and lace garments since Rosie seemed to have become incapable of decision. He tried to ease her embarrassment as the salesgirl brought out boxes and boxes of intimate fluffy soft underwear, tissue wrapped.

"In France," he whispered, "men are accustomed to choose pretty things for their ladies."

"It's very strange," she said distractedly. "Very strange."

They went to Worth's, which André explained to her was the finest couture house in Paris – indeed in the world. He could see that she was fascinated by the richness of the carpets, the glitter of the chandeliers, and the bowing attention she received, but he sensed she was impatient for it to be over. Then when the fashion show began, she seemed dismayed as she watched the mannequins who swayed out to show gowns for her inspection. And he realised that their confidence and beauty was filling her with an uncharacteristic insecurity. Something was definitely wrong.

Once again, he made the decision. He chose a white silk gown with pearls and diamanté, cut low to show her shoulders and the swell of her breasts. It was finished with a soft shawl collar that covered her upper arms.

He watched as she stared blindly at herself in the long mirror. Women fussed around her, adjusting, nipping, tucking with delicate pins, exclaiming that madame looked *ravissante*, but madame did not respond. And when the fitting was done, André insisted that the gown should be ready that evening, ignoring the wails of despair from the imposing head vendeuse.

"We would prefer to make the gown again for madame," she was saying, but André was adamant it should be ready that day. Sebastian clung to Rosie's hand and told her she was beautiful, but André could see that she felt nothing but impatience, and the joy faded from the day.

The carriage took them home, where Nou-Nou, her face as sour as if she had eaten a lemon, whisked Sebastian away.

He took Rosie's cold hand in his. "Now, my dear," he said soothingly, "we shall have a glass of champagne and then a little lunch. Then you must rest before this evening."

"This evening?" she said dully.

"We are going to Maxim's, and you are to wear your new gown," he said, as if speaking to a fretful child.

Suddenly her eyes were full of tears, brimming over, spilling down her cheeks, and she covered her face with her hands.

He felt her pain himself, and put his arms round her, resting her head against his chest.

"Oh, my dear one," he said. "What is it? You are not happy? You have not been happy all day."

"André, I can't." She was having difficulty speaking and somehow had lost control of her resolute lower lip. "Not tonight. Not Maxim's. Not love. Nothing. Oh, please André. I must get it over with. I have not slept for thinking of it and all day it has been growing. I want to get to Chigny and find him and be sure all is well. I can't wait any longer. I can't bear the uncertainty. And you, you who have been so kind. Oh, André, please understand."

He understood only too well, and for a moment the sadness was insupportable. Then he led her to a small sofa, sat her down, and perched on the edge beside her, facing sideways to take her hands in his.

"Rosie, now stop. No more tears. It is bad for your baby. You shall go to Chigny this very moment. I will take you myself." He made himself sound strong, though the thought of delivering her to another man was unbearable.

"No – please. I need to go alone," she said. "I couldn't be proper company. André, I'm afraid. I feel such an idiot. I'm not usually like this, honestly."

He had pulled her head onto his shoulder and was stroking her hair, determined to comfort her.

"Rosie, listen to me. You don't realise what strain you have been living with," he said. "Think what you have achieved to get this far. Of course you are afraid. You are like a soldier who has gone to the war bravely, marched forward, kept his shoulders back and his spirits up. Now, tomorrow, it is time to fight. Of course you need it to be over. It was wrong and selfish of me to try and keep you for a little longer. Believe me, I had no intention of –" he hesitated – "of troubling you

97

tonight. Not now I know more. It is your company I crave. You must stop crying and be brave again. You must be composed and resolute. Jean Paul will not welcome you if you cry. Men do not like tears."

"You don't seem to mind," she said dismally.

"I am an old man, in love, and to me your tears are beautiful. I could drink them from your face. Now, to your room and pack as quickly as you can. The carriage will take you to the station. Marius, my valet, will travel with you – not at your side, but nearby to make sure you are safe. He will deal with your baggage and find you a carriage to take you from Reims to Chigny, though it would be better that you rest the night in Reims."

"I can't do that," she said. "I have to get there."

"Very well," he soothed. "Now just get yourself ready."

Released, the eagerness with which she jumped to her feet pained him. Then suddenly she stopped.

"Oh, André – the dress. Can you stop them altering it?"

"I have no wish to," he said calmly, though had the dress been to hand he could have torn it to shreds. "The dress will be here, waiting for your return, when you will wear it for me. I shall take you to Maxim's and be the proudest man in Paris."

He instructed the maid to help with the packing. He insisted on changing her money from dollars into francs, and she was concerned that he had given her too much. He had given her a great deal too much, for he was fearful of what might happen to her when she reached Chigny. While she was upstairs, he wrote a list of addresses, including his own, and instructions on what to do if she were in any kind of difficulty. Writing the words steadied him.

Still calm and in control, he ordered Nou-Nou to bring Sebastian to say goodbye. The child was wearing his best sailor suit, his small face set in downward lines and as Rosie, her hands trembling, came into the hall, he began to cry. She bent down to hug and kiss him, and he could see that there were tears in her eyes as well.

"Please don't go," Sebastian wailed.

"I'll come back, I promise," she told him, and kissed him once more before hurrying through the door and into the street.

André followed her and helped her into the waiting carriage. He smiled at her reassuringly, and could not resist just brushing away an errant lock of hair that had escaped from under her hat.

"I shall telegraph ahead to make sure there is a conveyance waiting for you," he told her, handing her the soft leather wallet in which he had put her money. "I have written my address for you. It is in there with others that may be helpful if you have problems. Should anything go wrong you must return. You have sufficient money, and you go with my most heartfelt wishes for your happiness. And whatever

98

happens, you must let me know where you are, and you must come back one day to Paris. After all, you have promised Sebastian."

He saw she was near to tears again and could only nod dumbly as he closed the carriage door and gave the coachman the signal to be on his way. He watched until the carriage was out of sight and his smile had set into a grimace, and then he went back into his house and shut the door on the emptiness outside. Somewhere he could hear Sebastian crying and Nou-Nou's scolding voice. A vendor was calling his wares in the street below and a pigeon preened and cooed on his windowsill. He moved to shush it away, and suddenly André felt very old.

Marius took care of everything at the Gare de l'Est. He found Rosie a window seat in the first-class compartment, and made sure that her luggage, including the trunk, was safely aboard.

Once she was settled, he bowed and said: "I will return when we arrive at Reims, madame." He then slipped discreetly away.

She barely took in the green countryside and the soft hills that the train, trailing smoke, chugged through. The journey took no more than an hour yet it seemed interminable. The tension in her was so great that she needed to pace up and down, but forced herself to sit, hands clenched in lap while she stared blindly out of the window. She was aware of her ingratitude to André, but that she would have to think about later.

The light was beginning to fade as the train snorted into Reims station. Again Marius managed everything. She waited, one booted foot tapping, while he found the porters and then the carriage that was to take them to Chigny les Roses.

"The village is almost twenty kilometres away," he told her when he returned.

Kilometres meant nothing.

"How long will it take?" she asked.

He shrugged.

"There are two horses for the carriage. Around an hour and a half, perhaps. But the coachman needs the address."

"I have no address," she told him.

"No address?"

"It is the home of the family Dupuis. They live near Chigny les Roses."

Marius looked perplexed for a second. Then he said: "Well, we must go to the village and enquire."

The light faded quickly after they were through the narrow overhanging streets of the town. A creeping mist settled on the hillside in grey shrouds. It seemed a bad omen, and she decided not to look as the carriage trundled on. She could hear Marius talking to the coachman, but could not distinguish what he said. Outside, it was now dark, and from her seat she could see the glow from the two lamps on the carriage. Suddenly she was weary; careful that her boots did not touch the plush of the long seat, she stretched out. Sleep, she reasoned, would make the time pass faster and she would be rested before facing whatever lay ahead.

Later she was dimly aware of lights outside and voices calling, but no one opened the carriage door. She dozed on, half-asleep and dreaming, half-awake and fantasising that Jean Paul would welcome her with amazement, pleasure, kisses – and then love. In these last moments of her journey she was pushing aside the thought that he would not be pleased to see her at all, that it might be the reverse. But still there was the baby to consider and she held her hands protectively over her stomach.

She was wakened by the carriage stopping. This time she knew instinctively that they had arrived. There was silence, except for the snuffling of the horses, and then the sound of feet crunching over gravel. The door opened and Marius said: "We have found what we think is the house, madame. Do you wish us to drive in? It is some distance from the road."

She sat bolt upright, pushing her hat back into place and straightening her back.

"If you please," she said.

Marius bowed and closed the door again. Now, as the horses resumed their clip-clop, she strained to look out of the window, but it was dark and she could see nothing except the trees. The carriage was rocking and bumping; the road to the house was a rough one. Eventually she heard the coachman call 'Whoa' and the horses stopped again. She had been nervously pulling her dress into place, and settling her hair beneath her hat. It was too dark to see in her little mirror, but she pinched her cheeks and bit her lips before the door opened again and Marius helped her from the carriage.

She was standing in front of what looked like a large, turreted house. surrounded by trees. She saw by the carriage lights that there was a flight of stairs, and then a big double-fronted door. It seemed too large somehow for the impression of his home that Jean Paul had given her, and she hesitated.

"To be certain we are at the right house," she said in her careful French, "will you and the carriage please wait, Marius."

"But of course, madame," he said.

She took a deep breath and forced herself to walk forward. Now she was wishing she had waited. Waited until daylight, stayed in Paris, stayed in New York – stayed at home. Anything but this terrible suspense that was catching at her throat, weakening her knees and sapping her courage.

But, head up, she walked on. The carriage lights lit the door ahead and she saw a huge, shining knocker, fashioned in the shape of a bunch of grapes. She reached it and slowly put out her hand to grasp it and bang it against the door just once.

Then she waited.

All was silent for perhaps half a minute, and then she heard crisp footsteps and with a great creaking and snarling of bolts the door was opened.

A maid stood there, a maid in a long black uniform with frilled white apron and cap. She was young with a pert face and snapping black eyes.

"Yes, madame?" she said, looking suspiciously from the carriage and the two waiting men to Rosie on the doorstep.

"Monsieur Dupuis. Is he in?" Rosie managed to croak.

At that moment a door off the inside hallway opened and a man and a woman came out.

"Who is it, Marie?" the man said.

Rosie felt her breath stop at the voice and she took a pace that left her standing just over the threshold. Her heart was beating so loudly she felt everyone must be able to hear it. The man stepped forward. She saw the strong curly black hair, the satyr's eyebrows, and the dark eyes. He had grown a little heavier since she had last seen him, and he appeared better dressed.

"Jean Paul! Jean Paul!" she called. "Oh – Jean ..."

The hallway was going round. As she swayed, she was conscious of the anxious face of the older woman. The man hurried forward to catch her just before the world went black.

Chapter Eight

"She called me Jean Paul," Clovis said.

He was standing, not certain what to do, supporting the strange girl who drooped over his arm like a flower with a broken stem.

"Well, pick her up, you great lump," his mother scolded. "Pick her up and put her on the sofa in the parlour. Don't just stand there."

Clovis did as he was bid. The girl seemed very light as he carried her from the hall, her face tranquil, her long lashes making two dark half-moons on her cheeks. As he laid her down, she murmured, stirred and then her eyes opened. They stared up at him, amber brown and glistening with tears, but she did not speak. Outside he could hear his mother talking to the two men who had accompanied her. He could not distinguish the words, he was too intent on gazing at the darkly beautiful face that stared up at him.

"You are not Jean Paul, are you?" she said in hesitant, careful French.

"No, I am his twin brother," he told her.

She looked puzzled for a moment as if she did not quite understand.

"I see," she said finally, and pulled herself upright. "He said he had a brother. Are you Clovis?"

He nodded.

"But where is Jean Paul?" she asked.

"I don't know."

"Is he not here?"

"He has not been here for nearly three years."

She sighed, a long wavering breath, then clasped and unclasped her hands. Even in distress she was beautiful, he thought.

"I had convinced myself. I was so sure that he was here. It never occurred to me that he would not be." Her eyes closed and the tears began to flow. He stood silent, feeling large and helpless. He was debating whether he should get her a little cognac when his mother came bustling in.

"She is looking for Jean Paul," she said. "One of those men says she has come all the way from America to find him. Why on earth would anyone do that?"

He shrugged. He couldn't imagine, but it would be as well not to say that to his mother. She would take it as criticism of his twin.

"She doesn't sound French," he said as a compromise.

"He says she is American and that she can speak French quite well and understands if one speaks slowly." With a rustle of black taffeta she settled herself on the chaise longue beside the girl. "Madame," she said slowly and carefully. "Is it true you seek my son?"

The dark eyes were unveiled again, still full of tears.

"You are his mother?"

"Yes. You know my son?"

"Yes. Is he here?"

"No. We do not know where he is. Do you?" his mother asked.

"No, madame."

"I see. What is your name?"

"Rosie Brunner."

"Brunner is German."

"My father is German, my mother was French."

"There is a trunk on our steps that the men brought from the carriage. It has Anne Marie Cremont written on the side."

"She was my mother. I brought her trunk home again. It is full of vine cuttings."

"Vine cuttings?"

"Ones that will resist the phylloxera."

"Indeed!" His mother's voice was dry, unbelieving. "How do you know they will resist?"

"Your son said so."

She would believe it now, Clovis thought. God – her god – had spoken, even if at second-hand. And it was fortunate for the girl that she had French blood. His mother loathed the Boche with unforgiving passion for the years of the Franco-Prussian war that had inflicted so much damage on Champagne.

"And my son was your lover?"

The girl nodded.

"Well, that has its ironies." She laughed without mirth. "And what did you expect if he had been here?"

"A father for my baby," the girl said with dignity.

"Umm." Madame Dupuis rose and went to turn a lamp higher. She wanted a better look at the girl, Clovis thought. "For how long did you know my son before he left you?"

"Perhaps two months."

"And did he know that you were to have the baby when he left?"

"No. I did not know myself."

It seemed to Clovis that the girl might faint again, she was so pale. He had the fancy that if she unclenched her hands she would fall into small fragments.

"Mother," he suggested, "should we not let Madame Brunner rest and talk about this in the morning?"

"The morning? You mean, keep her here?"

His mother's expression was outraged.

"There is nowhere else she could go at this time of night," he pointed out. "I heard the carriage leave when you came in."

Madame Dupuis was not pleased. She stood tapping her fingers on the mantelpiece and then said to the girl: "Do you have money?"

"I have plenty of money, thank you, madame."

"Umm." The little sound always denoted thinking time for Madame Dupuis. "Well, maybe Clovis is right. You should rest the night here, and tomorrow we shall decide what is to be done."

"Jean Paul could be on his way here," the girl said eagerly. "It might be that he came more slowly than I. Perhaps this week or next ..."

Clovis interrupted.

"He will never come home again, madame. He cannot," he said gently.

"But why not?"

"That's all you need to know," Madame Dupuis said, indicating the subject was closed. "Now – are you hungry?"

Typical. His mother, uncompromising, unforgiving, could always disconcert by her sudden swings to compassion and kindness.

"As a matter of fact," the girl said hesitantly, "I am very hungry. I have not eaten today."

"And the other bags on our steps contain your clothing?"

"Yes."

"Then." She moved to the bell by the fireplace and pulled it fiercely. Marie, who had probably been listening outside the door, appeared in an instant.

"Marie, take Madame Brunner here to the blue room and get Henri to bring her baggage up. Then she is to have a tray of supper." She turned to Rosie. "Will a little pâté, bread and cheese suffice? With soup to begin?"

"But of course. You are very kind."

"*Bon!* Along you go then –" Her long, thin hands made shooing gestures. "Eat and sleep and we will talk again in the morning."

"Poor girl," Clovis said after Rosie had left the room with Marie. "She is confused, but so brave. Mama, we must be kind to her. Imagine her state of mind now. Indeed, what is she to do? And so pretty."

Mdame Dupuis had settled herself in her big chair at the side of the fireplace. Absently she stirred the logs with the big brass poker.

"What are *we* to do, is the question," she said. "Now we have given her our hospitality it will be more difficult to send her away. And if it is truly Jean Paul's baby ..."

"She did not look like one to lie."

His mother sighed. "Will the disgrace that my son has brought upon us never cease?"

Clovis's head was full of pictures of the American girl. The soft eyes and black, looped hair, her proud expression once she had recovered her composure. Her good manners.

"She is very beautiful," he said abruptly.

Madame Dupuis gave him a sharp look.

"In one way it is quite a relief to think that such a thing should have happened," she said. "No, you're right. The girl cannot be lying. No one in their right mind would dream of travelling so far without such a spur. She does not seem a slut and has courage. Tomorrow we will find out more. It will be good to have news of Jean Paul, no matter ..." Her voice trailed away. "I would have liked to have asked more, but she looked as if she might collapse."

"It must be a terrible shock to arrive as she has done and find him not here," he said, carefully feeding his mother's swing to sympathy. "Imagine her turmoil."

His mother sniffed.

"She should have had more sense than to get herself into trouble," she said. "But then Jean Paul can be very persuasive. And Americans are naive in the ways of the world?"

"They are?" His mother's opinion of Americans was new to him.

"Of course. Just riff-raff from all over the globe. I cannot think what possessed Jean Paul to go there." She took out a lace handkerchief and tapped her lips with it disdainfully. "The girl said he worked on her family vineyard. Doing what? I wonder. I trust nothing menial. Ah well – we shall find out tomorrow." She rose with a swish of her widow's black taffeta. "For now I am going to bed."

Clovis took himself to bed too. His room was on the other side of the house from the blue room where Rosie Brunner slept, but he imagined her in the soft feather bed, fearful of tomorrow. What could she do? Return to America – and face disgrace from her family, no doubt? Stay here? He wondered idly if Madame Frédéric would give her a place at the House. The American girl was beautiful enough – in fact, more beautiful than most of the girls Madame employed. Madame had taken pregnant girls in before, if it looked as if they might have promise in the work. And as the girl's honour had gone, what else could she do?

The thought had been an idle one, but suddenly Clovis felt a chill at the idea of Rosie Brunner being passed from man to man, and his

105

twin's child growing up in a brothel. He did not care for either possibility. Clovis rarely felt desire, and when he did, Madame Frédéric and little, round Claudette attended to his needs. To his surprise he was feeling desire now. This time not as a general need for a woman, but a positive need for Rosie.

The sensation increased as he conjured up the memory of carrying her into the parlour, and it came as a considerable shock. Women had never meant much to him. Jean Paul had all the sensuality, all the attraction. Though he and his twin looked alike, they were complete opposites. When they were young men the village girls had pursued Jean Paul (rarely to be refused) while Clovis had hardly been given a second look. Since their father's death and Jean Paul's enforced departure, he was heir to the estate and vineyards, and some women had shown interest in him. He was well aware of their reasons. As yet, none had attracted him. He was content to visit Claudette each week, attend to his business and keep his mother company. But now to find himself so actively aware of one particular woman was worrying. He lay on his back, his hand enclosing the tumescent evidence, wishing it was Rosie's hand and not his own.

Clovis believed that his chances of finding a woman to love who loved him in return were slight. He could marry for convenience, picking one of those attracted by his assets. Perhaps some girl whom no one else wanted would marry him and actually love him. But he wanted better.

It was then that the thought came to him – a simple solution to all the problems caused by the American girl's sudden appearance in their lives. He would marry her. The child would be a Dupuis, legitimately. His mother would have a grandson by the son who was unashamedly her favourite. He would have the remarkably courageous – if impure – girl, and for the first time in his life he would have taken something from his brother.

Beautiful Rosie, in her fur-trimmed coat, her pretty hat, her small elegant boots, was special. And he wanted someone special. How could she refuse him? In her situation there was no chance he would be humiliated by a rejection. She would be grateful and maybe she would love him out of gratitude.

He knew that compared to Jean Paul, whom she had followed so far, he was dull, dry and sometimes boring. But maybe with her as his wife he would blossom.

That was it, he thought contentedly as he stroked himself to peace, he'd marry her.

"*Bonjour, madame.*"
The voice that woke Rosie belonged to the young girl who had

opened the door and brought her supper the night before. For a moment Rosie could not think where she was. She blinked, bewildered at the unfamiliar blue hangings round the four-poster bed, but there was no sense of panic as there would have been a month or so before. She had woken to so many strange rooms and faces since she'd left home.

"*Bonjour*," she said sleepily, watching the girl arrange towels beside a steaming pitcher of water set by a blue patterned bowl.

"It snowed in the night," the maid said as she moved to draw back the curtains and let cold, white light flood into the room. "So pretty, but one freezes. How I hate the winter! You will need your warmest clothes, madame, and breakfast will be served in half an hour."

She spoke without drawing breath, then disappeared, leaving Rosie to work out what she had said.

As she sat up, a touch of morning sickness hit her again. Grimacing she lay back for a moment, trying to ignore the waves of nausea.

Memory was pushing sleep away. She remembered again the first sight of Clovis and her utter conviction that Jean Paul was found. Then had come the moment's doubt and the darkness. The second she had opened her eyes again she realised the man was not Jean Paul. She shivered. Clovis was no more than the husk of Jean Paul. The extraordinary resemblance was unnerving, sinister.

She lay quietly until the sickness passed and then carefully got out of bed and went to the window. It was, as the maid had said, pretty. The room where she had slept looked out over gentle fields that sloped downwards, glistening white and broken with patterned rows of black, twisted, sleeping vines. The view was soft, with slow hills and long, low ridges, waves in a sea of vines stretching as far as the eye could see. Small knolls crowned with bare trees stood guard here and there over the fields and she had the impression that way beyond a river might run. These were the first vines she had seen since leaving California; the terrain was so different, so hostile under the threatening sky, that she marvelled grapes grew here at all.

Leaving the view, she washed in the rapidly cooling water, dressed, and brushed her hair into a knot with care, fussing to make herself neat for Jean Paul's fierce mother. "Courage, Rosie," she whispered to herself as she opened the door of the sombre room and moved out into the passageway.

The house was big, and ornately furnished, but in an uglier, heavier fashion than André's in Paris. The walls of the wide hallway were lined with paintings, mostly of vineyards and workers. She wanted to inspect them, for there seemed to be differences between the way people were dressed and the equipment that her father used, but she was already late for breakfast, and uncertain of which way to go.

She found the stairs and descended into the broad hall where she had fainted the night before. The little maid was dusting and smiled as she pointed towards the back of the house.

"They are in the breakfast room, Madame," she said. "They are waiting for you."

Rosie could hear voices and, trying to ignore her nervousness, she walked to the half-open door that the maid indicated, knocked and went in. It was a small room and mother and son were already seated at a big, red-clothed table. Crumbs and half-eaten bread were scattered before them alongside huge coffee cups.

From the expression on their faces as she entered, it was obvious they had been talking about her. Clovis leapt to his feet and hurried to pull out a highbacked chair while Madame Dupuis poured coffee from a large red enamel pot.

"Good morning," she said. "Sit yourself down. Clovis, call to Marie to bring fresh bread."

Rosie murmured thanks and settled herself at the table, asking if all had slept well and praying that Madame Dupuis would speak slowly until her ear was attuned again.

But all Madame said was, "Tell me of Jean Paul."

Rosie sighed.

"I will try, Madame," she said, "but you must forgive my mistakes when I speak and correct me. Alas, Jean Paul had not taught me as much as I would have wished."

"He was teaching you French?"

"Yes, Madame."

As best she could, Rosie described how Jean Paul had arrived at the winery, and how her father had employed him. She omitted little, except for the details of their love affair and the incident with Peter. As she spoke, Clovis sat silently at the table, listening. Occasionally Madame Dupuis tried to help when she was lost for a word, correct her grammar and her pronunciation, but mainly she just listened, until Rosie reached the morning when Jean Paul had so precipitately disappeared.

Madame Dupuis pursed her lips.

"What else had he done?" she asked. "Had he stolen?"

"Oh, no." Rosie was shocked. "He just took as many of the vine cuttings as a man could carry – I believed to bring here. And he had a right to them. We did not even know they were of use until he told us."

"Nothing else at all?"

"Nothing," Rosie insisted. She could not mention the night in bed with Peter. Besides, she told herself, as she had told herself a thousand times before, there was probably nothing to it.

"Did he tell you he was the village school teacher here?" Madame asked, the sharp glare of her black eyes fixed upon Rosie's face.

Rosie shook her head. "No," she said, amazed. "He said he worked with the vines, but that since the coming of the phylloxera there was not enough to support all the family so he had left to find a new life."

"Nonsense!" Madame was displeased and banged her coffee cup into the saucer so that the liquid slopped over the sides. "There is sufficient for all in this family. And as for the phylloxera, it has not attacked our vines, and being remote, as we are, I doubt it ever will."

"Mama, Mama," Clovis said, putting a restraining hand on hers. "Our visitor is only telling us what she was told. It is not her fault. Calm yourself."

"The very idea –" Madame Dupuis muttered. Then addressing herself to Rosie again: "However, you are certain nothing else happened to make him leave? My son," she said, her voice suddenly dry, "is in the habit of disappearing when it is prudent to do so."

Rosie shook her head again.

"Was there some other reason he left here, madame?" she asked.

"Umm." A silence. "Yes. Maybe. "

"What was that?" Rosie asked the question cautiously.

"The reason is too complicated to explain now," Clovis said quickly. "More important, we have to decide what you are to do."

"Indeed," Madame said. "When is the baby due?"

"I think towards the end of June."

There was a long silence while Clovis and his mother digested the information. Rosie waited. Despite Madame Dupuis' fierce manner, her hawkish nose and hooded eyes, there was a softness about her mouth, and Rosie was warming to the woman. Clovis still gave her the shivers; he seemed soft and empty, bereft of all the life that animated his twin. In him the fire had never been lit.

"What do you want to do?" Madame Dupuis asked abruptly.

The question took Rosie by surprise. She had not thought beyond getting through breakfast with these two strangers in their strange home. All her attention had been on keeping her composure and understanding what was being said.

"I don't know," she said. "I would like to stay somewhere nearby just to see if Jean Paul does come home. I still feel that he will."

"He will not," said his mother positively. "There is no possibility of his showing his face in the village or, indeed, in all Champagne. Do you want the baby?"

"But of course." Rosie struggled for the words to explain. "You see, I have become accustomed to the thought of it and I know that I shall manage somehow. If it is a boy, I shall call him Jean Paul. I am sure it will be a boy."

"And how will you manage?"

Rosie straightened her back. "I have managed so far."

"It will be different when the baby comes. Alone, without a man, without respect."

Rosie listened, knowing that what she said was true. Clovis was fidgeting as his mother spoke.

"Mama." He had risen to his feet, and began to pace round the table. "I have the answer. I shall marry Madame Brunner and my twin's son will have a father. You will have your first grandchild, Rosie will have a husband and a home. It is the obvious way out of the problem."

Rosie could not believe her ears. She stared, dismayed, at the man standing smiling at her.

Madame Dupuis had also risen, her expression equally astonished. Her angular frame leaned threateningly towards her son as if she were an inquisitor.

"Why do you want to do this?" she hissed.

"Because, Mama," he said, his voice patient, "it is the logical thing to do. You cannot send this girl away, not when she is carrying Jean Paul's child."

"Please, please." Rosie too had risen to her feet. "That will not be necessary. I have money. I have a return ticket. I can manage. I can go home, or I can stay in an hotel nearby perhaps. I can say I am a married woman. Who will know? Clovis must not make this sacrifice for me."

He moved towards her and to her dismay took her hands in his. She felt herself recoil.

"It would not be a sacrifice," he said quietly.

Madame Dupuis was striding to the door and it seemed to Rosie that the woman's grey hair was standing on end at what was happening. She wrenched the door open to reveal an empty hallway.

"Huh!" she said. "For once that girl's not listening! Keep your voice down, Clovis. It's out of the question for you to marry her. She can stay here and be a servant until the baby's born and then she can leave it here and go home."

"Mama!"

Rosie was struggling to keep track of the conversation. Both were speaking fast, hissing at each other. She opened her mouth to protest that she would never leave her baby when Clovis said: "Does she look like a woman who would abandon her child?" He threw out his arms in a theatrical gesture, and had she not been so appalled at the turn of the conversation, Rosie would have burst into hysterical laughter. "Of course not," he went on. "Come, Mama, we both recognised her courage and her qualities last night. A servant! The mother of Jean Paul's baby a servant in this house? I am astonished you should even consider such a thing."

"You dolt! Stupid, just as you've always been. You only want her because she was Jean Paul's." Madame Dupuis' voice was rising. "Just like you always wanted everything he had."

"That is true, Mama," Clovis said with dignity. "I wanted his charm, his energy for life, his intelligence – and the love you gave unstintingly to him."

The room was suddenly silent. Madame Dupuis, her mouth shut tight, sat down heavily. For the first time, Rosie felt a little warmth towards the imposter in Jean Paul's shape. She sensed the pain of being always second. He had taken her hands again, and was staring into her face.

"Rosie," he said. "Will you marry me?"

She wanted to shout No, but the feeling of sympathy was still with her.

"Monsieur Clovis," she said, hesitantly, "you are so kind and generous, but you do not know me. You cannot marry a woman you do not know."

"I want to marry you."

The trapped feeling was lodged in her throat. She coughed nervously.

"But I do not know you."

"Does it matter?"

"Well –"

His voice was suddenly brutal. "I ask you, madame, who else would marry you?"

"Clovis!" It was his mother's turn to remonstrate, and he turned to her, his face flushed.

"But it's true, Mama. Who else will marry her? I was thinking in bed last night that she could go to Madame Frédéric's, but that would mean your grandson growing up in a brothel. Would you like that? Maybe Americans are different, but I'd wager no one will marry her if she goes home. Who will want her bastard?"

Appalled, Rosie felt the colour begin to fade from her cheeks, and her head started to spin.

"Now, look what you've done!" Madame Dupuis scolded. "Help her back into the living room, and settle her by the fire."

Seemingly glad of the excuse, Clovis slid his arm round Rosie's waist and gently led her from the room and down the passage. She felt so shaky that she was obliged to lean on him a little, and he made soothing noises, apologising for his unkindness as they walked.

"I just want you to understand how it is ..." he kept saying.

"Yes, I know. I know," she said distractedly.

By the time she was seated in one of the big armchairs in the parlour she was calm again. Madame Dupuis bustled in, looking

111

behind her suspiciously before she shut the door.

"Are you all right, child?" she asked.

Rosie nodded.

Madame settled her bony frame into the facing chair.

"He was cruel, but Clovis is right – unless of course you have sufficient money to live alone."

"I have quite a lot of money, madame," Rosie said, her voice deliberately cold and anger rising. "It was to be my dowry for Jean Paul, along with the vine cuttings. I thought that with both money and the cuttings, he would not refuse me. I am touched indeed that your other son should offer me his hand," she added, unable to control the note of sarcasm that had crept into her voice. But Clovis's ear was not sufficiently finely tuned.

"But I would marry you if you were penniless," he said, his tone fervent.

"So we know," his mother said dryly. "Now do be quiet for a moment. For once you may have made a sensible suggestion. But tell me, child. Will you marry him?"

Rosie looked from the suddenly sympathetic face of Madame Dupuis and then to the puppy-dog eagerness of Clovis. She needed time. She hesitated, then said: "In two weeks it will be Christmas. May I stay either here, as a paying guest, or nearby in an hotel until the New Year? If Jean Paul has not returned by Christmas, we will discuss the matter again."

Clovis made a sharp little sound of distress and turned his back on her. She got up and moved towards him, putting her hand on his arm.

"Please," she said. "I don't want to hurt you, but if Jean Paul is on his way home I believe he will strive to be here for Christmas. And should he return, it is his right to know of this child. So it is better to wait. But if he does not come, we can talk again."

"And you will marry me," he said with childlike happiness. "For I know that Jean Paul will never come back again."

He leaned to kiss her on the cheek, shyly and apologetically. His lips felt like ice, and his words were doom.

Madame Dupuis insisted that now it was all arranged, Rosie should stay in the house, and a slow friendship began to flower between the two women. Rosie learned how Madame Dupuis' husband had been a *vigneron* for the big champagne houses. Madame's father had been a champagne maker who bought his grapes from Claude Dupuis.

"Of course," Madame Dupuis confided, "he was not my class, and Papa was furious when I wanted to marry him. But I loved him so. He had such moustaches, such bravura, and shoulders like an ox. It was poetry to watch him plough a field, urging on his workmen, doing

112

better than ever they could do. And strong! He could topple the biggest boulders." Her eyes grew misty at the memories. "Papa realised in the end that it was a match of true love, and he helped Claude to get together the equipment to make his own champagne. We had such plans when we were young, Claude to be another Monsieur Bollinger or Monsieur Moët, while I took care of the boys. But in truth we were not ambitious, and when Papa died and his money and this estate, Les Hérissons, came to me, it seemed unnecessary to continue the fight to establish ourselves in the champagne world. Of our sons, Jean Paul was bright and clever and wanted to teach. Clovis – well, Clovis has no business brain. Like his father he excelled on the land, and believe me, child, growing grapes, particularly this far north, is hard. Everything in nature, it seems, is working to ruin the harvest. To be a *vigneron* in Champagne you need patience, muscle, and an indomitable spirit.

"And then Claude died. I still have not forgiven him for leaving me. Clovis took over the vineyards, and Jean Paul continued to teach. It was only a year later when Jean Paul left, breaking my heart again. Of course, it is wrong to have favourites, but he was mine. Rascal that he is. And then when you came with news of him – well, how could I turn you away?

"But Clovis is the better man. He is dull, perhaps even a little simple, but he is kind and true. Yet, oh dear, sometimes I yearn to shake some life into him. Perhaps once you are married you will be able to do that."

The two women were sitting in Madame Dupuis' own little parlour tucked between the breakfast room and the main living room. Both were embroidering baby clothes. And Rosie felt a chill at her words. It seemed that it was taken for granted she would marry Clovis, regardless of her own wishes.

"Tell me, Madame," Rosie said, choosing her words with care. "Why are you so certain that Jean Paul will never return?"

The confiding, woman-to-woman mood vanished. Madame Dupuis' mouth shut like a trap, and she put her sewing, untidily for her, back in her sewing box.

"To say I am certain is sufficient," she said coldly. "I must now go to the kitchen to see how dinner is progressing."

As the days slipped away, Rosie found herself curiously content. Her thoughts were with the baby, and neither Jean Paul nor Clovis seemed of great importance. Clovis watched her when they sat at table, but he was shy and said little. She had evidence all the time of how Jean Paul had lied to her. The Dupuis' were rich by her standards, though they had not the wealth of Lizzie or André. The house was twice the size of her home in California, there were servants – a cook and kitchen maid, Henri and Marie who ran the house, and any number of workmen who laboured on the vines.

Rosie had little to do except gossip with Madame Dupuis and sew for the baby. Madame explained that at this time of year life was always quiet as they were mostly snowed in and the house was remote from the nearest villages. It was as well, Madame said, that Rosie's presence was not public knowledge.

She learned Les Hérissons meant 'The Hedgehogs' and indeed the gentle slopes, covered with the blackened, winter-dead vines, did resemble ranks of gigantic hedgehogs crouching in the snow.

Madame Dupuis made her take little walks about the estate. She explored the winery buildings with their huge unused casks and complicated bottling equipment and thought that should Jean Paul return, they would bring the buildings to life again, fulfilling his ambition to create the finest champagne in the world.

But she was puzzled all the time as to why he had left, and why he had lied. It became an obsession to know the history of his departure from Les Hérissons. Neither Clovis nor Madame Dupuis would give her even a snippet of information and she decided that perhaps the ever-curious Marie might be more helpful. Marie missed little of what went on in the house, however much Madame Dupuis tried to hide things from her.

Rosie took to chatting to the little maid in the mornings. When the girl came to clean her bedroom, Rosie sat languidly brushing her hair at the dressing table, while Marie plumped the bed, replenished the fire, polished and dusted.

The girl chattered away about her family who lived in Rilly, a nearby village, and her beau, who worked on the land with Clovis. One day, choosing her moment, Rosie asked casually: "Did you know Monsieur Clovis's brother?"

"Monsieur Jean Paul. Of course," the girl said. "What charm! But too much charm for his own good."

"He went away, they say."

Marie gave her a sharp look. Rosie recalled how on the night of her arrival Madame Dupuis had been concerned that Marie had been listening at the door. Maybe she had not heard, and maybe she had accepted Madame Dupuis' story that Rosie was a visiting friend from America, for she said: "Yes. He had to."

"Why?"

"They didn't tell you?"

"I didn't ask. I'm sure they would if I did. But it seems perhaps a little – well, you know."

114

Marie was looking troubled. Rosie was holding a pretty tortoiseshell combe that André had bought her.

"This would look so nice in your hair, Marie," she said casually. "Now, what were you saying about Jean Paul?"

Marie's greedy peasant eye was on the comb in Rosie's hand.

"Well, madame," she said. "It was at the school. It was so bad it's not a thing one talks about. He was lucky really that the parents didn't get him. They would have, but he'd gone."

"But what did he do?"

Marie fidgeted.

"Perhaps you ought to ask Madame."

Rosie played ostentatiously with the comb, then half-slid it along the dressing table in the maid's direction. She was beginning to be fearful of what she was going to hear, but she wanted her worst fears confirmed. Marie's hand was stretching towards the comb.

"It was the boys. The little boys. He'd been – well, you know. One of them complained."

Rosie abruptly thrust the comb at the girl.

"I see," she said, fighting to sound casual. "How dreadful. Now take this, Marie, and run along, there's a good girl."

The maid's hand came out in a grasping grab and she ran. Rosie, her hands over her stomach, her eyes shut while slow tears trickled from beneath the lids, was contemplating the frightful truth of what she had heard, and remembering again, with blinding clarity, the night she had caught Jean Paul in bed with her naked brother.

Chapter Nine

Jean Paul was whistling softly to himself as he sat, slumped and at ease, on the bare boards of the old farm cart he drove. The head of his thin-ribbed horse hung low as they plodded up the muddy road, wheezing in the foggy air. It was as well, Jean Paul thought, as he tickled its rump with a willow switch, that the poor beast hadn't too much to pull. Just his few clothes – though more than he had set out with – and a big wooden box of vine cuttings.

Hans Brunner's thirty dollars had fared him well. It had been stake enough to prospect a little further, gain a little more knowledge and give him time until the heat had cooled down at the Brunner home.

In the distance now he could see the stone-built house and the shingle roof looming up in the mist. It was silent and still. Nothing stirred, though there was the sound of a flicker pecking away at the wood of a tree somewhere. In spite of his abrupt departure and the circumstances that had propelled him into leaving sooner than he had intended, he wasn't too concerned about the reception he would get. They needed him about the place. He grinned. They needed him for pleasure as well as for work – and that had to be an unbeatable combination.

Peter would have found some way to whine and lie his way out of what Rosie had interrupted. She would be hungry by now, and prepared to forgive him anything. Peter had no choice other than to accept him back. What chance had he of finding another lover? His tastes were not for publicising. It was strange that both brother and sister had the appetite, but in different ways. He grinned again at the thought that he had the appetite too. In every way.

He had reached the broken-down gates that marked the edge of the property, and sticking from the mouth of the rickety post-box was a letter. He laughed out loud, jumping down from the cart. He'd arrive with the news. It would break the ice, he thought, as he pulled the letter out.

But as he went to stuff it into his dungaree pocket he noticed that the postmark was French. The writing looked familiar, though he could not place it, and it was addressed to Mr Hans Brunner.

Had Brunner been checking up on him? he wondered. If so, it was fortuitous that he had arrived before the letter.

Without hesitating, he tore open the envelope and unfolded the single sheet of paper that was inside.

"Dear Papa," he read. "This is just to tell you that I am safe and well and will be arriving in France tomorrow. I don't expect you are worried, but I'm writing just in case.

"Also I want to explain about taking the money. I had to do it to get away, and I only took exactly a third of the cash. I didn't touch the gold because I figured that was yours. That's all still under your bed where you hid it.

"The third of the cash I decided I had worked for and earned. I reckoned the rest was yours and Peter's.

"Maybe I'll write again when I'm settled, but I am OK. Give my love to Peter, and hoping you are OK too and managing without me. Best wishes to you from your daughter, Rosie."

Jean Paul whistled faintly through his teeth at the implications of the letter. Rosie gone. Looking for him? She must have believed the note he left. And she'd gone off with money – but left gold. How much gold? Jean Paul was in a thoughtful frame of mind as he carefully tore up the letter, watching the fragments scatter on the light breeze.

At the house he pulled the old horse to a stop outside the verandah and jumped lightly from the cart. Nothing moved. He ran up the steps and banged on the door.

"Is anyone home?" he called.

There was a shuffling from inside, the door opened a fraction and the anxious face of Peter peered round the jamb. The blue eyes opened in stunned disbelief, and then the door was thrown back and Peter was upon him, hugging him, kissing, babbling words of welcome and demands to know where he had been. "It's been weeks! It's been weeks!" he kept repeating hysterically.

"Wait! Wait!" Jean Paul said, untangling himself. "Can I come in?"

"Of course." Peter was dragging him through the door, pushing him into the kitchen, dusting off a chair for him to sit on. "Oh, Jean Paul – it's good to see you. You just can't imagine how lonesome it's been since you went. I swear, I thought I'd die missing you."

Jean Paul pulled the chair to the table and settled in what had been his usual place.

"Lonely? Why have you been lonely?"

Peter pulled a long face.

117

"Well, Rosie went and three weeks after, Pa had a fall. It was the whisky. He fell down the back steps on his way out to the privy." His nose wrinkled in disgust. "I had to clean him up and get him in. He didn't seem to have hurt himself too much, but he couldn't get moving again. He kept on all the time about Rosie. I guess we both miss her. There's no one now to cook and clean."

"So I see." Jean Paul looked round the littered kitchen, the basin full of unwashed plates and cups, and the burned saucepans on the range.

"I try," Peter said defensively, "but there's so much to do about the place. Pa nagged from his bed at first, telling me do this, do that, until I came near to killing him. But then he got real sick. He's abed now. I had the doctor come once, but I had to go into Calistoga to get him. He won't come this far unless he gets paid first, and there isn't any money. Pa won't give me any. Every time I ask for some he just tells me to go find Rosie."

"You said Rosie had gone?"

"That's right. I guess it was about two weeks after you left. Perhaps a bit longer. Suddenly one morning she wasn't here anymore. She didn't leave a note, nothing. She'd just gone. At first we thought something bad might have happened to her. But then Pa went rushing upstairs as if something had just hit him, and I heard him banging around in his bedroom. Then he came down the stairs so fast I thought he'd fallen, shouting that she'd gone and I was to go get her back. He sent me off to Calistoga. He even gave me money, and said I was to follow her no matter what and bring her back. Well, they told me at the railroad station that she'd booked East. She'd gone to San Francisco and I went down there after her. I waited at the station, and she came in that next morning looking like a duchess. She was all dressed up, and with porters running after her, and getting on a Pullman carriage. I tell you, I couldn't believe my eyes. I just went right up and grabbed her and told her Pa wanted her home. She said she weren't never coming home, but I'd got hold of her arm real good and I'd have kept her off that train except some man said he'd make trouble for me if I didn't let her aboard that minute. So, what was I to do?"

Jean Paul was analysing the information. Peter was not looking him straight in the eye. Peter was lying a little.

"Why did she go East?" he asked.

Peter hesitated. "Don't know," he said.

He was definitely lying, Jean Paul decided.

"It was the way she was done up that just amazed me," Peter was saying. "Where did she get the money for those clothes in that time?" He paused and said suspiciously, "You didn't give her no money, did you?"

"I had no money to give anyone," Jean Paul said silkily. "But my guess is that she found money. Your father's money maybe. That's perhaps why he was so angry."

"You think so?" Peter said dubiously. "I just thought he was mad because there weren't no one to cook and clean no more. I don't think Pa's got any money."

Jean Paul shook his head slowly.

"It must be that she took money from him to go East. Where else would she get it? The question is – did she take it all?"

"Not Rosie. Rosie wouldn't steal. I can't believe it."

"Maybe she took just what she felt belonged to her?" Jean Paul suggested.

Peter shook his head. "I just don't know."

"Then why don't we find out. Where is your father now?"

"I told you. Sick. I think perhaps he might be dying, and then what am I going to do with myself? He's got pneumonia, the doc said. I have to keep the room all steamy with kettles of hot water all the time or he just can't breathe. He's real sick and I don't know what to do."

"First we go and see him."

"He oughtn't to be disturbed."

"We won't disturb him."

Jean Paul was on his feet and heading for the stairs. Peter followed reluctantly. As they went to the top of the house, Jean Paul reviewed his prospects. Though he had looked forward to another encounter with the daughter, it was perhaps just as well she was out of the way. And if the old man was dying, that could only be good news. With him gone and her gone and just Peter to deal with, nothing was going to be too difficult to achieve. He had thought he would have to marry. Now it would not be necessary. His spirits were high as he opened the door to Hans Brunner's room.

It was dark, with heavy curtains drawn over the windows and a small lamp lit in the corner. A pan perched clumsily on a trivet over the open fire belched steam, making the atmosphere thick and fetid. The old man was in the high-backed brass bed. Jean Paul moved to peer at the sunken face and heard the thick, rasping breathing.

"He seems worse," Peter said. "Think I ought to get the doctor?"

Jean Paul did not answer, but stood at the foot of the bed, his mouth pursed, staring at Hans. Then he turned and began to open the drawers of the chest that stood against the wall.

"Hey! What are you doing?" Peter whispered.

"Looking for money."

"But you can't."

"Why not? He's dying."

The man in the bed lay as if already dead. Peter continued to make

119

ineffectual protests as Jean Paul went swiftly through the room, drawer by drawer, cupboard by cupboard. It wouldn't do to go straight to the bed. He lifted the old rugs, looked in the few ornaments the room possessed and then he stood, as if thinking.

"You heard him banging about?" he asked finally.

Peter nodded, and the rasping, rattling breathing seemed louder in the silence.

"Under the bed. It's got to be under the bed," Jean Paul said. "Help me move it."

"No. You mustn't."

"Help me move it."

Peter whimpered and did what he was told.

Between them they pushed the heavy piece of furniture from the middle of the room until it was against the wall. Then Jean Paul knelt and began to knock on the floorboards. As he leaned forward, one of the planks moved. He pressed. It rose and his heart lifted with it.

"Got it!" he said, triumphant.

At that moment the figure in the bed sat up. The fierce old eyes were wide open, the bald head gleamed with sweat. Like some terrible apparition, he pointed one finger at Jean Paul and wheezed, "No! No!" He seemed to be struggling to get out of bed, and Jean Paul found himself mesmerised, watching as Peter rushed to quieten his father.

"We just want the money so we can get the doctor, Pa," he cried out. "That's all. Honest, Pa."

"Thief –" The word was a long drawn-out dreadful wail. Then the old man coughed – a cough which became a rattle as he fell back on the pillow.

Peter was standing over him, pale and terrified.

"Oh, Jesus, Jesus, Jesus," he whispered. "He's gone. He's dead. What have we done?"

"Found the money," Jean Paul said, his hands scrabbling in the hole in the floor. "Found the money. That's what we've done.

Jean Paul did not get involved with the funeral. He sent Peter to Calistoga to see the priest and the undertaker while he went out to the field that he had been clearing before he left.

He was pleased to see that someone – it must have been Peter – had continued with the work. Much of the scrub had been cleared, saplings chopped down, and there had been a rough attempt at terracing. Grunting with satisfaction, he set to work again. This slope was to be the foundation of his fortune.

It took three days before the business of disposing of the mortal remains of Hans Brunner was completed, and in that time Jean Paul slept in his old room above the barn. He hardly saw Peter, and he avoided the flow of visitors who rode out to pay their respects. Peter hardly came near him, probably out of some sense of respect for his father while the body was still in the house. The two young men ate together, but in near silence. Peter was obviously terrified of the future alone. That, too, could only help, Jean Paul thought.

The day after the funeral Peter came and joined him on the hillside. His face was blotchy and he had obviously been weeping. It was pouring with rain, falling from the sky in stinging wet cords. A grey chill rose from the ground, striking cold through the soles of the feet upwards.

"Jean Paul," Peter said nervously, standing like a schoolboy, his blond hair flattened on his head. "I'm sorry I've not seen you. There's been so much to do, and I sort of felt it was better to get it all over with before we talked."

"I understand." Jean Paul stopped work and leaned on the pick with which he had been trying to dislodge a stubborn rock. "Are you all right now?"

"I'm fine," Peter said, his shaking hands showing he was far from fine. "But I guess I'd like it if you'd come into the house now. You can have Rosie's old room. Not right you sleeping over the barn like that."

"It is not worth the trouble," Jean Paul said. "I shall be on my way soon."

"On your way!" Peter's voice had risen to a shriek. "But why? Where are you going?"

"To find my own place." He turned his attention to the rock again.

"But you can't go. You can't leave me here alone."

Jean Paul shook his head with great deliberation.

"But here, Peter, I am just the hired hand. I want something of my own."

Peter stepped forward, within touching distance.

"That's easy. You can have half of this. What would I do with it? How could I manage without Papa and Rosie? Stay and share it."

Jean Paul appeared to consider, and then shook his head again.

"It would not be right. I do not have enough money to pay properly for a share in a property of this size."

"Money doesn't matter. Oh, Jean Paul, please don't leave me. Please don't go. You can't imagine how much I've missed you. You're the only one who's ever understood. The only one I've ever been able to talk to. You can't leave me all alone."

Jean Paul straightened and moved to kiss Peter gently on the forehead. The boy shivered.

"It is too soon for these decisions. We shall talk tonight over supper."

He returned to his work, the rain beating on his shoulders. It could only help to let the boy sweat out the rest of the day. One way or the other all would be well. The small bag of gold dust that he had expertly palmed while Peter wailed over his father was pressed now against his groin. It was a comforting promise of better times ahead.

Dejected, Peter had turned and walked away. The Frenchman watched him go. The boy had a *derrière* like a peach, he thought, enjoying how the rain-soaked denim clung to the two curves below the narrow waist. Perhaps he would move into the house tonight. It had been a long time since Sarah. He laughed briefly to himself as he moved the rock with one last lustful heave. A long time – well, five days. But when one has the appetite ...

By dusk the rain had become almost insupportable on the exposed hillside and Jean Paul left immediately the light began to go.

There was no sign of Peter when he reached the house, so he began to straighten things out himself. He prepared supper and cleared up the kitchen. He loathed disorder of any kind.

There was a ham in the larder that could have been fresher, but he cooked four good thick slices in a bubbling pan of red wine, adding onions and some dried mushrooms and put some potatoes on to boil. As he began to light the lamps, Peter came in.

"I was in the winery racking the barrels," he said apologetically. "There was work to be done and it was dryer. Did you get very wet?"

"Very."

"I sure hope you don't catch cold."

"I never catch cold. Is there any bread?"

Peter shook his head.

"Don't know how to make it. Rosie always did it."

"Well, we'll have to do without," Jean Paul said, thinking that he did not know how to make bread either. Sarah, though, had made remarkably good bread. A slut who cooked like an angel. She would be useful here – if he could manage it.

Peter set the table, and they sat down together and started to eat. Almost immediately Peter blurted out: "You aren't really going, are you?"

"I have some dreams to make come true," Jean Paul said softly.

"What dreams?"

"To make champagne here in California."

"Why do you want to do that?"

"Because I am a Champenois."

Peter fidgeted uneasily.

"Is it possible here?"

"It will never be possible to make real champagne, but most certainly it is possible to make a sparkling wine by the same method."

"I never heard of anyone doing it."

122

"Well, I assure you, many people do. And have done so for many years. It is not as good as the French champagne of course, but I believe it could be made better."

"How do you know?"

"Because I have been to the vineyard here where it is made."

"Is that why you went away?" The boy's voice was so eager that Jean Paul knew he wanted this to be the reason.

"Yes. And I exchanged the wild vines I took with me for cuttings of Chardonnay – the white grape from which champagne is made, though we need some Pinot Noir vines also if the product is to be fine."

Peter chewed thoughtfully on his ham.

"Would they grow here? It's not too hot?"

"Not at all. This vineyard is cool in the late autumn, that I know. Is it cool in the spring?"

"Sometimes it's real cold."

"A climate not unlike Champagne, though it gets hotter here. The field we are clearing would be perfect."

"Then why not plant your cuttings there?"

"Because it is your land."

"You can have it if you stay. Like I said, you can have half the property." He gulped. "I love you, Jean Paul. I don't want you ever to go away."

Jean Paul reached out to hold Peter's hand and said: "You are so good. So *gentil*. But I cannot accept. You are young. You may find someone else, and then where would I be? No, Peter, my sweet Peter, it is better if I go. I would have no real rights ever."

The boy banged down his fork, his face scarlet.

"Look, I won't ever love no one else. But what we can do is we can make it legal, so it's half yours, all legal. Then you can do what you like."

"Would you be willing to buy the Pinot Noir slips?" He told himself to slow down. He was jumping ahead. He should not have asked so soon.

"If you want them. Honest, you can have the money too if you want. You found it. I'd never have found it –" his face reddened again in shame at the memory of the manner of his father's death. "I just wish we'd waited," he muttered.

"Well –" Jean Paul made his voice reluctant. His tickled trout was almost in his hand. "I don't know."

"Please! I don't want you to go away."

"Ah, Peter – you think I want to leave you again? Of course not. Together here we can be happy. I might even make you rich." He laughed and pressed the hand he still held. "Peter, you are so good, so generous. I hate to speak of the property in this way, but a man needs

123

something of his own. I have wandered so long. I, too, have been so lonely."

"Did you miss me where you've been? Where was it?"

"The valley of the Russian River, and of course I missed you. It's not far from here. It is part of the Sonoma Valley and there they make champagne."

"I heard Pa speak of that."

Their food was cooling on the plates.

"It's all settled then," Peter said happily. "We'll go into Calistoga and see a lawyer and we'll fix it all up, and then you'll stay."

"I'll stay," Jean Paul said, and with victory won, his mind was now on two firm, tight moons below a narrow waist. "And tonight, may I stay with you?"

"Oh, please! Oh, thank God!" Peter said. "Now. We'll go up right now."

They went to Calistoga the next day, and it was all fixed by a lawyer whose quick, darting glances at Jean Paul revealed deep suspicions, but Peter bulldozed the transaction through. Jean Paul had never seen him so positive.

They jogged back on the old wagon and Peter chattered happily, his delight obvious. He kept patting Jean Paul as if to make sure he was still there. Any distress and dismay at the loss of his father had disappeared. He babbled how exciting it was for the place to be theirs, and now they had Pa's money how many changes and alterations there would be.

"Let's go into 'Frisco and shop for clothes and see the town," he said. "My, that would be fun."

They were at the front of the house. Jean Paul swung down and began to unhitch the horses.

"No," he said firmly. "That money is going to be spent on building up the vineyard. We need phylloxera-resistant vines, and we're going to get them."

Peter pouted.

"We could spend just a bit."

"No," Jean Paul said again. "And you'd better get working. I want the long shoots cut off the field of Zinfandel and it's time we were ploughing, before the frosts come. Get going, eh?"

Peter's face was sulky, but he did as he was bid.

As the turn of the century neared they fell into a pattern of work. There was too much to do for just two men, and the house suffered. Jean Paul fretted over the dirt and the disorder, and finally over the cooking. Peter could not fry a slice of ham without burning it. He made foul coffee, and eggs in his care became either bullets or a sloppy, inedible mess.

"We need a woman around the place," Jean Paul grumbled one day. He was tired. He had been up at daybreak, carrying back the soil that had been washed down the slopes by the rain and redistributing it around the roots of the vines. The casks needed topping up, and that had to be done by the light of oil lamps after the grey chill winter night had descended.

Peter looked alarmed at the mention of a woman.

"It's better without Rosie," he said uneasily. "She made trouble between us."

Jean Paul grinned, but it was more a baring of the teeth. Peter would work without complaint as long as they worked side by side and as long as he was kept happy at night. He was greedy, Jean Paul had decided. He himself was becoming tired of bread and bread. He was beginning to think about women again. He was remembering Rosie's soft eagerness and passion. He thought of lascivious Sarah. He was restless for change.

"Rosie could cook," he said.

Peter looked anxious.

"I'll learn. I'll try," he promised.

"You do not have the gift," Jean Paul said dismissively. "But you have other, better gifts. We need a woman here to look after the house."

"Don't want no other woman here." Peter's face was set in sullen lines. "It might be like last time."

"Like last time?"

"You and Rosie."

Jean Paul raised his eyebrows.

"I know what happened between you and Rosie. She didn't come up to your room all naked like that for no reason. I know what you were both doing. I reckon she went away because ..."

"Because what?"

A beat of silence.

"Because she was looking for you."

Jean Paul contemplated. Most of his life he had gained what he wanted because he knew how to deal with people. Both Rosie and her brother craved love. He had given them both as much as his own nature would allow. He did not need emotional love, though the physical was of the utmost importance. Rosie had responded to his teaching, to his interest in her. But she was not to be bullied. On the other hand, while her brother was given the physical love, he could be bullied and cowed. Indeed, he was best bullied and cowed. He liked it.

"Rosie has gone. She has nothing to do with the matter," he said.

125

"But we need another woman in her place."

"We can manage."

"We cannot."

"I won't have it."

"Peter, *chéri*, we are partners now." He said it like silk.

Peter's Adam's apple rode up and down in his thin throat.

"An old woman."

"They have no energy."

"I don't like it."

"We will talk about it later then."

That night, while he pleased Peter, his mind was on lusty, musky, wide-spread Sarah. She was a slut, and would fight him, but she was malleable in the end. And her cooking was of the angels.

The next morning he prepared his own horse and cart. His horse's ribs had filled out in the peace of the winery. The journey back to Sonoma would not take long.

At breakfast, which he prepared, he gave Peter his orders. The land must be manured, the barrels topped up, the soil spread around the roots of the vines.

"I know," Peter said suspiciously. "Why are you telling me all this?"

"Because I shall be away for a few days."

"You can't go away. Why? Where are you going?" Peter's voice had reached its girlish high.

Jean Paul wiped his mouth with the back of his hand and rose slowly to his feet.

"Where am I going? Courting, my dear Peter. That's where I am going. Courting."

Chapter Ten

Clovis was not a happy man as he sat in the dining room of Les Hérissons, a large glass of Marc de Champagne in front of him. His mother and Rosie had retired to the drawing room, observing the formalities his mother always insisted upon at Christmas. In the past there had been three men left – his father, Jean Paul and himself. It seemed ridiculous to be sitting here alone with a drink he did not particularly want, waiting until he could decently join the ladies and be with Rosie.

The roast goose was sitting heavily on his stomach and he had eaten far too much of the chocolate log. He belched gloomily, thinking that tomorrow he could remind Rosie of her promise that they could discuss their marriage. The subject had not been mentioned since he had proposed. Would she change her mind? he wondered uneasily.

The past two weeks had not been good for Clovis. He had found himself more and more obsessed with the American girl who had come so unexpectedly into their lives. But she had taken little notice of him. She spent most of her time with his mother and they appeared to have become close friends. It was good that they should care for each other, but what depressed him was that Rosie seemed to prefer his mother to him.

"Imbecile!" his mother had said when he asked her if this could be the case. "How can she spend time with you alone? It would not be proper."

As much as he cared for Rosie, and in spite of his slow mind, Clovis could not help thinking that it was a little late in the day to be worrying about proper behaviour. And who would have known if they had spent time together? Only their own servants. They had few friends in the area since Jean Paul's departure. Rosie herself had said he could not marry a woman he did not know, but how was he supposed to get to know her? It seemed he would have to wait until after the marriage before he could so much as exchange a word with her alone.

The only conversations they had had were over meals, and always with his mother present. They talked about champagne and the growing of vines this far north. She showed an unseemly, unfeminine interest in the minutest details, and though it gave him pleasure to listen to her hesitant French and her unusual accent he wanted her to talk of girlish trivialities – not of what should be men's affairs.

Because she so filled his thoughts, he had hardly left the house except to work on the vines since her arrival. He wanted to be near her all the time, and her certainty that Jean Paul would come home had affected him. Each day when there was no whistle at the door he breathed a little easier. He knew that the chances of his brother returning could only be nil, but he had a superstitious fear that perhaps the fierceness of Rosie's longing would act like a magnet. He feared that Jean Paul might reappear, debonair, full of the electric energy Clovis had envied all his life. No doubt his mother had also been full of hopes for the return of her prodigal, he thought bitterly. But his brother had not returned, and he and Rosie should marry as soon as possible.

The thought of Rosie as his bride and their wedding night alone together aroused Clovis as he sat alone at the table. Then an awful thought struck him. Would he be able to make love to her without harming the baby? Or harming her, come to that? Would he have to wait to possess her until his brother's child was born?

Quite distracted he drained the Marc and got to his feet, staggering a little. As it was Christmas his mother had been generous with their best champagne. He stood staring glassily into space. Who could he ask if it would be safe? Not his mother. Not Rosie. Who?

In a flash of inspiration he realised that Claudette would know. He would go to Madame Frédéric's, he decided, and achingly aware of the need that the thought of Rosie had created, would kill two birds with one stone. It had been a long time since he had visited Claudette. Perhaps it was abstinence that was causing his constant ill-humour.

He slipped out of the house without a word. He could hear the light buzz of his mother's voice, chatting to Rosie, and the enchanting cadence of Rosie's quiet chuckle. He felt very lonely.

One of the stable lads saddled up his horse and Clovis set off through the woods to where Madame Frédéric's establishment was set back from the Épernay road, near to Rilly. A frosty moon shone but there were still traces of the angry red sunset that had turned the snow to blood as early dusk had fallen. The jogging of the horse made his richly fed stomach protest. He belched again, still miserable, and conscious that he had drunk too much. Clovis had little appetite for wine. It upset him, changed his normal placidity to bad temper. He believed in moderation in all things and was angry with himself for the day's excess.

But at Madame Frédéric's his welcome was warm. As he breathed in the familiar smell of perfume and dark tobacco, Claudette, in a black corselet and flounced petticoats, ran across the room making shrill little cries of delight and flung herself into his arms.

"*Chéri, mon chéri*, where have you been," she squealed, pinching at his earlobe with spiteful fingers.

"Claudette!" Madame Frédéric was making shooing noises at the girl. "Permit our guest to relieve himself of his cloak and settle. Welcome, monsieur. A glass of champagne?"

Her chins rippling, she clicked her fingers at the little maid who could have been no more than ten and was, Clovis knew, the child of one of Madame's girls. Jean Paul's child could have had the same fate had it not been for his generosity, he thought. And was angry again at Rosie's cavalier treatment of him.

Madame had taken his cloak herself and he took a glass from the full tray the child proffered.

"Sit yourself, monsieur. Warm yourself. It is a pleasure to see your face. And most particularly at this festive time."

Madame had never for one instant shown disapproval of the Dupuis family like so many of those who lived in the mountain region when the truth of Jean Paul's vices had been made public. Lowering her voice to almost a whisper, she said: "You are content with Claudette?"

Clovis stared, puzzled, into her rouged face. He did not grasp what she meant.

"But, of course," he said. "I have always been content with Claudette."

She nodded, satisfied.

"Ah, I had wondered. Since we have not seen you I thought perhaps there had been some little lovers' tiff." She looked at him coyly. "It is as well. Some of the girls have gone home today, but Claudette's family are too far away. I let the dear things go as it is Christmas. Besides," she added with a rare touch of honesty, "we did not expect too many of our clients, you understand."

A fat hand on which her heavy rings made thick swellings was on his arm as she led him to an armchair. He felt better already. A huge fire burned under the marble mantelpiece and the familiar nude painting – after the style of Reubens – that dominated the room stared down at him, pink and rosy, flesh in soft folds. Madame believed that a skinny woman was an affront to nature. A scraggy woman could damage a man's bones, she would insist, and her girls were all as fondant soft as the painting.

129

Once he was settled, she permitted Claudette to leave the little group of girls in their various stages of colourful undress to come and join him. The girl curled herself on his lap, taking his hand and placing it where her white breasts spilled from the corselet.

"Feel how my skin burns and my heart beats at the pleasure of seeing you," she sighed, then whispered in his ear, "and you will find that more than my heart is burning for you."

Clovis smiled, pleased. He prided himself that though Claudette was just a whore, he pleasured her. He was well-made, and once he had straddled her, he wasted little of her expensive time. She always groaned and cried out in a most exciting manner, telling him afterwards that it had been wonderful, and that he was the finest of all her lovers. He doubted that was true, but he felt that at least Rosie could not be too disappointed once she was in his bed.

Claudette teased him while he drank his champagne, saucily letting her hand rest where it should not, and raising her eyebrows and exclaiming at what she found there. He sipped his champagne and wondered if he would be happy for Rosie to fondle him in such an intimate manner. No, he decided, he would prefer his wife to be more restrained, less forward. And yet the thought of her touching him excited him again, causing Claudette to breathe more deeply and increase the gyrations of her fingers.

Claudette had a thick body with small breasts, but her face was pretty, with a small turned-up nose and cupid bow lips. Clovis had always thought she looked like a china doll. Today, critically inclined, he decided she had the face of a predatory piglet and wondered how he had been content with her for so long.

But he was fond of her, though she could not compare with Rosie, and at the thought of Rosie, suddenly all desire for the girl on his lap left him. Claudette's questing fingers faltered and stilled. She looked at him, her eyebrows question marks.

"Let's go to your room," he said hastily.

"But at once!" she said, jumping from his lap and taking his hands to pull him to his feet. "I have missed you so much, *chéri*."

She led him through the room where two of the other regulars who patronised Madame's were enjoying champagne. They nodded to him distantly. Before Jean Paul's departure, they would have smiled and bowed. Clovis noted that the hot eyes of one of them, a grower from Mailly, were furtively watching the child waitress. "Hypocrite!" he thought, knowing that if Madame saw a source of income in the girl her innocence would be short-lived.

Claudette was leading him from the ornately furnished room to where the curved stairs stretched ahead. Madame's *maison* had once been a small château, home of nobility, but Clovis doubted if then the

130

stairway had been lined with explicit paintings; paintings meant to increase the ardour of Madame's clients as they neared the girls' bedrooms.

The paintings had never appealed to Clovis. He found their wealth of detail gross, and today he did not even glance at them, nor at Claudette's black mesh-covered legs twinkling ahead of him. His mind was on how to frame the questions he wanted to ask.

Her room looked the same as always. The bed cover already turned back showing the white sheets, and the big green water pitcher and matching basin steaming with hot water. Another small slave had been busy. Claudette covered her walls with erotica, but there were also pictures of her family who lived in the Auvergne. It had never occurred to Clovis to ask why she had come here from so far away.

She instantly slipped out of her petticoats and walked towards him wearing just the long corselet, suspenders and black stockings. Her pubic hair was sparse, blonde and childlike.

"Let me help," she whispered, leaning to remove his cravat, the pink of her mouth deepening in anticipation. He stood staring out over her head at the heavy curtains that covered the long windows, and when her busy fingers began on his shirt buttons he said without preamble: "Is it safe to make love to a pregnant woman?"

"How pregnant?" Claudette's fingers had quietened.

"Perhaps four months."

She stepped back.

"Clovis! You have put a girl in trouble!"

He had not meant to be so blunt, and her words angered him.

"Of course not. Don't be a fool."

She attacked his shirt again.

"Why do you want to know then?"

"Curiosity, maybe."

She shrugged.

"At four months it is safe enough. The girls here when they are fool enough to become pregnant go on for much longer."

His shirt was being eased from his shoulders.

"And later, when they are – " he hesitated, trying to find the right word – "rounder?"

"Simple. They do it doggy fashion."

At first Clovis did not understand. He had only ever made love to Claudette, and then only with her beneath him, her head on the pillow, her legs coiled round his back.

"Dog fashion?"

"Like this, silly." She moved away from him and knelt on the bed, her legs wide apart, the white moon of her behind raised towards him so that he could see how the black elastic of her suspenders bit into her

131

flesh. She placed her elbows on the bed and looked round at him coquettishly.

"Try it," she suggested.

She looked obscene. She looked like the picture he disliked the most on the stairs, the one where the woman was positioned as Claudette was now, with a man entering her from behind, while another knelt before her, his penis in her mouth. He had always thought the scene bestial. Dog fashion was the right description. The thought of making love to Rosie in such a way appalled him.

"Come on." The girl on the bed moved her hips suggestively. "Try it. It's good. Goes in a long way."

"No thanks." He picked up his shirt from where she had thrown it and began to put it back on again.

"Clovis!" Her voice was a wail. "What is it?"

"I want another glass of champagne," he said in panic. "We'll do it later."

He was aware that he had offended her; her petulant expression made no secret of her displeasure.

"You'll have to pay twice," she said sulkily.

He didn't bother to answer but just left the room and made his way back down the stairs to the salon where Madame Frédéric hurried towards him.

"Is all well, Monsieur?" she asked, bright eyes quizzing him from the fat puffiness of her cheeks.

"I want a glass of champagne," he said belligerently. He had no idea how he was going to leave the premises without looking a fool.

"Of course." Madame knew how to soothe. She led him to the most comfortable chair in the room and clucked gently at him until the champagne arrived. He drank it very quickly.

"Another?" she suggested, and he nodded.

He noticed that Claudette had returned, half-dressed again in the flounced petticoats. She settled with the other girls; a black and white bird amongst all the brighter plumage.

"Claudette did not please?" Madame asked him softly.

"Claudette was fine. I was thirsty. Too much Marc celebrating after the goose," he explained.

"Perhaps we should bring you the bottle?"

"Yes, bring a bottle," he said.

In the event he had no excuses to make before leaving. Finishing the bottle finished him. Madame and one of the male kitchen staff carried him out, somehow toppling him onto his horse. He lay there in the frosty night, his arms round the horse's neck, gulping in great breaths of lung-freezing air. Then he was sick, and feeling better for it, managed to sit half upright in the saddle and kicked the horse into moving.

He was half-dozing as the animal made its own way back to Les Hérissons. He mentally dismissed the debacle at Madame Frédéric's and let his addled mind fill with Rosie. Jean Paul had not returned. She would marry him and he would never need to visit a brothel again. There was no reason now why she should refuse to marry him.

As he jogged through the night, the snow crackling under his horse's hooves, he found himself comparing her with Claudette. He thought of the lewdness of Claudette's posturing before him; the invitation to take her animal fashion. Rosie would never behave in such a way; he could not imagine such a thing, and yet the idea of her spreadeagled across the bed like Madame Frédéric's plump little whore filled him with the excitement that had deserted him in the bedroom. He felt that he had been remarkably patient with Rosie and, through the mists of alcohol, began to become angry at her indifference. It was time that he asserted himself. He had been too gentle, too considerate – and yet why should he have been when she was already expecting his brother's baby? In truth, there was little to choose between her and the girls at Madame Frédéric's. They merely had not had the good fortune to find someone willing to marry them.

And yet he did want to marry Rosie, and he wanted to know for sure that she would marry him. He would settle the matter that very night, he decided. His patience was at an end. He kicked his heels into the horse's sides and, startled, the beast broke into a gallop. Clovis clung on, drunkenly dodging the branches that whipped about his head. He had no idea of the hour. He did not care how late it was. Tonight he would be sure that Rosie was his for ever. And if Jean Paul did come home, even as soon as next week, it would be too late to change anything.

Rosie had been sitting by the fire, listening fascinated as Madame Dupuis told stories of Champagne in days gone by. The woman was a natural storyteller, and through her conversation Rosie was not only becoming more and more proficient in the language, she was building up a background of knowledge about the people and countryside where it seemed she was destined to live. Slowly she was discovering an affinity with the land, different though it was from her birthplace. It no longer looked forbidding and unwelcoming to her and plans were forming in her mind as she wandered about the property on her daily walks. She would persuade Madame to let her restore the winery and make champagne again. Then on the day that Jean Paul came home his dream would be at least part fulfilled.

She was happy. She had managed to put aside all thought of marrying Clovis. Her natural optimism had convinced her it would never happen. Somehow, something would prevent it. Madame might even side with her in the matter. Madame Dupuis was besotted with the idea of the baby, and had confided to Rosie that she had always wanted a daughter. Though she had not exactly said so, Rosie felt that maybe she had been accepted as that daughter, and knew that she had wholeheartedly accepted Madame as the mother she had missed for so long. She had been attempting for some days to ask if perhaps she could call the older woman something a little less formal than Madame, but an unusual shyness had held her back.

So it came as something of a shock when Madame rose to her feet to put another log on the fire, sat down and said: "I suppose we must begin to make some plans for your wedding. I feel it should be quiet; just a simple affair. Perhaps in Reims. Would you be happy with that?"

Rosie found herself unable to reply and Madame said gently: "You have virtually promised him, my dear. And what else can you do? I fear your hopes for Jean Paul's return will not be realised."

"It looks as if he will not come," Rosie said miserably. "But I did not mean to promise Clovis."

There was a brief silence and then Madame said: "Clovis is not Jean Paul, but for you, he may prove to be the better in the end. It is easier to love Jean Paul – I understand that very well. But you may find a happier life with Clovis. He is slower. He has not the magic of his brother. When they were small, I always felt that one, maybe Jean Paul, was the mirror, and Clovis the reflection. They look so alike and yet the Lord reversed their characters. Have you noticed that Clovis is left-handed? All the trying in the world could not change him. As children they tackled nothing in the same way – nor indeed as adults. But Clovis is good, and though it pains me to say it to you, Jean Paul is not. The reverse of the mirror. His heart is not as pure as his brother's and it may be that you have had a lucky escape.

"You will have no problems with Clovis. He will be your dog. Have you not noticed how he cannot take his eyes off you?" She laughed. "His disposition is good. He is only bad-tempered when he has been drinking. Then he becomes morose and full of self-pity. Now when Jean Paul drank – " she sighed – "but we must both forget Jean Paul. A new life will begin for us all when your baby is born."

Rosie was silent, staring into the blue and yellow flames of the fire. Madame had reminded her of the knowledge she had of Jean Paul's departure – knowledge she sometimes wondered if she would have been better without. Most of the time she managed not to think about what Marie had told her, just as she had put the prospect of marriage to Clovis from her mind. And even now she did not want to trouble herself with either problem. Her inner attention was on her baby. She felt sometimes that the baby was quelling all her natural restlessness and that her only function was to wait quietly until it was born. Not until then would she be her own person again.

"Where is Clovis?" she asked, in a small attempt to change the subject. "We've been here a long time now."

"Probably asleep over the table," Madame said. "He drank more than he can normally deal with today. But you haven't answered my question."

Rosie hesitated.

"Can we talk about it tomorrow? I think I, too, have drunk more than I can deal with. The champagne was delicious, *chère* Madame, but my head is not clear."

The older woman sighed.

"You will have to make your decision soon. But, very well, we will talk tomorrow."

They kissed on both cheeks as Rosie had learned to do, and then she lit herself to bed with a small oil lamp. A fire burned cheerfully in her room but still it was chilly, and she hurriedly undressed and got into the warm bed where Marie had placed a warming pan full of hot coals.

She lay thinking how different her life had become since she left California. Waited on, whereas in the past she had always been skivvy to all. Was marriage to Clovis the only way out for her and her baby? She thought about what Madame had said. It was true there was nothing truly wrong with Clovis; the revulsion she felt for him was unfair. He had done nothing, said nothing. He had only shown her kindness. It was not his fault that to her he seemed the husk of the man she loved. And knowing what she knew, she had no rhyme or reason to go on yearning for Jean Paul, but still her treacherous body wanted him each night.

In the warmth of the bed she lectured herself. Tomorrow she would make herself make plans for the wedding, and she would do it with good grace. Since there was no alternative, if she was forced to marry Clovis, she would make him feel that she cared for him and that they could be happy together. Even though his mother had said that in all things he and Jean Paul were opposite, maybe he would make her as happy in love. If only she could lose that sense of revulsion she felt whenever he was near ...

She slid into a deep champagne-induced sleep until suddenly she heard her room door open stealthily. It was still dark and the fire had almost died. She froze, keeping very still and trying to make her breathing sound as if she still slept, but listening all the while.

"Rosie." The whisper was hoarse, but still unmistakably Clovis.

She sat up in the bed, the sheets pulled to her chin.

"Clovis!" she hissed. "What are you doing here?"

"I must talk to you." He put the oil lamp he was holding on the table by the door and moved towards her. He wore a muddied cloak and he seemed to be unsteady on his feet.

"Are you drunk, Clovis?" she asked. There was something menacing about his stance that made her uneasy. "What do you want?"

"To talk to you and to make plans for the wedding."

She felt her stomach lurch.

"But it's the middle of the night."

"It has to be settled. Now." His voice was stubborn.

"Not now."

"Now."

She was beginning to be angry.

"Clovis," she said, "you have no right to be in my bedroom. Please leave."

He laughed. "Your bedroom. That's rich. This is my bedroom. I am the heir to this house. You are here because I say so."

"I am here at your mother's invitation," she said coldly.

"And that means mine. Les Hérissons is mine."

It did not seem the moment to argue.

"We will discuss it all in the morning," she said firmly and slid back down into the bed, turning her back on him and burying her face in the pillow.

She realised immediately it was a mistake. She heard his heavy pace and then felt the big quilt being pulled back and thrown on the floor.

"Don't turn your back on me," he said, his voice ugly. "Look at me."

She was aware that her nightgown had ridden up and that he would be able to see her bare legs. She tried to wriggle the garment down.

"I will not."

"You will." His heavy hand was on her shoulder and with a rough jerk he turned her round. "Now, are you going to marry me?"

"I most certainly will not marry you if you behave like this," she said, furious.

"Aren't you afraid?" he asked mockingly, his face distorted with rage.

The heavy odour of wine hung over him like the smell from a fermenting barrel.

"I'm afraid of nothing." It was true.

"Then you should be," he said. He threw his cloak onto the floor and began to tear at his belt with clumsy fingers and then at his buttons. She heaved herself over onto her side again so she did not have to watch.

"You are disgusting," she said. "Please go away."

"*I'm* disgusting! You there pregnant and acting as if you're better than Madame's girls. Very much the lady. Too grand to marry me."

She was not sure what he was talking about. She did not reply.

"Nothing to say? Well, I'm telling you that you're marrying me, and we're going to consummate the wedding right now."

Swiftly Rosie leapt from the bed and stood on the far side away from him. His trousers were on the ground and he wore only his shirt, hose and shoes. His huge erection threw a long shadow like a baton on the wall in the light of the oil lamp. She laughed out loud.

"Clovis, you look ridiculous," she said. "Go to your bed."

He moved round the bed towards her and she realised, now angry with herself, that she was trapped in the corner. He had blocked the way to the door, and he was, she saw, much more drunk than she had realised. He was muttering incoherently as he came towards her. She stood still, staring at him, still unafraid.

"Now please, Clovis, don't be so foolish."

He did not reply. One hand stretched towards her, snatching at the neck of her nightgown, and with a single pull split it down its entire length. It fell from her body to the floor.

"I've put up with enough from you," he said. "No gratitude . . . what else would you have done . . . only a whore . . . that's all. Just another whore."

She stood naked, suddenly more enraged than she had ever been in her life. For weeks she had contained anger, grief, anxiety and held herself controlled. She felt the layers of dignity she had wrapped round herself slipping and she knew that if he touched her again she would kill him. Yes, kill him, she told herself fiercely as she stared at him, trying to decide what to do. The sight of him swaying before her, rampant, filled her with disgust. She wanted to tear at his reddened face, but instinctively she put her hands over her gently swelling stomach.

He was staring at her, lascivious, dumb; his mouth seemed to be salivating and his breath was heavy. She could see he was about to pull her towards him. I mustn't be violent, she thought. I might harm the baby, but never, never would she let this drunken, slobbering lout touch her.

She made her decision as he made his move. She smiled, opened her arms wide to embrace him.

"Come, Clovis," she whispered. "Come, husband," and as he lurched towards her, she brought her knee up with all the force she could muster and caught him hard in the groin. At the same moment she clenched her hand into a fist and thrust it with all the strength she was capable of into his face. It struck his nose. Blood spurted.

He let out a cry of real anguish, and fell back, clutching himself. Quickly, while she still had the advantage, she leapt across the bed, freeing herself from the corner where he had pinned her. First she snatched up his clothes from the floor and flung them at him in a fury. He put up his hands, dazed, to protect his face as belt and buckle came flying across the room. And then she grabbed the candlestick from beside the dressing table and held it threateningly high, with every intention of using it, if need be. "Get out!" she hissed at him. "Get out before I kill you."

The pain and her assault seemed to have sobered him. He stood, groaning softly.

"I mean it," she said menacingly. "I shall kill you if you don't go."

Painfully he bent to pick up his clothes, and then straightened, moving with care, his face covered in blood. Without a word he walked to the door, very quietly opened it, and equally quietly closed it behind him.

Once he had gone, she stood panting and shaking uncontrollably. Her rage had not subsided. He had meant to rape her, she realised, and her sense of outrage was great enough to do him real damage should he return. Her body was her own, she told herself, to give to whom she pleased, not to be plundered by a drunken, slobbering half-wit. How dare he! How dare he! Suddenly she was crying, a young girl sobbing in a room six thousand miles from home. How could she marry a man who tried to rape her? But what else was she to do? For all her bravado and defiance, Rosie understood very well the life of an unmarried mother, and a life of shame was not what she intended.

Gradually her tears subsided. She was deathly tired, but afraid to sleep in case Clovis returned. She wrapped herself in the tattered remnants of her nightgown and crawled into bed, eyes wide open, but exhaustion soon defeated watchfulness.

When she woke in the grey morning light the heavy aroma of wine still hung in the room but Clovis had not returned. She lay awake, still angry, her thoughts chaotic, until Marie came in with the morning hot water. Then she began to think constructively. She could still go back to New York, but that was not the answer. Not yet. As she washed and dressed she made her plans. By the time she left her room she knew what she was going to do.

Clovis was hovering in the hall as she came down the stairs. His face was grey as a winter sky, his nose slightly swollen where she had hit it, and his eyes red-rimmed. Remembering how he had behaved, she felt herself shrinking back, but he moved forward to help her down the last three steps. She could feel his hand shaking in hers.

"Please, Rosie, I must speak to you," he said. "Before breakfast. It cannot wait."

Her face averted from him, she just nodded, and he led her through the front door and down the steps to the driveway below.

"Let's walk a little," he said. "Get away from the house."

She nodded again, still not speaking. He was silent too, until they rounded a bend and the house was out of sight. Their footsteps squelched dismally in the half-melted snow and without a wrap she shivered in the chill air.

"You're cold. I'm sorry," he said. "I'm not thinking properly. I won't keep you." He stopped and turned so he was facing her. Speaking very fast he said: "I don't know what to say. I'm sorry, Rosie. So truly sorry. It's no excuse, I know, but I was drunk. I don't remember a lot. I'd been drinking and thinking about us. I'm not good when I drink. I came home and I drank some more to give me the courage to come to your room, and after – " He stopped and said, his voice low: "I don't even remember after, Rosie, except I think I did . . . Did I?"

Her first thought was not to answer. Let him think he had succeeded, let him sweat, she thought, but then something in her would not give him the satisfaction.

"No, you did not," she said coldly.

"You stopped me?"

"I did."

"Thank God!" he said fervently. "I didn't hurt you? Or the baby?"

"I don't think so." She was choosing her words with care. He had not remembered her pretended capitulation or what she had done. He didn't even remember what he had done. Perhaps his amnesia was contrived, but even so, maybe there was an escape here. Yet at the same time he looked so crushed, so hangdog; the tinge of pity she was feeling for him grew.

"Can you forgive me?"

"I don't know." Her answer was truthful.

"I understand. But I do love you. I swear I'll never do anything to harm you or hurt you again. I swear it." He was beginning to sweat. "Rosie, you will still marry me?"

She hesitated.

"Rosie," his voice was anguished. "I know what you must be feeling, but I swear to you that I will never touch you again, never ask you for love, unless you want – well, you understand. If you will marry me, that part of it shall be your choice. If you never wanted me that way ever, I would accept it if you will only marry me. If you could love me as your friend, it would be sufficient."

His hands were clasped in front of his chest; he looked near to tears. She did not know what to say.

"Rosie! Marry me!"

Her mind was racing. Could she share her bed with him ever? Instinctively she put her own hands over her stomach where the baby lay.

139

"It's cold," she said. "We must go inside."

She turned swiftly and hurried back to the house, still determined to stay with the plan she had made that morning.

Madame Dupuis was already at the table, pouring the coffee into huge cups when Rosie hurried into the breakfast room.

"You look frozen, child," she said as Rosie settled herself. "Have you been out?"

"Just for a little air, madame," Rosie murmured.

The older woman gave her a sharp look as Clovis came through into the room.

"And where were you last night?" she asked, her voice dry.

"I went out to clear my head, Mama," he muttered. "It was the champagne."

Madame Dupuis clicked her tongue.

"You know you cannot drink," she said. "Just like your father – no head."

Clovis looked from under his eyelids at Rosie as if to confirm the truth of his mother's words.

They ate and drank in silence for a moment, and then Madame Dupuis said: "We had best be making plans for the wedding, had we not?"

Rosie heard Clovis's sharp intake of breath, but he said nothing. She put down her napkin and said calmly: "Yes madame, I had been thinking about it. Tomorrow I shall take the train to Paris to buy myself a gown and some garments for my trousseau."

Clovis dropped a knife with a clatter.

"You are running away!" he shouted.

Rosie kept her face expressionless.

"And where would I run to?"

"You'll go back to America – looking for him."

"Clovis!" His mother's voice was a command for silence. No one spoke until she asked: "Why Paris, my dear?"

"Is it not every girl's dream to be wed in a Paris gown?"

"Of course. Clovis shall come with you and see you safe."

"Oh, no, madame. That would spoil it all. In America, the groom must know nothing about the bride's arrangements. It all must be a surprise. Is it not the same here?"

Madame Dupuis looked at her quizzically. "And if I were to come with you, would you say that was against American custom?"

Rosie sighed.

"No, it would not be, but the truth is, madame, that I would like to make the journey alone. I need some time to myself to think. I shall be safe. Remember how far I have come alone already."

Clovis had thrown down his napkin in an angry gesture.

"Mama, don't let her go. She won't return. I know it."

"How do you know it?"

His mother's face was stern and Rosie wondered if perhaps she had some inkling of what had happened the night before. Clovis did not reply. He let his head fall into his hands.

"I will take Marie with me if you wish," Rosie said quickly. "She shall chaperone me at the hotel."

"Hotel!" Clovis sat up, his neck rigid, shoulders speaking indignation. "You are to stay at an hotel?"

"Just for one night," Rosie said cheerfully. "It will be my little shopping holiday."

"But you cannot. It is not seemly!" Clovis said.

"Clovis, Rosie has travelled halfway around the world. It is too late to speak of what is and what is not seemly," Madame Dupuis said. "If you wish to take Marie, you are welcome, Rosie. But go alone if you prefer. I have faith that you will bring me back my grandchild."

The woman's steady gaze was holding hers, and Rosie felt a pang of guilt. She said: "I shall be back long before he is born, madame, have no fear."

Clovis, with a muttered exclamation, left the table, his breakfast unfinished.

"He is worth a chance, my dear," his mother said quietly.

"I know," Rosie said. It was true, but she prayed that she would never have to take that chance.

Chapter Eleven

Dear Lizzie,

I so long to hear from you and hope that things are fine back there. By now you must have received my last letter and will know that at least I got here safely. Though I sometimes fear that my letters to you will never arrive and you will not know what has befallen.

Since I wrote I have settled into life here, and Madame Dupuis is good to me. She is most forthright, and stands no nonsense from anyone, but her heart is kind and she seems to have a regard for me. I like her very much.

My sad news is that Jean Paul did not arrive, and indeed it seems now as if he may not.

And so it looks as if I shall have to marry Clovis. I told you he had offered to have me, but I fear I can never love him.

Oh, Lizzie, I do not want to marry him, but what else am I to do? I know you will say that I could come back to New York and pretend to be a widow, or some such story, but I should be found out for sure. And what would I do to live? I would not be a burden to anyone. I could not bear it.

I am writing this to you on a train. I have been to Paris for a day and a night. It was a last attempt to alter my situation. Alas, it failed.

She paused and stared out of the train window at the gentle rolling countryside. Of course, it had been a crazy idea, but it was worth the try. Yesterday had been her nineteenth birthday, a fact she had not told either Madame or Clovis. She wanted to spend it with André, and perhaps to be given the best birthday present of all – a place under his roof. From the station she had taken a hansom straight to his house, anxious that she had no way of giving him warning of her arrival, but his welcome had lacked no warmth.

"I came because it is my birthday," she said by way of explanation after the smiling maid had let her in. Sebastian was beside himself with joy, and André's delight was apparent. He had ordered champagne to be brought, declared that they should have the dinner at Maxim's he had promised her, sent his valet to Worth with her gown to be let out a touch, and installed her back in the room where she had slept before.

And then he had introduced her to his son.

They were taking tea with Sebastian who had been excused the nursery in her honour when she heard a deep voice in the hallway, speaking to the maid.

"That will be Philippe," André said. "He is back from New York. It seems that young Sebastian is to have the pleasure of his father's company for a while."

Sebastian was already jumping from the table and running from the room, calling: "Papa, Papa, I am here. Ah, Papa, you must please meet my friend, Rosie. She is *très gentille* and it is her birthday. She is nineteen years old. Imagine!"

André laughed and shook his head.

"He speaks of you all the time," he said. "You are without doubt his favourite person."

"I was wondering," Rosie heard herself blurting out, fully aware it was not the best moment, "if I could be his governess. I'm not too well educated, but I could maybe learn myself while I taught him."

André looked startled, but before he could reply, the door was thrown back with a bang and Sebastian burst through, clinging to the hand of a tall, blond man.

"*Chère* Rosie," he was shouting. "This is my papa."

"Gently, gently," the man was saying as André got to his feet.

"Philippe," he said, "this is the legendary Mademoiselle Rosie Brunner."

The man took her hand, bowed and kissed it.

"*Enchanté*, and happy birthday," he said. And in that moment Rosie felt that same shock wave of recognition, the pull at the gut that she had felt at the first sight of Jean Paul. And as she stood smiling foolishly at André's son, she asked herself how could a heart play such tricks? How could she feel again exactly as she had felt before for someone so totally different?

For where Jean Paul had been of medium height, this man was as tall as his father. He had a long silky blond moustache and sideburns that curled down to meet it. His face was youthful with a small neat nose and light blue eyes that were regarding her with a gentle, enquiring expression. He was a big man, and when he bent to lift Sebastian, the child looked lost in his arms. Bemused, she suddenly realised that this was how her dear André must have looked when young.

143

"I hear you have been very kind to my son," he said. "I am grateful to you."

"It is no hardship to be kind to Sebastian," Rosie said. "For when he is good, he is very good."

"And when he is bad he is wicked?" his father suggested.

They all three laughed and Sebastian pouted.

"Not wicked," he said crossly.

"And what about when you threw soup all over Rosie?" André asked.

Sebastian hung his head and was silent.

"But he was forgiven that," Rosie said quickly. "Weren't you?"

Now alone on the rocking train, her pencil still in her hand, she had only to recall that meeting, Philippe's hand holding hers, his lips lightly touching her flesh, to recreate the sense of warm desire. And she was alarmed to find that on analysis, thoughts of Jean Paul no longer produced the same hot, sweet feeling.

As the train lurched along, she continued her letter:

It was my birthday and André and I went for the dinner that I missed the last time. My Worth dress was a little tight, but not too much so. I do not seem to be really swelling just yet. Madame Dupuis says it will all begin at four months. And so, though perhaps it is not in the best of taste, I have decided to wear the gown for my wedding. It is beautiful, and for me has such happy memories that I shall think only of them when I become Madame Clovis Dupuis. I have bowed to fate, dear Lizzie, but I shall not let fate defeat me.

It was the most wonderful evening that I had with André. I am sure that Mr Webster will have taken you to Maxim's when you came to Paris and had I not been shown New York by you I would have been even more impressed. But it was the beauty and confidence of the women that I found so fascinating, Lizzie. I promised myself then that one day I should be the same. I see no reason why not. I have managed so much already, but I want more and André has made me see that with courage and determination it is possible for a woman to have the life she wants.

Over dinner I told him all my circumstances; how I did not want to marry Clovis, and I took all my courage and asked him if I could be governess to Sebastian. But he said it was not possible, in the kindest and most gentle way.

So many things unsaid, she thought as she paused again. And why was it easier to tell André the intimate truths than to write them down in a letter to her friend?

144

She had explained the events of Christmas night to him and he had listened gravely but he smiled when she told of the conversation in the driveway in the morning.

"And what do you want to do?" he asked when she stopped.

"I want never to go back to Les Hérissons and I want to stay in Paris and be governess to Sebastian," she said without hesitation.

He sighed, and stroked his chin thoughtfully.

"You tempt me, my dear. To have you under my roof . . . But my son will soon be here permanently. I am too old for you, and you seem to have forgotten your baby. Les Hérissons is where your child should be – with his family. Americans have little sense of family. Maybe because you have left it all behind. We French care about our ancestors and our offspring. Would you deprive your Madame Dupuis of her grandson? Remember, once you have your baby, your position will be secure. And," he said, his eyes twinkling, "for a lady with ambitions, it does not seem to be such a bad position. The Dupuis have money, they have land. If you pursue your idea to make champagne, perhaps you will become another Madame Pommery, or Madame Cliquot. The world of champagne is the place for ambitious women with energy. I will make you a promise. When you produce your first vintage, my son will sell it for you. How's that, eh? And I will always be in your life if you need me. For as long as I am here, that is," he added ruefully.

"You make me sound like a child," she said crossly. "You are humouring me. You don't understand. How can I marry Clovis when I don't want to sleep with him?"

"It seems you do not have to. I think he will keep his word. His pride will not let him importune you. But you would be wise to find some way to do your duty as a wife."

He was smiling at her so kindly that she resisted the retort that was on her lips. She wanted to say it was all very well for men; it was all very well to tell her to acquiesce, but there was no justice for women. But then, as if he had known what she was thinking, he leaned to take her hand and hold it between his own.

"Listen, my dear. The world is not easy for women. Even women with the spirit and enterprise you have. You cannot see it now but you have fallen on your feet. Your Clovis is dull and slow. That night he was brutish – but he was drunk and frustrated. He may never be that way again. And it seems he loves you. At Les Hérissons you have the chance to bring up your child in a safe, loving home, adequately provided for. And if that is not enough, you can create your business. I believe that the young Clovis will do anything to make you happy. There is a school of oenology, wine studies, in Épernay where they are learning to combat the phylloxera. Philippe is planning to take a course there. There is no reason why you should not go too. Learn. Use

145

your brain. You have the energy and the enterprise to save your vineyards, for unless something is done, the phylloxera will certainly destroy Champagne as it has destroyed other regions. When your Jean Paul told you the vines must be replanted with American stocks, he was right. There is plenty for you to do with your life, my dear. Marriage to a man you love is not essential. A fine thing should it happen, but most of us marry for convenience in the end."

"Did you marry for love?" she asked.

"No, I married the woman my parents chose for me. I have loved many times. I am in love now – " he gave her a dazzling smile – "but I was happy enough with my dear wife."

"And your son?" This was the question she wanted to ask. "Did he marry for love?"

He smiled.

"I permitted him to marry for love," he said. "But love dies, as you will one day discover, and then the mystery is, where did it go? What happened to that burning desire that was once the most important, urgent thing in the world?" He sighed and then looked directly at her. "Philippe wanted to join us tonight. But I am a selfish old man and I wanted you to myself. Would you have liked it had he been here?"

She nodded, and said simply: "Only because he is so like you."

"Like me when young?" he suggested.

"Maybe," she said.

"Then you will be glad that I have told him he must give you lunch tomorrow and see you safe on the train back."

She could not control the flush of pleasure that rose on her cheeks.

"You see," he said and sighed. "Youth calls to youth."

"Not always," she said, remembering the last night on the ship.

He smiled at her. "No, not always," he agreed. "But, my dear, it could not have worked for you and me. I am old. You would be holding a white handkerchief at my funeral far too soon, and then you would be alone again. No. Go back to your new family. Have your baby and make your life mean something. You will, I know. Women rarely realise the power they have. Teach your Clovis how to be a lover. You have the gift; you can mould him how you will." He smiled at her. "Your pretty black corselet should not be wasted on an old goat like me."

"You laughed at it," she said sadly. "And you're laughing again. Why?"

"Because it tells me so much about you, my sweet Rosie. The girl who yearns to be a lady, but a woman as well."

"I don't understand," she said, still not mollified.

"It is a garment that a lady would not wear – only a lady who was also very much a woman and knew how to please a man. And that is

146

something you know instinctively. I am not criticising, my Rosie. It is a fine compliment that I pay you. All your life men will want you as I want you now."

He had come to her room that night, shy and ready to be turned away, but she had welcomed him. If he loved her, she knew that she loved him in a special way that had nothing to do with what she felt for Jean Paul or could feel for Philippe. The sexual hunger she had felt on the ship had gone, but in loving gratitude she wrought magic with hands and mouth until he was content and then she told him he was the best birthday present she could ever have had.

Remembering, she sighed. Outside the windows of the train, the world was dark. They would be waiting for her at the station with the carriage. It was so different from the last time. She sighed again and returned to her letter.

> And so Lizzie, I go back to face my fate. But I go with hope. André's son, Philippe, escorted me to lunch and then onto this train. He has persuaded me that I should put my energies into the estate if Clovis will permit it. Later in the year Philippe is going to a special school in Champagne where they are studying the grape and the most modern methods of producing the wine. For him it will only be for a short while. It seems his company insist that their employees know every aspect of their trade, but he says that I must go too, and that perhaps I could become a true expert. My only fear is that the family will not think it seemly for me to do so, but if I pay my own way, they cannot refuse me. I may be marrying to give my child a family, but that family will never own me.
>
> Clovis has already promised me that he will plant the cuttings that I brought in their own special vineyard. Yes, they arrived safely and are nestled in sand, waiting for the day when they can be grafted. I shall use my own money to buy more if he will not. But Madame is so excited about the baby that I think she will deny me nothing, and Clovis does seem to care for me. It is sad that I cannot care for him. How idyllic life would be then.

As she wrote, her mind was still on Philippe for whom she could care. She had found it again – the style, the class that instantly appealed to her. Lizzie's style; André's. Madame Dupuis had it too. But not her children. She wondered briefly what the dead father had been like. Did he have a touch of roughness that had attracted the formidable Madame Dupuis? And was she, Rosie, always to be attracted to men like Philippe and André because they possessed this quality she wanted for herself?

147

Philippe had been so correct, so charming, but all her instincts told her, loud and clear, that their attraction was mutual. Now she knew the look in men's eyes and it no longer surprised her. She could read desire, and for her the old yearning was back; the wound was reopened. She clasped her hands over her gently swelling stomach and asked herself how it was that she could experience – and savour – these stirring feelings for a man she barely knew. But she was certain that one day she and Philippe would be lovers. How and when were barely considerations.

So, for the meantime, with the thought of that future as a consolation, she would go back and marry Clovis. She would wear her Worth gown, be a beautiful smiling bride and do as Madame Dupuis and André in their wisdom told her. When the baby was born, her life would be her own again. Then anything would be possible. Anything at all, she told herself. All she had to do was wait.

California, May 1900

Peter was in no hurry as Castor and Pollux ambled gently along the sun-drenched road. They twitched their ears against the flies, and Castor snorted protest at the weight of the wagon behind him. The horses were getting old, Peter thought, his mind on Jean Paul's promise to buy a proper little carriage so that they could go into Calistoga looking like gentlemen and not impoverished dirt farmers.

He was supposed to be hurrying, but he had no intention of doing so. Peter could always postpone unpleasantness. And months of buried frustration from living with the slut, as he called the skinny, evil-tempered girl that Jean Paul had brought home five months ago and announced as the new housekeeper, had left him pitiless on her behalf. She had arrived pregnant with Jean Paul's child, and there had been the frightening moment when he had thought for a while that Jean Paul would marry the bitch. Then to his infinite relief he discovered that the Frenchman had told the girl that he was already married, with children, back in Champagne. Maybe it was true. Peter doubted it, and clearly so did Sarah Saunders.

He wondered how many lies Jean Paul had told. When Peter had accused him of sleeping with Rosie, Jean Paul swore that he had never touched her, but Peter did not believe him. The memory of her naked body in the lamplight that night still filled him with a curious combination of his own jealousy and also pain for her embarrassment. He wondered, too, about the truth of the stories that had been told about the Frenchman's background. Jean Paul's tastes, his education and his manners seemed not to belong to a family who would have been totally

148

dependent on the vines – as he and Rosie and their father had been. And yet why should a man of some refinement take up with Sarah Saunders? Sarah was good-looking in her scrawny way, but she was personally none too clean and she was without education. It was true she cooked like an angel; also, as Jean Paul was fond of saying when he wanted to provoke Peter into more and more sexual excesses, she was a devil in bed.

"She makes it understandable why men make love with women, my dear Peter," he would say. "I would share her with you if you were interested. Such a pity you are not; you truly do not appreciate what you are missing. Ah, to enjoy the two of you at once!"

Sarah was not as naive as Rosie had been. She had immediately understood her lover's relationship with Peter; jealous and angry, just as he was, she taunted him daily about his lack of manhood. Peter just prayed that she would never be taken into Calistoga where she might well talk. Then he and Jean Paul would be tarred and feathered for sure. His only consolation was that she could hardly tell without involving her lover and the father of the child to which she had been painfully and noisily giving birth when he left the house.

He had been sent to fetch the midwife from Calistoga, and Jean Paul had told him to get a move on; the girl was near her time.

"Let her suffer," Peter had muttered to himself as he leisurely harnessed up Castor and Pollux. And he had no intention of hurrying now.

In Calistoga the midwife was out, but he left a message with her aged mother who shouted instructions as to what must be done as he set off back down the path.

"Just keep the baby warm if it comes," was her last reminder.

"All right, all right," he shouted back, setting his horses on their way with a sharp crack of the whip.

Even the thought of the baby depressed him. As it was, he only had a couple of nights a week with Jean Paul – and at first Sarah had refused to cook on those days until Jean Paul had beaten her, and then, surly as a bear, she had almost thrown their food at them and Jean Paul had had to beat her again to stop her deliberately burning their meals.

The baby could only make matters worse, separating him and Jean Paul even more. And if it were a girl? Peter's pretty nose wrinkled in disgust.

One thing that Sarah had not been able to change was the determination of both men to make the vineyard their fortune. They were at their happiest when working together away from the house. Peter had been fired with Jean Paul's ambition to make the best champagne in the United States, but it was taking time and hard work, though neither had any doubt that they would succeed. Some of the fields had been replanted with different grapes, using the wild vines and the grafts that Jean Paul had brought back with him. It would be three years before they knew if their plans would succeed, and in the meantime, to give themselves some income, they planned to continue to make the same red *vin ordinaire* that old man Brunner had produced.

Peter could see his home now, the stone walls shimmering in the late July heat. Everything seemed quiet. The horses clopped up the path, the wagon leaving a trail of yellow dust behind. At least there were no shouts and screams coming from the bedroom Jean Paul shared with the slut, Peter thought, as he jumped down from the wagon. The baby must have arrived.

With little enthusiasm he went into the house and up the stairs. It was hotter indoors and he realised that his shirt was sticking to his back. There was no sound to be heard, but the main bedroom door was half open. Cautiously he peered in at the bed. He looked at the blotchily blood-stained sheet and for a moment thought Sarah was not there. Then he saw that the sheet carried all the way up to the bedhead and over the pillows, and realised with a shiver of horror that she was under the stained material, her face covered. Nothing moved. Sarah was dead.

The knowledge of his own wickedness fought briefly with the involuntary flash of triumph and gladness that she had gone from their lives. But maybe Jean Paul would be bereft. Peter had no idea how he would react. It seemed wise to compose his features into a careful expression of sorrow.

There was no need. Jean Paul was sitting on the big old chair by the window, and in his hands he cradled something red that squirmed. He looked up, and Peter saw that his eyes were shining with a sort of wonder.

"You're supposed to keep it warm," Peter stammered, suddenly awed himself.

Jean Paul did not seem to hear. He said, as if it were a declaration, "I am a father. I have a son."

BOOK TWO

Chapter Twelve

Champagne, September 1900.

Philippe had meant to take a brisk walk to the School of Oenology from his newly rented apartment in Épernay. He was aware that his life left him little time for any physical exercise, and as the school was a good mile and a half along the Reims road, it seemed just the right distance to fill his lungs with good, clean country air.

But in the event he found the silence of Épernay, compared with the nightly dull rumble of noise that blanketed Paris, so peaceful that he overslept. And after bathing and dressing hastily, he realised that in order not to be late for the first morning of the course, he would have to take a hansom cab.

As horse and carriage swayed and bounced down the rutted road out of the town, he found himself thinking, not for the first time, about the young American girl that his father had met on the ship. He wondered if she would be there this morning. She had been so anxious to join the school and he could still remember his own sense of anticipation at the thought of it. But his father had said that it might not be possible because the beautiful Rosie Brunner was expecting a baby.

The news had shocked and dismayed Philippe, for he knew the girl was not married and she seemed so young to bear such trouble alone. Then his father had told him the whole story of Rosie's incredible journey to find the father of her child and explained that she had come to the house on the Île de la Cité for advice on whether or not she should marry the man's twin brother.

"And what *did* you advise?" Philippe had asked.

"I told her to marry him," his father had said.

"Does she love him?"

"Not in the least."

Philippe felt outraged. The conversation was taking place over breakfast on the morning after Philippe had taken Rosie to lunch and then put her on the train for Reims. A picture of her, amber-eyed and black-haired, was very much in his mind. For a man who had not looked with any interest at another woman since the death of his wife, he had found her astonishingly appealing.

"Was that a good idea?" he asked, rather stiffly.

His father shook his head indulgently.

"You are as romantic as she is. Of course it is a good idea. What will she do otherwise? She complained that the world is not a fair place for women, and of course she is right. For women there is little justice. But with a child it is better to be respectably married. And better for the child, too."

"I suppose you are right," Philippe grudgingly conceded. Somehow he did not care for the owner of those bewitching eyes to be trapped in a loveless union. Not when he himself knew the joy of a marriage based on love. He could not conceive of marriage without passion. Rosie, he was sure, was a woman of passion.

He had thought about Rosie Brunner frequently since, wondering how she was faring. Sebastian had often asked after her too, complaining that she had not been to Paris. Philippe was inclined silently to echo his complaints. And he found that a bowl of scented roses, a single white rose nodding in a country garden, the women selling long-stemmed red roses at the Madeleine, brought her to mind. He had asked his father about her once, and André said that she had indeed married the twin brother, and that she seemed to have come to terms with her situation.

But now, almost a year later, André had been vague when Philippe enquired if she had kept her resolution to go to the school at Épernay.

He was well in time for the lecture when the cab pulled up at the white-painted buildings that housed the School of Oenology. Feeling like a new schoolboy, he paid off the driver and walked towards the entrance. It was then that he noticed the girl coming from his right where the private horses and carriages were tethered. She had not seen him, but he felt a small beat of excitement. It was Rosie Brunner; he was certain of it.

She wore a pale blue coat, richly embroidered down the front and fur-trimmed, with one lapel folded back to show a lining of old rose velvet. The waist was tightly cinched, emphasising how charmingly slender and curved she was. A high collar of rose velvet nestled under her rounded chin, and she wore a large velour hat with a dashing bow of old rose, her dark hair piled beneath.

She looked anxious as she hurried towards the path, one blue gloved hand lifting her skirts from the mud.

He stopped and waited as she neared. She still had not seen him.

154

"Good morning, madame," he said.

She looked at him, at first a little haughty, and then her face lit up and the amber eyes smiled.

"Oh!" she said. "How delightful. It's André's son, Philippe, isn't it?"

"Indeed it is," he said bowing. "And you are Rosie, but not Brunner any more."

"Rosie Dupuis," she said, holding out her hand to him. "And what a pleasant surprise to see you. Though you did threaten to come, I recall."

"As indeed did you," he said.

There was a strange little awkward silence as they looked at each other. Her eyes seemed very large and shining, almost as though she was going to cry.

"May I escort you in?" he asked.

"I should be grateful," she said. "For I find myself a little apprehensive. But with you ..." Her voice trailed away, the sentence unfinished.

He had been allocated the seat directly behind her, and as she sat, her head bent to take notes while the lecturer droned on about pests in the vines and the latest chemicals for dealing with them, he found he could not concentrate at all.

A faint perfume drifted back to him and the nape of her neck was tantalisingly near ...

Mentally he shook himself and forced his attention back to the lecture, trying hard to ignore her disturbing presence.

When they were released from the room, he fell into step beside her.

"How did you get here?" he asked. "By carriage?"

She shook her head. "I took the train from Rilly-la-Montagne. My home is very near to it, less than three kilometres. And then a carriage from Épernay station."

"Oh," he said, puzzled. "This morning I had thought you were walking from the private carriages."

He saw the blush rise on her cheeks, and realised, though without understanding why, that he had confused her.

"No," she said abruptly. "It is a little too far for a carriage from home. But Henri, our man, will meet me at Rilly when I return."

Without stopping to think he blurted out: "Must you return immediately?"

She blushed again, hesitated, and then shook her head without speaking.

"I was thinking, you see," he said, afraid he was going to stammer, "that I could take you back to Épernay, and perhaps you would join me for dinner before you leave. I have taken an apartment there

155

for the length of the course, and it is not agreeable to eat alone."

"A meal in your apartment?" Her voice was devoid of expression, but she did not look shocked or outraged.

"I had not meant – " he started to say. Then he changed his mind.

He looked straight into her eyes, and saw expectancy and something else that could have been desire.

"Yes," he said. "In my apartment."

"Very well," she said quietly.

There was no cab rank by the school, and in the end they walked back into Épernay. It was a soft late-September afternoon and already a few leaves were falling with the chestnuts. As they walked, she talked enthusiastically of her attempts to make Les Hérissons live again as a champagne house. She told him how she had persuaded her mother-in-law to take back the old *chef de cuvée* who had blended the wines for the Dupuis in days past when they produced their own champagne.

"He is called Eugène and he is a little man, like a brown nut," she said, "and already he has taught me so much. He makes me taste all the famous marks, and I can now tell a Krug from a Taittinger and a simple Moët et Chandon from an ordinary Bollinger."

"And of those last two, which is the best?" he asked, smiling at her.

"Eugène says that in the end it is a matter of taste, but I prefer the Bollinger and he was kind enough to say I had good taste."

"In which case, I too have good taste," he said. "But I prefer Dom Perignon above all. We shall have a bottle with our meal."

It seemed to him to be an enchanted walk as she told him of her ambitions. He welcomed every kerbstone, every pothole that permitted him to take her arm. He felt as if he could feel her skin burning below the soft wool of the tight sleeve on her coat. He wondered if she could feel the heat of his hand, and wondered also at these sudden stirrings that he had not felt for so long. He was puzzled, almost embarrassed, at the strength of his feelings, yet at the same time elated. He knew he should be telling himself she was a married woman, but then he knew she did not love her husband.

But there was one question he had to ask.

"My father said that you have a baby."

His father had said no such thing, but he needed to know.

At first her face lit up, and then she looked doubtful; anxious.

"Yes, I do," she said.

He could see she was going to tell him more, but now he suddenly did not want to know. "Ah, look, we are almost there," he said.

His apartment was in one of the large houses on the Avenue de Champagne itself. He led her up the short drive and the flight of steps to the front door.

"I'm afraid there are rather a lot of stairs," he said. "It is an attic apartment, but perfect for the few weeks that I shall be here."

In fact, the apartment was large, and she exclaimed with pleasure as he led her into the big drawing room where gabled windows looked across the soft hills of the Marne Valley. Someone had furnished the room with taste. There was a charming chaise longue, and some rather stiff but well cared for Empire pieces, and gold damask curtains to match the upholstery on the soft furniture. A large oriental rug covered the floor.

"It is charming," Rosie said. "And not small at all."

"No, there is a bedroom," he said, and stopped, embarrassed.

"And of course a kitchen," she said quickly.

"Which is where the Dom Perignon is," he said. "Please sit down and I will bring it in."

"You have no servant here?"

She sounded a little surprised, even apprehensive.

"Not until tomorrow," he explained. "He brought some things yesterday and he will be returning with the rest. There is really not enough to do here to keep him permanently occupied, so he is helping out in Paris. Marius is getting rather old."

The mention of his father's house seemed to relax her. She sat down on the chaise longue, loosened the collar of her coat and absently began taking pins from her hat while she looked around the room.

"Please," he said, "let me take your coat."

He moved towards her and she rose and moved towards him. They both stopped. Her hands hovered at the first button, and he said again: "Let me."

He began to unbutton her coat slowly and intently, his eyes never rising to her face. She stood quite still until he moved to slide the garment from her shoulders. Then, almost imperceptibly, she swayed towards him.

He had not intended it, but his arms went round her, and he held her very close. She did not draw away, but leaned her head on his shoulder. They stood motionless until slowly, timidly, her arms went round him.

"Rosie," he breathed. "Oh, Rosie."

"I know. I know," she said.

He pushed her away from him, but only to look at her. The amber eyes glinted. Her colour was high, and her lips just slightly apart. Her expression was a question. Very gently he took the hat with its brave bow and set it on a small table; he peeled her coat from her shoulders and let it drop to the floor. She stood as still as a mannequin in a shop window until he took her face between his hands and leaned forward to kiss her.

Her response was a shock. Her mouth clung to his, her arms tightened round him with a kind of desperation and she moaned

157

faintly as he tentatively slid his tongue between her parted lips. Gently her mouth opened, and he was able to taste and explore her until he felt the flickering of her own tongue exploring him. He found himself dizzy with desire.

"Wait," she said eventually, and drew back, a little breathless but still smiling. Her quick fingers were at the buttons of his overcoat, and in seconds she was taking it from his shoulders just as he had done for her.

"Now kiss me again," she said, her voice husky. "Long, long kisses that I have dreamed of from you."

"And I from you," he confessed.

They clung together, mouth to mouth, her hands clasped behind his back.

"Help me with your dress," he whispered in her ear. His hands had found a line of buttons at the back that he feared would defeat him.

Obediently she turned round and presented a neat back and a long row of blue wool-covered buttons that ran from the nape of her neck to the curve of her rounded bottom.

"It is not so difficult as it looks," she said softly.

He was not really listening. His clumsy fingers were attempting to undo the buttons, and then he realised that these were buttons with no buttonholes. Below was some sort of stud, and by giving both sides of the back of the dress one sharp pull, it separated, revealing the white curve of her back before the dress fell to the oriental carpet to rest with the matching coat.

She instantly turned to him, her face serious. Above her long sheer black petticoat she wore a black corselet edged in lace and with a few diamanté scattered over the right breast.

Such a garment was the last thing he had expected under the chic outfit she had been wearing. He felt his breath falter and his body strain against the tight black trousers that he wore.

"Oh, Rosie," he said, and took her back into his arms, biting at her neck, her ears, nibbling her lips and then thrusting his tongue deep into the soft, warm red cavern of her mouth.

As they kissed, he was pushing her back towards the chaise longue, afraid to suggest the bedroom, though that was where he wanted to take her. She was aware of his movements, and made no resistance. When her legs found the gold damask surface of the chair behind them, she slid away from him and sat down.

He sat beside her, just looking at her beauty, while she, her head tipped back, looking straight at him, unlaced the corselet slowly and provocatively. He watched, mesmerised, as the white of her full breasts spilled forward, tumbling, released from their confines.

She did not hurry, and when the last ribbon was undone, she let the garment fall behind her, and placing one hand under each breast, offered them up to him.

He devoured them with his eyes first, the deep red nipples standing proud, the purply blue veins on the milky whiteness of the skin, the soft droop that her hands supported. Then when he had looked and stroked his fill, he thrust his face between the twin globes before taking each nipple, one between his teeth and one between his fingers, twisting, biting and squeezing until she lay back, moaning with ecstasy.

Then to his delight he felt her tentative hand running from his chest and down until her fingers closed over the hard protuberance that was imprisoned there. She began to stroke and knead him through the fabric until, fearful that she would cause it all to be over for him, he had to stop her.

He clasped her hands between his and drew back, still hardly able to believe that this beautiful young woman was sitting in his rented apartment in Épernay, her breasts bared, her hair tumbled, apparently willing to let him make love to her.

"Rosie," he began. "It has been a long time ..." he hesitated, not sure what to say next.

She nodded. "And for me," she told him. "But then, I have been waiting for you."

"For me?" He did not understand.

She nodded again.

"When you walked through the door that day in your father's house, I wanted you. When you took me to lunch, I was certain of it. I have been waiting ever since, for today, when I hoped and prayed that this would happen." She laughed, throwing back her head. "Ah, Philippe, I do not always wear such things as this –" she touched the black of the corselet that lay beside her. "I wore it for you. I prayed you would see it, because it is a garment that a lady would not wear; only a lady who is a woman and wants to please her man."

"You wanted me to make love to you?" he asked. His head was spinning, trying to relate the candour of this girl with the few other women he had known. She should have sounded shameless, like a whore, but she sounded only sincere and honest, and her gaze was unshrinkingly direct. "You still want me to make love to you?"

She smiled at him.

"Of course, and I think the bedroom would be more comfortable than this scratchy old seat!"

She laughed, and he was laughing too.

"My darling girl!" he said, and stood before bending to sweep her into his arms. Her head on his shoulder, he carried her through to the bedroom where, gently, he laid her on the four-poster bed that dominated the room, and sat down so that he could more easily slide her petticoat and black lace undergarments from her body. Obligingly she raised her hips from the bed and the movement aroused him so much that he feared again that he would not be able to please her.

She lay, naked, on the velvet coverlet, smiling up at him, as he stroked the luxuriant hair that covered her mount of Venus, slipping his fingers lower until her hips rose again, but this time with urgent need. Her fingers were finding their way through the maze of the bow of his tie, and the many buttons and fastenings of his clothing, until he too was naked.

Their lovemaking, and her ardour, were a revelation to him. But it was as he feared. The first time he plunged into her eager, open body, he could not wait, and the surge of feeling left him drained spread-eagled across her, as she soothed and stroked his back with long, tender caresses. He thought he slept for a moment or two, but he woke to find her head no longer beside his. To his astonishment, she had turned her body and was curled at his side, her mouth closed over him, licking, teasing, gently blowing warm air, then taking her mouth away and rubbing her hand in long, firm strokes, until he leapt to hard, vibrant life again.

He pulled her up again so that he could kiss her mouth that tasted of him and of her, and suck again at her nipples. Her eyes were closed, her legs spread, and he took the invitation to kiss her from mouth, to throat, to breast, to belly and then below to the musky, warm depth of her, until she cried out for him to take her.

This time he could wait, and he turned her body, changing their positions as he plunged into her. She was so light, she seemed to be an extension of him, speared on his body. All the time he rode her her hands were guiding him, touching him, squeezing and stroking his eyes, his mouth, even his ears, and then probing in places where he had never been touched. Then again the floodgates opened for him – and also for her. She cried out loud and he thought he might have done so too. And they lay panting, wet with sweat, the sharp smell of their passion filling the room. And then they both slept.

He woke first, easing himself carefully away from her, trying not to wake her before padding out naked into the kitchen. There he took a bottle of Dom Perignon from the ice-box. He found two glasses, and some cold chicken legs that his manservant had left. He took them all back into the bedroom on a small tray before finding himself a dressing gown. He kept thinking of what had happened between them, still astonished by the intensity of their lovemaking. Her response had been something he had never experienced before. He looked at the sleeping girl, now so innocent, so soft and childish, her mouth slightly open, long lashes on her cheeks, her naked limbs relaxed in sleep, and marvelled that she could be so much a woman.

It was the pop of the champagne cork that woke her, and she stretched and smiled lazily at him, like an amber-eyed cat, he thought.

"Champagne," she said sleepily. "How lovely. Someone once told me it was a wine for love, now I can find out if it is true."

"Oh, it's true," he said pouring her a glass, and handing it to her with a bow. "The only wine for love. Are you hungry?"

"Ravenous," she said.

"There are only chicken legs," he warned.

"Perfect."

She sat up, and sipped deeply from her glass, unselfconscious in her nakedness.

"Um. That is delicious."

"So are you."

She sighed a sigh of contentment.

"Sit by me," she commanded, patting the bed, "and talk to me."

"If you let me cover you," he said. "You could catch cold or I might not be able to control myself."

"I don't want you to control yourself," she said, laughing, as she let him pull the bedcovers over her.

"Do you think I'm shameless?" she suddenly asked, the chicken bone in her hand, her mouth shining with the fat from its skin.

"I don't know," he said, believing it best to be honest. "You see, I have little experience of love. My wife and I loved each other very much. We were childhood sweethearts. In fact, looking back, we *were* only children. From what I experienced with you today, we were only playing at being grown-ups. But we managed to make Sebastian. She never really recovered from his birth, and when she died, I believed that I would never want anyone else, and that love was dead for me." He paused, and added quietly: "I cared for her a great deal."

He felt a great relief at having told someone, at long last, his feelings at the loss of Nicole. He had never let even his father see the devastation that he had felt at her death. His main purpose had been to protect Sebastian.

"After she died," he went on, "I began to travel for my firm. They were very good to me. They knew I wanted to get away from Paris. I had two years in London, and nearly three in New York before coming back last year. You were the first woman who had attracted me. I think I had been numb, but that first day we met, you warmed a little corner of me. Today you have warmed me right through. So the answer to your question, on reflection, is no, I do not think you are shameless, anymore than I was shameless just now. I think we may be in love."

"I know I am in love," she said quietly. "And I think I always will be."

He did not know what to say. He was overcome with emotion, and he knew that he could easily have cried. So, in silence, they drank the champagne, until she said, suddenly flustered, that she must go. The moments they had shared were temporarily lost as they dressed rapidly and hurried from the building. He was aware that their movements were a little furtive and it worried him. But he walked her to Épernay station where she would not let him wait for the train with her.

"We shall see each other tomorrow," she promised.

"And I may kiss the back of your neck in the lecture room," he told her.

She laughed, blew him a kiss, and hurried into the station with just one backward look, and he did not know how he could bear to let her go.

He walked back to the apartment which still smelt of her, and of their lovemaking, his mind full of pictures of her, both naked and dressed. He pulled the scent of the afternoon into his lungs, and tried to settle himself down to read a Zola novel.

But even Zola could not distract him. He found himself dreaming of Rosie. The intensity of passion they had shared was new to him and had left him uncertain as to whether the pleasure was God- or Devil-given. He had not understood that these things could happen so wildly between a man and a woman, and if it was wrong, wicked, evil, he felt he did not care. He wanted it again, and again, and again.

But what sort of woman was she? There was so much about her that he did not know. So much neither of them had said. But there was all the time in the world to find out.

Just as long as her husband did not find out about them, he thought, and shivered a little in spite of the warmth of the room.

Champagne, 1911.

Clovis was in a mood of rare contentment as he stood, his daughter's hand in his, on the hillside above Les Hérissons. His home on the slope of the valley below looked tranquil and well-loved in the warm sunlight of a clear early April day. The barns, long since restored, were housewife neat around the big house, and the lawns which surrounded the turreted building glowed green and lush with bands of pale dun where they were split with neat gravel paths. At the back of the house the forest stood sentinel, the varied greens of many trees shielding the buildings from the narrow path that joined the road to Épernay.

From where he stood he could see the occasional workman come into the courtyard rolling a barrel, the sound of iron bands grating on stone rising clearly in the silence of the day. Whichever way he turned, the land belonged to the Dupuis family, and he was proud to see how elegantly cultivated it was, in geometric patterns of newly sprouting vines.

Rosalie was shaking his hand urgently. "Papa, when is Mama coming back?"

"Tonight or tomorrow, Allie. When she's finished all her business," he said, his mind still on the vineyards. He was suddenly anxious, wondering if the new field that Rosie had insisted they bought down in the Marne Valley where the grapes yielded finer wines would be safe should there be any trouble. She had bought other land on the other side of the mountain, closer to Reims and down near the Vesle River, but though that was equally distant, it was not on his mind.

"Will she bring Sebastian?"

"If Sebastian wants to come."

"Surely he will?"

Clovis did not care if Sebastian came or not, but he thanked heaven that surely at the age of sixteen his manners would be better than they had been at nine. But Rosalie adored him; always had since Sebastian and his father had come to Les Hérissons after Rosie and he had produced the first of their own champagne, seven years ago.

"He's not a child any more, Allie," he said gently so as not to hurt her. "He's nearly a man. There may be other things he wants to do."

Her face fell, and he pulled lightly at her thick dark plait of hair.

"Cheer up," he said. "You've always got me."

"I know." She squeezed his hand. "But I do want to see Sebastian. It's been *months* ..."

"I think Mama may be bringing you home another young man," he said, feeling a prophetic twinge at the thought of the men who would surely cluster around his daughter one day, just as they did her mother. He loved Rosie as much as he had from the first moment he had seen her, but he was now reconciled to never owning her or even understanding her. She was somehow tantalisingly out of his reach and always had been.

But Allie was different. Allie, now ten years old, was the light of his life. She was also a miniature version of him. He saw his face in hers; the same pointing eyebrows, the long thick lashes, the dark thick curly hair and the full mouth. After her birth it had disturbed him that he also saw Jean Paul in her, but as she grew, the child's nature was all Rosie's. She was resolute, happy, brave and, above all, intelligent, which he, Clovis, had never been. But to him it was more important that she was honest and true. Two qualities his brother had never possessed.

He felt himself to be honest and true also, and the sharing of these qualities convinced him that Allie was therefore *his* daughter. To his way of thinking, it was no more than an accident of fate that she was not, and he had successfully dismissed Jean Paul's involvement in her birth completely from his mind. Indeed, he never even thought about it, for he was tranquil in the thought that Allie was meant to be his to care for.

And the child made up for all his disappointments. She loved him without question; accepted his faults and wrapped him in her love.

"Is Mama bringing someone else home then?" Allie asked, leaning her head against his arm. "Someone nice or someone business."

"Someone nice, I think. Her American friend and her son."

"Is that the one she writes to all the time? The one who lives in New York?"

"The very same," said Clovis.

"And do you like her?"

Clovis felt that inward smile that his daughter's quickness so often brought. She had sensed his uneasiness regarding the visitor, an unease he did not quite understand, except that any mention of America always made him feel a shortness of breath and a momentary anxiety. He had long since forgotten why this should be. He simply accepted, as he accepted so many things, that the mention of America made him nervous.

"I don't know," he answered. "I've never met her."

"If you don't like her, I shan't like her," Allie said positively.

"I think we should both try to like her for Mama's sake," Clovis suggested. "And her son is seventeen, older than Sebastian, so you may have two young men to flirt with."

She pushed out her full lower lip.

"I am content with Sebastian, Papa," she said gravely, "but we will both be nice to Mama's friends, as you say."

Gazing down over the valley, his arm round Allie's shoulders, he wondered what the woman would be like. Over the years he had become used to the letters from New York arriving about once a month, and as busy as she was, running between the estate, Reims and Paris, Rosie always found time to write back. It was long ago since she had told him the story of how Lizzie Webster befriended her on her journey across America, but that was another piece of history that Clovis had dismissed from his mind. He had almost managed to convince himself that his wife was a true Frenchwoman, born and bred in Champagne. He did not care to recall her background.

It had been just about a week ago that the telegram had arrived when they were at breakfast one morning. Both he and his mother had assumed that it was just another business matter, but Rosie, still in her deep pink peignoir, her hair loose over her shoulders and sleepy-eyed as she always was at breakfast, had let out a shriek of delight as she read it.

"Oh, Mama, it's wonderful," she said to his mother, her face aglow. "My friend Lizzie is coming from America. She wants to know can she visit. Would you mind? Can she? Oh, Mama, it would give me such joy to have her here."

His mother smiled indulgently as she always smiled on Rosie since Allie had come to give them all so much happiness.

"My dear girl," she said, "this is your home. You can have here who you like. Of course your friend is welcome."

"And her son too, she says." Rosie had finished reading the cable. "He is seventeen now. He was just a little boy when I stayed with them in New York."

Clovis knew that nothing would stop Rosie telling the history of their kindness again, and nothing would stop his mother listening, indulgently. He did not want to hear the story, concerning as it did her life before Champagne, and he had left the table and gone to look at his vines.

He was proud of his vines. Only one field, that nearest the road to Épernay, had suffered from the phylloxera. While other *vignerons* in Champagne were still fighting the frightful insect using the foulsmelling, poisonous gas, carbon disulphide, the Dupuis had never spent a sou on that dangerous remedy. The gas did kill off many of the phylloxera bugs when it was injected from a primitive machine into holes drilled at the side of the root of the vines. But at what a price! The gas itself was expensive, lives had been lost from explosions, and still the phylloxera lived on.

But not in his fields.

Rosie had insisted from the day she had arrived eleven years before that grafting was the only answer. After their marriage, she had turned some of the old barns into nurseries and hothouses where their new stock had flourished until it was strong enough to plant out into the fields. And now, here in the spring of 1911, he was one of the very few *vignerons* to have his entire crop settled on the strong, tough roots of imported American vines.

Those older *vignerons* who could not believe that fine grapes could grow from a wild, alien species, not much more than a weed, insisted that he had been lucky. They argued that his fields were free because of the remoteness of his land and because he was on the mountain and not in the valley. But that was not true of his vineyards in the Vesle Valley, so much nearer to Reims.

Some vine-growers had grafted their secondary growths, their inferior stock, still hoping to keep the original roots of their finest vines. But it was a futile effort. In the past year the phylloxera ravaged four times as many acres of ungrafted stock as those that were replanted with grafted vines.

165

Rosie's interest in the most modern methods of dealing with disease and pests gave Les Hérissons protection against other threats too. They had barely suffered from the mildew which had disastrously blighted the Champagne harvest for the past three years. But the *vignerons* were jealous of the progress that Les Hérissons had made in what were troubled times. Clovis believed they resented that the estate now produced its own champagne – even though he was in the market to buy their grapes. Even with the new fields, Les Hérissons could not yet grow sufficient for all their needs.

The Dupuis' success had made for unpopularity, and that was probably why all the muttering about his brother's antics all those years ago had never died down.

He knew there were whispers about his wife, too. They still considered her a mystery woman. No one had forgotten her dramatic appearance in a fine carriage in the village one winter evening long ago, asking for the Dupuis family. And the villagers could count. He knew they were trying to remember when it was that the American girl had come to Chigny les Roses. They had married quietly in Reims, but at Allie's christening he was aware that people wondered if the baby could be his. He believed the child's resemblance to him had silenced their tongues, but Les Hérissons and its inhabitants were still not accepted by the village. His only contact with local news was gleaned on fortnightly visits to Claudette at Madame Frédéric's. Claudette kept him informed.

He had been to see her the night before, while Rosie was in Paris, and he had heard news that disturbed him. His concern must have shown, for Allie was asking him: "Why are you sad, Papa?" while rubbing her head against his arm just as his dog did.

"Not sad, Allie. Worried," he said.

Her face immediately set into lines of anxiety, responding to his mood.

"What about?"

"Business things," he said. "Nothing to worry you with."

"Mama worries about business things, not you," she said cheerfully. "You worry about the grapes."

He laughed. "Well, I suppose it is the grapes. I'm worried about the new vineyard in the valley."

It was in the autumn of 1910, six months before, that Rosie had bought the piece of land in the Marne Valley, near to Ay and the main road to Épernay. She had had Clovis plant it with grafted stock. If the field flourished, it would defeat the arguments of the traditionalists and perhaps make them realise that her way was the only way to beat the phylloxera. But the field was too far away from Les Hérissons for his liking, particularly in the present climate of unrest.

166

"Why are you concerned about the new field?" Allie was asking him in her grave, grown-up fashion.

"Because the word is that there may be trouble in Ay," he said. Claudette had told him this in the quiet of her bedroom as, like an old married couple, she crocheted while he rested on the bed. "There's talk of riots tomorrow. There are troops in Épernay supposed to prevent it, but they can't protect the fields. I would be sad if the new stock came to harm. It's too far away to watch."

"Why should anyone riot?" Allie wanted to know.

Words and explanations were not Clovis's strength, but he tried.

"Your mama could tell you better," he said. "But the growers are downhearted because the harvests have been so bad for so long and they've no money left. There's been a lot of trouble already because some of the big champagne houses have been using cheaper grapes from other areas instead of paying our *vignerons* the right price and using the right grapes. We haven't been doing it, Allie," he said hastily. "Your mama won't hear of it. She says we must just make less wine until the harvest improves. But you must ask her for the truth of it all. I just worry about the new field."

The unrest was serious, and he felt that the vine-growers had right on their side. Some of the big, established Champagne houses had been using cheap wines from the south in their champagne to improve and recover from the bleakness of the last three harvests.

Rosie would have none of this. She argued that they had not fought so long and so hard for their reputation as a small but reliable maker of champagne to lose it all for a quick and easy profit. Only grapes from their own vines and those bought from the local *vignerons* went into their barrels. And besides, financially the Dupuis' could ride the storm.

Normally Clovis never worried his head about the business side of their enterprise. His whole pleasure was in the changing of the seasons of the fields, the tiny delicately scented flowers on the vines in the spring, the slow sprouting, the hard, green pellets, harbingers of the grapes to come, and the final sight of the tightly packed fruit on the bough, waiting to be harvested.

He never minded the endless labour, the fight against every pest that God had seen fit to inflict on a vineyard. He sometimes felt that it was almost as if the wine at the end was a reward for persistence and patience in the face of adversity. Like his father before him, Clovis loved the land, and the thought of the fresh green shoots of the Ay field, trampled under marauding feet, worried him.

And he worried all the way home, as Allie skipped ahead of him, picking a bunch of wild flowers from the pale soil at the edge of the fields. They were, she said, for her mother.

"It's a pity there are no poppies yet," she said regretfully as she showed him the few flowers she had found. "Mama loves poppies."

"And so do you," he said, smiling down at her.

"Well, yes," she agreed. "They are such a happy colour. But if Mama doesn't come home tonight, these will all be dead. I shall have to give them to Grandmama." She looked at the sad little bunch impatiently. "Why do wild flowers fade so quickly once they're picked, Papa? Why can't we tame them so they live longer?"

He didn't know the answer, but the question made him think of Rosie. He didn't know how to tame her, either.

"I don't know," he said with a little sigh, taking her hand. "But you mustn't be sad if she doesn't come home until tomorrow. She has so much to do, you know. Your mama works very hard."

Rosie sat up in the big double bed and stretched luxuriously. She was content, sated with love and kisses, and she had slept after the second time they had made love. Philippe was not beside her, but she could hear him moving in the bathroom of the little apartment he rented in Paris, supposedly for their work but in reality so they had a place where they could be alone.

She slid down into the bed again, pulled the heavy linen sheet over her and lay staring up at the small chandelier that lit the room. The curtains were drawn, but spring sunlight crept through the chinks. It was a lovely day, and perhaps there would be time for a walk along the Seine before she met Lizzie.

She thought about the lovemaking she and Philippe had just enjoyed and shivered. If it was possible, he had been more intense than usual. Their meetings were so curtailed – perhaps once every three weeks if fate was on their side – that each encounter was conducted as if it was the first and maybe the last time they would ever couple.

Today had been somehow different. He had kissed her frenziedly, and started to undress her almost as soon as she was through the door of the apartment. Then he had led her unprotesting to the bed, where with no pretence of foreplay he had taken her, riding her hard and fast, panting above her, his face contorted with desire.

The second time had been different, soft and loving with sighs and kisses, and murmurs of delight. Their joining had been long and slow, and they had twisted and turned, and strained to be closer for timeless minutes until the crescendo had come for them both. Then they rolled apart and slept, he with a caressing comforting arm thrown protectively over her breasts.

Awake now, desire spent, she wondered about the fierceness of his passion. He had seemed frantic.

Suddenly uneasy, she threw back the sheets and swung her legs over the side of the bed. Her clothes made an untidy splash of colour on the pale beige Chinese carpet. Stepping over them she walked naked across the room to where her oyster-satin peignoir lay over a small Empire chair. Normally she would have joined him unclothed, but something half-remembered seemed to be warning her to cover herself.

Very gently she knocked on the bathroom door. "Philippe, darling," she called.

"One moment." She heard the key turn, and the door opened. He was dressed, but his fair hair was wet, plastered to his head.

"I thought there might just be time for us to walk by the river," she said. "But we should have to leave in a moment if I'm not to be late. A walk would end this beautiful, wonderful unexpected day. God bless Lizzie!"

She had made her tone light and happy. It was true that this meeting was a bonus; a surprise pleasure. And it was Lizzie who had given her the excuse to come to Paris. On the day the telegraph had come, Rosie had told Clovis and Mama Dupuis that she would go to Paris to meet Lizzie. She said that she would also take care of some business before bringing Lizzie home. Then she telephoned Philippe at his Paris office, asking – for the Dupuis' benefit – if they could have some discussion about last year's *vendange*. They made the appointment, and he had been waiting for her at the apartment when she arrived.

Now he picked up a towel and started to rub his hair.

"I'd rather stay here," he said. "We must talk."

The sense that all was not well grew.

"We must indeed," she said gaily. "I have an idea I want to discuss with you."

"Well, let's sit down," he said. He seemed very formal after the uninhibited lovemaking of the afternoon.

She walked through to the small salon and he followed her, seating himself in a chair, leaving the settee for her. She resisted the urge to settle herself on his lap.

"What I was thinking," she began, "is that this year we'll have more bottles than ever before, but still not enough to become a great name. It'll take another four years before we can double the output, unless we buy in more grapes. And hire cellars. But I'd rather use our own crop. It makes for a more reliable wine. And I thought we could dig some caves in the hillside, like Madame Pommery's at Reims, to make more cellar space. We could cut through to the old Roman cavern. The temperature would be perfect.

"I want to make really fine champagne, Philippe, but I don't care about being famous. Your father said to me, long ago, that I could be another Madame Pommery, or Veuve Cliquot, but I don't think that's what I want."

169

"What do you want?" he asked, but his voice was stilted. Normally when she unfolded her plans to him, he would tease her a little. Superficially he had always treated her as a woman playing at *les affaires*, turning their business discussions into a light flirtation, he the strong man pandering to the whims of a pretty woman. But at heart he had always taken her suggestions seriously. Between them they had created the small success which the champagnes of Les Hérissons enjoyed. She and Philippe were business partners and friends as well as lovers.

"What do I want?" She shook her head. "I want you with me every minute of the day, and in my bed every night. I want your children. I want to be your wife. But as I can't have any of that, I'll use my energies in becoming very rich. But if I were famous as well, it would be harder for us to meet. There could be a scandal. As it is, no one in Paris knows of Madame Dupuis, and it's safer that way."

He looked momentarily stricken, but she hurried on, leaving him no time to reply.

"I do want to make superb champagne, and I had an idea. Could you sell what I produce to perhaps just a few influential people? Not merchants? Sell direct, perhaps to a member of the English or Russian royal family, or a head of state. People of that kind. And what we'd do would be to let them have their own label designed and printed so they could call it *their* champagne. It would have snob appeal, don't you think? We could turn over all our production to individuals. Once we'd sold to them, think of the trouble it would save. Think of the profit there would be."

He was nodding his head slowly.

"I think it is being done already," he said, "but only with inferior marks. To do it with fine champagne could work. You would have an advantage because usually the makers of the great *cuvées* don't wish to hide their lights behind their barrels!"

She laughed a little too much at his small joke.

"So shall we try it this year?" she asked.

"If you wish. I am going to Washington next week which would be a good enough place to begin. But you may decide you'd rather be famous."

"Why should I do that?" She asked it cautiously, her nerve ends telling her that now he was going to tell her what was on his mind.

"Because I am getting married," he said baldly.

Rosie felt the colour drain from her face. As if she had been cruelly stripped she clutched her peignoir protectively round her throat so that no flesh showed.

"Married?"

He nodded.

She could think of nothing to say. She sat staring at him. Then her voice came out in a whisper as she said painfully: "You don't love me any more?"

"Rosie!" He rose to his feet and walked across the room, pulling her from the settee and holding her close to him and gently rocking her. "Rosie, I love you more than life. But it can't go on like this. You have a life. You have a husband and a child and a proper home. I have only Sebastian who is growing up and will leave me very soon.

"I need a woman, a home, a hostess, a companion. I need you, but I cannot have you. It's been so long, waiting to be able to meet you, needing you, longing for you and not being able to have you."

The painful truth of what he said struck at her heartstrings. She fought to recover composure by breathing slowly and deeply.

"Who is she?" she asked, keeping her voice low and trying to sound reasonable, though she wanted to scream the question.

"She is the daughter of an old friend who owns a château in the Loire. He makes fine wine. Her name is Lorraine, and she is eighteen years old. She is very beautiful, we are both very rich, from the same world, and it is a very good match."

He told her as if he was reciting, yet still each word was a knife.

"And you love her?"

"Not in the slightest. She imagines herself in love with me."

"If you don't love her why do you want to marry her?"

"Do you love Clovis?"

"You know I don't."

"Well?"

"But that is different."

"Is it? You married him out of a need. I am doing the same."

"It isn't the same," she insisted. "Philippe, ten years we've been together. Haven't I been enough for you?"

"Yes and no," he said slowly. "When we are together, I know you are the love of my life. And I've known it on all those long, cold lonely nights, imagining you sharing your bed with Clovis –" she opened her mouth, but he gently put his hand over it. "Let me finish. I would have married long ago," he went on, "but for Sebastian. Sebastian always wanted you as his mama. It was difficult because he was too young to understand that you belonged to someone else. Now he's older he does understand. He likes Lorraine, but he sees her as a rather boring sister. She is very young. And Sebastian is right. Sometimes she is boringly young."

"And you don't love her?"

He shook his head.

"Then how can you make love to her? How can you be a proper husband?"

"My sweet romantic Rosie. You'll never be truly French. Do you make love with Clovis?"

It was a question that had never been asked in ten years. Rosie felt her whole body burn with the sudden heat of embarrassment.

"Yes," she said quietly. "Always after I leave you. Never at any other time."

His expression was a question, but he had paled.

"I had to," she said. "Supposing I had become pregnant by you? What would I have done? What would you have done? I made love with him out of necessity."

He had gone quite white. His hurt was visible. He appeared near to tears, his mouth pulled down hard to keep it in place, but all he said was: "The poor bastard."

"I know," she said. "We have all suffered, but he, without even knowing it, has suffered the most."

The room was so silent she could hear the clock ticking and it seemed the noise from the street below was suspended. Philippe had walked away from her, and stood looking out through the long windows onto the Champs Élysées below. With his back turned to her, he said: "Must it change anything?"

She felt her heart lift a little.

"What do you mean?"

"I mean we have been lovers for ten years. We cannot marry. There's no possibility. You are married. If I am married too, why can't you still be my mistress?"

"I don't think I could bear to think of you making love to someone else," she said painfully.

"I have borne it."

He was forcing her to face things that had been buried for far too long.

"And now your wife must bear it too?"

"She will never know."

"She is a woman. She will know."

"She is a Frenchwoman. In time, when she tires of her aging husband, she will take a lover."

"As Clovis has his *poule* at the brothel."

"Does he? Who can blame him?"

"Not I," she said sadly. "Ah, Philippe, if only we had met sooner."

"My father, who loves you as much as I do, says there is no point in regrets. And since we are speaking so openly, my darling one, did you once make love with him?"

"No, never." The question was a shock, the lie spontaneous, spoken as instinctively as she would have leapt from the path of a falling rock.

"I wanted to know," he said. "Nou-Nou said that you had."

172

"Nou-Nou!"

"She is jealous of you. You see, once, long ago, when she was young and ardent, I made love with her. And I discovered that so had my father."

Rosie found herself both shocked and dismayed. She felt the revelation put her in the same grubby package as the servant, and she had never seen her encounter with André as anything but loving and romantic.

"I can't believe it," she stammered, picturing the nursemaid's sour face and demeanour. "I would rather not have known. How could you both?"

"Because we are men, and because we are Frenchmen," he said with a sort of smugness.

She understood but hated his sudden cruelty. She had hurt him. He needed to hit back. But it was all too much. The apartment where they had been so happy seemed to be closing in on her. She had to get out. She was, she realised, angry.

"Philippe," she said, moving to go back into the bedroom, "I must go. I shall be late. I can't talk about it any more now."

She was snatching her clothes from the floor. It seemed as if he realised he had gone too far in hurting her for the hurt she had imposed on him. The swaggering mood disappeared.

"I must know if we can still be lovers," he said frantically. "Rosie, I cannot live without you, but I cannot live alone any longer. Please tell me. I can't bear not to know."

"I have to think about it," she said, her voice cold. "Give me a little while to think."

He bowed his head and was silent. As she swiftly dressed she could feel his misery and was glad of it. Then quite deliberately she put her arms round him, and kissed him passionately, pressing herself against him, searching his mouth with her own. He groaned as she moved away, hurrying for the door.

"Will your child bride kiss you like that?" she asked contemptuously before she closed the front door with exaggerated quiet.

That, she thought, as she ran down the stairs to the street, was something to remember her by; something to feed his hunger when she was away. She was angry and confused, but she was sure of one thing. He would never be able to give her up. Ever. The question was, would she be able to give him up?

"Surely we must be nearly there, Alexander. Shouldn't you get the baggage together in case we can't get out in time?"

Lizzie was wringing her black leather gloves between her hands as if they were wet as she leaned forward in her seat, her shoulders rigid and her mouth trembling.

"Please relax, Mama," Alexander said patiently. "We are going to the end of the line. I promise you that the train will not run away with us."

His mother showed no signs of relaxing. She continued to twist her gloves even more fiercely, and her feet made a small tattoo on the carriage floor. With a hidden sigh, her son left his seat and began to bring down the expensive baggage from the rails in the private compartment before piling it carefully near the carriage door.

"Look at the view, Mama," he coaxed. "Isn't it pretty? So much greener than home."

Distractedly Lizzie looked out of the window at the spring salad green of the French countryside.

"Very pretty," she murmured, just to please him, but her mind was not on views. Her mind was back in the mansion on Park Avenue where her husband and daughter would be wondering and worrying where she and Alexander were and what they were doing. At least, she prayed they would be wondering and worrying. She felt a tear begin to fall and, anxious not to alarm Alexander, looked resolutely out of the window while groping for a small, lace-trimmed handkerchief. A quick dab at her eyes, a twitch at her large fur hat so it hid one side of her face, and she was ready to face him again.

A pang of guilt washed over her. She should have explained to Alexander. But how? There was no one she could tell the awful truth to except Rosie, who had been her friend, and with whom she had shared so many confidences. Only Rosie's ears could hear the dreadful news, because Rosie lived so far away, knew no one she knew, and was wise and kind.

"What an adventure we are having!" she said, making herself sound as happy as possible.

He frowned.

"Yes, it is, Mama, but you are certain Papa knows where we are? I wish we had said goodbye."

Perhaps it had not been right to flee like that, without a word. But then what Mr Webster had done was not right either. It was too cruel and frightful. What other choice had she but to run away? Especially when Jenny, her only daughter, had been part of the betrayal.

Now, as the long journey neared its end, doubts and fears were assailing her. Suppose Rosie was not at the station when they arrived, then what would they do? Alexander's schoolboy French had served them very well at Le Havre, but should they be abandoned in Paris, how would she find her friend? How would she get herself and all the baggage to that place right in the country where Rosie lived?

She put the anxious thoughts away, angry with herself for being so upset this late in the journey. She had borne up amazingly well on the ship. She had even surprised herself by flirting with a gentleman who was travelling alone and who had obviously been taken by her. She realised now that she must have been in a state of euphoria at her own daring and cleverness at booking the passage and escaping without being caught. But now her destination was near, she was fearful, wishing that her husband was by her side to take care of all the tiresome little details of life, just as he had taken care of them since they first married.

But for Alexander's sake she had to be brave and smile. She was afraid that her eyes would be gleaming unnaturally with tears; he knew her so well that he would spot her distress immediately.

"Well, Papa won't know where we are at this very minute in time," she told him, begging the question, "but as soon as we arrive we shall telegraph him with our address."

Her tall, tow-headed son looked relieved. His bony, handsome face, all angles and shadows, brightened.

"I think we are nearly there," he said. "Look, Mama, there are more houses beside the track, and it is becoming industrialised. This must be the outskirts of Paris."

She looked out of the window at the unprepossessing view.

"You are right," she said. "It is an adventure, Alexander. We have managed it. We have arrived."

In no more than a minute, the train, belching clouds of grey steam, was creeping the length of the platform. She went to stand beside Alexander who was staring fascinated out of the window.

"Even the people are different in Paris," he said, in an awed voice that sounded very young.

It was true. There was not a black person to be seen anywhere. Not a single Negro porter or passenger. The waiting crowd seemed a mixture of fashionably dressed folk or small, dwarf-like men in blue blouses and rough blue trousers with bib and braces.

"We shall find a porter?" she asked her son anxiously, unnerved by the lack of black faces and red caps. Not to be able to find a porter suddenly seemed a disaster. Mr Webster had always been able to find a porter.

"Of course, Mama," he said, for the first time sounding a little impatient. "I shall find a porter."

She looked at him in dismay. He had abruptly changed to being grown-up and exasperated with her as Mr Webster used to be when she was silly. He was not a boy at all, but nearly a man. Soon she would lose him too. Some other woman would take him away and she would be totally alone in the world.

It seemed to Lizzie that her life was collapsing in fragments all about

175

her. And suppose Rosie did not come? Suppose Rosie did not want to see her? Where would she be then? What would she do? Return home, like a beaten puppy, having to accept the unacceptable? Her misery seemed bottomless, and she stood staring out of the window at the unfamiliar, frightening crowd that clustered on the platform, tears pouring down her cheeks, heedless of what Alexander might think.

Her life, she decided as she groped for the lace handkerchief yet again, was surely over.

Chapter Thirteen

Sebastian was at the Gare St Lazare with at least a quarter of an hour to spare. He wanted to be well ahead of Rosie so that he could greet her on arrival. He had it all worked out. He would creep up behind her and surprise her with a huge hug. She would be amazed when she saw how tall he had grown in the six months since they had last met and how grown-up he had become.

He had been looking forward to seeing her for days now, ever since his father had said she was coming to Paris and that he could, if he wished, spend a few days at Les Hérissons with her. To go to Les Hérissons was the greatest of treats, away from his tutor and away from sour Nou-Nou, now advanced to a kind of housekeeper since he no longer needed a nanny. He could not think why neither his father nor his grandfather got rid of her. She depressed him, and always had. Rosie understood that. Even when he had been little, she had always refused to have the nursemaid at Les Hérissons and had looked after him herself, no matter how busy she was. The only snag had been sharing her with Allie, but then Allie was mostly with her father.

Rosie couldn't have been more different from miserable Nou-Nou. Rosie made him happy. They laughed together and she always had time for him, which was more than anyone else did these days since he had grown up.

He dressed with great care for their meeting. He wore trousers of a fine English tweed, held up by a broad leather belt and tucked into tall soft boots. His loose, informal shirt was cambric. He had tied a floppy bow under the big collar, and over his black curls he placed a broad-brimmed felt hat which he tipped forward over his eyes. A searching look in his long glass told him that he looked good; a little rakish, but elegantly artistic, and very much dressed for the country without being boringly rustic. Rosie would be impressed.

He was beginning to think that he must have missed her. It was almost time for the train from Le Havre to arrive, and he couldn't imagine her being late to meet this old friend of hers.

And then he saw her. She was paying off a cab, almost throwing money at the man. Her face was scarlet and she looked more agitated than he had ever seen her. Nevertheless, he decided to carry out his plan. Stealthily he crept up behind her and flung his arms round the narrow waist and hugged her to him.

"Who ..." She spun round still in his grasp. Her full red mouth was close to his, and he could see the small flecks in her amber brown eyes. They were very angry eyes, but the anger faded as she recognised him. "Sebastian! I don't believe it! How marvellous!"

She planted a great smack of a kiss straight onto his lips, a kiss which caused the most disturbing feelings to run through him.

"You weren't expecting me?"

"No, I'd no idea."

"I'm welcome?"

"Welcome? You're the nicest thing that has happened to me all day."

Sebastian was aware that she had been with his father and could not control his doubtful look.

"It's true. I promise," she said. "Are you coming to Les Hérissons?"

He threw his arms wide open.

"Haven't you noticed? I'm dressed for the country."

"And you look truly fine," she told him.

"And I'm taller?"

"You are definitely taller."

"And more handsome?"

"More handsome than ever." She was relaxing, laughing at him, and whatever it was that had upset her seemed to be receding.

"And you are as beautiful as ever," he said.

"And getting old."

Then he knew what had upset her.

"Rosie, to me you will never, never be old," he told her fervently. "I shall not permit it."

"Who can prevent it?" she said sadly.

He was out of his depth in that moment, and it seemed safer to change the subject.

"Your friend's train should be in," he said. "We should go to the platform."

"Shall I recognise her, do you think?" she said as if she, too, was glad to speak of something else. "Ten years is such a long time. But she will have a boy of about your age with her. That will help."

He put on an affronted expression.

"A boy? Of my age? I am no longer a boy, Madame Dupuis."

"To me you will always, always be a boy," she mocked.

"Yes," he said, placing his hand where his heart lay under the cambric shirt. "The little boy who fell in love with you."

She looked uneasy and he realised that perhaps the words were too near the truth to have been said, and he took her arm and hustled her towards the platform.

"Looking for Lizzie, that's what we are doing," he said.

As it was, the two women recognised each other immediately and fell into each other's arms with cries of joy, calling each other's names and planting kisses on cheeks, standing back to look and wonder, oblivious of all around them. The tall thin fair boy who must have been the son drew back, slightly embarrassed, and Sebastian, feeling the same way, moved to stand with him. They looked at each other ruefully, with an unspoken understanding between them.

"My mother is a little *dérangé*," the American whispered, in slow, careful French. "She has been crying."

"And Rosie is crying, too," said Sebastian, taking the opportunity to practise the English Rosie had insisted he learn. "It is a moment of great emotion for them both."

"True." The young American paused, and then pushed out his hand in an awkward gesture. "My name is Alexander Webster."

"And I am Sebastian Lefevre."

Alexander's face lit into a smile of surprising beauty, a smile Sebastian reckoned would take him through life on oiled wheels.

"Ah, I have heard of you. You are like the adopted son of Madame Dupuis, is that so?"

Sebastian grimaced. In his new clothes and with his mouth still stinging from Rosie's spontaneous kiss, he was not too certain if he wanted to be regarded as the adopted son. He was, he felt, more of an admirer.

"Well, once it was like that," he said cautiously.

They fell silent, watching the two women. The greetings seemed to be over. Rosie was laughing and mopping at her friend's eyes, telling her to stop crying.

Madame Webster was a pretty woman, Sebastian decided, though miles older than Rosie. But she was still pink and white, rather English looking, and very well-dressed. He liked the way her blonde fringe curled from under a huge black fur hat, and she wore a tailor-made costume, tightly fitting, that was trimmed with the same fur. She didn't look French at all. But she looked soft and tasty, like a delectable creamy cake, and he judged that he would like her.

"Come and help me with the baggage," he said to Alexander. It was time someone took charge of the situation. Feeling a little self-important, he took Alexander's arm. "The women will be kissing and

179

crying for ages yet. And if we do not get them moving, we shall miss the train for Épernay, and that means we shall miss dinner, and I promise you, dinner at Les Hérissons is not to be missed."

Very much the man in charge, jingling his money in his pockets, he led his new friend to where the porters waited.

As a special treat, and because Sebastian was there, and more likely, Allie suspected, because she could speak English, she was allowed to stay up for dinner with the grown-ups that night. Her grandmother had been determined to impress these wealthy Americans. The meal was set in the big dining room which was normally only used at Christmas and the rare special occasion. As there were only six of them dining, Henri had taken out some of the leaves from the long table before all the best family silver was removed from the felt bags which normally held it safe from the air. Marie, who was agog at these visitors from so far away, had set the table. She had fussed and polished under Madame Dupuis' instructions. Now the cutlery and their best china all gleamed in the light from the candelabra above and the fine silver one that was placed in the centre of the long linen-covered table.

Allie's English did not seem to be in much demand. Her mother, seated at the head of the table, had placed the nervous American woman at her right and her silent son on her left. Sebastian was next to Lizzie, and Allie sat opposite him, beside Alexander. Her grandmother, her beloved Mimi, was at the foot of the table. Clovis, worried by the rumours of trouble, had gone to keep an eye on the new field near Ay.

Allie wanted to talk to Alexander. He was not a patch on Sebastian, of course, but he was very good-looking in an unusual way. Sebastian's clothes had much more dash and bravura — he was wearing a bright red cummerbund tonight — but Allie liked the quiet elegance of Alexander's more formal evening wear. He could be an actor, she thought, he was so good-looking with his blond hair and sensitive face.

Neither he nor Sebastian was taking the slightest bit of notice of her. As usual, her mama was holding court. And it was not surprising since she looked so ravishing in a long, slender dress in brilliant green. It had no waistline, but was tied with a narrow black and white patterned sash under the breasts. It was cut daringly low, but her breasts were concealed by a finely ruched chiffon insert and the same chiffon had been used to make long, tight sleeves. It was a daring dress, very modern, and Allie knew her mother had bought it in Paris from a famous designer whose name she could not remember. She thought that her mama made Lizzie, in her dove-grey waisted and frilled frock, look very old-fashioned indeed. Not that her own demure frock in taffeta gingham check was much better. She momentarily fretted again that her mother insisted that she still wore such boringly childish clothes.

Since no one seemed to have anything to say to her — Alexander was hanging on her mother's every word, and Sebastian was being polite and entertaining her grandmother — Allie slipped into one of her daydreams. In it, she was wearing a dress just like her mother's and dining at this very table. She was alone with Alexander and Sebastian, and being even more gracious and amusing than her mother. The two men could not take their eyes off her, as she laughed and flirted, her dark eyes sparkling in the light from a hundred candles. But then, dramatically, there was a thunderbolt knocking. The dining room door was thrown open and the Boche burst in. There were four of them, big brutal men. As Sebastian and Alexander leapt to their feet, they were instantly bundled back into their chairs, knives at their throats. The Boche officer, swaggering in boots, with a monocle in his eye and a scar on his cheek, snatched her from her chair, whispering: "It is you I want. You are coming with me."

Allie knew at once that he intended to ravish her. She had no personal experience of the Boche, but her grandmother had definitely said they were brutal and ravished people.

She was struggling in the brute's arms as he tried to carry her away, but spurred by her plight, both Alexander and Sebastian escaped their captors. Snatching the carving knives from the sideboard, they duelled with the soldiers, while she kicked, fought and bit at the man in whose grasp she was caught.

"Be brave," Sebastian shouted. "All will be well."

One Boche fell, mortally wounded. There was blood on Alexander's shoulder. "Oh, no!" she cried when she saw it.

"Allie," her mother said sharply, and Allie nearly jumped out of her skin. "Your grandmother is speaking to you."

"Excuse me, Mimi," she said, dragging herself back to reality. "I didn't hear you."

"Dreaming again," her grandmother said to Sebastian. "Such a dreamer, and if she is not dreaming, her head is in a book. I was asking if your father had said when he was coming home."

"When the trouble is over, if there is any trouble," Allie said. "He will be safe, Grandma, won't he?"

"Of course," said her grandmother heartily, but Allie felt the underlying anxiety. "But he would have been better to stay here, out of harm's way."

She was explaining to Sebastian where Clovis had gone and why when Henri sidled into the room, his face anxious.

"Excuse me, madame," he said quietly to her mother. "But the gateman says that there is a mob of men on the road, and he believes that they are coming here."

It was so like her fantasy that Allie blinked and felt her mouth fall open.

Her mother instantly put down her knife and fork, and stood in her usual decisive way. "Is the gateman here?" she asked.

"Yes, madame."

Her mother turned and excused herself from the table and hurried into the hallway. Sebastian leapt to his feet and followed her.

"Is anything the matter?" Lizzie asked anxiously, addressing her question to Allie.

It was the perfect excuse.

"I'll go and find out," she said promptly and hurried after Sebastian.

Tomas the gateman was standing by the door flanked by Henri and Marie. He looked frightened.

"About thirty men, I'd say, madame," he was telling her mother. "All armed, and with burning staves. They're shouting, and I reckon they intend to burn the house down. It's hard to understand in all the noise, but I reckon that's what they intend. I've locked the gates. That'll hold them up for a while. But they'll get through soon enough."

Listening, Allie felt a strange little thrill, half terror, half excitement. This was the stuff of her daydreams, but real.

"Have you any guns?" Sebastian was asking her mother.

Rosie shook her head. "I think Clovis took them. But guns aren't going to be the answer. Not in a house of four women and two boys."

"I told you," Sebastian said, drawing himself up. "I am not a boy."

Nor did he look like a boy at that moment, Allie thought, her heart swelling with pride at how splendid he was.

Grandmother had now appeared, asking what was the matter. Embarrassed no doubt, Allie told herself, at being left at table with two Americans with whom she could not converse. And close on her heels came Madame Webster and Alexander, both looking bewildered.

"We must put up a fight," Sebastian said. "We can't just stay here and let them burn the place down."

Her mother didn't appear to be listening. She was, as Allie knew, thinking, and when her mother was thinking she might just as well have been blind, deaf and dumb until it was all sorted out in her head.

"Henri," she said. "Take Marie and anyone else you can find, and go quickly to the cellars and bring up some champagne, the best we have." She turned to Tomas. "Thirty men, you say?"

He nodded.

"Twelve bottles, and thirty of our best glasses with napkins and some dry biscuits on trays. Fetch it all to the hall, as quickly as you can."

182

"We are going to have a tasting?" Sebastian said, eyebrows raised.

"Exactly," she said. "When they arrive, we shall go out onto the porch. You will stand on one side of me, Allie on the other." She turned to look at her daughter.

"Allie, you are brave enough?"

Allie was insulted by the question. "Of course I am, Mama," she said indignantly.

"Good," her mother said, with a small encouraging smile. "Mama, you stay inside and look after Madame Webster and young Alexander."

Allie saw her grandmother's nostrils flare and her lips purse.

"If we are having a tasting," she said, "I intend to be present."

Rosie laughed.

"Of course," she said smiling. "It is your home."

She turned and spoke rapidly to Madame Webster: "Lizzie dear, it's too complicated to explain at this moment, but we are about to get a visitation from some gentlemen who are not as friendly as they might be. I think it best if you and Alexander stay inside while I deal with it. There's no real problem. It will be perfectly all right."

"I think Mama should stay inside," Alexander said, "but I would like to be with you and Sebastian if I may."

Allie thrilled. He was as heroic as he looked. But her mother was looking doubtful and he could see it.

"I shall not stay inside if you are in any danger," he said quietly, and it was just like one of her stories she made up.

The rattle of glasses on a huge silver tray that must have weighed kilos and kilos could be heard coming down the hallway. A white-faced Henri carried them. Marie, who looked as excited as Allie felt, the kitchen maid and Cook followed, carrying bottles in their hands and tucked under their strong Champenois arms — Allie was surprised they hadn't balanced them behind their ears or between their teeth.

"Is it the best we have?" her mother asked.

"Yes, madame," Henri said.

"Good," she said calmly. "Now we wait. Sebastian, can you manage the tray? It's heavy. Mama, Alexander, Allie and I will take two bottles of champagne each. Henri, would you start opening them, and you must remain in here with Madame Webster and the other bottles, until I call you."

Henri looked as if he were about to argue, but just bowed.

The sound of the mob was distinct now. It sounded like the howling of the wolves in the winter in the forest, Allie decided, working out how she would describe the scary noise later when she told her father of their adventure.

"They're through the gates, madame," said Tomas. Poor old Tomas looked quite terrified. It was his job to take her to her dancing classes in Épernay once a week, and he never stopped grumbling at the inconvenience. Being frightened served him right.

"Now," said Rosie, "it's time we met our guests."

The lights were lit on the big porch, and by the time everyone was armed with the champagne, the tray and the biscuits the mob was just a few yards from the house, the burning staves lighting the gravel path and throwing strange shadows from the trees. Enjoying the little trembling sensation of fear, Allie placed herself beside her mother, copying her upright stance, but her stomach did a flip-flop as the men howled and screamed. They did not sound like people. The flames they carried caught and flashed on angry, contorted faces as the Dupuis family and friends came through the door.

Her mother, head up, completely calm, moved to the stairs leading up to the porch, blocking the way, a champagne bottle in her hands. Like a fountain stilled, the shouting died away, replaced by an uneasy, muttering silence.

"Good evening, gentlemen." Her mother's clear voice and faintly accented French floated out into the starry night. "Welcome. I am sorry that my husband is not here to greet you, but of course you already know the Widow Dupuis and my daughter, Rosalie. These others are guests, friends from America and from Paris." She indicated Alexander and Sebastian as she spoke.

"I think I know why you are here. You are angry that your hard-won grapes are being overlooked for the inferior. You are angry that those who make champagne are spoiling its fair name. They debase a product both unique and rare and you are right to be angry."

She clarioned the last four words, then paused, and the men grouped before her shuffled their feet. It seemed to Allie they shuffled backwards.

One, still bold, shouted: "And what would you know about champagne?"

"My father grew grapes and made wine all his life," she said proudly, her voice ringing clear. "What I know of champagne I have learned from you since I made Champagne my home. I, too, value and respect the purity of our wines. And I believe I have earned the right to call them our — yours and my — wines." She stood even straighter, threw back her head and held the bottle in her hand high, and her voice became a passionate shout. "I believe as you believe, that no grape other than a grape grown in this region should sully this fine and noble wine."

Allie felt a shiver run down her spine. Her mother was magnificent. The men who stood uneasily before her felt it too. The mob had become an audience. The burning staves became lights to illuminate Rosie's rapt face. Reluctantly, a few of them gave a thin cheer.

"This wine," she said, presenting the bottle to them in her two hands, just as the priest gave the sacrament, "has come from the grapes of Les Hérissons. And from the grapes of M. Lasserre in Ay. A fine *vigneron*. I ask you, my friends, to taste this vintage. You will find it a true product of our region. And with this noble wine, let us drink to better times than those we have lived through." She turned and nodded, and her mother-in-law, equally under Rosie's spell, began to pour the frothing wine into the glasses that Sebastian held.

Allie joined them, bringing the first two she filled down the stairs to the men nearest her. She noticed one was M. Rombaud, who used to work for her father before he managed to get enough money together to buy his own small field. She knew M. Rombaud had had hard times since, and she was genuinely pleased to see him. Smiling, she handed him his glass and said: "Monsieur Rombaud! What a pleasure to see you. I trust you are well."

The man took the glass sheepishly, half-bowed and said:

"I am well, mademoiselle. And you?"

"I am well, too," she said. "How is Stephan?" Stephan was his son, and ten, like her. "I have not seen him for so long."

She could not understand why he looked so uncomfortable when she was being so polite, but she really did want to know how Stephan was. To make him more easy, she smiled again and went to fill some more glasses, shouting back over her shoulder: "Please tell Stephan to come and see me."

Her mother had beckoned the men to come nearer, and some of them stood on the steps to the porch, taking their glass of champagne and draining it quickly, murmuring thanks. Within four minutes they had all turned and walked back down the drive, looking somehow bedraggled and sad, as if they were soaking wet, which they most certainly were not on this bright April night.

"What's the matter with them, Mama?" Allie asked.

"They are ashamed," her mother said, her voice low. "They are good men. They have reason to be angry. But I wish I had not shamed them."

Her grandmother put her arm round her mother's shoulder, something that Allie had never seen before.

"Don't grieve," she said. "What you did was right. They would have been more ashamed tomorrow if they had burned down this house, and perhaps harmed the children who are here. It was a brave, bold think that you did, Rosie, and I am proud of you."

Allie watched, standing back near the front door. She could see the expression of adoration on Sebastian's face, and the wonder that lit Alexander's as both looked at her mother. She felt something like bile rising in her throat, and wanted so much to be the one that they admired. At that moment, she felt a curious feeling of despair that her mother would always be first in the affections of those she, Allie, loved. She would always be second best. She badly wanted her father. She wanted to tell him that she had been brave, too; that she had faced the mob and she was only ten years old.

Later, Rosie could not remember or begin to understand how she had come through that most dreadful of days. The meal had never been resumed; no one had the appetite, though Madame Dupuis had insisted that they all drink a large Marc de Champagne against the effects of shock.

"But what was it all about?" Lizzie cried. "Why did those men want to burn down your home?"

"Because we are the haves and they are the have nots," Rosie said. "Those men are starving. They only want what is their right and their due. They are growers of grapes, proud of the harvest they produce, except that for the past three years here in Champagne the harvest has failed them. It seems that God has sent every pestilence known to the *vigneron* to this area. In order to live, those men have had to ask a high price for the few grapes they do have to sell. Some makers of champagne here have not been prepared to pay their prices, and they have gone further south to buy at much cheaper prices.

"Of course, what they have produced with these inferior grapes is not true champagne. True champagne can only be made from grapes grown in this area. Those makers have cheated not only the *vignerons* of this area, but the wine itself, and in the end themselves."

She stopped, and shook her head.

"I'm sorry to be so fervent," she said. "It's really even more complicated than that. But I wanted to explain so that you would not think that you have come to a country of ruffians. Those are honest Frenchmen, who have been cheated. They were not to know that here at Les Hérissons we were not part of the plot."

And dear Lizzie's eyes had been full of tears when she had finished her explanation.

When the day was over, Rosie knew that the best of it all was that she and Lizzie could well have seen each other only a week before. All the closeness and warmth they had shared eleven years before was still there. Their letters, and the chemistry of friendship that had sparked when they first met, still held them together. Nothing had changed. But she was dismayed that Lizzie must feel she was in an unsafe place, and so she made her explanations and kept calm and smiling, though she felt drained. She longed to sleep.

It was Madame Dupuis who released her. The older woman had kept a sharp eye on them all. When she judged that everyone was more

186

relaxed, and the excited conversation and mutual congratulations were dying away, she firmly sent them all off to their rooms.

Rosie fell into her bed exhausted after she had seen a shaken Lizzie into hers. She had also put Allie to bed, hugging her and praising her for her bravery. Her normally chatterbox daughter was strangely quiet. This silence filled Rosie with alarm that her daughter might be harmed by what she had seen and experienced. She also felt terrible guilt that she had subjected Allie to danger. She was aware that it could have been truly dangerous, even though her instincts had said that the men, however angry, would not harm women and young children. As it transpired, they had not. But the gamble could have gone wrong. And if anything had happened to Sebastian, Philippe would never have forgiven her. If anything had happened to any one of them, she would never have forgiven herself.

She was glad that Clovis had not been there. Without doubt, somehow or other he would have mishandled it. But to have taken control from him had he been present would have offended her mother-in-law, and probably provoked one of his drinking bouts. And those she could not bear.

She lay flat on her back, staring up at the ceiling where the fire cast orange shadows that were all too reminiscent of the burning vine props the mob had carried. At least, she thought ruefully, the incident had taken her mind from the problem of Philippe. And maybe without the anger that still burned in her at the thought of his marriage she would not have had the nerve to confront those men. But she had felt regret for their hangdog, bowed and beaten look when they drifted away.

She put the night's incident out of her mind as something that was over and done with, and turned to the agonising problem of Philippe's marriage. Could she prevent him from marrying this highly suitable child? It was a nonsense even to think about it. If he had made up his mind, there was nothing she could do. In the ten years she had known Philippe, as much as she loved him, there had been times when she had clearly seen the core of iron under his charm. The same core that his father possessed, and that maybe Sebastian had too.

It hurt, hurt, hurt to think of him with another woman, but how could she complain when tomorrow night she would seduce Clovis into making love to her? Not that it was love. It was sex, nothing more. It was hardly even sex.

Clovis had kept his promise never to approach her, but after she and Philippe made love for the first time, she found herself terrified that she might become pregnant. She was haunted by the thought of how impossible it would be to explain away such an occurrence. The only thing to do, she realised, was to make love with her husband. She was not proud of the decision or the deception, but tempered her guilt with the thought of Clovis's pleasure. For he was both awed and delighted to be forgiven and welcomed to their marital bed on that first occasion. It still troubled her to think of it. Right from the first they had shared a room and a bed. Clovis had asked if this could be so that his mother did not realise that they were married in name only. She had agreed, and they lay each night uneasily, frightened to touch even accidentally. Then after one year, after the first soul-seering time with Philippe, she had been forced to turn to Clovis, for whom she felt nothing.

She learned quickly how to please him. Little was required. Then she had tried to teach him how to please her, so that hopefully their encounters would become more tolerable. The lessons were learned. He dutifully touched her breasts, he dutifully searched for the spot between her thighs that could drive her mad with desire, but she sometimes felt that he confused making love with ploughing his fields as he scrabbled about her body. He had never been able to arouse her. Even the lightest touch he could manage on her nipples still hurt and made her jump. Yet when Philippe deliberately inflicted a little pain, it was ecstasy.

She sighed, desperate for sleep, but her brain boiled with questions. The biggest was whether she would continue to be Philippe's mistress. More immediately, she wondered what she should do with Lizzie, who seemed sad and low. And then how to deal with the oddly disturbing presence of Sebastian. He had completely changed in the six months since she had seen him last. And it was bewildering to be confronted by a sparkling-eyed, flirtatious man instead of a little boy. He must have found a mistress, she decided.

She was just beginning to doze when she came abruptly awake at the sound of a whimpering cry. Allie's cry. She was out of bed in a second, pulling on her robe as she went running to her daughter's room. Allie was sitting up in bed, tears trickling down her face. When she saw her mother, she held out her arms.

"Oh, Mama, Mama, I had such a terrible dream. I was so frightened."

Rosie sat on the bed and held her close.

"It's all right," she soothed. "It was only a dream. Don't cry, just tell me about it, and then you'll forget."

"But I can't remember," Allie said, rubbing her knuckles into her eyes. "But, Mama, I was frightened."

It was hardly surprising that the child was suffering a nightmare. Rosie rocked her and stroked her dark hair, and then she whispered: "Do you want to come in with me tonight? We won't tell Grandmother or Papa. Would that help?"

Allie was hugging her, hot arms round her neck. "Oh yes, please," she said frantically. "Oh I do love you, Mama. I really do. I promise I do."

"Shhh, no more tears, no more words, just come with me," Rosie said, lifting her daughter out of the bed. Allie slid her arms round her neck and seemed to be content to be carried like a baby along the passage and into her mother's room.

And once they were both in the big bed that she had shared for so long with Clovis, the child slept. Listening to her soft, slow breathing, Rosie found sleep too.

She slept late and it was a gentle tapping at the door that eventually woke her.

"Come in," she called, and the door opened slowly and Lizzie's blonde head appeared cautiously as if she was not sure if she was in the right place.

"Allie said you were still asleep," she said apologetically.

Allie, Rosie realised, was no longer at her side.

"No, no," she said, untruthfully, "I've just been lying here, dozing."

Lizzie slid into the room and quietly shut the door behind her.

"I'm sorry to break in on you like this," she said, speaking very fast, "but Rosie, I must talk to you. If I don't talk to you soon, I think I may go mad. You see, the most terrible, terrible thing has happened."

Rosie sat bolt upright in bed.

"What is it?" she said, suddenly fearful that the mob had returned while she slept so deeply. "Is everyone all right?"

"Everyone is fine," Lizzie said, beginning to search in her long sleeve for a handkerchief, "except me, and I am the unhappiest woman in the world."

Her eyes were brilliant with tears.

Concerned, Rosie got out of bed, and went to take Lizzie's hand, pulling her so they could sit on the bed, side by side. "Come and sit down. I'll send for coffee, and then you can tell me all about it."

"Yes, send for coffee," Lizzie said distractedly as Rosie blew into the speaking tube by her bed and gave instructions to Marie in the kitchen below. "You have had no breakfast. It's too bad of me to do this to you, but Rosie, I'm so unhappy."

She buried her face in her hands, and Rosie put her arm round her shoulders and hugged her tightly.

"Now what is it?" she asked. "Nothing can be this bad."

"It is. It's terrible. Can you believe – Mr Webster has a mistress!"

Her head was on Rosie's shoulder, and she was sobbing so hard that Rosie could feel the hot tears dampening her nightgown. But the words came as a considerable shock. They could have been a message sent all the way across the Atlantic to point out the painful reverse of a married man and his affairs.

"Tell me about it," she said, stroking Lizzie's soft hair.

189

"It's so shameful," Lizzie said painfully. "It's been going on for years and I never ever knew. Everyone in town knew except me. He sometimes even took her to functions – not the kind of function that I would dream of going to, of course. Can you believe, she's older than me, and though I don't want to sound boastful, Rosie, I don't think as pretty.

"I found out when Tiffany's telephoned to say that my bracelet was ready. I didn't know what they were talking about, but I thought that Mr Webster must be buying me a surprise present. I just told them that perhaps they had better let him know at his office.

"Well, after a few days when he hadn't given me the bracelet, I was in Fifth Avenue right by Tiffany's, so I thought I would just pop in and look at it – just to see if I liked it.

"I explained to a young man that I had come for the bracelet that Mr Webster had ordered, and they looked at me very suspiciously. And then another salesman came – a new man I didn't know – and he said: 'Is it an emerald and diamond bracelet that you are referring to, madame?'

"I had to say I didn't know. And then he said very coldly, 'Mrs Webster has already been in with Mr Webster to collect her bracelet.' I opened my mouth to say that couldn't be, I was Mrs Webster, and then the awful truth struck me, and I just fled from the store."

"Oh, poor you!" Rosie said, hugging Lizzie tighter.

"It gets worse. When I got home, I just cried and cried, and Jenny found me and wanted to know what was the matter. I really felt I shouldn't be telling her, not showing up her father, but I just had to talk to someone, and she was always my sensible girl. I told her what had happened, and she said; 'Oh, Mama – you've found out. How frightful.'

"It took me a minute. I was so upset, and then I realised that she knew. My own daughter knew. I accused her, I was so angry with her for hiding the truth from me, and all she could keep saying was that she'd hoped I'd never find out, and that she hadn't told me because she thought Papa would get bored with this woman.

"Jenny told me that the woman is a notorious creature, and when Mr Webster came home that night, I confronted him with my knowledge. By then I was calm again, just very angry, and very hurt. And all he could say was that it was for sex, nothing but sex, and that she meant absolutely nothing to him. I said why was he giving her bracelets from Tiffany's, and he went very pale and wanted to know how did I know about that? And then he said that I wasn't to worry, and he'd buy me one exactly the same. Can you imagine a worse insult. To suggest that I would want a piece of jewellery the same as that – that harlot!"

Rosie could not speak for the moment, for try as she might she could not divorce herself and her situation from Lizzie's tale. She heard "it was just for sex, nothing but sex", and found herself wondering if Philippe might say the same to his new bride if caught out.

"And then," Lizzie went on, "I told him that I did not want anything that he might think suitable for his whore, and my heart nearly broke when he said: 'If there had been a little more of the whore in you, I would not have needed to do these things.'

"Rosie, I couldn't believe it. How could he say such a thing. I just fled from the room in tears, and locked myself in our room. He tried to talk to me. He banged on the door all the evening and tried to get in, but I would not even reply to him. I was packing. I knew I must go. I knew I must get away from him, but I couldn't think where to go. Then I thought of you. The next morning, after he had gone to work, I found out that the *Atlantique* was sailing for Le Havre that very day. Alexander was home, and I told him we were going away for a while. I didn't tell him why, and fortunately he had not seen his sister, so he had no idea what had happened.

"We were gone that very morning, and here we are, and now I don't know what to do. You see, Rosie, I find I miss him so very much. I am so hurt and so angry, but it has made me see that I do care for him. For years I thought he did not matter. You know the circumstances of our marriage and I have always thought before that I was deprived of romance. That's why I felt so strongly for you when we met. You were experiencing pain, but you knew what love and romance were. Well, I guess I was deprived of romance, but I see now how much more Jim gave me. He was just right for a silly, giddy thing like me, and it's only now that I appreciate it. But how can I ever go back when he has done this dreadful thing to me?"

Her head went back onto Rosie's shoulder and the tears began to flow again.

"Now sit up," Rosie said gently, fishing her own handkerchief from under her pillow, pushing her own problem away, "and stop crying. It's a pity you're not French. You'd find it easier to understand." Inwardly she winced at her own hypocrisy, she who had been told that very same thing only yesterday. "Listen, Lizzie, men are like that. They're all the same. Even poor Clovis has a mistress."

Lizzie's sobs were stunned into silence.

"He does? And you know? And you stay with him?"

"Umm," Rosie nodded. "He sleeps once a week with a little round blonde whore at Madame Frédéric's brothel on the road to Épernay. He really should have married her. They get on remarkably well. And she obviously doesn't mind his lovemaking, and the once a week seems to be sufficient for him."

191

Lizzie's cheeks were turning pink with embarrassment.

"Don't blush, Lizzie," Rosie said gently. "We are two women talking together, and we have the same problem. The difference is I don't mind. Tell me, did you enjoy making love with Mr Webster?"

Lizzie averted her face.

"Not really," she whispered. "I don't think I like sex very much."

"Neither do I with Clovis," Rosie said, "but I liked it very much with Jean Paul." And even more with Philippe, she thought. "Maybe you would like it better with someone else."

"I think it's dirty," Lizzie said, her voice surprisingly firm. "And I only ever did it because wives have to. There is no choice. But I did it as little as possible."

"Then you really can't blame Mr Webster for having a mistress," Rosie said, realising she meant it, and that perhaps she had become more French in her attitudes than Philippe had allowed. "I am very happy for Clovis to be taken care of by his Claudette."

"Well, I am not happy for Mr Webster to be taken care of by that dreadful woman."

"Then you will have to make the effort to keep him in your bed."

"How?" said Lizzie.

Rosie could not help but laugh.

"If I were to tell you, you would truly blush, my dearest Lizzie. But maybe if you hate it so much you will just have to learn to pretend, as I do with Clovis. Clovis is not a good lover. Maybe your husband is not a good lover either. But neither of them are bad men, so we are fortunate in that. And society says that if they give us their names and make homes for us, we must play our part – and that means in the bedroom as well as in the salon."

She stopped, conscious of sounding as if she were preaching, and on this subject she had no right to preach.

"But I am a good wife and a good mother," Lizzie said indignantly. "I don't understand you, Rosie. Surely men should not expect things from their wives that whores give them? I have always done my duty towards Mr Webster. I have never refused him, ever."

"Ah, you have never refused him, but have you ever accepted with joy and pleasure?"

Lizzie's face was scarlet with embarrassment. "Oh, Rosie," she said sadly. "I thought you would understand."

"I do. I promise you I do," Rosie said. "I understand more than you know, but you wanted my advice, and I have given it, though maybe you won't be able to accept it. Does Mr Webster know you are here?"

"He does not."

Suddenly Rosie remembered all those years ago when André had insisted that she wrote to her father to tell him where she was.

"You must let him know immediately," she said. "It's cruel to frighten him so. He will be imagining the most terrible things."

"Indeed, I hope he is." Lizzie's voice was fierce. "For I shall never, never forgive him. And I intend to leave him to worry about where Alexander and I are for a long time yet."

Rosie was saved from replying by Marie tapping on the door, and the rattle of cups on a silver tray.

"I will pour it, Marie," she said as the maid put the tray down on a small table. "Just pass me my robe, if you will."

Marie would have noted Lizzie's tear-stained face, and there would be great gossip in the kitchen this morning. But the few moments it took Rosie to pour the coffee gave Lizzie time to blow her nose briskly, wipe her eyes again, and take the cup that Rosie offered with something like composure.

"We won't talk about it any more for the moment," she said resolutely. "We will talk about you. We have not had one minute alone yet, what with all the to-do last night. You're the same, Rosie, but somehow different. You seem so strong. Grown-up is the only word I can think of that describes you. You were such a child with all your troubles when we met. But you've coped with everything and come through, just like you coped with those men last night." She shook her head in wonder, and then asked: "Do you ever think about Jean Paul?"

"Never." Rosie turned the word into two syllables in her positiveness. She wasn't sure she wanted to talk about him even now. "Today I can see what a child I was to be taken in so. Jean Paul was a bad man, Lizzie. It was lucky I never found him. I thank God Allie has nothing of him in her at all. And she adores Clovis, which makes up in part for the fact that I can never love him. But I respect him now. He is dull and slow, but he has many qualities. His mother was right when she told me that he was the better of the two. Though it must be said," she added, laughing, "that if I had not had the business and a life of my own, I think I might have run away back to America and you out of sheer boredom."

"I wonder where he is?" Lizzie said thoughtfully.

"Who?"

"Jean Paul, of course. He must be somewhere."

Rosie shrugged.

"Making wine maybe. Perhaps in New York state. Philippe tells me they are beginning to produce quite good wine there."

"You never said much in your letters about you and Philippe."

"Didn't I?" Rosie knew perfectly well she had said little about Philippe. There was little she could say that Lizzie would have understood. For one girlhood slip, the bitter loss of innocence, Lizzie's kind heart would bleed, as it had all those years ago. But she would

193

never have approved of a married woman with a lover, a secret apartment, and the kind of passionate love life that was as necessary to Rosie as food and drink. It was sad that maybe Lizzie would never experience the wonder of the kisses and caresses from one truly loved, and never realise the velvet pleasure of where such kisses and caresses could lead. And it was sad that she could not talk of it to Lizzie. Suddenly she felt a great wave of loneliness and a need to talk to someone, anyone. But who was there without Philippe?

"No, you didn't." Lizzie's look was remarkably sharp.

Rosie finished her coffee and got up to pour another cup for them both.

"We wouldn't have the business without him," she said. "He sells the champagne for me, and he has helped us to get quite a good clientèle in Britain, America and Russia. We have to make it sweeter for Russia. Of course, it's difficult because we're in competition with the big names. I'm trying to make fine champagne. I don't want to produce the stuff they sell at the grocers – unless, of course, the grocer is Fauchon. I intend to get very rich, Lizzie."

"But you always did. You hated not having any money."

"And I hated having to steal to get here. Do you know, I still have some of that original money left – just two gold coins. One day I'm going to give them back to my father – if he's still alive. I wrote to him once from the ship to tell him I was safe, but I never wrote again. I suppose he would never have forgiven me. But he's probably dead, and I do sometimes wonder what happened to Peter. I suppose I should have written ..."

Her voice trailed away. Lizzie was making her think of things that had remained long buried. Neither Clovis nor Madame Dupuis liked her to speak of America and neither cared to be reminded of how she came to be with them. The subject had become taboo. Rosie was certain that they had both convinced themselves that Allie was Clovis's child, and she herself was a born and bred Frenchwoman.

"Your Alexander is a charmer," she said, changing the subject. "It was so manly of him to stand with us on the porch, braving those men last night."

"He is brave and true," Lizzie said simply. "I confess I am proud of him. And your Allie is a fine child."

"You think so?" Rosie said, pleased with the compliment. "It was sad for her I just had the one."

"Would you have liked another?"

"Oh, yes, but they did say when Allie was born that it was unlikely it would happen. I did not have an easy time with her."

"In spite of all that morning sickness," Lizzie teased. "Do you remember?"

"Will I ever forget! And you guessed right away. But, oh Lizzie, the wonder and joy of it when the baby comes." She shook her head remembering, experiencing again the swelling, exhausted triumph she had felt when Allie was born. "It was worth all the pain; worth having to marry Clovis; worth all the fear and misery just to hold that little thing in my arms, feel her at my breast and watch her grow – the only thing in the whole world that truly belongs to me." Tears were hovering, and she made herself laugh, and added: "But all mothers must feel the same. Did you?"

"Oh yes!" Lizzie said, fervently. "But it is too unkind of God to make being with a man the only way to be given such joy."

Rosie closed her eyes, imagining the joy it would be to carry Philippe's child. Gently, so that it was not too obvious, she steered the conversation into the safer waters of times past.

But the first opportunity she had, she sent Henri into Épernay with an urgent message for the telegraph.

Allie had slid carefully out of bed without waking her mother and pattered back to her own room to wash and dress. She could see that the sun was shining, even through the heavy curtains with which her mother preferred to keep the room dark. There were times when Rosie had difficulty getting to sleep and light in the room woke her too early.

It always puzzled Allie, how much her mother liked to sleep. Once she was up, she was the busiest of people, but she liked to breakfast in bed after Clovis had gone to the vines, and she would sometimes go upstairs very early, long before the rest of the household, with a book that rarely seemed to be read. Mimi said she was one of those people who needed time to themselves.

Allie liked going to bed early too, but only when she had a very good book, and then she would be awake all hours reading it, sometimes right to the very end. Her mother would often come in to confiscate the bedside oil lamp if she thought it was getting too late.

She went downstairs to the breakfast room feeling faintly uneasy about something, but wasn't sure what. She stopped wondering what it could be when she found Alexander sitting at the table, looking rather lost and lonely.

"Good morning," she said cheerfully. "Has anyone given you breakfast?"

"Yes, thank you," he said in a grave kind of way, as if she was asking about something serious and important, like religion. And then he smiled his beautiful smile and added: "You speak great English."

She pulled a face. "My mother insisted. When I was little we had to talk it all morning, and she still makes me sometimes. Often she's the one who forgets the words these days. My governess is English, too, so I get plenty of practice."

He nodded. "I also thought you were very brave last night," he said. "Does that sort of thing happen very often here?"

"Goodness, no," Allie said, appalled that he should think such a thing. "But you were brave, too, and Mama was magnificent."

As she said it, the reason for her uneasiness dawned on her. The horrible jealous thoughts she had had about her mother last night. In the sunny light of morning, she felt very ashamed.

"But you are young," he said. "How old are you?"

"Ten – but I'll be eleven in June. How old are you?"

"Seventeen."

"That's really grown-up."

"It is," he said, and smiled again. "I only wish Mama would realise it."

"Oh, does she treat you like a child, too?"

"I'm afraid so," he said.

"Well, I hope mine has stopped by the time I'm seventeen," said Allie with a theatrical sigh.

She was pouring herself coffee when Sebastian came through the door, behaving much more like a whirlwind than a person. She looked at him critically.

"You are noisy, Sebastian," she said.

"I've always been noisy," he said cheerfully, taking the coffee pot from her. "What's the matter? You used to like it." He spotted Alexander and switched to English. "Good morning, Alexander, did you sleep well after all the excitement?"

"You do have the most terrible accent," Allie told him, leaving no time for Alexander to reply. She suddenly felt scratchy again when she remembered how Sebastian had not paid the slightest bit of attention to her last night.

"They say women find it attractive," he said, grinning at her.

"Women!" she snorted. "You are only a boy. Alexander is seventeen."

"And you," he said, still cheerful, "are only ten, as is perfectly obvious."

He had never said anything so unkind to her before. They had always been such good friends. Wounded, Allie got to her feet and said stiffly: "I am going for a walk before I have my lessons."

Alexander pushed his coffee cup away and put his napkin on the table. "May I come with you?" he asked.

"Of course," she said.

"Off you go then." Sebastian was piling apricot jam onto a piece of fresh bread. "I'll catch up with you later."

She hesitated, wanting him to come with them after all.

"I'll show Alexander the cellars," she told him. "That's where we'll be."

He did not seem very interested in where they were going. He just nodded. And he was making a dreadful mess with the jam. She tutted and swished out of the room, Alexander on her heels.

The young American was truly impressed with the cellars where, in chilly candlelit gloom, thousands and thousands of champagne bottles lay stacked from floor to ceiling.

"We're right under the courtyard now," Allie explained, "but the cellars go almost into the fields, and down to the gates. Before I was born they just went under the house itself. Mama had them extended about six years ago now. She says there still isn't enough space and she wants to make more cellars in the hillsides. It's easy enough because we have chalk soil here."

She felt very important and pleased with herself explaining all this to such an attractive young man. She led him a floor lower to where the bottles were set, neck down, in triangular wooden racks.

"See that man there?" she said pointing to where a man in a blue *blouson* squatted on a stool, turning two bottles at once with a twirling, barely perceptible movement.

Alexander nodded. "What's he doing?"

"Very gently shaking down the sediment in the bottle," she told him. "When it all gets lodged in the neck we take it out so the champagne is clear."

"How do you do that without losing the champagne?" he asked.

"Easy, we freeze the neck of the bottle, which freezes the sediment into a sort of plug. Then when we take off the cork, the bubbles push the plug out like a little explosion. I'll show you later when they are working in the *dégorgement* room. It's fun to watch."

It was freezing down here in the lowest cellar and she could see that he was cold, so she explained that this cellar had to be cold or the bottles might explode.

"Papa says that in the olden days everyone lost lots of champagne through breakages. But today, of course, we know much more about it."

She was leading him back upstairs and they walked through the courtyard into the stone building where the resting and fermenting wine was stored in huge oak casks.

"We keep it like this until it's ready to bottle," she told him. "But there are so many different things that have to happen before then. You ought to spend a year here and then you could see exactly what is done."

He said in his solemn way that that would be interesting, and then

197

asked if she wanted to be a businesswoman like her mama when she grew up.

"Oh, no!" she said. "I shall live in Paris and have my own apartment and be an actress. The greatest ever actress, like Sarah Bernhardt. Or, if not, I shall be a writer. I haven't really decided yet. The only problem is my name. Rosalie Dupuis sounds so ordinary, don't you think? I thought that when I was old enough I would change it to Blanche le Beau. But then if I grow up to be plain – and Mama says I mustn't bank on being good-looking – le Beau wouldn't do at all, and anyway, I suppose if I do grow up plain I would have to be a writer and perhaps something more serious would be a better choice."

"I want to be a writer," he said.

"You do?" She looked at him consideringly. "But you are so good-looking you could easily be an actor."

He went quite pink.

"I think my father wouldn't approve of that. He won't approve of me being a writer either. He wants me to go into the family business."

"And what is that?" she asked.

"Railroads, mostly, but I think he's getting into things like electricity and automobiles as well. I don't really understand, but things that are new and make lots of money."

She shook her head, feeling sorry for him. "It sounds very dull, and who cares about money!"

"Well, I suppose poor people do," he ventured.

"Yes, like Monsieur Rombaud. I think Papa ought to give him some money. After all, we have plenty."

"Who is Monsieur Rombaud?" he wanted to know, but a loud English voice shrilled through a window from above.

"Rosalie, where are you? It's time for your lessons."

Allie groaned. It was too bad, she was having an English lesson anyway, talking to Alexander. But Miss was not to be argued with and when she tried, her mother always took the governess's side.

"Coming," she called back, and said to Alexander. "I'm sorry. I have to go. Duty calls." She pulled a face and ran into the house, turning briefly to wave at him, wondering as she went what he thought of her, and fervently hoping that he liked her.

Sebastian made no attempt to follow Allie and Alexander. He wanted to see Rosie. All night his head had been full of pictures of her. He thought he would never forget the sight of her confronting those brutes last night. She had been like the figurehead of a ship, a warrior woman, blazing like the red and orange light from the burning vine props. She was beautiful and proud, her head high, the breeze blowing her dress back to outline her woman's body. Sebastian felt he had never really seen her properly before. He had always loved her, but as he might have loved his mother – had she lived, or Nou-Nou – had she been a warmer and kinder woman.

Rosie's rescuing of him aboard the ship was one of his most vivid childhood memories. And he still remembered his bewilderment when she had fled from his grandfather's house that winter's day when she first came to Paris. Though he was only five at the time, he had known for sure that she was not happy. After her departure, he had grizzled and been so naughty that finally Nou-Nou had spanked him and put him to bed. But he recalled how his grandfather had come to his room and comforted him, and promised that Rosie would come back one day.

"We shall both miss her," his grandfather had said, and the old man's sadness had made Sebastian sadder than ever.

He never forgot her. He was nearly nine when she came again to the house on the Île de la Cité. She accompanied his father, who looked pleased and proud to have her at his side. Sebastian now knew that she had started the business with his father and he was beside himself with joy to see her. Even though big boys of nine did not hug and kiss, he had flung himself into her arms as if he were still only five.

Now he was older, he realised that Rosie had given him the only love and tenderness he had ever known from a woman when he was small. And she had continued to do so ever since.

But he had wondered as time went by exactly what she was doing with his father. Sebastian, who had a natural worldliness and who had never quite been an innocent child, had begun to suspect that perhaps there was something between her and Philippe Lefevre. Once he met Clovis he suspected it even more. How could his beautiful Rosie have chosen to marry such a clod of the soil? For years he had hoped that maybe she would run away from Les Hérissons and come to live with him, his father and grandfather in the Paris house. She never did.

Of course the problem was and always had been Allie. Allie adored her boring father, and Rosie was too kind, too good to separate them. Nor would she leave her daughter behind. Sebastian knew in his bones that this was the answer.

At first it had made him resentful of Allie, but as they grew older and he understood things better, he began secretly to regard her as his sister, pretending that perhaps really his father was her father too. Though one look at her disproved his fantasy; she was the image of Clovis in looks, if in no other way.

And now he was angry with his father. His father was going to break Rosie's heart. He was sure of it.

He heard her footsteps clattering down the staircase and left the breakfast room quickly in case she had breakfasted in bed. She was heading for the back door of the house, and he called out to her. She stopped, turned and came back towards him.

"Aren't you taking breakfast?" he asked.

"I had coffee in my room."

"And where are you going in such a hurry, looking so much the emancipated lady?"

She was wearing a simple blouse, not unlike a man's shirt, a straight wine-coloured skirt and a plain tailor-made jacket in matching wool.

"To work," she told him.

"Can I come? I want to talk to you."

"You can come with me, but you can't talk to me. I have to decide upon the *cuvée*."

She had turned and continued her walk to the back of the house while he followed. She opened a door and went through a narrow passage that led to the annex of the house. Through another door and they were in a spotlessly clean room containing chairs round a long table on which were a spittoon, glasses narrowing at the brim, several unlabelled bottles and a collection of tall glass measuring beakers.

She opened the bottles and placed a beaker ready, consulting scribbles on a notepad.

"I've really already decided," she said, "but I wanted to check just once more, and then I had to go to Paris to meet Lizzie. It must be decided today so the blending can begin before the weather starts to get warmer."

"What exactly are you doing?" he asked, enchanted by her work-manlike manner, so different from the impassioned advocate of the night before.

"To put it simply, deciding on the mixture of different wines of different qualities to make this year's champagne," she said. "It's the first year I've chosen the blend myself. Our *chef de cuvée* – he'd worked for Madame Dupuis years ago and came back when we started up again – died last November. He taught me as much as he could. He made me drink different champagnes, and then try to blend our own wines to approximate them. Not easy. But he was kind enough to say I had a reliable palate and a good nose."

"A very pretty nose," Sebastian said.

"Thank you. But it is better to have a good one than a pretty one for this job."

"Explain to me," he said plaintively.

She laughed. "A good champagne is not one, it is many wines," she told him. "I'm mixing wine from black grapes, Pinot, and from white grapes, Chardonnay. I'm putting in some old wine from the cellars that we reserved from good years – like 1906 – into the blend. When I've decided on the mixture, we will put the exact same proportions of all those different wines into huge barrels, blend them and add yeasts to start the second fermentation – the one that adds the bubbles. Then in three years' time, I'll serve you a glass. And there endeth your lesson on champagne."

She was silent for a while, pouring and measuring until one of the beakers was full. Then she started on another.

He watched fascinated, until eventually she had made four different mixtures of wine. She then poured four glasses, sipped from each, rolling the wine around her tongue and then spitting into the spittoon.

"You try," she said. "Which do you prefer?"

He took them and tried them one by one. They all tasted much the same to him, and then he remembered that Rosie had shown more satisfaction when she sipped the glass that was nearest to his right hand.

He chose it.

She beamed at him.

"Well done!" she said. "That's the one I had chosen myself."

It seemed a shame to disappoint her, but peace and quiet had never been Sebastian's aim.

"I guessed," he said. "You seemed to like that one better."

She pursed her lips and gave him a reproving look which, he thought, made her look no less attractive.

"I presume you are not following your papa into the wine business?" she said dryly.

"No," he told her. "I'm going into the army."

He had startled her.

"Does your father know this?"

"No. But Grandfather does."

"And what does he think?"

"He thinks I am mad. He says there is bound to be another war with the Boche, and that fighting wars is no way for a civilised man to behave. But I told him that he knows very well I have never been civilised. And he sighed and said that maybe the army would make me. But then he added that he doubted it."

"Your papa will be unhappy," she said slowly, looking into the glass of the wine that was to be this year's *cuvée*.

"I think not. But anyway, I have no wish to stay at home. You know he is marrying?"

He watched, waiting for her reaction, but she did not let him see her face.

"I know."

"Lorraine is boring. Pretty, but boring."

"Well, she is young."

"I am young, but I am not boring."

201

She laughed, looking up at him, her eyes suddenly sparkling.

"That is true, Sebastian. You are not boring."

"What I am saying," he continued, patiently, determined to get his point over to her, "is that I have no wish to stay in a household where I have a stepmother who is two years older than I am." Then greatly daring, without thinking too closely what he was saying, added: "I would far rather have a mistress who was fourteen years older than me." That was the exact age gap between himself and Rosie. She had reminded him of it enough when he was little and constantly vowing that he would marry no one but her. Catching sight of her frozen face, he qualified his statement: "Or rather, that my father had a mistress fourteen years older than himself, if not one the same age."

"Your father's life is his own," she said quietly. "He has been alone for a long time. And, as you say, you will soon be away and he will be alone."

He snorted. "He'll be alone with that one, I tell you. She is a true bird-head. Stupid. She will drive him mad. She would drive me mad, and I am, as you pointed out, and as Allie pointed out this morning, only a boy."

"Men want different things at different times in their lives," she said, and he could see that she was near to tears. He made himself stop teasing her.

"Listen," he said. "Must we spit out this wine? Can't we drink it? I'll have the ones you didn't choose, you have the *cuvée*, because to tell you the truth, I couldn't taste the difference."

"Philistine!" she said, as she handed him the glass.

Clovis made a small detour on his way home from Ay. He stopped at Madame Frédéric's. He was weary and aching; he had spent the night in a hut on his field near Ay. He had seen the fires and heard the shouts of the mob as they rampaged through the little town, but no one had been near his field. Claudette would both warm him and soothe him. He was not anxious that she might be working when he arrived. These days few of Madame's clientèle asked for Claudette. She was more than a little overweight, and her squeals and coquettishness sat ill on her tubby little frame and heavily powdered face.

But Madame Frédéric kept her on, perhaps just for him, though his weekly visits could hardly pay her keep. He wondered if perhaps Madame was grooming her to take over one day, for Madame's health was not good. Now she was so monumentally fat that she could barely get out of her chair, and the slightest exertion made her huff and puff like an old steam train.

But she greeted him in her usual effusive manner, holding out her hand, which was more like a side of pork, to be kissed. The rings had

202

long since gone, cut away by a jeweller from Epernay because they became so buried in flesh that there was fear they might become embedded for ever.

"A pleasure to see you again so soon," she said, "and you will find Claudette in her room. She is mending some of the linen, but there is no hurry for it to be finished."

He walked up the stairs, passed the picture that always made him avert his eyes, and found his way to Claudette's room. Madame had put her in an attic chamber since the demand for her had dropped. But Claudette was content. She had been allowed to surround herself with her own treasures – brightly coloured cushions, soft, cuddly toys, trinkets won at the fair, and a collection of little boxes that Clovis had bought for her over the years.

She, too, looked surprised, but pleased to see him. She jumped to her feet and put down her needlework. She was dressed in a black robe, cut like a Japanese garment, and he could tell that she was embarrassed at being caught looking so homely.

"No, no, sit," he said. "I just want your company for a little while before I go home." She sat back down again, picked up her needle, and listened while he explained how he had spent the night in the field, and how nothing had happened.

"But in Ay it was bad," Claudette said. "They burned down poor Madame Bissinger's house, they hacked up all her pictures and stole all her silver and her jewellery. And they burned down the buildings of the houses of Deutz, Ayala and Gelderman. It will be a long time before they can produce again. The damage to the town is terrible, they say."

"But Deutz and those others would never use inferior grapes," Clovis said. "Why did they pick on them?"

"They were mad and drunk," said Claudette positively. "Just wanting to create damage. The dragoons were in Épernay and so they couldn't do their worst there. That was why they picked on poor little Ay. It is said they may have destroyed as many as five million bottles of champagne, and the damage to the fields is wicked. But the infantry have moved in. That'll quieten them."

"It's terrible," Clovis said.

"True, but it's over now." She put down the sheets that she was patching and said: "Do you want ..."

"No, like I said, just your company. I can't face Les Hérissons until I've rested a little. It's full of Americans. Friends of my wife."

"Americans!" she said "Imagine."

"And besides," he added gloomily, "I expect that tonight she will want to make love. She went to Paris to meet her friend. Whenever she comes back from Paris or Reims she wants to make love. I wouldn't mind if it was like that with you, but she's always wanting me to be

203

doing things. *Asking* me to do things. It is not seemly for a woman to behave like that. And anyway, whatever I do never seems to please her."

He was aware that he had grumbled in this vein to Claudette before, but there was no one in the world to whom he could talk, other than to her. What he would do without her, he didn't know. For as much as he loved Rosie, there were things about her that puzzled his slow brain. Claudette posed no such problems.

"Perhaps she's like a man," Claudette suggested. "They do say the men get to be wanting a woman after being on trains. Maybe it's the same for her."

"I don't know what it is," Clovis said. "But I wish she would just let me do it my way. I'd manage better then."

"But then you wouldn't need to come to see me," Claudette said with a touch of her old coquetry.

"Don't be silly." He was quite put out. "I'll always need to come and see you. Who else can I talk to?"

She giggled. "That's not what you're supposed to come for," she reminded him.

"Well, none of us is getting younger," he said placidly, stroking his moustache.

"And it makes a change for me to have a chat." She bent to her needlework, and said quietly: "I'm always very pleased to see you, Clovis. I shouldn't say it, but I do think of you as my best friend."

He was enormously pleased and suddenly found himself wishing he could introduce Allie to her, then with regret he put the thought away.

"I'm pleased to hear it, Claudette," he said, and moved to kiss her cheek. And as his lips touched her soft, powdered flesh, he realised this was something he had never done before.

She looked up, her eyes glistening. She touched her cheek where his mouth had been.

"Oh, Clovis," she said softly.

"I must go," he said.

But in spite of his tiredness and aching bones, he went home whistling, letting his mare jog along at her own pace. At Les Hérissons he stoically bore his mother's scolding for leaving them to face the mob without the man of the house to protect them, did his best with the language problem so as to be polite to Lizzie, whom he found he couldn't help liking. In fact, he liked her enough to wish that she spoke French. And her son seemed a good enough lad, too.

Rosie, it seemed, had been a heroine, and so had Allie. He told them both he was proud of them, but they seemed a little subdued to him. Sebastian was noisy as ever but looking surprisingly grown-up. Harassed by all that was going on, Clovis took refuge in his fields and among his barrels until late that evening. He waited until everyone had eaten supper in the dining room, and then had his in the kitchen with Marie and Henri for company. He told them all he knew about the riots, and they told him all they knew.

And as he feared, when he climbed into bed, Rosie's hand went out to touch him. To both their surprise, nothing happened.

"Sorry, Rosie," he muttered into his pillow. "I'm not feeling too good."

He felt her hesitate and then stroke him again.

"It's no good," he told her. "I must sleep," and even as he spoke, he slept.

Chapter Fourteen

"And what do you think of that one?"

The boy, spruce in a white sailor suit with navy blue trimming and silver-buckled navy shoes, took the glass from his father's hand. With the exaggerated gravity of a ten-year-old, he sipped, considered and spat into the cuspidor.

"Rather better than the last, Papa," he said.

Jean Paul laughed out loud, and slapped his thigh.

"Quite right, son," he said. "That's the real thing. French champagne. Bollinger's best. We haven't achieved that quality yet, but we will. That's the target; that's the goal."

"So you've told him a million times." The woman stretched out on the big leather sofa had one arm languidly draped over its back. A thin white hand crowned with a huge ruby ring made a lazy circle towards the bottle in Jean Paul's hand.

"Spitting out Bollinger is a sin. Pass me a glass of it to swallow."

Jean Paul took a crystal goblet from the shelf behind the desk where he sat, and poured the delicate amber wine. Hundreds of tiny clear bubbles rode to the surface, and he nodded his satisfaction.

"Here, Pierre," he handed the glass to his son. "Take this to Auntie Clara."

Pierre took the glass from his father and crossed the oriental carpet, careful not to spill a drop. He would be in trouble if he spilt any, and he would be in even bigger trouble if he emptied the wine into Auntie Clara's lap. Which was exactly what he wanted to do. Auntie Clara was most certainly not his auntie, merely the latest in a long line of aunties, who got younger and younger and sillier and sillier, but who seemed to be necessary to his father for some unknown reason.

"Thanks, kid." Clara's hand came out, ruby flashing, and took the glass. She drank it rather too quickly, Pierre thought. He hoped she would get the hiccups.

"Want a glass, son?"

"Yes, please, Papa," he said meekly.

His father took another crystal glass and half filled it.

"The kid's too young to drink." Clara lifted her chiffon-clad arm to point at the bottle. "I keep telling you, that stuff isn't for kids."

She wants it all for herself, the pig, Pierre thought.

"It's not drinking, it's learning," his father said sharply. "If he's going to inherit all this, he needs to know one champagne from another."

A look passed over Auntie Clara's face that she could not quite control. It said clearly that she had other thoughts about who was going to inherit the Champagne D'Or winery and all its treasures. Pierre sipped from his glass in a grown-up way and enjoyed the thought that she was in for a surprise. The aunties lasted only while Peter was in New York or Chicago or New Orleans. The minute he came back, they disappeared, to be replaced by another when Peter went travelling around the States again. This particular auntie was one of the worst. But she didn't dare complain about him to his father. Stupid she might be, but she had cottoned on quickly that the seemingly angelic little boy was the apple of his daddy's eye. His daddy wasn't going to hear a word against him.

But of course he wasn't an angelic little boy. He had put a snake in her bath the night before last. It was a perfectly harmless snake, but as she came from San Francisco, she wasn't to know that. The sight of it, he thought with satisfaction, had frightened the life out of her. Her screams could have been heard in Calistoga.

He had also discovered it unnerved her when he just stared at her, not letting his eyelids blink. She'd fiddle with her blonde hair when he did it, get her mirror out to see if she had something on her face. Finally, she'd have to ask: "What's the matter?" And then he would just let his eyes slide away, smile and say: "Nothing, Auntie Clara." And she'd mutter something about creepy kids.

She had an enormous wardrobe, mostly bought by his father, and a collection of silly huge hats which she wore on the side of her head, making eyes from the other side at any man who was about.

He'd found a nest of baby mice in the cellars, and carefully moved them with their mother to a home in her largest hat. She hadn't found them yet, but when the screams started, beautifully behaved little Pierre would be the first to rush to assist her.

He sipped his champagne appreciatively, wondering how he could get another glass. Pierre enjoyed wine a great deal more than his father realised.

"Aren't we going to do something?" Clara was saying petulantly.

"Later," his father said. "I've work to do. Why don't you go and have a sleep or something, so you're fresh for tonight." His father smiled that particularly unsmiley smile, no more than his lips rolling back in a straight line. He wasn't really smiling at all. When he was little, Pierre had been frightened of that smile, but that was before he realised that all his father wanted was for him to be perfect. Now, as long as his father *thought* he was perfect, life was easy. He only had to please his father – nobody else, except perhaps Peter, but then he didn't mind pleasing Peter. He liked Peter. Being perfect only applied to his father, who didn't mind how difficult he was with the servants, or even his governesses. But Pierre had been about six when he realised that to let people believe you were truly good worked out better. Then you could be wicked and naughty in your head or do things like the mice and the snake secretly, and no one ever guessed. He thought Clara might just have guessed, but his father would never believe it.

Auntie Clara was dragging herself to her feet and sulkily making for the door, trailing along in her red and white spotted chiffon which his French governess said was most unsuitable for daytime wear. But as Clara never went out of the house, she probably didn't know whether it was day or night.

He just hoped Peter would come home soon.

As soon as she had gone, his father stamped on the bell push under his desk, and after a while Angelo, their winery manager, knocked and came into the room. Angelo was smart. Peter had found him some-where in New York on the East Side, and brought him back to California. That was about six years ago, just before the earthquake which had financially almost wiped out all their neighbours. Pierre had thought the world had come to an end that day as the ground trembled and bucked like a young horse. But when his father talked of it, he would tell of Champagne D'Or's amazing luck. They had lost only a few thousand bottles of champagne, and the wine in casks had not been touched. Most of the other vine-growers had not been so lucky. Peter, who had been in San Francisco on the day, would tell stories that held Pierre spellbound – how the ground rocked and split and how people used their own Californian wine to put out the fires in their homes. In 'Frisco millions and millions of gallons of good wine had been lost.

Angelo, a short, dark stocky man with hairy arms and bowed legs, was standing waiting to be spoken to.

"What's the situation on the loans?" Jean Paul finally asked, looking up from some papers he had been studying.

"From whose point of view?" Angelo asked with a wolfish grin.

"Ours."

"In that case, good. There's hardly any rent money in at all this month."

"Could we foreclose on any of them?"

"A couple maybe. The two Yugoslavs are way behind."

Jean Paul pursed his lips, considering. Pierre understood exactly what they were talking about. His father always told him what went on with the running of the estate. Pierre was the heir, and as young as he was, his father insisted he had to know what it was all about.

What this was all about was that his father had bought as much land as he could lay his hands on when Pierre was just a baby. The problem was that once having paid the cash for the land, Jean Paul had no money left to hire hands to cultivate it. Then he had a brilliant idea. Peter went to the big cities, and several times to Ellis Island in New York where the immigrants came in, and found peasants who couldn't speak much English and who had worked with vines in their own countries. He offered them a plot to work, a tiny salary, some food and the chance to buy the land for themselves. But nine-tenths of the crop they raised belonged to Champagne D'Or until they had purchased the land. All they had to do was pay five dollars a month until the plot became theirs. Pierre, who was good at arithmetic, reckoned this would be hard to do.

At first, because they needed the money, Jean Paul and Peter had made sure that their tenants paid the five dollars. As time went by and the financial problems became less pressing, they left it to the workers to pay of their own accord. The money was rarely paid. The immigrants never could get five dollars together – and Peter used to say it would take about a million years, give or take a few, before Champagne D'Or had to hand over any of that land.

"Are the Yugoslavs producing?" his father asked.

Angelo shrugged. "Not much."

"Give them back what they've paid and get rid of them, then."

Pierre thrilled at his father's decisiveness.

But Angelo was looking doubtful.

"I don't know," he said. "They're Reds."

"You think they'll make trouble?"

"They were going on about the number of children picking in the autumn."

"It is not my fault if our tenants use their children as labour," his father said primly. "We do not pay the children, we pay the parents."

"Yeah, but the law ..."

"Keep the Yugoslavs." His father had changed his mind. "But tell them they'll have to improve their output or we'll be forced to cut their wages."

"Just as you say."

His father abruptly switched the subject.

"How about that spoilt wine? Was the chemist able to do anything about it?"

"Nope. He says it'll make terrible champagne. Suggests you chuck it."

"No, keep it as still wine and bottle it for the tenants. Give 'em a little treat. Any other problems?"

Angelo launched into a complicated conversation about space in the cellars. There was never enough and Jean Paul had suggested that they start digging into the hillside to make more room for the stock. But in the meantime, there were problems finding storage space for their output.

Losing interest in the conversation, Pierre noticed that Auntie Clara had not completely finished her champagne and he quietly sidled across the room so he could drain the dregs. His father did not notice. Bored, he wandered out through the long windows onto the back lawn, where, had he known it, Peter's sister, who was nearly a real aunt, once fed chickens.

He wasn't sure what to do with himself. It was Sunday and there were no lessons. His French governess had gone into Calistoga without asking him if he would like to go too.

He wandered into the old barn, the one that was never used any more, but which Peter would not have torn down. There was a mouldering bedroom above it where Pierre sometimes went and pretended that it was his, and played at being a poor scientist. He hadn't been into the barn for ages, and opening the door he frightened a colony of bats that hung from the beams. Pierre was afraid of nothing in nature so he shut the door quickly behind him so that he could observe them. He liked all animal and insect life. He could tame a wild cat, the biggest spider only fascinated him, he had a fine butterfly and moth collection and he liked snakes. He even knew how to pick up a rattler.

He stood quietly until the bats settled again, and then turned his mind to the problem of getting one into Clara's room. That achievement might even make her go before Peter came home. As it was, she kept whining that the countryside was dull and she was bored. She wouldn't be bored with a bat in her bedroom!

He sighed. At least catching a bat would keep him occupied for a while. Sometimes he wished he could go to school like other children, or at least have someone his own age come to visit him. But his father did not like him mixing with other boys and girls. The house was so huge, with the two modern wings built each side of the old original stone building, that it sometimes made him feel very small. His father had given him every toy imaginable, he had a library to himself with all the latest children's books sent from San Francisco. There were swings

210

and slides and even a full-sized carousel in the garden. But it got so lonely that naughtiness, particularly towards the aunties, was the only diversion.

He did wish Peter would come back.

When Angelo had gone back to his own office in the new winery buildings, Jean Paul sat thinking for a while, working out how he could extend his cellars. He was convinced that the climate, near as it was to that of Champagne, was not quite right and this was the reason he could never match the perfection of a fine Bollinger or Krug. He accepted it was perhaps asking too much to re-create a Dom Perignon in California, but he felt there must be a way to make a Californian champagne so good that even an expert could not tell it from the average best that France had to offer.

He had already won a fine reputation in the States – but with American sparkling wine. He simply could not produce true champagne to his own standards.

Caves built into the mountainside might be that fraction cooler than his cellars and could make the difference. But it would be a hell of a task to make them; not like digging into the chalk hillsides of Champagne. But if he was to expand, new caves or cellars had to be constructed in the rock.

There was no financial problem. In this spring of 1911 Jean Paul was a very rich man. And now, apart from his tenants and the labour he extracted from them, everything in his empire was sparkling honest and above board.

His champagne was made in the best conditions, from the best grapes and with nothing left to chance. He employed a brilliant *chef du cuvée* to blend it for him, and his own palate aided the decisions. He had the most modern machinery. The chemicals he used were acceptable, even in Champagne itself.

But it had not always been like that.

Originally there had not been sufficient money under the floorboards of old Hans's bedroom to do all that was needed to make the winery profitable. For the first year he was forced to continue with the same table wines that the Brunners had been making while he grafted stock to save the vines from the phylloxera and tried to buy more land to plant the white Chardonnay grapes.

His first champagne, made when Pierre was not quite four years old, was surprisingly good, but there wasn't much of it. He knew he could not command a decent price for a totally unknown brand and would be out of pocket.

So he bought a small printing press and paid an engraver a great deal of money to reproduce the Moët et Chandon label. Then he bottled his wine under the French company's colours. The corks he could not copy, but nevertheless he packed a protesting Peter off to Chicago with two wagonloads of bottles and told him to sell it as French and at French prices, and leave fast.

Peter did, and they repeated the fraud for two more years, each time picking a Mid West town where Jean Paul reasoned that palates might not be so sophisticated as in New York, Boston or San Francisco. And where hopefully they wouldn't look at the cork.

He bought more land, imported more immigrants from the East for labour, and gradually the financial problems receded. The earthquake of 1906, which left him with most of his stock intact, was the final breakthrough. Most other growers were smashed for the season, while he was able to get French prices for his product, under its own label. Champagne D'Or, called after the bag of gold that launched it, was on its way.

Sitting now in his fine linen shirt and red velvet waistcoat, he poured himself another glass of the Bollinger and lit up a Havana cigar. He had just settled back in his chair when the telephone rang. He took the receiver from its hook and put it to his ear. It was Peter.

"How did it go?" he asked.

Peter's voice wavered over the wire from Washington.

"Fine," he said. "I found two big new outlets. They'll take a thousand cases a year. Can you cope?"

"Peter, you just sell all you can, and I'll make all you can sell," Jean Paul said.

Peter's chuckle echoed over three thousand miles.

"We've lost one account, though," he said.

"Who to?"

"A French company. They've got a clever sales gimmick. They bottle their champagne – and it's good – under the buyers' own label. Several Senators have gone for it and we've lost the wholesaler they bought from. I was wondering if we ought to try the same thing."

Jean Paul thought about it briefly.

"No," he said. "I'd rather make us a famous name than pander to a bunch of Senators' vanity. But we'll talk about it later. You coming back?"

"Yep. Catching the transcontinental tomorrow, so see you at the beginning of next week."

They talked for a few seconds more, and then Jean Paul hung up. Peter had done very well, he decided, but then Peter was Jean Paul's hand-raised pie. Jean Paul had eradicated the dirt-farmer in him, insisted he spoke grammatically, let him spend money on the clothes he coveted and helped him develop taste. Peter had grown into a handsome, charming young man with a gift for selling. He had a diffident manner and was still a little nervous, but his quietness seemed to sell champagne better than the usual salesman's brash approach.

Also, he liked travelling. The little sexual encounters he had on his journeys kept him content. His youthful protestations of only ever loving Jean Paul had long since been forgotten. Though they were still a couple in both their private and business lives, their sexlife had declined over the years. Jean Paul found he had become more interested in women, and chose a new one for every trip that Peter made East. He did not under any circumstances want a wife. He had his son, his pride and joy, and a wife would only get in the way of their relationship.

He was bracing himself to send Pierre, whom he had named after Peter, away to school. Peter had been on about it for ages, insisting it was not fair that the boy had no companionship of his own age. But Jean Paul did not wish him to mix with the local children. His long-ago days as a teacher had taught him how children chattered, and how interested they were in other people's business. He worked on the theory that the less anyone outside the family knew about *his* business, the better.

So, if and when Pierre went to school, it would have to be in the East. A long way from Calistoga. The boy was undoubtedly bright, and though he wanted him to be well-behaved, sometimes Jean Paul worried that he was a little too good to be true. There was no doubt he'd have to go away, though the wrench would be almost more than he could bear. Pierre was all that was left of his own flesh and blood.

The languid, elegant figure of Clara was drifting back into the room. She picked up her champagne glass from where she had left it, grimaced when she saw it was empty, and wandered to the desk for a refill.

"Have you finished work?" she asked.

He nodded.

"What shall we do?"

"Make love?" he suggested.

She giggled. "Why not? Right here!"

"No, Pierre might come in."

She looked as if she wanted to say something, but just nodded.

"Your room or mine?"

"Yours." It was further from Pierre's

She went to pick up the remains of the bottle, but he stopped her. "We shall have a fresh, cold one," he said.

"Great," she said, and as she drifted upstairs, wafting perfume and chiffon, he went to the ice-box and brought out another bottle of Bollinger. Then, not hurrying, he followed her upstairs.

It was a pity that she had only a few days left. She might even leave right away, so he might as well enjoy her.

She was waiting for him in the bedroom, the chiffon gone, and in its place bands of black leather clamped round her wrists and ankles. She wore nothing else. She was a twenty-one-year-old natural-born whore, and her breasts were large but firm with huge, dark, upstanding nipples. Her generous pubic hair was black, proving that she was not a natural blonde, but he did not mind that.

He was slipping off his clothes. "Get on the bed," he ordered.

Meekly, she did as she was told, spreadeagling herself, legs wide apart, arms above her head. He knew which drawer held the leather thongs. He found them, then with a few practised movements, tied her arms to the bedhead and her feet to the bedposts. Then he took a piece of black silk from the same drawer and blindfolded her.

Without speaking, he lay down at first beside her, biting at her breasts and her neck, hard enough to make her writhe, but not hard enough to draw blood. He then took his biting mouth to what was exposed below, until she groaned and half-screamed as he explored with fingers, tongue and teeth.

Then he rolled over on top of her and entered her, roughly. It did not take long. In less than three minutes he was standing at the bedside, getting dressed.

"Is that it?" The voice came plaintively from under the black silk.

"That's it," he said.

"Then untie me."

He sat down on the bed and removed the blindfold.

"I've something to tell you," he said, his satyr eyebrows drawn into a frown.

She was frowning, too. Her face was flushed, and her mouth wet. Small bruises were already forming on her body.

"What is it?"

"You're going to have to go."

She did not understand.

"Go where?"

"Back to San Francisco. East. Anywhere you like. But away from here."

"Why?" She was trying to pull her hands from the thongs, but he had tied her too securely.

"Because my wife is coming home."

"Your wife!"

"My wife."

"But you never said you had a wife. No one ever said you had a wife."

"I must have forgotten to mention it."

She lay there looking at him, and he was pleased her hands were tied. She would certainly have tried to scratch and bite him.

"Untie me," she said, teeth gritted.

"In a minute. If you leave in two or three days' time, that will be fine, but you might just prefer to go today since that's the way things are. You can take all the clothes and jewellery with you, and you'll be given five hundred dollars. That should take you anyplace you want."

"Untie me," she hissed.

"In a minute. I'll just go and get the money now."

He leaned forward holding her in a painful grip. Swiftly he put the black silk not round her eyes but in her mouth, making a gag of it as she rolled her head from side to side in a vain effort to escape him.

"Won't be long," he said, and left the room.

But he was. Half an hour went by as she lay there, impotent, full of rage, unable to move.

It was Pierre who found her as he slipped through her bedroom door, a bat carefully hidden in his cap. She gave him such a shock, lying there, naked and bound, her eyes rolling above the black gag, moaning through the silk, that he inadvertently dropped his cap.

The bat, released, darted and swooped about the room, searching for escape. Clara's muffled screams and her rigid naked terror sent the boy rushing from the room. The first that Jean Paul, who was enjoying a cigar, knew of what his son had seen, was when he heard Pierre's panic-stricken voice calling for someone, anyone, to come and help.

Lizzie and Alexander had been at Les Hérissons for just two weeks, and Rosie was desperate for some time to herself. Lizzie was sad, ill at ease, unable to communicate with either Clovis or Madame Dupuis, and Rosie felt obliged to stay with her friend for most of the time, keeping her company, and doing her best to cheer her up.

Happily she was not too busy. Now the *cuvée* was chosen, Clovis was in charge of the blending and bottling, and with Philippe in America, she had no reason for business discussions that might take her away from Les Hérissons.

She kept silent about the telegraph that Henri had sent; indeed, she was wondering if it had ever arrived.

Sebastian had returned to Paris after staying for four days, and she missed him. He would have helped raise her spirits. Young as he was, his obvious admiration of her had eased the sense of rejection that the news of Philippe's forthcoming marriage had brought. She could not shake the thought of Lorraine, about to become Madame Lefevre, from her head. It was as if she had a buzzing fly or a monotonous tune in her brain, and she longed to talk to someone who might exorcise it. She needed to clear her thoughts and decide what she must do with her

215

life. At one moment she wanted to run to Philippe, taking Allie and leaving Clovis behind for ever; then sanity prevailed and she knew that this could not be done.

To pass the time and try to interest Lizzie she had taken her for drives in the bright red double saloon Léon Bollée car that she had bought earlier in the year. It had cost a fortune, but neither Clovis nor Madame had thought to question her decision. She sometimes thought that if she sold the house over their heads they would not complain. She could not decide whether their reliance on her was a good or a bad thing, but most of the time she merely continued to make decisions. It was easier.

Everyone was very impressed with the large comfortable car. It could drive at sixty miles an hour, but more important, from Henri's point of view, it boasted a covered seat for the driver. At this time of year when showers fell without warning, it made excursions so much pleasanter, particularly since his bones were becoming a trifle rheumatic. He drove them several times to Reims where the ancient buildings, fine squares and narrow streets did stir Lizzie to some enthusiasm, and then one morning Rosie suggested that they went to Paris – but by train. Henri preferred to drive at a leisurely pace, and at his speed they would not be able to get back the same day.

So it was all arranged. Allie would have the day off lessons and take Lizzie shopping with Alexander while Rosie attended a 'business' meeting.

It wasn't exactly a business meeting. Rosie had decided there was only one person in the world to whom she could unburden herself: André Lefevre. She wanted to talk to him. She was uncertain about telling him the full extent of her troubles, but she was sure that the sight of him would calm her. He had never ceased to be her friend, and she tried to see him whenever she was in Paris, but, of necessity, she had been unable to tell him all that passed in her life.

She telephoned the house on the Île de la Cité and left a message that she would be there at eleven o'clock the next morning.

She left Lizzie and the two young people in the Champs Élysées, having given Lizzie the address of Poiret, whom she believed to be the most exciting of the Parisian couturiers. She thought it was time that her American friend acquired some Parisian style. And then she took a cab to André's home.

On the Champs Élysées, the horses and carriages were crowded out by the motor cars. It seemed impossible that things could have changed so much since she arrived in Paris almost eleven years ago. But André, whom she had not seen for six months, had changed very little, and his *ménage* not at all. She was greeted with smiles by the servants, and he was waiting for her in his little sitting room, perhaps greyer, perhaps not so upright, but still handsome and still, she thought, desirable.

"Rosie!" he said. "What a pleasure to see you," and kissed her on both cheeks, holding her away from him to look at her better. "But you look tired. We shall have champagne to cheer you."

She sat quietly, enjoying the peace of the room while he fussed with the cork of the bottle that was already waiting in an ice-bucket. He handed her a glass, and then said: "Now, why are you tired and sad?"

"You're not supposed to notice," she told him. "You're supposed to tell me how beautiful I am looking."

He wagged a finger at her.

"Sebastian tells me you have American guests. Your friend Lizzie and her son. They are still there?"

She nodded.

"Too long. That is why you are tired. Guests and fish stink after three days."

"It's only that they don't speak French," Rosie said defensively. "It is difficult to leave them with anyone."

"So we know now why you are tired," he continued, stroking the velvet lapel of his smoking jacket, "but why are you sad? Shall I hazard a guess, my dear? Can it be to do with my son?"

She half-smiled at him, thinking how stupid she had been to think that he would not already know.

"My son is marrying, and this makes you unhappy, perhaps. Is that why you have come to see me?"

"I needed to talk," she said quietly. "André, there is no one in my world that I can talk to anymore – except you. I had not realised how alone I was."

He nodded and said dryly, "Most of us are alone, my dear. But could you not confide in your friend?"

"No. She has troubles of her own and she would never understand."

"That you have a lover?"

She nodded, not really surprised at his frankness.

"You knew?" she asked.

"I have known for years now. I was madly jealous for a while, but then happy for you both."

Her eyes filled with tears at the thought she might have hurt him.

"Oh, André, I do love him. I love you, too. I have always loved you, always will. But you once said that youth called to youth, and that is what happened between Philippe and me."

He just nodded, encouraging her to continue, and the bottled up words began to flow.

"I never told you about the wedding. I did it because you said it was the thing to do, and you were right. There was no choice, but how was

217

either of us to know how much I would love Philippe? But you see, even loving him might not have been the answer. He might not have accepted another man's baby. I never asked him if he would have considered it, because whatever the answer it would not have helped my situation. And remember, in the end you did not want to accept that either." He made a little protesting movement, but she hurried on. "So I married Clovis. André, it was the most dreadful day of my life. We married in Reims, quickly and furtively because of the pregnancy. There was just Madame Dupuis and Clovis, all stiff and awkward and unhappy in his best suit. I wore my Worth gown, the one you bought for me. It was a gesture of defiance really. I was trying to say that I was still me, Rosie, who loved you better than this young man who was to be my husband.

"I don't really remember the ceremony except that it wasn't like a wedding, not in a church, no priest, just legal, and then Madame Dupuis took us both for a meal at a big fashionable restaurant. I don't remember much about that, either, and then we hired a carriage and went back to Les Hérissons. Suddenly, without wanting to be, I was Madame Clovis Dupuis. And I longed and longed to be in Paris, safe with you.

"You were right about Clovis not approaching me. Thank God, he kept to his word. But he asked if I would share a bedroom with him for his mother's sake. What could I do but agree? André, imagine, night after night, year after year, sharing a bed with a man who physically repels you. Trying not to brush up against him, trying to sleep rigid on one side of the bed. I didn't want to arouse him. Then there were nights when he would come home drunk, and I would sleep in the armchair rather than chance his losing control. And yet all the time I longed, ached, burned for love."

"And you never made love with him?" he asked gently. "I seem to remember I told you that you would be wise to try."

She sighed.

"I did, but not until after Philippe. Then I had to. In case I became pregnant." She said it baldly and waited for his reaction, but he merely nodded, as if what she had just confessed was a normal aspect of married life.

She took a nervous sip from the champagne glass in her hand and said: "Once I was married, I began to assert myself, and no one seemed to mind. I started buying more grafted stock, and ordered the fields replanted. I began improving the cellars and building more outhouses and sheds for the work of making champagne. I persuaded Madame Dupuis to take back their *chef du cuvée*. He had really retired, but he saw my enthusiasm, and he taught me how to blend wines, and recognise a good champagne from a bad one.

"Clovis seemed to enjoy it all and Madame Dupuis never interfered. As far as I was concerned, I had to do something, or go mad. Just before Rosalie was born, I was frantic to be busy. I even insisted on helping Marie, our maid, to clean the house. Madame Dupuis thought I had lost my mind, and perhaps, in a way, I had.

"But, André, her birth healed so much. I loved her from the moment the midwife put her into my arms. She wasn't crying, just lying there, her eyes tight shut, making little puckering faces. Madame Dupuis was with me, and we both cried, and we were both so full of joy at this tiny bundle that was mine really, but that I would share with her. If my wedding day was the worst day of my life, the day Allie was born was the best. Nothing could ever compete with it. And Madame and I have been so close ever since. From that day I called her Mama, and I love her very much, but I cannot speak to her of my unhappiness. It would break her heart. You see, she has managed to convince herself that Rosalie is Clovis's child, and that Clovis and I are happy. I think she has even wiped from her memory that I am not French, and that it was her prodigal son who fathered her granddaughter."

"And none of that is bad," he said firmly, one finger stroking his moustache. "You needed a new life, and Rosalie gave one to you."

"I know. But you see, there was Philippe. Since that day when you sent him off to lunch with me, I had never stopped thinking about him. I think there must be something amiss with me. When I find a man I care for, I'm obsessed. I want him near me, I want to be making love; it's like having something in the blood that I cannot control.

"I was like that with Jean Paul and with you. It has been like that with Philippe for eleven years now."

She was silent, afraid that she was saying too much.

But he only said: "If it is any consolation I believe he has the same obsession for you. Had he not, he would have married long ago."

"Maybe I've spoilt his life then," she said, wondering if this could be so. "You see, I pursued him at first. I knew he found me interesting. I could tell it when we had lunch that day. And he'd told me he was going to the School of Oenology that next autumn, so I told Mama and Clovis that I was going there too. I expected opposition, but they were both so enchanted with Rosalie and pleased with me for giving her to them that I could do no wrong. Neither said a word, so I went and registered for the course. They signed me up without a murmur, and didn't even seem to mind that I was a woman. Perhaps that was because, as you once told me, Champagne has always permitted women to come to the fore.

"And, of course, come the autumn, there was Philippe. Do you remember? He had taken a little apartment in Épernay for the time that he was to be here. That became our refuge.

"Again it was all my fault. That first day of the course I got there early and I waited until I saw him arriving. He came in a cab, and he was just as I'd remembered; so like you. He saw me, so, thank God, I didn't have to chase after him, for when he saw me he looked so pleased that my heart just rose. Oh, André, I was so in need of love.

"He sat behind me at the lecture, and afterwards he suggested that we share a meal. I deliberately misunderstood him; pretended that I thought he meant at his apartment. He meant nothing of the kind, but he immediately accepted what I had said, and I knew then he wanted to be alone with me. My heart was singing. He should have thought me forward for agreeing to go, unchaperoned, but I believe he understood, and I found afterwards that you had told him my circumstances."

André nodded.

"As the door closed behind us, he began to help me with my coat, and I just went into his arms. I remember he held me very tight, rocking me, and it reminded me of you and the comfort you gave me. I felt as if I had come home again. All the loneliness and longing went away. And then he tipped up my face and kissed me." She hesitated and said, lowering her voice: "It seemed so natural to make love after that, and I wanted him so badly.

"That was how it all began, and that was how it continued until two weeks ago."

"When he told you he was to marry?"

"Yes. When he told me he was to marry."

The room was quiet for a moment, and then André said: "And now your heart is full of schemes to run away and be with him for ever? Is that not true?"

He was right, and she nodded without speaking.

"But your head tells you this is not wise?"

She nodded again. "But he wants me to continue to be his mistress," she said. "It is too much to ask."

"What else can he ask of you?" he said. "Do you want him to *ask* you to brave the scandal and leave your husband and child? Do you want him to *ask* you to leave his life for ever? You have no choice but to be lovers."

"He has a choice," she said passionately, knowing she was being unfair. "He does not have to marry."

"That is true, but perhaps *you* are asking too much. Philippe is a modest man. Perhaps you do not realise how well-regarded he is in his world of wine. He has given his life to his career because he had no other life, but even a career needs a background, a home. A man should not live with his ageing father and his young son. A man should live with a woman."

"You never remarried. You chose to live alone."

"I was over sixty when we met, my dear," he said, his eyes twinkling as he accepted her point. "Philippe is thirty-five."

"But an eighteen-year-old girl!" She did not care if she appeared complaining. "He is twice her age."

"She is young," André said, sounding almost complacent. "But then I chose her for him. She is also stupid, my dear Rosie. While she has sufficient money to spend on clothes and fripperies, she will be content, I assure you. And with the right staff, she will make a very decorative hostess for the entertaining that Philippe should be doing to enhance his business. And her father's connections can only do Philippe, and indirectly you, much good."

Rosie was speechless.

"So, my darling girl, why do you not continue exactly as you have been for these last ten years? As Philippe's business and your business thrive, there will be more chance, more time for you both to be together. You have your little flat in Paris, and another in Reims, I believe."

"You know about those?" Suddenly she was embarrassed.

"Of course, but Lorraine never will."

She was silent, and then moved from her chair to sit at his feet, her long skirt wrapped round her toes, her head resting against his leg.

"Oh, André," she sighed as he stroked her hair, "what would I have done if we had never met? You have always been my strength. Why didn't I talk to you before? I have wanted to for so long, but I did not know if you would ..." she hesitated.

"Mind? Approve?" He chuckled. "As I said, I did mind at first, but then I thought how fortunate it was that I could keep you in the family."

"On the fringes of the family," she said sadly.

"In the family," he said firmly, leaning to kiss her forehead. "But once in the family, you ceased to confide in me."

And it was that small tableau that Lorraine Delperrier interrupted as Nou-Nou, an uncontrollable smirk on her face, ushered her into the room.

It seemed to Rosie that she had done nothing for weeks but get herself to the Gare de L'Est in a state of mind confused between blazing fury and deep distress. She was almost glad to have met the harmless, silly Lorraine Delperrier, though she would have preferred advance warning. She could have done without the conversation, though it had answered many questions for her. She needed a focus for her anger, and she fixed it on Nou-Nou. It was not Nou-Nou's place to show guests, unannounced, into her master's private sitting room; indeed,

André's butler had hovered behind, his face clouded with disapproval and anxiety.

André had been totally unperturbed. He had pressed his hand to Rosie's head to signal her to stay where she was, smiled at the girl standing in the doorway, and said: "Come in, come in, my dear. Forgive an old man for remaining seated. Georges, since you are here, pour mademoiselle a glass of champagne, if you please."

Relieved, Georges hurried in.

"You may go, Nou-Nou," André said, a note of steel in his voice that Lorraine would not have recognised. When the nursemaid's starched back had disappeared, he said: "And, my dear Lorraine, the lady at my feet, where of course I believe all ladies belong, is my dear friend Madame Dupuis, visiting from Champagne. Rosie, my dear, this is Mademoiselle Delperrier, visiting from Tours."

The girl, her hair a mass of blonde puffs under a huge, high-brimmed hat which she wore coquettishly to the side of her head, looked uneasy, uncertain how to deal with an introduction to someone sitting on the floor.

To put her out of her misery, Rosie sprung to her feet, and held out her hand. Both women murmured '*enchantée*' before Rosie settled herself back on the floor. She felt that, however unconventional, that was what André wanted her to do.

"Sit over there," André commanded the girl, pointing to the chair where Rosie had previously been sitting. "And enjoy your champagne."

"You must forgive me, monsieur," Lorraine said, settling herself down with little wriggles and twitches of her skirt. "I had no idea you had a guest. No one mentioned it."

She had a high, girlish voice that was not unattractive in someone so young. Her complexion was cream and fondant pink, and she had big round pale blue eyes which she blinked a great deal, just like Allie's favourite china doll. Her clothes were the height of fashion; her dress high-waisted with a hobble skirt, and her pointed and buckled shoes were, Rosie calculated, extremely expensive.

"Rosie is not a guest," André said. "Rosie is almost family. She is like a daughter-in-law, if not a daughter to me."

Rosie knew that his eyes would be twinkling with mischief, but she dared not look at him. She knew she would break into hysterical laughter.

"Indeed?" said the girl, again slightly disconcerted. She pursed her little rosebud mouth before nibbling at her lower lip with small white teeth. It was, Rosie decided, her little facial trick and to men it probably appeared quite charming.

"You are visiting Paris for long?" she asked Rosie politely.

"Just for the day. I have brought some American friends here to shop," she said. "I am not fond of shopping so I came to see André."

"I have been shopping," the girl said, suddenly animated. "I adore shopping. And I have been shopping for my wedding gown. I have been to Worth and I have been to Poiret, but I do think that perhaps Poiret is a little too modern and daring for me. It is my firm conviction that brides should be traditional above all things, don't you agree? But I have not decided yet on the gown. It will take care and thought. After all, one only marries once, does one not? It is absolutely essential to find exactly the right dress. There will be the photographs for ever after to chide one if one has not made the right choice." She clapped her hands together and made a little pouting face. "Oh dear, I should have explained. You see, I am to marry dear monsieur's son when he returns from America. Is it not exciting!"

Rosie felt as if her stomach had fallen to her knees.

"He is a very lucky man, mademoiselle," she murmured.

"How kind of you to say so," she said graciously before addressing André. "Mama wanted me to ask you about the guest list," she said. "Papa has set his heart on the Ritz for the reception – we are to be married in Paris," she explained to Rosie, "it will be so much more convenient for the guests." She turned back to André. "Papa says that he has been able to change the room for a larger one, and if you and Philippe would like to invite more people, you are very welcome to do so. I am so thrilled. So many more of those one loves will be present."

André's hand was on Rosie's shoulder, steadying her.

"How kind of your papa," he said. "But you will have to talk to Philippe about it. At my age one begins to run out of friends."

Rosie could not stop herself speaking.

"When is the wedding to be?" she asked, astonished that her voice came out perfectly normally.

"June the twenty-first, the longest day," Lorraine said, clasping her pretty pale hands in a prayer-like gesture. "Quite the best month for weddings, don't you think? Then we are to tour Italy for a fortnight. It is sad it is so short, but Philippe says that he cannot spare more time from his business." She pouted. "I tell him that one only has one honeymoon, but you know how men are when it is a question of *les affaires*. But he says that I shall have enough to do, preparing our apartment, and indeed there is much to be done."

Rosie felt herself go cold. An apartment? Please God not *their* apartment.

"Where are you to live?" she asked.

"Philippe has bought an apartment in a new block at Neuilly," the girl chattered on. "Of course, I am more accustomed to living in the country, but I personally believe Neuilly to be the perfect compromise. You have no idea how many trees there are, and the avenues are so

223

wide, and yet it is only fifteen minutes to Philippe's *bureau*. We even have our own park to wander in, and it will be almost private since there are only four other apartments in the building. Philippe has promised I may have a little dog so I shall not be lonely when he is away on his travels. I thought a poodle, a white one, they are so adorable, though a pug would be less trouble to groom. Oh, I shall have much to please myself with, and, of course, I can always visit with dear monsieur, or go home to my family in Tours. But hopefully I shall soon have a little one to occupy my time."

André's hand tightened on her shoulder, to give her courage.

"Madame Dupuis is a business colleague of Philippe's," he informed Lorraine. "Madame is a maker of fine champagne, and she is one of Philippe's clients."

"I think I have heard Sebastian speak of you," she said. "Did you not rescue him on a boat when he was very little?"

"Not exactly rescue," Rosie said. "He was only lost. In no danger." She began to get to her feet, conscious that she could not bear too much more of this. She felt a pang of pity for Philippe. The girl was a self-indulgent bore, and curiously middle-aged. Pretty she might be, but a threat to the passion that she and Philippe shared – never.

"It was nice of you to lend me Sebastian," she said to André as she smoothed down her dress.

"There is nowhere else he would rather be," André said. "Do you not think he has grown?"

"He has become a man," she agreed.

"And insists on going into the army."

"He told me. He said you don't approve."

"Killing is no business for a gentleman," he said, his voice sombre, "though few would agree with me. I am convinced that there will be trouble with the Boche again. And next time, a modern war with modern weapons will create carnage."

Rosie shivered. He was the wisest person she knew, and his anxiety transmitted itself to her. Not to Lorraine who was saying brightly: "But he will look so handsome in his uniform."

"Indeed he will," André agreed, suddenly hearty. "He will have his pick of all the girls."

"Be tolerant. She is only eighteen," he whispered as he saw Rosie to the door after she had said her polite farewells to Philippe's future bride. She even wished her a happy wedding day, though the words nearly jammed in her throat.

"Eighteen going on forty," Rosie whispered back. "And a silly forty at that."

"But no danger," he said.

"No danger at all."

No, no danger at all, Rosie thought, as she walked the distance between the Île de la Cité and the Gare de l'Est. It was a long walk, but she had time to waste before she was due to meet Lizzie, Alexander and Allie, and then catch the train home. She had planned to spend most of the day with André, but there was a limit to what she could stand listening to if Mademoiselle Delperrier intended to stay for lunch. Weddings, babies, new apartments, pet dogs – shared with Philippe – were the things she had always wanted. But could never have. Envy burned as if she had drunk bad wine.

No danger, true, but silly little bird-head Lorraine would be his wife. And have all those important things and first claim on him. But how could he bear to live with her? He would bear it, she realised, because of her. It would be a sham marriage. She knew he should have a real marriage, a happy marriage, but she stood in the way. André was right. They must snatch at whatever happiness they could, because normal, wedded happiness was not for either of them.

She ate a solitary simple lunch in the brasserie opposite the Gare de l'Est, lingering over her coffee. Then she took a brisk walk down the Boulevard Magenta to the Place de la République, and back. Girding herself to hide her misery, she stood waiting for Lizzie and the others.

The twenty-first of June would truly be the longest day, she thought. The longest day ever.

Chapter Fifteen

It was fortunate that Lizzie was in a happier frame of mind than Rosie had seen her since the day she arrived. She had bought a great many clothes, and all three of them, Lizzie, Allie and Alexander, were laden with bags and packages with expensive looking wrappings.

"I have been so naughty, Rosie," she said gaily. "I declare I have spent a fortune, and I fear I shall have to ask you for the loan of some money until Jim comes."

They were settled comfortably on the train, speeding past the suburbs of Paris. Dusk was falling, and the gas lights twinkled in the streets outside. The two young people were in the corridor, looking at the view.

Jim? It sounded like a change of heart.

"You have been in touch with Mr Webster?" Rosie asked cautiously.

"Not yet, but I think I should tomorrow. I do miss him, I'm afraid. Of course, I am still very angry with him, but it is not possible to stay away for ever." She sighed. "I think perhaps the separation will have done us good. Do you think he will have missed me?"

"I'm certain of it," Rosie said stoutly. "And tomorrow, first thing, we will send Henri to the telegraph office with a message to say where you are. Do you think he will come to get you?"

"I'm certain of it," Lizzie said, a touch complacently. "He will be astonished that I managed to get here alone, but I am certain that he will not let me make the return journey by myself."

Rosie nodded, privately hoping her friend was right. She was wondering why there had been no reaction to the telegraph she had sent the morning after Lizzie's arrival. It would be quite dreadful if Mr Webster had taken the excuse to go off and live with his mistress. Lizzie could unwittingly have handed him his freedom.

Having made the decision about Mr Webster, Lizzie then proceeded to tell Rosie about her day. She had shopped and shopped until she thought her feet would drop off, but then they had taken a little snack lunch at the Crillon. It had, she said, been the most lovely day. And when Mr Webster arrived, she was planning to take him shopping in Paris, too.

"He will be amazed at how I found my way around," she said. "You know, Rosie, this has all been very good for me. I see now that I am not such a silly person as I always thought. I can do things for myself, and I think perhaps I am not so unattractive. I may be nearly forty, but there was a gentleman at the Crillon who was giving me the most admiring looks. Even Alexander remarked upon it."

"You are a very pretty woman, Lizzie," Rosie said, full of foreboding that maybe Lizzie would have need of her newfound independence if Mr Webster had bolted for freedom.

"Well, when I am home again, I propose to try to do what you say, Rosie." She was beginning to turn a little pink. "Would you tell me what to do to keep Jim with me? I realise you are right, and that it is my fault. All that is necessary to men, I suppose," she said, her voice resigned.

"I'll try," Rosie said, blanching at the thought of explaining. "But the best way would be to ask Mr Webster what he would like you to do, and then try to ... do it ..." her voice trailed away.

"I must change my attitude, I can see that." Lizzie nodded her head firmly, giving instructions to herself. "Now I no longer have him all to myself and have been away from him, I realise I do love Jim, and if I am to keep him away from other women I must be a wife in every way. That is the difference between us. I think that you can never love Clovis, and so you do not care."

Rosie only nodded, wishing she had never sent the telegraph. If she had not sent it, she would not be feeling this sense of foreboding. She swore to herself that never, never again would she interfere in matters that were not her concern.

Lizzie had leaned back her head and closed her eyes, a little smile on her lips. The two young people had their heads together in the corridor. Compared with Sebastian, Alexander was young for his age, Rosie thought. He seemed content with Allie as company, though it was true that Allie was engaging company for everyone, and of all ages. Rosie had noticed that her daughter had been hurt for the first two days of Sebastian's visit because he had taken little notice of her, whereas in the past they had been inseparable, like brother and sister. But fortunately, as her English was more fluent than Sebastian's, Alexander had naturally gravitated towards her. His attentions had appeared to mend her broken heart quickly enough.

But then young hearts only dented.

She dozed for a while, and only stirred as the train pulled into Rilly-la-Montagne station. There was a fuss and a confusion as they tried to get all the parcels together. Each one of them was loaded as they climbed down onto the platform, laughing at the amount they had to deal with.

"Henri will cope with it," Rosie was saying, when suddenly Lizzie dropped all the parcels she was carrying, turned white and swayed on her feet.

"Lizzie! What's the matter?" Rosie gasped, grabbing her friend's arm.

"It's all right," Alexander cried as he started to run down the platform. "It's Papa."

Striding down the platform was the solid figure of Mr Webster, the heavy black moustache now white, the hair thinner and the face redder. But he looked what he was – a man of power and purpose.

Lizzie had not moved, and then, when he was just three paces from her, she gave a little gulping cry and flung herself into his arms. He held her very tight as she sobbed her heart out on his shoulder. And at that moment, Rosie felt the most enormous sense of relief.

Lizzie must have sobbed for a full two minutes, while her Jim patted and soothed her, and then he gently pushed her away from him, looked into her face, and said: "Now that's enough of that."

But Lizzie's tears flowed on as she babbled her relief. "Oh, Jim, I can't believe that you're here. How did you know how to find me? Oh, Jim, you must love me to have found me. I wasn't going to tell you where I was. Well, I was going to tomorrow, but not before. I wanted you to miss me and be sorry you hurt me. But you found me, all this way from home. Oh, Jim, only you could do it."

A look of faint puzzlement spread over Mr Webster's face, and Rosie, standing well behind her friend, caught his eye and put one finger to her lips, her expression pleading silence and promising explanations later. Mr Webster was not a leader of men for nothing. The message was received.

"Of course I found you," he said, stroking her hair. "I would have gone to the ends of the earth to find you."

Rosie nodded approvingly.

Lizzie gave a huge, gusty sigh and laid her head on her husband's chest, groping for the handkerchief in his top pocket as she did so.

"Oh, Jim, I forgive you," she said. "I love you. To think you found me ..."

Mr Webster gave Rosie a most un-tycoon-like grin over his wife's head, and then seeing his son's wondering face, became serious again.

"Good to see you, son," he said, thrusting out the hand that was not holding Lizzie. "I guess you've been looking after your mother."

"No." Lizzie drew back from his grasp haughtily. "I have been looking after both of us."

"I see," he said, and Rosie could see that puzzlement was setting in again.

Quickly she said: "Why do you think we always meet on railway stations, Mr Webster? But welcome to France, and to Champagne."

"It's good to be here," he said, gently disengaging himself from Lizzie. "There were times when I thought I'd never make it. Boy, have I had difficulty making myself understood. But your Henri helped. He's outside with that incredible automobile of yours. I've got to have one just like it."

Rosie understood his problem. There was no one at Les Hérissons who spoke a word of English.

"You must have had a terrible time," she said, "but obviously someone managed to tell you that we were in Paris."

"Not really," he said. "Your Henri dragged me here to the station. At first I thought he was just trying to ship me off. But when I tried to get on a train, he wouldn't let me. Sensible guy, that Henri."

Rosie began to relax. It seemed to be working out even better than she could have planned, not that she had actually planned anything other than to get Mr Webster to France. As long as he didn't spoil it all by mentioning the telegraph.

Happily he didn't say a word, and once they were back at the house, and Lizzie had rushed upstairs to tidy herself, Jim Webster wanted to know what it was all about. He and Rosie were alone. The young ones had gone to feed Allie's rabbits, Madame Dupuis had bustled off to instruct Marie and the cook, and there was, as usual, no sign of Clovis.

"Didn't Lizzie send that telegraph?" Mr Webster asked.

Rosie shook her head.

"No, I did. Rather, Henri did, and I suppose he forgot to sign it. I didn't tell her what I had done, though, because she was determined to worry you. I just thought it was unwise to make you too anxious. You might have started calling in the police or something. But she was so angry with you she didn't care."

"Don't I know it!" he groaned. "I went crazy when I found she had gone, but I guessed she wouldn't do anything too terrible since she had Alexander with her. But I couldn't think where she could have got to. I've had half New York looking for her. I guess it never occurred to me that she'd do anything as daring as getting on a boat and going to a strange country, all on her own."

"Well, she was with Alexander," Rosie smiled. "And I think you might find her rather a different woman for the experience. More interesting, maybe," she added with a naughty twinkle she couldn't resist.

He frowned.

"She hasn't – "

"No, she hasn't done anything except think hard about herself and your marriage. I think she's going to try to play her role, if you don't break the rules."

"She told you?"

"Yes."

"You think I'm a bastard?"

"Not really."

"Not shocked?" His face was red with embarrassment.

"No, not really. I've been living in France a long time, Mr Webster. Attitudes are different here. I gather you didn't have much choice."

He sighed.

"Not a lot. I'm fifty-two, time's passing by. I've made a packet, and I love Lizzie. Loved her from the moment I saw her; always will. She's the best little woman in the world ..."

"But you wanted a bad little woman for a while," Rosie suggested, smiling.

"That's about it." He suddenly stared at her. "This is no way to talk to a lady. I'm sorry."

"All you should be sorry about is that you didn't talk to your wife more like this," Rosie said. "It might have saved you a lot of heartache." Was she lecturing? It was time to change the subject. "Anyway, why did it take you so long to get here? I was beginning to believe that you'd taken the opportunity to run off with this other lady."

"Well, to tell you the truth I was so damned mad with Lizzie for frightening me like that I thought I'd let her sweat for a while." He hung his head like a reproved schoolboy.

"I see. Well, since she thinks you've been combing the world for her, I wouldn't mention that," Rosie said dryly. "Maybe you'd better take her on a second honeymoon since you're in Europe. It might be better than the last."

His face brightened.

"I was thinking exactly the same thing myself," he said. "I was wondering about Italy. What do you think?"

Italy! The man was saying Italy!

"A good choice," she said evenly. "Italy's very popular this year. Why don't you tour?"

It was decided that Alexander would stay at Les Hérissons while his parents went off on their second honeymoon. An arrangement that delighted Alexander and did not displease Allie.

Rosie felt that all was well that ended well, too, since Mr Webster, on hearing her plans for personally labelled champagne, had immediately said it was a brilliant idea and he would buy a great deal of it for the Pullman carriages in his trains.

Rather defensively, Rosie had said that trains were not exactly what she had in mind. Even Pullman carriages. And she had taken him and Alexander to her tasting room and given them a blind tasting of Dom Perignon, a Pommery vintage 1904, and her own 1906 vintage.

Alexander enjoyed all three equally, and found the tasting room fascinating. Mr Webster, a man who knew his champagnes, gave the matter some thought before he pronounced the Dom Perignon the best of the three, but insisted there was little difference between the Pommery and her wine.

"I'm flattered," she said, "but now you see my wine is very good – and very expensive."

"In which case, to hell with the passengers," he said. "I'll have it for the boardroom! But you won't sell anywhere near as much."

"I'm not looking for a huge market," she told him. "I want to make really beautiful champagne and sell it to people who will appreciate it, and won't mind paying the right price. I don't want to make wine for grocers."

He nodded and said: "I'll take another glass of your 1906 if I may. That is most certainly not for the grocer."

After Mr Webster had taken Lizzie off to Italy, life at Les Hérissons settled back into its usual, and more peaceful, routine. Clovis, as always, spent his days in the fields, and Alexander, observing the life around him, thought that Rosie seemed to sleep a great deal. She seemed like someone trying to lose time.

But he was content with Allie for company. He was fascinated by the girl. He had never met anyone like her. Though she was only ten years old, coming on eleven, as she insisted, there was a maturity about her that was quite unlike American girls of her age. She adored teaching him things – French, the way the winery was run, how grapes were kept healthy, how to make the best mustard from your own mustard seeds, the life and death, including the birth cycle, of a rabbit.

The outpouring of information was never boring, because Allie had the trick of turning everything into a story. Her head was crammed with stories. They only had to see an old man or a young girl, anyone, on the streets of Chigny when they took their long afternoon walks and Allie had a story about them.

But she could listen, too. He told her about his own life in New York, and how he was to go to university – Harvard – because his father thought it had more class than Yale. He told her how obsessed with class and getting it right his father was. He told her things that he had never told anyone else.

231

For a while it puzzled him that someone who chattered as much as she did – when she wasn't reading a book – could know so many stories. Then it dawned on him. It was because she listened as well. People told her their stories and she stored them all in her head, like the squirrels in Central Park stored nuts in their cheeks.

He thought quite seriously about marrying her when she was older. The age gap was only seven years – nothing like as large as that between his parents He discovered that she longed to see America.

"You know that Mama is really American, of course," she said, "but nobody likes to speak of it. Grandmother likes to pretend that Rosie is Champenoise. I don't really know why, but there is some great mystery there that one day I shall find out about.

"Mama sometimes tells me about America, and the time when she stayed with you in New York. It sounds wonderful. One day I shall definitely go."

It was all 'one day' for Allie. One day she would do this. One day she would do that. Alexander felt that she would probably achieve all the 'one day' dreams, and therefore when she was grown-up she would not consider marrying anyone as quiet and dull as he.

For she was very pretty. Her mama might have warned her that she might grow up to be plain, but he thought the chances were small. Her glossy dark hair fell in long waves down her back, except when "Miss", the governess, insisted it was braided during lessons. Her whole face, with the dark eyes, the pointed, thick black eyebrows and full mouth, would not change now. She would have hundreds of suitors.

It was madness for him to be thinking this way about a ten-year-old girl, but madness or not, he told himself, 'one day' he would marry Allie.

April slid into May, the grapes flowered early, it was hot and dry and in early June Lizzie returned from her second honeymoon to collect Alexander and take an ocean liner back to New York.

She confided to Rosie that she still did not like 'it' too much, but that changing her attitude had helped.

"But men do want to do very strange things, don't they?" she said, her voice both resigned and puzzled.

They both cried at saying goodbye, and Lizzie begged Rosie to come to New York, and bring Allie with her.

"Alexander is quite enchanted with her," she said, "and she has told him how she longs to see New York, and America, the land of your birth. Please do visit with us, dear Rosie. It would be such joy for Jim and me."

"I will, one day," Rosie promised.

It was just a few days after her guests had gone – and Les Hérissons seemed strangely quiet without them – when Philippe telephoned her.

It was something he rarely did, and she was afraid that her heightened colour and excitement would show as she went to take the call.

"Rosie?" Her heart lurched at the sound of his voice. "Philippe, here. I have good news for you."

For one joyous moment she thought he was going to say that his marriage was not taking place; that he had changed his mind.

"Have your circumstances altered?" she asked cautiously.

"No." He said it abruptly, understanding what she meant. "It's a matter of business. But we must meet to discuss it. Shall I come to Reims or will you come to Paris?"

She remembered the Parisian presence of the dreadful Lorraine.

"Better you come to Reims?" she suggested.

"Yes, probably. Can we meet tomorrow? Around midday? At the office?"

She hesitated, and he added: "Please."

"I'll be there," she told him.

She shut her eyes after she had hung up, and stood, the column of the telephone clutched in her hand. She had meant to say 'No', she had meant to say it was over. But at heart she had known she would do no such thing.

She fussed about what to wear before leaving for Reims on the following morning. Of course she was not going to let him make love to her, but nevertheless she took out her newest and prettiest pure silk underwear. It had been a present from Lizzie, bought on the day's shopping spree in Paris. But looking in the chest of drawers in which she kept her underthings, she came across the black corselet she had bought so long ago in San Francisco. She smiled, remembering the last time she had worn it on that first day with Philippe, and the other occasion when it had seemed to bring her happiness. On an impulse, she decided to wear it again that day. Just in case.

He was already waiting in the apartment when she arrived, standing, looking out of the window. He spun round as she came into the room, having let herself in with her key.

"I wanted to see you arrive," he said, "but you must have walked under the window."

Normally she walked on the cathedral side of the road so that he could see her coming down the street. Today she had quite deliberately not done so. Without replying she put down her umbrella and carefully took off her hat, fussing with the pins.

"How are you, Philippe?" she asked, her voice cool. "The trip was a success?"

"It was a great success," he said gravely.

Knowing he wanted to kiss her, she moved so that a small table set in

233

the middle of the room separated them. She was having to restrain herself from rushing into his arms, she was so pleased to see him. But he looked tired and thinner, and she noticed that his moustache was losing its bright blond colour. Her heart contracted at this sign of his getting older, just as she was getting older herself.

"I'm pleased for you," she said.

"You should be pleased for yourself, too." He moved a pace nearer to her, and she almost backed away, afraid of what would happen if he came too close. "You asked me to sell your champagne to a member of the British royal family, and I have done it."

She gaped at him and he grinned.

"You should know your wish is my command," he said, bowing. "Your client, who has given detailed instructions, even a drawing of how his label must be, is a royal duke. And you are commanded to meet him at Their Majesties the King and Queen of England's Garden Party at Buckingham Palace in July."

"Say all that again," she said faintly.

He opened his mouth, and she waved a hand to stop him.

"No, I think I understood. I just can't believe it."

"You are to attend in your own right as the proprietress of a company making wine for a member of the royal family. Clovis is not invited."

"How strange to invite a woman on her own," she said.

"And I am to be there in my own right, as someone who supplies the royal family with wine," he said. "My future wife is not invited."

She did not know what to say. While she hesitated, he said: "Shall we go to London together, Rosie?"

His blue eyes were beseeching her. She looked at his bony, intelligent face, the mouth with the sensuous lower lip, and the silky blond hair, and loved him so much, wanted him so much.

It was time to stop playing games. She nodded.

"And there is more," he said. "I have sold your Les Hérissons champagne to Congressmen and Senators in Washington, and to tycoons in New York. You are invited to a wine congress that takes place in New York at the end of July. There will just be time to take the boat from England. Shall we go to New York together as well, Rosie?"

She drew a deep breath, hardly able to believe what she was hearing.

"Yes – if it is possible, Philippe," she said meekly.

He lifted the small table that separated them and the collection of tiny ornaments that decorated it slid about alarmingly. He set the whole thing aside, and took her in his arms. With a sigh she stayed there.

"Rosie, my Rosie, I love you so much," he said. "Do you realise that this will be the first time we will ever have been free to be together for a long, long time – day and night."

"Will it be possible, though?" she asked, her head buzzing with the difficulties. "What will Mama and Clovis say?"

"They will be thrilled when you show them the invitations," he assured her. "An invitation from the King of England!"

She clung to him.

"Dare I?"

"If I dare leave my bride of one month, can you not leave your husband of eleven years?"

"But Philippe, you know it's different for women."

"These invitations are not to a woman, they are to the proprietor of the champagne company," he said stubbornly.

"Then they should have gone to Mama."

He laughed and hugged her.

"But I wouldn't have gone to all that trouble to get them for your mama-in-law."

She had to laugh, too.

"But seriously, they will be shocked unless I take one or other of them. It will look improper to go alone with you. Even if you are a married man by then," she added tartly.

"Then take Allie," he suggested. "The experience will do her good."

It was one solution. She thought about it and said: "Lizzie was most anxious that Allie should visit New York. Alexander is quite smitten with her, young as she is."

"But what shall we do with her in London?" he asked.

"I shall have to have her with me," she said slowly. "I know no one in London. And we would have to have her with us all the time on the boat, unless, of course, we took Miss as well. Miss could look after her, but we would have to be so careful."

"Rosie, to have you that close for so long would be sufficient for me, even if I never even put my arms round you," he said, hugging her tighter to him. "Maybe Miss could take her off somewhere in England. After all, neither of them is invited to the Garden Party. We shall only be in London for two days."

"And what are you going to say to your new bride?" she asked, moving out of the circle of his arms. "I am told that the wedding day is the twenty-first of June and that for your honeymoon you are touring Italy before you return to a charming apartment on the outskirts of Paris where, if one used one's imagination, one could imagine oneself in the country."

He looked startled.

"How do you know these things?" he asked.

235

"Didn't your father tell you?" She walked away and looked out of the window at the cathedral.

"No. I have hardly seen Papa since I returned. What should he have told me?"

"That I went to visit him and your Lorraine arrived to discuss the wedding plans. Have you been informed that you are permitted more guests since her papa has been able to hire a larger room at the Ritz than was expected."

He was looking decidedly uncomfortable.

"She told you all that?"

"Yes, her entire conversation consisted of your wedding, your honeymoon and her plans for your future family. She assured us both that she will soon be busy with a little addition to the Lefevre family."

"Oh, my God!" he said softly. "I am so sorry, my darling."

"It's all right," she said, her voice resigned. And now she had spilt out the weeks of remembering that nightmare conversation, it was all right. But she was still not quite ready to stop baiting him and added, turning to smile at him: "She's very pretty."

"That is true."

"And very stupid."

"Rosie! Please."

"But isn't she?"

"She is very young."

"And stupid."

"Yes, if you insist, she is stupid. And that is why you and I will be able to go to London and New York together, because we will both be married to stupid people." He paused, and then, as if he were interrogating her, demanded: "Did you make love with Clovis after the last time?"

The question took her by surprise.

"No. He didn't want to. I think he had been to see his whore, and he can't manage it too often." The truth seemed best.

He looked concerned.

"Was everything all right?"

"How would you feel if it wasn't?"

"Rosie, if you were carrying my child, I would be the happiest man on earth. Are you?"

She shook her head without speaking.

"Ah, my darling," he said sadly. "We are storm-tossed, but we will go away together, taking what happiness we can. Just please stop being angry and bitter with me now. It is so unlike you that I don't think I can bear it."

She melted at the words, and moved to hold him tight to her.

"I'm sorry," she said. "Truly sorry. But it hurt to meet Lorraine and

236

to hear her talk of having your child. You must understand that."

He hugged her back, and bent to kiss her lightly on the mouth.

"No more quarrels," he said. "Just tell me if you will come away with me?"

"I will come away with you," she said.

"And shall we still be lovers?"

"We shall still be lovers."

"In which case," he said, "may I make love to you now?"

Madame Dupuis was beside herself with pride when Rosie showed her the thick white engraved card that invited her daughter-in-law to be a guest of the King and Queen of England.

"But it is unbelievable," she said, awed, "for such a thing to happen. You will go, of course, Rosie. What tales you will have to tell us when you return."

"I think our champagne is becoming famous, Mama," Rosie said, choosing her words with care, "because I am also invited to the International Congress of Wine in New York the following week, after the Garden Party. There will just be time to get there. All this, of course, is due to Philippe Lefevre. He has worked hard to get our champagne internationally known. We should be very grateful to him. We are to supply a royal duke, one of the old King's sons, with our champagne, especially bottled for him. That is why both Philippe and I have been invited to Buckingham Palace. And in New York, members of the government are buying our champagne, so we have been invited to take part in a competition to find the best champagne in the world."

Madame Dupuis looked troubled.

"Monsieur Philippe will be going too?"

"Why, naturally," Rosie said, making herself sound surprised at the question.

"I see." Madame Dupuis frowned. "Is it wise to travel with him?"

"I thought I should take Allie and Miss with me," Rosie explained. Madame's face cleared and she let out her breath in relief.

"It will be a marvellous experience for Allie," she said. "But if I may make a suggestion, Rosie dear ..."

"But of course," Rosie said.

"Perhaps we will not mention to Clovis that Monsier Philippe is to travel with you. It will only make him anxious."

"If you think so, Mama," Rosie agreed gravely, unable to believe that fate had presented her with an unwitting ally in her mother-in-law.

The longest day passed by without too much pain, for Rosie was so occupied she scarcely knew the date from day to day. And besides, in the shorter days to come, the days of high summer, she would be with Philippe. She could afford to wait.

Letters were written to Lizzie, accepting her invitation, and she was busy about her business, constantly supervising the endless routine of creating fine champagne. The champagne she intended to present at the congress had to be chosen and dispatched. It must be at Philippe's warehouse in New York in good time so it could rest before entering into competition with sparkling wines from all over the world. Madame was appalled at the idea of what she contemptuously called grape fizz from Italy and Spain, and indeed America itself, being compared with the true, the only veritable champagne.

"How can this stuff call itself champagne when it does not come from Champagne!" she snorted.

Rosie explained that she believed that there were different categories.

"I should hope so," Madame said, with an audible sniff.

Rosie saw little of Clovis. He was busy in the fields with his workmen. As if to make up for the past three years the weather was perfect for the wine-grower. And Clovis was content. He, too, was proud that his wife was to visit the royal family, just as long as he did not have to accompany her, for he said that he would explode with misery if he had to be among all those people jabbering in a foreign language. In his eyes it was a perfectly natural thing that his wife should meet a real King and Queen, for she was a queen among women herself, and by the time he had told it to all her clièntele, Chigny les Roses was buzzing with the news. And it was not a mere garden party that Rosie was to visit, but a tête-à-tête with the new Queen of England, a German lady (which was not in her favour), but nevertheless said to be *charmante.*

The vineyard workers and the cellar men were equally proud that the fruits of their labours were receiving their rightful due and sliding down the throats of royalty. At Rosie's urging, Clovis cracked a few bottles of their 1906 vintage for the staff and created a little party in the main cellar where the men drank to the success of their champagne. And, again at Rosie's urging, Clovis announced a bonus.

Miss, being English, was also highly impressed with the news. Miss's name was Thoronson, a word almost impossible for French tongues to climb round, so she was simply called Miss by everyone at Les Hérissons. Allie was fond of her, even though Miss was strict and allowed no nonsense. She was a quiet girl, aged about twenty-two, whose father was a vicar in the south of England. When Rosie told her she was to accompany Allie, she was enchanted.

She had come shyly to Rosie and asked if perhaps it would be allowed for her to take Allie to her home while Rosie visited Buckingham Palace.

"To be honest, madame," she said, "I would like very much to see my family, but I also think it could be of help to Allie's education to see how the English live, and I do have younger brothers and sisters who would amuse her."

She explained she lived between Winchester and Southampton, and therefore it would be simple for her to meet Rosie off the Southampton boat train after the visit.

Rosie had to make journeys to Paris for new clothes. She endured long hours at Paul Poiret's salon until a wardrobe for the trip was at last designed and finished. She was a little aghast at how much money she was spending, but Philippe had promised her that her presence at both these occasions could only contribute towards the success of her champagne house.

The trips to Paris allowed visits to her dear André, and happily the odious Lorraine did not appear again. André twinkled at her news, and enquired if his son was to travel with her. When she told him yes, he smiled and said: "Am I to assume that he is to be forgiven for his temerity in marrying?"

And she sighed, smiled ruefully and said: "You may assume so."

Her departure, accompanied by Allie and Miss, was announced in *La Champagne*, their local newspaper, and the occasion became a party. All of Les Hérissons came to the station at Rilly-la-Montagne to see them off, Madame Dupuis, Clovis, Marie and Henri were there, even the little kitchen maid and some of the cellar workers and field hands turned up to wave them on their way. Rosie spotted the faces of some of the *vignerons* from whom they bought grapes and who obviously felt they had a part in this honour which had come to Les Hérissons. Since the night of the Ay riots, the attitude of the local people had imperceptibly changed. Neighbours who had barely said *Bonjour* before were waiting on the platform. The priest came down from his little old church at Chigny to bless their departure, and the priests from Rilly and Mailly, not to be left out, came too. The stationmaster, who was guard, ticket seller and cleaner (when his wife refused to sweep the platforms), wore not only his official uniform but his peaked cap as well. All that was missing was a brass band.

Rosie felt her eyes smarting as the crowd gathered on the platform in front of the little station building. They were happy and noisy because she was spreading the fame of their wine, just as many had done before her, and more would do in the years to come. She was producing her own *cuvée*, but the champagne itself was the thing, and to broadcast the special qualities of their region's wine was all-important.

"*Vive les Hérissons! Vive Madame! Vive la Champagne! Vive la France!*" they shouted, fists punching the air as the train pulled slowly away, leaving them behind while she, suddenly full of guilt, was on her way to join her lover.

*   *   *

239

"You were without doubt the most beautiful woman there," he said sleepily, his hand clasped over her breast.

"Flatterer!" She moved her head from the pillow for just the distance that it took to kiss his cheek.

"It is not flattery," he assured her. "It is truth. I would swear to my Maker that you were the most beautiful woman there."

She let out her breath in a long, slow stream.

"It was wonderful," she said. "It was the most exciting thing that has ever happened to me, with the possible exception of making love with you."

"Flatterer," he said lazily, in turn.

"I would swear to my Maker that I must be forgiven my sins because making love with you is the most exciting thing in the whole world."

They lay silent for a moment or two, bodies entwined, her legs curled between his, his arm under her shoulders, touching wherever it was possible to touch.

The rosy light of the setting sun filtered through the long windows of their hotel suite, bouncing off the grey ripples of the River Thames below. The room was large, but the single bed a little small for the two of them. But that did not matter.

She lay there in perfect peace, thinking about the afternoon they had spent. She pictured again the green lawn and fine gardens and lake, all enclosed by a high wall, sheltering the well-dressed people; men in top hats or colourful uniforms, women in soft summer dresses and extravagant hats. There were two military bands, one at each side of the vast camomile lawn, playing either military music or tunes from the operettas, and three huge marquees, all decorated differently. On the way in she had caught a tantalising glimpse of the interior of the palace before emerging onto a long terrace overlooking the King's garden. There had been an air of elegance and style such as she had never seen. She had the feeling, one that she had had just a few times in her life before, of having found her natural habitat, and the added triumph was that Philippe was there with her – not with Lorraine.

But they had agreed to forget Lorraine's existence for the next three weeks.

"I liked the Duke," she said sleepily. "What a splendid beard he had. And such charm."

"He quite fell in love with you. He was like a schoolboy at your feet. I doubt if he had ever encountered such a beautiful woman, surrounded as he is by those horse-faced English women." She knew he was teasing her and giggled. "If you had beckoned with your little finger, you could have sold him every drop of champagne that you make. It was not me that he invited to the royal marquee, but you," he said, tweaking her nipple so that she squeaked in mock alarm. "Had I

240

been without you, I should have been taking my tea and strawberries and cream with the mob. And had I been a jealous man, I would have challenged him to a duel."

"Umm," she said, rubbing the point of her chin into the hollow of his bare shoulder. "I thought some of the women were very pretty. Not as well dressed as they might have been, maybe, but so fair and doll-like. You could tell the ones whose dresses were made in France. I thought King George very handsome – I like his beard, too, and what extraordinary pale blue eyes he had. Did you not think that Queen Mary was an absolutely regal queen? She must have been a most beautiful young girl. But why did they ride among their guests in a carriage?"

"To prevent being jostled, maybe, and to see and be seen. And they noticed you in your buttercup yellow."

"Monsieur Poiret said that royalty always wear bright colours so as to be easily seen. He insisted on the buttercup yellow so that I could compete."

Rosie knew she had been seen. She knew that when she and Philippe had wandered through the crowd of aimlessly milling people, all searching for royal faces, eyes had turned to watch her; the women's with some envy, raking from her high, feathered hat down the length of the floating muslin gown to the small matching buttercup-yellow shoes. The men's eyes registered something quite different.

But she had held Philippe's arm and curtseyed deeply as King George and his Queen drove past in their carriage, presiding over their first Garden Party as reigning monarchs. Rosie wondered if they were nervous since they had only been crowned the day after Philippe had married, just three weeks before.

It was after the royal couple had passed that they happened upon the Duke, resplendent in naval uniform. His eye had also lit upon Rosie, and recognising Philippe, he sent his equerry to bring them to meet him.

The equerry enquired her name in a whisper. She whispered it back, and he then formally presented her to his royal master. She curtseyed low, trying to look as if she met royalty every day, and with eyes demurely lowered, reminded herself not to forget that she was really only little Rosie Brunner from Calistoga, U.S.A.

The Duke had addressed them in perfect French, and invited them to take tea in the King's marquee.

"So much more comfortable than the public marquees," he explained. "And the cakes are made by the palace chef and not a catering company. I can tell you from experience that those from the catering company are decidedly inferior."

The three of them, the equerry a pace or two behind, had walked

241

across the camomile lawn, chatting about champagne.

"My father, the late King, always called it 'the boy', you know," the Duke told them. "When he was shooting, a boy would follow him, carrying a bucket of champagne bottles on ice. He would cry for the boy to bring up a bottle, and in time it became known as a bottle of the boy."

"And which make did he drink, Your Royal Highness?" she asked.

He laughed, throwing back his head: "That would be telling,"he said.

Rosie had been conscious of whispers as the crowd parted in front of them and realised that people were asking who she was. And as she walked, head high, one hand lifting the brilliant buttercup-yellow muslin of her floating dress from the turf, the other holding a matching parasol (for Paul Poiret had promised her rain at an English garden party), she could not help feeling a sense of triumph. Perhaps taking tea with the British royal family was not the most important thing in the world, but just for that moment she decided to permit herself to think that it was.

Inside the marquee, the Duke told his equerry to see that they were seated and served, and then he took her hand and lifted it to his lips.

"You must excuse me, Madame Dupuis," he said. "I must do my duty and mingle with the crowds. I hope we shall meet again. Perhaps we may share a bottle of your admirable champagne one day. "

"That would be a great pleasure, sir." she said.

"For now, I suggest you remain here. As you see, you can watch the crowds outside without being jostled, and in a short while Their Majesties will enter here to take tea themselves. You will be able to get a very good look at them, if," he said, his look mischievous, "you as a good democratic French woman are interested in such things."

"Sir," she murmured, "there are few of us who are not interested in such things, and most who deny it are not speaking the truth."

He laughed, inclined his head towards her in a miniature bow, and said: "I trust we shall meet again."

"I too, sir," she said.

Remembering it all, she smiled to herself.

"Is he married?" she asked Philippe, to tease him, one hand scratching at the light blond hair on his chest.

"Who?"

"The Duke, of course."

"I don't believe he is."

"Just think," she said yawning. "If I played my cards right, I could be a duchess."

"You are a duchess, and a queen and a princess, and stop talking about the Duke. Pay attention to me."

242

"I did. Just now. I thought you wanted to sleep."

"I have changed my mind," he said, and rolled over to lie on top of her, his legs pushing between hers, his mouth kissing first her eyes, then her cheeks, and then descending on her mouth.

"I can't breathe!" she said plaintively.

He lifted his body from her, leaned on his elbows and smiled down at her.

"You *were* the most beautiful woman there, you know."

"And you the most handsome man."

"More handsome than the Duke?"

"More handsome and younger."

"You prefer younger men?"

"I prefer you."

"Good." He rolled off her, kissing the tip of her nose in passing. "Because tonight we are dining with a very elderly lord who wanted to meet you before deciding whether or not he will graciously permit you to make his champagne for him."

"Is he rich?" Rosie asked.

"Very."

"Then we will be making his champagne," she said, all confidence. "Lead me to him."

Philippe stood naked, hands on hips, his lean body most beautifully muscular, she thought.

"I will," he said. "Just as long as you put some clothes on first."

Allie was not at all sure she was enjoying this trip. It had been something of a blow to discover that she was not invited to the royal Garden Party, but instead would be spending two days at a country vicarage with Miss.

Miss's parents turned out to be elderly; a pair of wispy, dried-up people who looked as if they were made from fallen leaves. But they were kind and glad to see her, and so pleased to see their daughter – whom they called Pam – that Allie was glad that they had come. She really thought that the older Thoronsons did not look long for this world. Their younger children were slightly patronising. Since their French was excruciatingly bad, and her English was extremely good, Allie thought their attitude somewhat misplaced. And they asked such silly questions about France and life there, as though they thought that on the other side of the Channel was a barbaric land.

Also the huge rambling vicarage was freezing cold, even in July, but the garden was beautiful, full of flowers, most of which Allie had never seen before. It was so gloriously scented in the evening that she took to standing in the middle of the smooth green lawn and taking long, deep sniffs. Allie wished her mother could see it. They even had poppies growing in flower beds, cultivated for their beauty and not pulled up as weeds.

But it was a little dull, and she was missing her parents. She told herself philosophically that she would only be away from her mother for two days, and therefore bore with equanimity the watery greens and overcooked meat that seemed *de rigueur* in the vicar's household. Happily the early raspberries and the late strawberries and the most amazing thick cream from a local farm made up for Mrs Thoronson's cook's terrible treatment of food. And she liked the pretty little village where the Reverend Thoronson's church stood, and thought it much, much more charming than any village in Champagne.

Mrs Thoronson cried when Miss said goodbye, and Allie made up a story of how Mrs Thoronson had only been waiting for her Pam to come home before dying, quietly and at peace.

But when she said to Miss that she was sorry her mother's health was not good. Miss looked quite startled. She said that her mother was in rattling good form and fit as a flea, and whatever gave Allie that idea? So Allie decided that maybe English people just looked dried and desiccated like that. She wondered if it was anything to do with not having wine with their meals.

At Southampton, Allie was a little puzzled to find that they were travelling with Sebastian's father. She did not know why, but his presence made her uneasy. And she was disappointed to find that she and Miss were sharing a berth a deck below where her mother had a state room. She was put out by this, as she had shared her mother's cabin on the voyage from Le Havre.

The state room was large and comfortable with portholes so you could look out and see the sea, but on balance, Allie thought, her narrow little cabin with the two berths and the sink and washbasin was a great deal more exciting. The state room looked just like any old bedroom.

Allie was fascinated by the ship. It was at least ten times the size of the vessel that had taken her mother and Miss and herself over the Channel. Almost before they set sail from Southampton she had found her way around the liner, discovering the library, the restaurant, the games rooms, the decks that were permitted to the passengers and those that were only permitted to the crew. She determined to find some way to see those that were forbidden.

She loved the underlying sound of the engines, particularly at night when it sounded as if the boat had a great beating heart, just like a person. And when they were out into mid-Atlantic, she was awed by the vastness and loneliness of the grey, rolling sea.

There were disappointments. Her mother and Monsieur Philippe ate at the Captain's table; she and Miss were tucked into a corner. She chose the seat where she could watch her mother beguiling all in sight. Her mother was definitely one of the best dressed and most beautiful women on board, she decided, though she had no jewels to compete with some of the older, chic women. But her mother did not need jewellery, Allie thought, half-proud, half-envious. She dazzled without diamonds.

Right from the time they had left Chigny, Miss insisted that she still do her lessons. It was boring struggling with the arithmetic, but for her French and English lessons, she had to keep a diary of what she did each day. It was a little frustrating because, as Miss would mark her work, she could not say all the things that she wanted to, like about the watery vegetables and the superior attitude of Miss's sisters and brothers. But she got round the problem with a little secret notebook, so she would not forget to tell her father a single thing when she arrived home again.

All this writing meant that most of her time was taken up sitting in the ship's library, scribbling away and trying not to make blots with the new fountain pen that her grandmother had given her at the end of June for her birthday.

She took tea each day with her mother in one of the liner's lounges. Sometimes Monsieur Philippe was there, and sometimes he wasn't. She preferred it when he did not appear. She could sense a closeness between him and her mother that worried her and made her wish that her father was with them.

"Are you enjoying yourself, Allie?" her mother asked when they had been at sea for three days.

"Very much," Allie said, truthfully. "But I wish I could eat my lunch with you and not with Miss."

"What! And leave Miss to eat on her own?" her mother said.

"She could eat with Monsieur Philippe," Allie suggested.

Her mother laughed rather loudly.

"But Allie, Monsieur Philippe and I are here on business. We are promoting your father's champagne. We are sitting at that table for business reasons. It is you who are having the holiday."

"Then why is Miss making me do my lessons?" Allie said crossly.

"Because it will pass the time for you until we get to New York."

"But there are a million things I could do on this ship." Allie protested. "Could I stop the lessons, please, Mama?"

Her mother relented surprisingly easily.

"If you wish," she said. "But you may get bored."

"How could I get bored here?" Allie said, genuinely astonished that her mother should think this possible. "Mama, you have no idea how much there is to explore."

"Then be careful," Rosie said. "Ships can be dangerous places.

245

Keep away from the side."

"Mama!" Allie was on her dignity. "I am eleven. I am not a baby anymore."

"All right, my sweet." Her mother put down her teacup and rose to her feet. "I'll tell Miss that you are to be liberated from lessons."

Monsieur Philippe was walking across the thick carpet of the lounge and, dropping a kiss on her daughter's head, Rosie went quickly to meet him. It was as if she had forgotten that Allie was there.

Allie would have liked to explain how she felt to her mother, but she seemed to have no time for her. It was all Monsieur Philippe this and Monsieur Philippe that. And though Allie had always liked him because he was distinguished, *gentil* and Sebastian's papa, she was indignant because he monopolised her mother.

In her wanderings around the liner, she explored the lifeboats, wriggling under the tarpaulins that covered them to see what went on underneath and how they worked. She made up a story that they were shipwrecked and as the ship dramatically sank, holed by a huge rock, she, single-handed, dropped a lifeboat into the sea to rescue her mother who was already in the water and desperately swimming for her life. Monsieur Philippe was on the deck and her mother was crying to him to save her. But he could not swim and he was desperate to know what to do. It was she, Allie, who saved them both, bundling Monsieur Philippe into the lifeboat, and then dragging her mother from the sea.

"How can we ever thank you?" they both cried, and then she graciously forgave them for ignoring her.

But even if they were ignoring her, she was not lonely. In her explorations the other passengers would chat to her, and she found the sailors friendly. On deck they would point out different birds – sea birds which they assured her she would never see on land. She saw an albatross, which reminded her of the English poem Miss had made her read about the poor ancient mariner doomed to sail the seas for ever. It had been a very difficult poem, she remembered, full of funny words. But watching the setting sun turning the sea to glorious molten copper, she thought that wouldn't have been such a bad fate except for the dead albatross round his neck. It was a rather big bird and surely would have smelt quite dreadful.

It was watching the sunset that made her decide to get up early enough to see the sunrise. She decided not to mention it to Miss. Miss had taken to coming back to the cabin quite late and a little dishevelled, creeping about while Allie pretended to be asleep. Miss was not displeased that her pupil was liberated. She was having a gentle flirtation with a rather stiff young Englishman who was travelling to New York alone. He seemed quite smitten by Allie's governess and

246

threw lingering, longing looks across the dining room while they lunched. Allie knew Miss would much rather be lunching with him, but since Allie was made to go to bed early, they could dine and dance together every evening. As a consequence of these late nights, Miss was finding it difficult to get up in the morning.

The sailors said that five o'clock was the best time to see the sunrise and on the last day Allie made herself wake at five o'clock. She did it by banging her head on the pillow five times before she went to sleep. It worked. She woke to the minute, and carefully climbed out of her berth and dressed. Then quietly, so as not to wake Miss, she slipped out of the cabin and into the stuffiness of the dimly-lit corridor outside. She liked the corridors. The closed doors in rows made them secret and intimate. The corridors were full of stories.

Walking on tiptoe so as not to disturb anyone, she went up the companionway to the corridor where her mother's state room was. As she rounded the corner, imagining her mother sleeping peacefully, a door opened. Instinctively she shrank back into the shadows, but the figure leaving her mother's room was hurrying, head down, also on tiptoe, in the opposite direction. Allie held her breath and saw to her astonishment that the hurrying man was Monsieur Philippe, looking very guilty and strange. But why, she wondered, was he leaving her mother's cabin at five in the morning, and why did he look so furtive?

As he disappeared round another corner further down the corridor, it dawned on Allie that he must have done something dreadful to her mother to be there at that hour and looking so guilty as well.

In a sudden panic, forgetting to be quiet, she ran the few yards to her mother's door. It was not locked, and she burst in, crying, "Mama, Mama, are you all right? What has he done to you?"

Then she stopped. Her mother was seated at the dressing table, frozen still, a hairbrush in her hand, her expression a mixture of terror and dismay. The bed behind her was rumpled, and there was an untidy heap of clothes on the floor.

But the most terrible thing was that her mother was quite, quite naked.

It took Rosie five panic-stricken heartbeats to recover her wits as her daughter stood in the doorway of the state room, staring, horrified, at her.

And then the sense of survival that had never let her down yet returned.

"Allie, my darling," she said calmly. "Is something wrong?"

As she spoke, she was casually picking up her peignoir from the back of the dressing table chair and slipping it on before moving towards the child. She put her hand on Allie's forehead as if feeling for a

247

temperature, saying: "Don't you feel well? Not another headache!"

"I'm not ill, thank you, Mama."

Her child's voice and demeanour were hostile.

"Then what are you doing out of bed at this hour?"

"I was going to see the sunrise."

"Yes?" Rosie coaxed gently.

"And I saw Monsieur Philippe coming out of your room. He was creeping. I thought he had done something awful to you."

"To me? Philippe? Why would Monsieur Philippe want to harm me?"

"I don't know. It was the way he was moving. He looked guilty, as if he was hiding something."

She was still unbending, suspicious, her dark eyes staring straight into Rosie's, unloving, hostile.

"I expect he was trying not to wake anyone up. Poor Philippe was not very well. He came to me for some seasick and headache powders. He was in great pain."

"Why didn't you have any clothes on?" The words came out strangled. "What would Papa say?"

"Allie, my dear child." Rosie made her voice exasperated, bordering on angry. "You don't think I had no clothes on when Monsieur Philippe was here! You are a very naughty girl for even thinking such a thing. I was just getting back into bed when you burst in, frightening the life out of me. Don't ever do that again. You should not be out of bed, nor should you be wandering around the ship at this hour, and you should most certainly not be giving me such frights."

She could see to her relief that the scolding tone was having its effect. Allie began to hang her head.

"I am sorry, Mama," she said.

Rosie stifled a long sigh of relief.

"It's all right, darling," she said, giving Allie a hug. "It was nice of you to be concerned. Let's forget it now and go and look at the sunrise together since we're both completely awake. Would you like that?"

"Oh, yes please," Allie said.

"Very well then. Just let me get dressed."

Together they watched the sun come up in a blaze over the wake of the ship, turning the sea to fire, and Rosie hugged her daughter to her on the pretext she was cold. Allie, at first a little stiff, eventually snuggled to her side.

"Would you like to have breakfast with me, in the state room?" Rosie asked.

Allie's eyes shone at the thought, and her eagerness and pleasure gave Rosie a pang of guilt for how little time she had spent with her daughter since they left France.

"Good," she said. "You go back to your cabin and wash and dress properly and come back to me in about an hour, and I'll order an English breakfast for us both. How will that be?"

That was perfect in Allie's view, and she went scampering off while Rosie made her way swiftly to Philippe's state room.

She knocked very gently, and after a minute, sleepy-eyed and in a dark blue silk dressing gown, he opened the door.

He looked startled to see her.

"Is anything the matter?" he said as she slid under his arm and into the room.

"Yes, terribly the matter," she said, turning to face him. "Allie saw you leaving my room."

"Oh, my God!" he said. "But how?"

"She was on her way to watch the sunrise. You know what a romantic little thing she is. She just happened to pick the moment that you were leaving."

"What happened?" he asked.

"She burst in. She thought because you looked guilty, as she put it, that you'd done me some damage. I was sitting there, stark naked. I nearly died."

Swiftly she told him exactly what had happened, and what she had said, finishing: "I think she believed me. But, darling, today you must stay in your cabin. You're ill, and have decided to rest. I can't think of anything else to do. I've asked her to have breakfast with me, so for goodness' sake stay here. It will only be for a day. We berth tomorrow, and you can make a gentle recovery." She was near to tears as she said: "Oh, but Philippe, I would have given the world for it not to happen. I am so angry with myself. I love her so much, and have sacrificed so much for her, and now perhaps I have spoilt it all, because of this one chance to be with you. You and Allie are the two people I love most in the world, but I think perhaps I love you the most, and no mother should feel that. If she realises, if she understands the meaning of what she saw ..." Her voice trailed away. "She adores her father. If she thinks I am betraying him ..."

"She's too young to understand," he said firmly. "I'm sure of it, and you handled it beautifully, my darling." He took her in his arms, and rocked her. "Don't worry. She'll have forgotten the whole thing by tomorrow."

Rosie was not so sure. She knew her daughter's intelligence and quick mind. What she did not know was how much she understood of life. They had had no conversation on the subject, and as Allie did not go to the village school she had little chance to learn from the whispers of children her own age. But Rosie remembered her own instinctive understanding of such matters when she was a child. And she was fearful

249

that maybe once left to think, Allie would doubt her explanation.

But there was little she could do about it, except contain her own guilt, act naturally – and pray.

*   *   *

Dear Diary,

Today has been the very best day of the trip so far though it did not start out well and I thought something dreadful might have happened.

I had decided to watch the sunrise so I would be able to describe it in my diary for Miss, and I went all on my own at five o'clock in the morning. I had just got to the passage where Mama's state room is when I saw a man creeping from her room, all sly and furtive and looking as if he should not be there.

Then to my dismay, I saw it was Monsieur Philippe and because he looked so guilty I thought he must have done Mama a mischief so I rushed to save her.

The worst thing was that when I went into her room Mama did not have any clothes on at all, and it was a shock because I have never seen a grown-up without clothes before. I could not help staring at her and seeing how shapely she was, and that she had hair on her body, down there. I wonder if this is normal.

She covered herself with her peignoir, and she was angry with me for breaking into her room and thinking bad things about Monsieur Philippe. He had visited her for headache powders because he was not well. I could not help being glad that he was not well because it meant that Mama spent the last day on board the ship with me. She came and watched the sunrise with me, cuddling me to keep herself warm, and then I had breakfast with her in her state room.

But best of all, I was permitted to sit with her at lunch at the Captain's table. I had to promise not to chatter, but I did not even want to say a word. I just wanted to listen to what everyone was talking about. The people were so well-travelled, and talked of countries everywhere, all the places I shall go one day. Some of them were planning to journey to America next year on the newest most luxurious liner ever built. It is called the Titanic. One man said they should take all the pleasure they could because he believed that we would be at war again soon, which will really upset Grandma if it is the Boche all over again.

They all seemed so impressed with Mama, and enquired most kindly after Monsieur Philippe and they were very nice to me. The Captain wanted to know what I thought of his ship, and when I told him that I wanted so much to see the bits that no one was allowed to see, he laughed and said I should have a guided tour if Mama would permit it. She said she would permit it – if she could come too.

It was marvellous, dear diary, we went onto the bridge where they drive the ship, and down into the engines so I could see where the heartbeat comes from and we were even permitted a peek at the kitchens where you could not imagine how many people were working.

It was unkind of me, but I became gladder and gladder that Monsieur Philippe had a headache.

Mama even let me stay up later than usual, but she had to dress for the Captain's ball that night. She wore all white, with beautiful shiny beads all over her dress, and had white feathers in her hair. I was allowed to kiss her and see her leave for the ball, and then Miss was allowed to take me so I could see all the people going. Mama was definitely the best and Miss was cross because she wanted to get to the ball with her young man and I wouldn't leave until I saw Mama dancing.

I saw Monsieur Philippe there. I suppose his headache had gone. He was dancing with Mama and looking into her eyes like on the cinema. I wish he was not here, and I wish Mama had had her clothes on this morning. It does not feel right to have seen her without them, even though she was only like a lady in a picture in the Louvre.

And I think it best not to tell Papa about any of that. I think it would upset him. And I think that Mama might be cross with me, too.

I have to stop now, dear diary, and write in my official diary, but I shall just tell about the guided tour in that. The bit about Mama is private.

Philippe warned Rosie not to set her heart on winning any gold medals at the Congress.

"We're here to find clients," he said as they presented their credentials at the Waldorf Hotel where the Congress was to take place, "and to introduce you to the international world of wine. And to have some time together."

She smiled at him, and whispered: "The last bit is the best. If, of course, you have any time for me."

She was teasing him because she had been impressed to find that he was at the congress as a judge, not of champagne but of clarets. She now knew what his father had meant when he said that she did not understand in what high esteem her lover was held in the world of wine.

"I had not realised that you were so famous," she whispered after the tenth person had greeted him in the foyer of the Waldorf where he had taken a suite.

"I don't tell you everything," he said lightly, "but I'm only this popular *because* I am a judge. Those men are all exhibiting their wines. But since all the bottles are wrapped uniformly and the corks removed by an attendant, it's theoretically impossible to tell whose wine is whose, so they are wasting their time being charming to me. The judges are simply looking for the best. And, anyway, as you'll find for yourself, no competitor is allowed to be present when his wine is being judged."

In spite of his warnings, she still had hopes that maybe her Les Hérissons champagne would receive some mark of merit, if only to please Madame and Clovis and everyone back home. But at the receptions and small private parties which the various exhibitors gave – and she and Philippe seemed to be invited to them all – she listened, learned and found that the competitors were flatteringly interested in her.

The Europeans still talked of phylloxera and she was able to tell of her own success with imported cuttings; most of them were at last coming to the same viewpoint.

The talk from the Americans – who were enchanted to find that she was one of them – was of the prohibitionists. Would they gain power, or wouldn't they? She was shocked to find that prohibition could mean the United States government outlawing any kind of alcohol and that indeed there were already places in the United States where people were not permitted to buy wine.

"I could understand them not permitting people to drink whisky and gin," she said to Philippe, "but to forbid champagne, wine, and fine cognac is a crime against nature. Mama will never, never believe such a thing. But then, she has always thought us Americans barbarians."

"Us Americans?" he twinkled. "What's this?"

She laughed, a little embarrassed. But it was true that she did suddenly feel pride in being an American. New York was more amazing than ever. The bustle of it, the electricity in the air excited her. She knew she would probably never return there to live – France had become her home – but, looking at the tall buildings, how miraculously modern everything was and feeling the energy of the people, she felt this was not a bad heritage to share.

She was seeing very little of Lizzie and Jim Webster. Allie seemed content and occupied with Alexander to look after her. He was home for the summer before going up to Harvard, and happily showed an excited Allie his home town. Rosie was truly busy, only returning to Lizzie's mansion to sleep and to breakfast. She longed to stay at the hotel overnight with Philippe, but it was too dangerous. And besides, she was satisfied just being with him. She was finding his company as pleasing as his lovemaking. She felt that they were truly a couple.

Mr Webster, who had greeted her with great warmth, threatened to put in an appearance at the Congress.

"I'll bring along a millionaire or two," he promised. "They can taste that remarkable champagne of yours. I guess you don't mind millionaire customers, even if Pullman carriages won't do."

She laughed, and said if he really meant it, she would give a party for them all.

Afterwards the *New York Times* said in its social columns that her party was the highlight of the Congress. Philippe had drawn up the guest list, and though most of those invited were French and titled, he had included a fair sprinkling of British nobility, old-money Americans, and even Japanese and South Americans.

And then, of course, there were Mr Webster's millionaires, plus Lizzie, beaming with pride at her friend's success.

Under the heading "Call Me Rosie" the *Times* social columnist wrote:

> Is she American, or is she French, the beautiful young woman whose party in the Presidential Suite at the Waldorf last night eclipsed all other parties at the International Congress of Wine? Ask Madame Dupuis, or Rosie, as she prefers to be called, and she says in her charmingly accented English: "I was born here, but returned to my mother's homeland where I now make champagne."
>
> And what champagne! Connoisseurs were impressed. I was impressed, and so was an assortment of French counts, barons and princes, rubbing shoulders with British lords, earls and knights.
>
> I spotted a Rockefeller and a Vanderbilt or two and tycoon Jim Webster, who was there with his charming first-family Bostonian wife who assures me that Madame Rosie is an old friend of the family. Jim Webster had also brought along some millionaire friends who were charmed by their ravishing hostess.
>
> Her business partner, Monsieur Philippe Lefevre, who is a judge at tomorrow's claret tasting, is one of the foremost Parisian wine merchants and known as a world authority on the wines of Bordeaux. He assures me he has great respect for our native wines, and reminds me that a Californian wine won a gold at the last Paris congress.
>
> Madam Rosie is hoping her champagne will do well.
>
> "We have only been producing for seven years," she said, "but I would not wish to become a household name. We grow our grapes and blend our wines on our estate with only the connoisseur in mind. No expense is spared to please the client who wants

a fine champagne, carefully produced, and which we will bottle for him under his own label. I do not make wine for grocers."

Madame Rosie has made it big since her return journey to France. She supplies her Les Hérissons (it means the hedgehogs, folks!) champagne to a brother of the King of England, and a host of other titled personages.

Whether or not her champagne wins the coveted Gold this week, Madame Rosie is the toast of the Congress – a lady in the same mould as her predecessors in Champagne, Madame Pommery and the Widow Cliquot.

All New York wants to meet this elegant, charming expatriate who has a reputation for being one of the best-dressed women in Paris.

Last night she wore an outfit designed by the famous Poiret. Another envious lady guest described it as inspired by the Orient, with an unconstricted skirt topped by a short patterned tunic and worn with a turban and slave bangles – quite the latest thing.

Welcome home, Madame Rosie. Why don't you stay?

"But it's not true! I never even spoke to him!" Rosie gasped, as she read the article at breakfast the next morning. "Where did they get all that stuff from?"

"Me," said Mr Webster smugly. "Nothing like a little publicity to get the product moving."

Rosie was speechless and then she began to laugh.

"Mr Webster," she said, "you are a wonder! What would have happened to me if I hadn't met you on that railway platform that day?"

"Guess you'd have done all right," he said, beckoning the maid to pour him more coffee. "You're the kind no one and nothing can hold down. Like me. I recognise it. Did you like the 'call me Rosie touch'? Democratic, that's what you've got to appear in this country. If you're classy, rich, a bit of a snob and democratic at the same time, you can't fail. And speaking of that, isn't it about time you called me Jim?"

She was surprised to find that Philippe was delighted with the report, and he said much the same things as Jim Webster.

"I don't like it not being really true," she said doubtfully. "It makes me sound like some renegade blue-blood."

"It's true enough," he said cheerfully, "and you want to be rich, don't you? Now everyone really does want to meet you. Americans understand the value of advertising. You're a New York celebrity overnight."

She shook her head and giggled.

"I must say it's rather fun," she said.

The invitations to parties increased, including one to a soirée at the Vanderbilt mansion. Not to be outdone, Lizzie gave a superb dinner party for a carefully selected few, with Rosie as the guest of honour. She served only Les Hérissons champagne with a meal of caviare, fresh bay lobsters, perfect filet mignon and mountains of strawberries and cream.

It was a party that again led the *Times* social columns.

"I feel quite dizzy with it all," Rosie confessed to Philippe on the morning that the champagnes were to be judged. "I wish I could be there to watch the judging. After all, it is what we came for."

"I'll watch for you," he said. "You go shopping."

She did as he said, and spent a small fortune on gifts for home and for the new friends she had made. In a spirit of mischief, she bought Lizzie some very naughty underthings.

Her champagne did not win the gold medal, but it received the honourable mention awarded to a first-time entrant to the Congress. She was disappointed that it had not done better, but when Philippe told her the mention had been won above twenty-odd other new-comers, she was consoled.

"And the day after tomorrow we go home," she said sadly, after lunching in his suite. "Me back to Clovis and you back to Lorraine."

"Who is Lorraine?" he asked, silencing her with a finger on her lips before he kissed her.

There was to be a final dinner and ball to which every competitor was invited. Rosie decided to wear the white and silver dress that she had worn for the Captain's ball on the ship. It was the most striking gown that she had with her, and Philippe was anxious that she should be the best-dressed woman there.

"None of them must forget you," he said in his suite, and shyly proffered a small, wrapped box.

He had never bought her presents because of the difficulties of explaining them away at Les Hérissons, and she took the parcel and looked at him, eyebrows raised.

"I don't know what you'll say to everyone at home," he said, "you can throw them over the side of the ship on the way back if you want, but please wear them tonight, for me. They are my thanks for the happiest days I have ever spent."

Slowly she pulled away the wrapping paper, and underneath, in a blue box engraved with Tiffany's name and tied with white satin ribbon, were a pair of long, diamond earrings in the shape of two bunches of grapes. They lay in the box, glinting at her, and her eyes filled.

"Oh, Philippe, they are the most beautiful ..." and she burst into tears, flinging herself into his arms, sobbing uncontrollably.

"I can't bear to leave you," she cried. "Can't we stay here, together, for ever? Make a new life. Lots of people do now. I can't go back to Clovis. I can't. I can't."

She was clutching him desperately.

"Rosie, we can't," he said, stroking her hair. "What about Madame Dupuis, and Allie? What about the life you have built up? What about my papa and Sebastian? We can't abandon them all."

"You don't want to be with me," she accused him.

"Of course I do. But we both know it's not possible."

He let her sob until she regained control of herself and began looking around for a handkerchief. He pulled out his, and gently dabbed her eyes with it.

"I'm sorry," she said. "But it has been so wonderful."

"And we will have more times like this," he soothed. "Now we have been away together, people will take it for granted that we have business matters to deal with."

She was blowing her nose briskly and then suddenly asked:

"Did you tell Lorraine I was going to be here?"

He looked uncomfortable.

"Well, no. Did you tell Clovis?"

"Well, no."

They looked at each other, and suddenly she giggled.

"We are wicked," she sighed.

"We are, indeed. Now try on your earrings. They weren't meant to make you cry."

The earrings looked superb with the white and silver dress. Rosie had gone back to Lizzie's to get ready for the ball, and Lizzie's maid, who had a gift for dressing hair, was arranging her dark curls into a mass of high puffs which left the diamond grapes swinging and glittering against her olive skin, enhancing the matching glitter of her amber eyes. They were the first precious stones she had ever owned, but it was not the fact that they were diamonds that made them precious. It was because they were a gift from Philippe. She had already made up the lie to explain them. She would say that the earrings were her prize for winning the honourable mention. Clovis would never think to question it. Mama might just raise her eyebrows, but Rosie would explain how incredibly rich Americans were.

Jim Webster nodded approvingly when he saw her.

"Did I ever mention that you grew up real pretty?" he said. "And with class. You were looking for class and you sure found it."

Rosie could have cried, but that would have made her nose red again, so instead she sniffed, and hugged and kissed him, while Lizzie looked on, smiling.

"Jim is right," he said. "You look beautiful. I'm so proud of you."

The two of them, with Allie and Alexander, came to the front door of the mansion to hand her into the family Cadillac.

"I feel like Cinderella going to the ball," Rosie said as she waved them goodbye.

"But you look like a princess, Mama," Allie called as she was driven away.

Philippe was hovering anxiously in the doorway of the Waldorf when she arrived, and he hurried to take her into the foyer, removing her white fur wrap and handing it to an attendant.

"You look most incredibly beautiful," he said, and she could see in his eyes that he meant what he said. "I'm proud to be with you."

"It's the earrings that do it," she whispered, shaking her head gently so that they swung.

They went into the reception where the winning champagne, a Roederer, was being served, and instantly Rosie was surrounded by an admiring crowd.

She was talking to a group of growers from New York state when she realised that she had become separated from Philippe. Missing him, she gently disengaged herself from the group and began to look for him. He was a few feet away, facing her, and talking to a blond young man whose back looked oddly familiar. Rosie made her way through the crowd towards them, and as she neared she saw Philippe smile and say something to his companion.

The man turned just as she reached them. She began automatically to say 'Good evening', and stopped dead.

She was staring into the face of her brother Peter. Older, sophisticated, but quite definitely Peter.

Peter could not believe his eyes and ears as the incredibly attractive woman in silver and white flung her arms round him, hugged him and said: "Peter! Oh, Peter! I don't believe it! What are you doing here?"

It was beginning to dawn on him that the woman in the diamond earrings was his big sister. Cautiously, as she drew back to look at him, her face glowing with pleasure, he said: "Is it Rosie?"

"Of course it's Rosie!" she said. "Don't you recognise me. I recognised you immediately. Oh, Peter, I can't tell you how pleased I am to see you."

Peter's head was spinning as she turned to Lefevre, the judge, who he'd been talking to on Jean Paul's instructions. Jean Paul had said to get to know all the judges.

"Philippe, this is my brother, Peter Brunner. I've told you about him. Isn't it marvellous!"

The judge must be Rosie's husband, thought Peter, but how the hell did she ever get to marry a Frenchman?

"I wouldn't have recognised you, Rosie," he said feebly. "You've changed a lot."

"I'm eleven years older," she said. "But you look just the same. Are you here for the Congress? Have you come from home? How is home? How is Papa?"

Philippe Lefevre had taken them both by the arm and was leading them to a quieter spot in the room.

"You need to talk," he said, "but do you mind if I listen?"

"Papa is dead," Peter said baldly. It was the only thing he could say with safety until he had sorted things out in his mind. One thing had hit him with blazing clarity. He mustn't let Rosie know that he was with Jean Paul and that Jean Paul had returned. It had suddenly dawned on him why she had married a Frenchman. She must have gone to France looking for Jean Paul.

Her face had clouded over at the news.

"I'm sad," she said, "but I thought he must be. When did it happen?"

This was bizarre, Peter thought, looking around him frantically. A party where he was supposed to be making his mark for Champagne D'Or and he had to meet his long-lost sister, a sister who, under the circumstances, he never wanted to see again.

"Not long after you left. He had a fall and got pneumonia."

"Peter, how dreadful. And you were left alone. I am so sorry. How did you manage?"

"Well, I decided to go into champagne," he began cautiously.

"How extraordinary. I make champagne, in France. What a coincidence! Are you still in the same house with the same land?"

"I've improved it a little," he said. "And bought some more land." He didn't want to give too much away in case she decided it was worth coming back.

"And have you married?"

"No. Never had time."

"I should think not, running all that by yourself."

There was an awkward silence, broken by the loud, nasal voice of the Master of Ceremonies calling them into dinner.

"Why don't you arrange to meet Peter later?" Philippe suggested. "It's not a good moment to talk with all this going on. Go up to the suite for a while after supper. You can meet here at, say, ten thirty."

"Shall we do that, Peter? I want to hear every single thing about you, and everything that's happened."

"Of course," he heard himself saying, though he knew that while she might want to know, he was not going to tell. "Ten thirty, right here."

She gave him another impulsive hug and kiss and then, with a backward wave, went into the dining room with her husband.

Peter debated. Should he leave right now, or should he eat his supper? He made the decision to eat. After all, he had paid for the meal, and he could always get away before the speeches started. In the crowd, no one would notice him go.

But two things were certain. He wasn't having a long heart-to-heart with his long-lost big sister. And he wasn't going to tell Jean Paul that he'd met her.

Rosie could hardly contain her excitement all through the dinner.

"We were so close when we were little," she explained to Philippe. "There was just Peter and me against our father. We relied on each other so much, and I can't bear to think of him being alone there at the winery when father died. I should never have left him. He would only have been a kid, just about sixteen, and he hated being on his own. I'm so proud of him. Didn't he look handsome and successful? I would never have thought my little Peter could have done all that on his own."

She was impatient for the meal to be over, and kept asking Philippe to look at his watch to make sure that it was not yet ten thirty.

"Relax," Philippe said indulgently. "He's not going to run away."

But Philippe was wrong. Rosie waited, and waited, pacing up and down in the reception room, enquiring if anyone had seen a blond young man. It was nearly eleven thirty when Philippe came to look for her, and found her sad and near to tears in all her finery.

"Oh, Philippe," she said, her voice tragic. "He never came. I don't understand. Why? Why? Why?"

All the way back to California as the train rattled over mountain and plain, Peter thought about the incredible coincidence of meeting Rosie and in such a place. Now he had funked it and run, he was curious. What did she mean she was in champagne when her husband was an authority on claret? How had she got herself to France all those years ago? He remembered the man who had humiliated him on the station, and then how his father had humiliated him when he got home.

He had no reason to love Rosie, he thought, even if they had been close as children. She had abandoned him. What would have happened to him if Jean Paul had not returned did not bear thinking about. He decided to forget that their brief encounter had ever taken place.

Jean Paul was not pleased that Champagne D'Or had won no prizes.

"Couldn't you have influenced the judges?" he asked.

"It's not like that," Peter protested. "They taste blind. There was no way I could have tipped any of them off about which was our wine."

"Who did win?"

"A Roederer took the gold medal, and in the first entrant class it was also a French champagne that took the commendation. I brought you home the label. It's something to do with hedgehogs, they say."

259

"Hedgehogs!" Jean Paul seemed suddenly very interested. "Let me see that label."

"It's in my attaché case."

"Well, go and get it."

Jean Paul was pacing up and down the room when he got back with the Les Hérissons label. Jean Paul snatched it from his hand and stared at the drawing of a hedgehog in front of fields of pruned vines which looked like a giant hedgehog themselves. In the background was a turreted house.

"Les Hérissons," he read. "Chigny les Roses, Champagne. Well, well, well."

"They're the company that took the Washington account from us," Peter said, suddenly uneasy. Jean Paul's expression was very strange.

"Are they now," Jean Paul said. "Successful, you'd say?"

Peter shrugged. "They seem to be, but I don't know anything about them. Do you?"

"Not a thing," Jean Paul said slowly and somehow unconvincingly. "But I think I might find out a little more."

Philippe felt very tired as he climbed out of the new big Panhard car that Lorraine had chosen. The new chauffeur, also chosen by her, had met him at the station. He felt deeply depressed at the idea of going back to a new apartment, a new wife, new servants, and he toyed with the idea of going to his father's for a rest and some conversation before going home.

His conscience and the thought that he had been married only six weeks and away for a month of them sent him to Neuilly. But his heart and his head were still full of Rosie and he was not sure how he would react to his wife. The truth was that at that moment, until he had bathed, slept and refreshed himself, he did not wish to see her at all.

The new chauffeur, whose name he could not remember, gave a discreet toot on the horn of the Panhard as he neared the front door of the apartment. It opened immediately, and an impassive butler, called Quilliam, whom Lorraine had imported from Tours, stood ready to take his coat.

"Madame is out, sir," he murmured as Philippe came into the marble-floored hall. "She said to tell you she will return shortly."

He heaved a sigh of relief and turned into his own small study off the hall. There he settled down in a spacious black leather armchair and took up the book that he had been reading before he left.

The apartment seemed unnaturally quiet, and then he heard muffled sounds, as if someone were creeping about outside the room. He was wondering irritably why the servants could not walk in a normal manner when suddenly the door of his study burst open. Lorraine was

260

standing there, her face lit by a huge smile, behind her an assortment of grinning people.

"Welcome home, darling!" she cried, rushing to fling herself into his arms. "And look, we have a party to celebrate!"

People were crowding into the small room.

"You did it all wrong, darling," Lorraine was laughing. "We were all hidden, waiting for you in the drawing room, but you didn't come in."

He was forcing a smile, shaking hands, trying to appear pleased.

"I think we'd better go to the drawing room, *chérie*," he said, gently disengaging her arm from round his waist. "We'll all stifle in here."

"Of course," she said, leading the way. "Come on everyone, back to the drawing room. The champagne is there."

There must have been fifty people in his home, and he wasn't sure that he knew as many as ten. To his relief he saw his father standing with Sebastian by the long windows that overlooked the park, and he made his way across to them.

His father looked amused.

"Good trip?" he asked.

"It went well," Philippe said.

One of the new servants thrust a glass into his hand, and to his annoyance he took one taste and realised it wasn't Rosie's champagne. Just a non-vintage Mercier, his nose told him. He put down the glass.

"Rosie was highly commended for her champagne," he said, "and she fell in love with the Duke."

"I trust not, Papa," Sebastian said.

Philippe leaned to kiss his son on both cheeks.

"You get more grown-up every time I see you," he said. "Is everything all right? Are you happy here?"

"It's fine, Papa," his son said gently, as if he was consoling his father.

Lorraine, in a pretty pink muslin tea gown, fluttered to join them.

"Isn't it the most marvellous thing to have him home again?" she demanded, sliding her arm through his, and clinging to him like a piece of fluff on a black jacket. "Were you surprised? Were you expecting a party?"

"I was surprised, and I was not expecting a party, *chérie*," he said, smiling down at her and unwillingly responding to her enthusiasm.

"I just adore parties," she said. "You know, my own papa always says that I will take any excuse for a party, but today what a perfect excuse, the home-coming of my darling husband. And I have arranged for twelve of us, including your darling papa and Sebastian, to dine in the private dining room of the Café Anglais. Is that a good idea?"

She was waiting for congratulations. She looked so young and eager that he found himself putting his arms round her, telling her that it was all brilliant, a marvellous surprise, and that he could not imagine a nicer home-coming.

"And the trip was successful?" she asked, but before he could reply she was calling over a tall, thin young man who carried a handkerchief foppishly in his hand. "Didier," she said, "you have not met my husband. Philippe, this is Didier le Brune, an old friend of our family. He was at the wedding, but I think you were never introduced to each other."

She darted off, hands signalling delight as a newcomer was ushered into the room. Philippe and his father found themselves making uneasy conversation with Monsier le Brune.

It seemed an interminably long evening and it gradually dawned on Philippe that his problem was that the guests were all so young. Lorraine had invited her friends, and they seemed abominably noisy to him. Over dinner at the CaféAnglais they shrieked at each other across the table, made jokes he did not understand and did not wish to understand. Lorraine, at the far end of the table, had the good fortune to have his father and son at her side, and was obviously enjoying it all immensely.

He charmed the boring young women who sat by him by listening to every word they said and encouraging them to talk. They talked mostly of fashion, the best restaurants and where they had travelled. He could think of nothing to say to them.

It was gone one when the party broke up and the cars and carriages arrived to take his wife's rich, boring, juvenile friends home.

He was deathly tired, and knew that his smile and charm were becoming rigid. He hoped no one noticed.

In the Panhard, Lorraine snuggled up to him and whispered provocatively in his ear: "Soon we'll be alone, my darling one."

He groaned mentally. He had discovered that his new bride was as rich, silly and shallow as he had expected. But her middle-aged, sometimes hectoring manner disappeared when they were alone. Then she played the little girl. He found this equally tiresome. But there had been one bonus. She was surprisingly interested in bed. Her response and passion had helped what could have been a difficult situation, and she was able to arouse him. She was certainly not experienced, and he found a certain pleasure in teaching her. Their wedding night had not been the disaster he feared. And once she was no longer a virgin, she was keen to experiment, and he found that though conversation with her was torture, lovemaking, though not to be compared with what he and Rosie shared, was bearable.

But tonight? Tired, full of rich food, bored, and with the memory of the last night on board ship, and being in Rosie's bed, Rosie's arms and, indeed, in Rosie ... he did not think that he would be able to perform for his hungry young wife.

"I am very tired, *chérie*," he said, aware of sounding feeble.

"Poor you!" she said, still so wide awake at nearly two in the morning. "Don't worry. Your little Lorraine will wake her Philippe up."

And she did. Philippe would not have believed it possible, but her soft flesh, her flowery perfume, her fluttering, tentative hands, and her clinging mouth did indeed wake him up. As he felt himself spring to life, and as she whispered questions asking what would please him, he was lost. And he hated himself, hated his flesh that responded to a woman, any woman, when all he loved was Rosie. When it was over and he lay panting on his wife's childish breasts and thinly covered mount of Venus, he groaned, feeling himself an adulterer, with Rosie the one betrayed.

"I told you I'd wake you up," she said in a self-satisfied little-girl voice. "And I did, didn't I?"

He did not wish to be reminded of his treachery. He did not reply.

"My darling," she said, fluttering her eyelashes on his cheek. "Don't sleep. I want to talk."

"Lorraine," he said, desperate, "I have been up since dawn. It must be three in the morning. I'm tired."

"You won't be when you hear my news," she said smugly.

"What news," he said wearily, too exhausted to think.

There was a long silence, and then a small giggle from his wife.

"You're going to be a papa again."

She was right. His tiredness vanished.

"What did you say?"

"I said you're going to be a papa again."

He felt as if someone had stepped on him, squeezing the breath out of his body. And then it began, the slow growth of pride and excitement. The sense of being a man. A feeling of wonder and joy such as he had forgotten since the day, long ago, when Nicole had told him that Sebastian was in her womb.

He sat bolt upright, and the mother of his child-to-be giggled.

"Told you I'd wake you up," she said again, wriggling closer to him.

The giggle and the wriggle ended his moment of euphoria. He could think of only one thing.

How could he tell Rosie?

Champagne, May 1912

The morning of the fifth of May dawned dull and chilly, as most of the year had been already. It was not good wine weather, Rosie was thinking as she walked through the house to her office. Last year had been perfect; early flowering of the vines, a superb hot, dry summer,

263

and the vintage was in by early September. The wines promised to be excellent, probably the finest since 1874, Madame Dupuis assured her, and the unrest in the Champagne had calmed under sunnier skies and a bountiful crop.

This year Les Hérissons looked set fair to make serious money. Philippe had continued to find her an impressive clientèle. This not only enhanced her business, but gave them the opportunity to meet frequently. In November they had been invited again to England to attend a ball at the Duke's country seat. They had managed to stretch the time by two enchanted days which they spent together at the Savoy in London, before beginning the journey home.

Lorraine was never mentioned.

As she settled down at her desk, Rosie considered whether or not she should take a brief trip to Paris later in the week. It had been nearly a month since she had heard from Philippe, and he was not travelling. He had told her that he would be in Paris for most of March and April.

She decided she would telephone him later and see which day would be best for both of them.

She had just settled down to work when she heard Allie's scurrying footsteps half-running down the hallway.

"Mama, Mama," she was calling. "Come quickly. I have a surprise for you."

Rosie put down her pen on the blotter as Allie rushed into the room and grabbed her hand.

"You'll never guess," she was saying excitedly. "It's a lovely surprise."

Amused by all the excitement and a little curious, Rosie let herself be dragged back down the hallway to the front door of the house. It was closed. But Allie opened it with a flourish.

"Behold!" she said.

Outside, at the foot of the steps, mounted on a glossy chestnut mare, was Sebastian. But what a splendid Sebastian, in black shining spurred boots, red trousers, belted and buckled blue jacket and a red-trimmed officer's forage cap.

As he saw her, he saluted smartly, and dismounted before running up the steps to kiss her on both cheeks.

"Sebastian," she said, "you look magnificent!"

He had grown a small moustache as well as an inch or two in height. He seemed to have filled out too, but the cheeky grin and the knowing eyes remained the same. There was no doubt he was a grown man now.

"Like it?" he asked. "I've joined Grandfather's old regiment. I'm a cuirassier. I've been in six weeks now."

"Six weeks!" she said. "Why didn't you let me know?"

"Well," he said. "I did it in a bit of a hurry. I wanted to get out of the way before the baby was born. I managed it by two weeks."

Rosie was genuinely puzzled.

"What baby?" she asked.

Suddenly he looked ill at ease.

"Lorraine's baby," he said reluctantly. "My new baby sister."

Rosie thought she was going to faint, just as she had long ago, on this same doorstep. Somehow she managed to hang on to her senses, but she was unable to speak.

"Mama, are you all right?" she heard Allie say as if from another planet.

Sebastian had moved to take her arm, and she could feel him willing her to stand upright.

"I'm fine, Allie," she said, fighting for control and survival. "I just felt dizzy for a moment. I hadn't realised the baby had been born, Sebastian. I thought it wasn't due until later in the year."

He gave her a sharp look.

"You did know?"

"Of course," she lied. "How is Lorraine?"

"Making the most of it, languishing in bed, covered in pink frills," he said cheerfully, relieved that he had not been the bearer of bad news. "It seems a nice enough little baby. And Papa, of course, is besotted."

Her voice still calm, she asked: "What are they calling her?"

"Françoise. After Lorraine's mother."

"That's nice," she murmured. "Your grandfather must be very pleased."

"He hasn't seen it. He's still in Menton."

André had decided that his old bones could not stand the winter chill of Paris. As soon as the chestnut leaves had begun to fall in the Champs Élysées he had gone to the south of France for the winter. Was it too far-fetched to think that he had gone away rather than be involved in the deception?

Shock and dismay were gradually turning to anger. As she asked Sebastian about his new life, another corner of her mind was racing with the cruelty and duplicity of Philippe's behaviour.

How could he have taken her to London, made love to her so ardently? How could he have continued with those idyllic hours in the Paris or Reims apartments without ever once saying that his wife was pregnant?

Fury was churning her stomach into knots, but she could not, would not let Sebastian see how hurt and angry she was.

"Does your father know you're here today?" she asked.

"No. He's far more interested in Françoise than me at the moment. I expect when the novelty wears off he'll ask how things are going."

In spite of his grin and joking manner, Rosie detected a core of hurt in him, too. He was vulnerable in spite of the dashing uniform and the soldier stance.

"Well, I want to know every single thing that's happened," she said, turning her mind from her own misery. "Come inside and tell me without missing out a thing."

He put his arms round her and hugged her.

"The nice thing about you, Rosie, is that you're always here," he said, and she knew then that he had felt very alone.

She forced herself not to think about Philippe's deception while Sebastian was in the house. He needed to feel loved and wanted, and reassuring him helped to calm her. But when he rode off, kissing her a fraction too near the mouth, and promising to return soon, she felt the rage grow again.

"Isn't it lovely that Monsieur Philippe has a baby?" Allie said innocently as the family ate supper. "Do you think I could be allowed to go and see it one day? I like babies."

Madame Dupuis lifted her head and scented the air.

"A baby? Philippe?" she said. "When did this happen?"

"A month ago I believe," Rosie said, cutting into her lamb chop with great care.

"How extraordinary. Did you know?"

"I think he might have mentioned it."

Her mother-in-law gave her a shrewd look, and then pursed her mouth tight.

"How odd to keep it secret from everyone."

Rosie did not reply.

"What is it?"

"A girl. Called Françoise."

Madame Dupuis frowned.

"It's hard on Sebastian," she said.

"Yes. I think he feels rather left out."

Madame Dupuis had always had a soft spot for Sebastian.

"Tell him to come and stay here whenever he wants. But I must say I do find it all very peculiar."

"Perhaps he thought he would look silly, having a child so late," Clovis suggested, and the way he said it made Rosie wonder if he had ever thought of perhaps having a child of his own and regretted it had not happened. She realised that the rawness of her own misery was making her sensitive to the misery of others.

"It's probably all a misunderstanding," she muttered.

But there was no misunderstanding. Philippe had deliberately deceived her. Upstairs in her own little sitting room, pacing up and down, she tried to reason it out. Obviously he had been afraid to tell her – but she had never before thought of him as a weak man. Obviously he had to sleep with his wife and therefore she was likely to get pregnant. Indeed, Lorraine had said she intended to get pregnant as soon as possible. All these truths did not help. The anguish did not lessen.

And he was besotted by the child, and he had not been in touch with her for over a month. The control that had taken her through the day vanished like smoke. She found she was crying.

Anger suppressing pain, she seized pen and paper and began to write frantically, a wild scrawl that gave vent to her emotions.

Philippe,

How could you, how *could* you hurt and humiliate me so? For me to hear, from Sebastian, that you have a child, to realise that you had not the courage to tell me your wife was pregnant or even confess that the baby was born, is perhaps the cruellest and most dreadful thing that I can imagine.

I feel my heart is rent. I feel I can never bear to see you again. Oh, I realise that it was necessary for you to sleep with her. I know she wanted a child . . . but not to tell me. To let me hear in such a fashion. It is unforgivable.

Now you have done this, there is nothing left for us. Besotted, Sebastian says you are by your daughter. Besotted by your wife, perhaps, that she has given you this gift. I wanted to give you a child, but what chance was there? I wanted to be your wife, but it was never possible.

I know I am being unreasonable and self-pitying, but I do not care. I am desolate.

Now you have a daughter, what place will there be for me? She must come first; it is a bond that you and Lorraine share which leaves no room for me. I shall be on the fringes of your life – your mistress if I accept the role. Well, I do not choose to any more, and never will be again.

I almost hate you for the shock you have given me. If you had been honest perhaps I could have borne it. But I ask myself why you did not tell me. You will answer that you knew it would pain me. But if I had been prepared, the pain might have been bearable.

I despise you for your cowardice while understanding it. What we have shared should have made you treat me better. But maybe now there are others more important than I am.

Philippe, it is over. This is goodbye. Please do not attempt to change my mind. My tragedy is that I shall always love you.

Rosie

Drained, she sat thinking, the letter on her lap, staring into the fire until the room darkened. Then she went quietly downstairs and slipped through the front door. She walked through the woods to the top of the hill where the land opened up and the many hectares of vines made orderly rows against the lowering sky. The ground was damp, but she sat, her arms round her legs, chin on her knees, watching the light change, dry-eyed; mourning.

It was dark when she went back to bed with Clovis, who grunted and turned in his sleep, accidentally flinging one arm over her as she lay, eyes open, staring at the ceiling, still thinking.

The next morning she shut herself in her sitting room and took the letter she had written from her locked drawer. She read it and shook her head before tearing it into as many small pieces as she could. She placed the confetti in the fireplace. It made a brave blaze for a few seconds and then fell to ashes. She took a fresh sheet of notepaper and, tight-lipped, without tears, did the controlled and considered thing:

> Dear Philippe,
>
> I write to congratulate you on the birth of your baby daughter. Sebastian told me your good news when he called to see us all here at Les Hérissons yesterday. He tells me you are 'quite besotted' with little Françoise and that she is giving you great pleasure.
>
> As I love you, I am therefore glad for you. And bow to the inevitable that your life now has meaning and it is time for what we have shared to end.
>
> I would be lying if I did not say that I am bitterly hurt, indeed angry, that you kept this secret from me. It was a cruel deception; a harder blow than the truth would have been.
>
> I understand that you would find it difficult to tell me, but where was your courage and your honesty, Philippe?
>
> Our business affairs are too entwined to disentangle, so if you find it possible, could we continue as partners and friends?
>
> Please do not try to dissuade me from this decision or even ask me to discuss it. I do not have the strength or courage to talk of it with you, anymore than you had the strength and courage to talk of it with me.
>
> The kindest and most loving thing that you can do now for both of us is to accept the inevitable.
>
> Please believe that I wish only for your happiness. A new life has begun for you, and you should be free to live it to the full.
>
> Rosie

She did not read the letter through when the words were on the paper. She took an envelope and addressed it to Philippe's Paris office, marking it Private and Confidential.

And then she rang for Henri and asked him to be sure that the letter went in the first possible post.

BOOK THREE

Chapter Sixteen

"Oh, madame, it has arrived, it is upon us."

Marie, the partridge-plump Marie, with her fluff of dark fringe and her snowy apron, stood in the dining room of Les Hérissons twisting her hands, her face streaked with tears.

The Dupuis were eating their dessert. Both Madame and Rosie put down their spoons and forks, and rose to their feet.

"How do you know, Marie?" Rosie asked, her voice calm.

"The posters for the mobilisation are on the walls in Épernay and in Reims," Marie said, choking back sobs. "My Robert has already left to enlist. Oh, mesdames, to think it should have come to this!"

"What is she saying?" Clovis asked.

"It must be war," Madame Dupuis said quietly. "If they are mobilising ..."

"Of course it is war," Rosie said. "It had to be war. Why do you think that the dragoons and the infantry left Reims last week. Dear God, more than three thousand men in red and blue with rifles on their shoulders and bands playing as if it were the fourteenth of July. The flag with a guard of honour. It's obscene. A parade! A march to death more like it."

"Rosie!" Madame Dupuis' expression indicated that Rosie had blasphemed. "Marie, you may go."

"No, Marie," Rosie said. "Tell us what has happened."

Marie was making no attempt to hide her tears.

"Madame, it is true. It is the war. The posters are in the Place Royal and the Hôtel de Ville and at all the crossroads. All able-bodied men must enlist. They say we will be informed in Chigny tomorrow. Oh, madame, my Robert has gone already."

"Where has he gone?" Clovis asked.

"To the Hôtel de Ville in Reims," Marie said. "Oh mesdames, it will be the most terrible war."

Rosie felt a cold shiver and remembered André's words. The next war would be carnage.

"Forty-four years," Madame Dupuis said as if speaking to herself. "Forty-four years since the Boche set their filthy boots in the Hôtel de Ville, and now it happens again."

Clovis was rising to his feet.

"I must go," he said.

"Clovis, no," his mother protested. "Wait."

"Wait?" said Clovis. "If Marie's Robert has gone, I must also do my duty."

"Duty! Duty!" Rosie said passionately. "Is it your duty to die, Clovis? I don't want you to die," and as she spoke she realised that she meant what she said. "War, disgusting war! What has it to do with us, the ordinary people? We live our lives as best we can, and politicians and statesmen bring us to war. For what? Clovis, killing men is no pursuit for a gentleman."

She was near to tears herself, fearful for all those she loved. She had heard Madame Dupuis' tales of the horrors of the Franco-Prussian war that had left much of Champagne a wasteland, but this time, as André had said, it would be a modern war with modern weapons, and so much worse.

"It is the end of *la belle Époque*," Madame said sadly. "Maybe the end of much more. But we must fight, Rosie. Our men must fight, to keep us from the heel of the invader. There is no choice."

"But there should be," Rosie cried. "There should be a choice for all of us."

There was none. War was declared the following day, August the second. The newspapers spoke of enormous German losses, and the heroic resistance of Belgium as the Boche once again marched through this little neutral country and also into Luxembourg.

Angry, impotent, Rosie watched as the men marched from their villages, singing optimistic songs, their mood euphoric. Never could men have faced war with such enthusiasm. Clovis, who had not understood what she meant or felt, had been among them, carrying a few things packed in a knapsack. She had not heard from him since. But then Clovis hated writing.

A week later, the *Éclaireur de l'Est* was headlining Victory. The Germans might have invaded Belgium but they had been chased from Liège. The French army was in Alsace. Britain had declared war on Germany. Rosie did not trust this optimism, and was chided for her scepticism and called a defeatist.

The troop trains trundled eastwards through Rilly each day, with scrawled, joking messages chalked on their sides; "Pleasure train for Berlin", "En route for a season at Baden-Baden", "Special train for the execution of the Kaiser".

The reality was different. The handsome dragoons who had left the Remois girls crying at their departure were massacred in Belgium. Few of the young men of the local 132nd Infantry regiment would ever return to the chalk soil of Champagne, but lay buried in the mud of the Somme and Flanders.

"No doubt they'll build them a fine monument," Rosie said bitterly.

André, the old soldier, had explained it all to her when she had visited him in Paris in early July, barely a month before. He was certain that war was inevitable and doubted that the French army could stand against the modern might of machine-guns and the huge field guns that the Germans had built up.

"And," he said in disgust, "our troops march in red pantaloons, for God's sake. They will be sitting ducks for the machine-gunners. Going to war in red and blue! What folly! And do you know why they wear red?" he asked angrily. "Money, my dear Rosie, it is all to do with money. France has invented a new fast red dye. The manufacturers want to break the British monopoly in red dye. What better way to advertise than to dress the poor, unfortunate soldiery in red trousers?"

"Sebastian will have to fight?" she asked fearfully.

"And Philippe. He will no doubt join my old regiment and fight alongside his son. No one will escape. Not even your poor dull Clovis. There will be no choice for any of them."

He sat, his head bowed, an old man brooding.

"If I could, I would go in their place. I did not raise my son and his son to see them die by a piece of red-hot metal. At least the sword was clean and had honour."

She finally received an ill-spelt, scrawled letter from Clovis on August the 26th. He was with the 4th Army in the Ardennes. All he said was that the men were brave and true. Allie cried when the letter arrived, for she had been distraught since her father had left, sleeping badly and suffering nightmares. Though she was fourteen, and tall for her age, Rosie had brought her into her bed most nights.

She needed comfort herself.

She had received a stiff and formal letter from Philippe two days after Clovis left that had left her shocked and fearful:

My dear Rosie,

I must tell you that today I have enlisted in my father's old regiment, and I leave for the front in a couple of days' time. Sebastian has already gone.

I have left both your and my business affairs in the best possible order, though what will happen to the wine trade of France in these troubled times is hard to forecast.

Monsieur Brunel, who happily is too old to have to fight, will take over your clients and do what he can for them and you. He is a good man and will do his best, though again it is hard to judge whether or not there will be any export business until this war ceases.

The General Staff are assuring us that it will be short – all over by the late autumn, they predict. We can only pray they are right.

I pray also that your life will not be too disturbed, and that the fair fields of Champagne will not be sullied by tanks, guns and marching men.

My thoughts, as always, are with you and yours.

Philippe

It was no good. She could not stop loving him, and the thought of him going to war filled her with terror. Since she had written to him more than two years before, there had been little contact between them. He had continued to handle the sales of her champagne, and the business had flourished. In spite of her reluctance to become famous, her wines were known by the *cognoscenti* as being of fine quality, and she had been forced to limit her clientèle to those who could buy in bulk.

As war was declared, the new cellars in the chalk hills had almost been finished. Rosie had been able to tunnel through to the old Roman chalk pit on the estate. It was like the chalk pits of the Pommery cellars in Reims, a dizzy thirty metres below ground. Previously it had been inaccessible, with no more than a narrow opening at the top which had to be fenced for safety. At the foot of the drop there was a fine, big chamber that would store a great deal of wine.

Until the second of August dawned, everything had been going perfectly, except that never for one moment had she stopped loving and missing Philippe. Without him, she felt arid, as if the sap had gone from her. Time and time again she reproached herself for her foolhardiness in sending him away. But she knew that it had been the right thing to do. It was hard enough that they could not openly be as one. To have to share him with a new family would mean that she would be pushed further and further into the background of his life. Yet she could not put him from her mind or from her heart.

But in these bright, warm days of August, while the grapes ripened perfectly on the vines, it was hard to think of anything but the war. The mood of optimism was fading. The department of the Marne had been designated a war zone, and every day the fighting rumbled nearer as the French army fell back from the frontiers. Marie and Henri kept Les Hérissons informed with news from their relatives who worked in Reims and Épernay.

"The trains are coming back, madame," Marie said sadly, "full of

274

our wounded. They are taking them to the hospital in the Place Belle-Tour. So many of the dragoons. It is a terrible sight, and they say there are hundreds of thousands more dead, and madame, I have not heard from my Robert."

Marie was weeping, and Rosie tried to comfort her, saying that no news was good news. Robert, a good, strong Champenois lad, well able to look after himself, would be home again soon.

But she did not believe it herself, though the authorities coninued to declare that Germany was repulsed and the end was in sight.

In mid August the refugees began to arrive in Reims and the surrounding villages. The Belgians came first in cattle wagons, into Reims station, exhausted, haggard, homeless men and women who had to be found a place to stay. After them came a flood of Frenchmen and women from the Ardennes and by the end of the month from the Marne itself.

Madame Dupuis and Rosie placed a dozen beds in the outbuildings, and set up a kitchen.

"But it's so little," fretted Rosie. "We must do more."

On September the second Henri came with the news that soldiers of many different corps had retreated to Reims.

"They sleep on the pavements, madame," he said, tears in his eyes. "Exhausted men. Beaten and hungry. And still they retreat. I fear we are lost."

Rosie went to stand high on the hill where she could look down at the road winding its way through village and vineyard and on to Épernay, further south. Columns of French soldiers marched, still in their brave red, rifles on shoulders, tired feet in puttees pounding the road, yet disciplined and orderly even in retreat. Their weary progress raised the fine, choking chalk dust of Champagne, making a halo of white around each marching man. Later a thin and straggly column of dragoons on weary horses went by. So tired were they, they barely made the speed of the earlier men on foot.

It could not be long before the Germans came.

That night they heard for the first time the background rumble of gunfire, distinct and threatening, silencing the bullfrogs. The sky was lit by blue and orange flashes, not unlike that of the fireworks that they had watched so happily on 14 July.

That evening, after supper, Rosie, Madame and Allie gathered in the parlour along with their staff. And on the table were six bottles of the Les Hérissons 1906 vintage, with one of the finest family crystal glasses for each of them.

"First," Rosie said, standing with her back to the fireplace, Madame Dupuis beside her, "we are going to drink to France, to our brave loved ones, and to victory. And then we must decide what we are to do for our own safety, and the safety of the estate. Tomorrow or the day after the Germans will be here, and we must not be unprepared. Henri will open the wine, and Allie, you may pour it."

There was complete silence except for the inappropriately festive pop of the corks as Henri opened the bottles. Then, so quiet was the room as Allie poured, that Rosie felt she could hear every bubble fizzing.

Allie handed everyone a full glass.

"*Vive la France!*" said Madame Dupuis, her voice ringing like a bell. "To victory. Long live our loved ones and may we all live long, too."

Solemnly they all raised their glasses and drank. Marie was crying.

"Oh, madame," she said. "I'm so frightened."

Madame Dupuis stepped forward as if she was going to hit the girl.

"Nonsense!" she said. "I forbid you to be frightened of the Boche. If they come here, we will receive them with our heads high and we will take no nonsense. This is our home. What can they do but kill us? And I would rather die than show them fear."

"Yes, madame," sniffled Marie, not looking as if she agreed.

"Yes, be brave, Marie," Rosie said. "And think what we can do for the best. Now, are there any guns in the house?"

There was silence as everyone thought.

"Somewhere in the attic is an old hunting rifle of my husband's," Madame said. "And that old powder musket on the wall in the back hall. But nothing else."

"Hunting knives?" Rosie asked.

"One in the pantry," Henri said. "Cook sometimes uses it to skin a rabbit."

"Anything else that might make a weapon?"

"My big kitchen chopper," Cook said with relish, "and those heavy iron bars we never got round to putting back in the pantry window."

"Do you wish to try to fight them, madame?" Now Henri was looking nervous.

"No, not at all," Rosie reassured him. "But I think everything that might be used as a weapon should be hidden somewhere we can find it, and they cannot. Just in case we need them. They would certainly confiscate any guns."

"They did last time," Madame said grimly.

"Right, Cook, will you be in charge of finding a hiding place?" Rosie asked.

Cook, a surprisingly thin and lugubrious woman who was never happier than when jointing a pig, smiled a rare smile.

"I know just the place," she said. "At hand in the kitchen, just in case I ever get the opportunity ..."

"No one is to do anything foolhardy," Rosie warned. "And next, we must hide as much of the champagne as we possibly can, particularly our blending wine, and our vintage bottles. It is a shame to have to move them, but it would be worse to see them poured down German throats."

"The refugees will help, madame," said Marie, who having become interested in the proceedings, had forgotten her tears. "They are very grateful to you."

"Maybe we can put barrels into the Roman chalk pit," Rosie said, "and then close up the tunnel leading to it again."

"Can't we conceal the entrances to all the new tunnels, Mama?" Allie asked. "We could hide a lot there."

"We could indeed," said Rosie. "It would be good to keep those tunnels secret. But there simply aren't enough of us to move everything. And anyway it would look suspicious if they came here and found nothing."

"Last time," said Madame Dupuis indignantly, "they just stole our champagne and actually shipped it back to Germany."

"Could we get some lads from the village school?" asked Miss, who had been appointed English teacher at the little Chigny red-brick school when the schoolmaster enlisted. "I know the ones who are reliable."

"Why not?" said Rosie. "But everyone must be sworn to secrecy about what we do and where we hide anything. Agreed?"

They all agreed, and over more glasses of champagne, campaigns and strategies to foil the foe were plotted. The Les Hérissons household went to bed reasonably cheerful.

Rosie, who found that for some inexplicable reason she missed Clovis in her bed, could not sleep. Her head was buzzing with how to move the huge barrels without damaging them. What farm equipment and machinery could be called into play? she wondered. For once in her life she needed the practical Clovis. But he was not here.

Rosie rarely prayed, believing as she did that God helped those who helped themselves, but tonight she said a silent prayer for Philippe, and Clovis and Sebastian and Marie's Robert. For they were all truly in His hands. And then she slept.

A soft, tapping noise, like a branch blowing on the window, woke her. Drowsily she listened, but it had stopped. And then a second or two later it began again. She climbed out of bed and crossed the room. Outside, the thunder of the guns had stopped, and a thin moon was lighting the back courtyard and the vines beyond. As she drew back the curtains, there was the tapping noise again and a dark, indistinct shape, blocking the view.

At first she was alarmed, but then reasoned that anyone wanting to do her harm would not be trying to attract her attention. She moved to undo the latch and saw the moonlight gleaming on the steel of a cuirassier's or maybe a dragoon's horned helmet.

She opened the window.

"Who is it?" she whispered.

"Sebastian. Rosie, please let me in. For God's sake, before I fall."

Immediately awake and alert, she pulled him through the window and into her bedroom. As his boots landed on her carpet, he groaned, and sank to the floor.

"Thank God!" he whispered. "Thank God."

She knelt beside him busying herself removing the comic opera helmet and loosening the tight collar of his uniform.

"What happened, Sebastian? How did you get here?"

"We're on the run, Rosie," he said painfully. "My horse was shot from under me the other side of Reims. I think everyone else is dead. I walked here. Like I said, Rosie, the good thing about you is that you're always here."

"Shhh," she said. "Get up. Let me get you on the bed."

He sat bolt upright.

"Are they here? The Germans?"

"No, not yet. There's time, I think." She had pulled him to his feet and sat him on the bed while she lit the gas lamp.

"Now let's look at you. Are you hurt?"

"Not physically," he said, "only sick unto death."

In the soft bluish light, his young face was white, with black bruises under his eyes. He had aged ten years and was exhausted.

Without speaking she began tugging at his boots, and with some difficulty pulled them off. Then she lifted his feet onto the bed. If he could just sleep ...

"Lie still and talk to me," she said. "Tell me about it."

As he lay, her fingers were removing belt and revolver and unbuttoning gold buttons in an effort to make him more comfortable. He barely moved, his eyes closed.

"Lie beside me and I will," he said finally. "Bring me back to reality, Rosie. Tell me this war is a bad dream."

"Alas," she said sadly, stroking his forehead. "This war is a terrible reality."

"You cannot imagine it," he said, his eyes still closed. "I shall see it to my dying day. Young men, men like me. We went so gaily, it was a game, and they are dead, all dead. The head wounds, Rosie, you cannot believe. They had their heads split open, their brains trailing like maggots. They had their brave, red-trousered legs shot away from them. They were cut in half in their Napoleonic tunics. They hadn't a chance. The wounded howled and cried or were pitifully quiet, and we could do nothing for them. And the blood; so much blood. Did you know blood smells? Sweet, as if it might be good to drink. It must be, the earth drank it so quickly. I know now, Rosie, what hell is like. This war is hell. No game, Rosie, no game." He was beginning to cry, but the words continued to pour out.

"The men were courageous enough for any commander. The infantry kept their ranks, they marched in formation in the heat and the dust, the white dust here in Champagne. It's choking dust. I'd never noticed it before. Then the howitzers began from behind us, and the machine-gunners began their rat-a-tatting, and we all took to the fields away from the road. It didn't help. The shells came hurling on, screaming over our heads, whistling. Death comes with a whistle, Rosie. Then they got our range. More and more shells thundering over. We officers weren't supposed to take cover. We have to encourage the troops, you see. We mustn't lose control. A few brave fools stayed upright, while the men crouched, desperate for cover, any cover. They blew my mare's legs off. I had to finish her off, poor thing, with a bullet in the head and then a *poilu* used her poor dead carcass to hide behind. But then some were using the dead men for cover. There were enough of them. But God help me, I stood up, brandishing my revolver, like a schoolboy playing at soldiers. And nothing hit me.

"So the officers died standing up, and the men died crouching. It didn't matter which way they died. They died. And I lived."

He had begun to shiver, and determined that he should rest, she tugged at his clothing, somehow managing to undress him down to his underclothing. Then, with more difficulty, she managed to pull the bedclothes over him. She lay beside him, on top of the bedclothes, holding him very tight. He was very hot, and he smelt bad, as if the odours of blood and death had clung to him.

"You're safe now," she soothed. "Try to sleep. You need sleep."

"I need sleep," he said bitterly. "What about those who will sleep for ever?"

She wanted to make him think of something else.

"You walked here from the other side of Reims," she reminded him. "Of course you are tired. Are you hungry?"

"I may never be hungry again," he said. "And tomorrow I must walk to find my regiment."

"Tomorrow is another day," she said. "Just try to sleep. Please."

He was quiet for a full minute, and then he groaned, and turned in her arms, pulling his from beneath the sheets to hold her tight.

"Rosie, you smell clean. You smell of woman and of civilisation. You smell safe."

Without warning, he was kissing her, frantic, passionate kisses of an intensity she had forgotten could be found in just the meeting of lips. Without meaning to, she was responding, and the sigh of relief, almost joy, that her response brought from him alarmed her. She tried to pull away. But he had found her breasts beneath her thin summer nightgown and was undoing the buttons that ran to her waist. His mouth closed over the breast nearest to him, and he lay, breathing deeply, suckling, for the moment at peace.

She knew she should stop him, but could not. She knew what was inevitable, but did nothing. "What harm?" she asked herself silently as his mouth pursed and suckled, and a guilty response grew in her. If her body could defeat his dreadful memories even for just a few moments, what harm? How could it possibly be wrong?

She let him suck, trying to pretend it was just like her baby, her Allie, suckling. But it was not.

His hands were exploring her, and when he found her damp and moist, ready, he hesitated fractionally, and then he whispered: "Rosie, can I? Please? You know I love you. I have always loved you."

She did not speak, but wriggled her nightgown off her shoulders and down her body. Then, after he had rolled over onto her, she helped him remove what little clothing he was still wearing, and guided him into her.

It took very little time. His thrusting was as urgent as his kisses had been, and then a last frantic push, a long drawn-out groan and he collapsed on her.

"You always save me when I'm lost and crying," he murmured. "I love you, Rosie." And then he slept. Eventually, exhausted, she did, too.

He had gone before she woke in the morning. The same way as he had come. Through the window. There was no word, but his regimental badge – a replica of a blue grenade – had been carefully pinned to her pillow.

Allie thought that 3 September was definitely the most exciting day of her life, and noted that fact in her private diary. Her mother was up much earlier than usual, but she seemed preoccupied as she directed operations to save Les Hérissons. They had mustered as many people as they could. The refugees were either elderly or women, but they could help a little. Miss had managed to find willing young pupils who regarded the hard work as fun and part of the war effort.

Their elders were grimmer, but all day everyone toiled, moving bottles and barrels, blocking entrances to the cellars in the hillsides and piling rubble in the cellars below the house to close off some of them. It was an impossible task to hide everything, but they did well. And Cook, whose father and brothers had been killed by the Boche in the Franco-Prussian war, worked as hard as anyone, seeing that all the helpers were kept fed.

Henri's cousin came by with news from Reims in the late afternoon, and everyone stopped work to gather round and hear what he had to say.

"Reims is dead," he said, his voice full of emotion. "The shutters are closed, only a few shops have opened, the army has disappeared from the streets. General Foch is in Sillery, no more than ten kilometres away, but he has decided that Reims will not be defended. Dr Langlet, the Mayor and his counsellors are at their posts. Dr Langlet has posted a communiqué asking us all to stay calm and do whatever is necessary to come through this terrible test. He asks for our silence, our dignity and our prudence. Alas, the Germans will take over the town tomorrow."

"The fourth of September," Madame Dupuis said softly. "The same day as in 1870. A day that has lived again."

"The swine," Cook breathed. "The murderous swine!"

Everyone was silent. Marie was crying, and Allie noticed that her Mimi's eyes were too bright. She moved to take her grandmother's hand and squeeze it tight.

Her mother was speaking, quietly, but so intensely that every word could be heard. She was dry-eyed, but seemed almost feverish as she stood, her head back, just like on the night when the mobs had come to Les Hérissons.

"It is a setback," she said, "nothing more. We must be brave, we must keep in good heart and spirits. It is too late for defeatism now. For the sake of those men who are dying dreadful deaths for us out there, we must be strong and guard what we can of their true lives for them. Because never fear, in the end, we shall win. Right must and will win against might."

"Vive la France!" Cook cried.

"Vive la France!" they all echoed, and Allie felt a strange prickling of the skin, a feeling of being at the beginning of something momentous. There was no need for fantasies today. She was living one.

Chapter Seventeen

The Prussian Guard entered Reims the next afternoon, but not without incident. First they took reprisals. Their general, von Bülow, believing incorrectly or wishing to believe that the men he had sent to Reims, bearing the flag of truce, had been kidnapped, gave the order to open fire. The savage and senseless bombardment hit the centre of the town, two hundred Remois were killed or wounded, and in the late afternoon the Germans marched without incident into the cathedral city.

And many marched on. Through Champagne. For a while Rosie began to hope that on their secluded hillside they would escape the force of the fighting; hidden in trees, the house had not been shelled. But soon she was seeing with her own eyes what Sebastian had so painfully described. From her hilltop she could see the ant-like columns on the roads, the skirmishes between Frenchman and German. She heard the clatter of the machine-guns, and watched as the shells from vast black guns on wheels tore into the ground, destroying both vines and men. She saw lumbering tanks like prehistoric beasts, and the occasional plane buzzed low overhead.

She returned home sick at heart.

And all the time the French were retreating. Many of the Germans pursuing them were drunk and the roads were littered with broken champagne bottles, often causing damage to the wheels of the supply cars, though long wagon trains, pulled by horses, were more often in evidence.

The enemy was moving fast, first shelling and then occupying each small village. They swept through Chigny, inflicting much damage, and the word was out that both Epernay and Château-Thierry to the south of the Marne were to be evacuated.

"They have been fighting on some of our fields," Rosie reported to Madame Dupuis. "Mama, it's dreadful, there are dead men on our fields."

Madame lowered her head, and Rosie realised she was praying.

It was the morning of the sixth when two German cars appeared before the gatehouse. Old Tomas let them in. He had no choice. Nor could he warn anyone at the house what was happening, but Allie spotted them halfway up the drive and rushed to tell her mother.

By the time the vehicles had come to a halt at the foot of the steps, Rosie and Madame Dupuis were standing above them on the porch, waiting.

An undersized, sallow-faced young man wearing a spiked helmet leapt from the front seat of the first car and hurried to open the back door. Then he stood rigidly to attention.

The man who climbed out of the back of the car was older, well into his fifties. He wore field grey, with crimson and gold collar patches, gold-plaited epaulettes, and crimson stripes down trousers that tucked into black boots. He was squarely built, with heavy features and curled moustache and beard. He looked a little fat, but his face was not unpleasant.

Once his superior was safely out of the car, the younger officer relaxed his salute, marched to the foot of the steps and said in poor French: "You will have to leave. Lieutenant General Maurer is taking over this house."

Rosie felt Madame Dupuis bristle.

"Indeed he is not," she said, her voice deceptively mild. "This is my home, young man. You and your compatriots may be permitted to be our guests, but I and my family will not be leaving."

Rosie stole a look at Madame. The fierce nose was raised haughtily, her grey hair stood out around her head, and her thin figure was ramrod straight. Rosie almost laughed at the young officer's momentary confusion at being faced with this defiance. Then he put his hand on the butt of his revolver, threateningly. Madame did not flinch; she just stared at him contemptuously.

The general barked a question. The younger man, his face red with anger, replied to him in German, saluting before speaking.

Rosie tried desperately to remember some of the German of her childhood, but none came. She attempted another ploy.

"The Widow Dupuis is correct," she said in English. "Surely German gentlemen do not turn defenceless women and children from their homes?"

The older man looked at her sharply, and replied, also in English.

"You are a Britisher?" he asked.

"No, I am German American. My name was Brunner. We came from the Rheingau. My husband is a French serviceman."

"I see," he said. His English was accented, but appeared better than the lieutenant's French. "And who is this woman?"

"She is my mother-in-law, the Widow Dupuis."

"And what did she say?"

"That you were welcome to be our guests but that you would surely not expect us to leave our home." Rosie felt a little softening of what Madame had really said was in order.

"I see." He was smiling a little. "She is formidable, your mother-in-law, no?"

"Sometimes," Rosie said, and smiled back, as if they were sharing a conspiracy.

He pursed his lips, nodded his head contemplatively several times, while regarding her.

"We need a headquarters. This is the best house in the village."

"A large house, General, inhabited only by women, children and old men. I am sure we can find you good accommodation without anyone becoming homeless."

The young lieutenant's round face was set in disapproving lines, and he fidgeted with the braid hanging from his shoulder epaulettes.

His superior officer spoke to him sharply for almost a minute while Rosie and her mother-in-law stood, unmoving, above the two men, blocking the way into the house. Four more men, who appeared to be N.C.O.s, were leaving the other car, pulling at their high collars in the heat of the early autumn sun.

"I have told him that you may stay, providing you do not interfere with us," the older man finally said. "I myself will require the biggest room in the house. You will all be permitted to stay, but only after my men have chosen their own quarters."

Rosie nodded submissively.

"May I explain to my mother-in-law?" she asked.

He nodded brusquely, but he was watching her with a look that was familiar. Rosie felt her heart lift. She might be able to cope with this.

The lieutenant was a different matter. His face was petulant, and his mouth very red, the lower lip too full and turned downwards. It gleamed moistly. His eyes were narrowed under the helmet, and there was something about him that made Rosie uneasy. It was an uneasiness that had nothing to do with the war or his nationality, but a gut conviction that the man was bad.

After Madame had deliberately overplayed the hostess and welcomed the Germans into her home, the lieutenant, who was the general's A.D.C., stomped about, looking in room after room with Madame Dupuis and Rosie close behind. Madame's expression said that if he were not watched he would surely steal something. Equally, he behaved as if he were deeply suspicious of them. He rooted in cupboards, looked under beds, and insisted on seeing every room.

They came across Allie in the kitchen with Cook, and Rosie saw him lick his lips as he inspected her daughter as if she were a piece of merchandise.

"Who is this?" he asked in his bad French, jabbing an autocratic finger to where Allie stood by the kitchen tāble.

"My granddaughter," Madame said frostily.

"And the old woman?"

"Our cook."

"You will be cooking for us now, old woman," he informed her. "And it had better be good."

Cook looked as if she had not understood him.

Before they left the kitchen, he turned again to look at Allie, his red mouth gleaming, and Rosie felt her stomach clench.

She realised it was a long time since she had looked seriously at Allie. The child was becoming a woman; the little girl was vanishing. At fourteen, she was almost as tall as Rosie, and her breasts were formed. She had her father's black curly hair and his delicate features. Her deep blue eyes were even wider than the Dupuis' brothers', and her skin fairer. She was an extremely beautiful girl, with an alert, questioning manner. Her face in repose was thoughtful, almost Madonna-like, but when she smiled there was mischief and fun there.

"You might like the refreshment of a glass of champagne," Rosie murmured to take his glance from her baby. "Our maid will serve you in the parlour."

He gave her a look of deep suspicion.

"I think it would be better to finish the inspection first," he said. "In case there should be something you do not wish me to see."

Rosie shrugged and they continued the tour.

The general commandeered her room and the lieutenant chose Allie's, a room full of the child's girlish treasures. Whether out of politeness or to avoid the old woman's sharp tongue, they left Madame where she was. But Henri, Marie, Miss and Cook were told to leave their rooms. The house had four reasonable spare bedrooms, two of them in the attic. Rosie gave these to the staff and converted her little upstairs sitting room into a bedchamber for herself and Allie. She thought it was better if the child stayed with her.

As they carried bedclothing into the sitting room, Rosie said to her daughter: "*Chérie*, stay away from the young lieutenant. Just try to keep out of his sight."

Allie looked at her gravely and nodded.

"Don't worry, Mama, I will. He's scary, isn't he?" she said.

Rosie breathed a sigh of relief that Allie was aware, too. To be aware, she felt, was a great protection.

The day passed with the inhabitants of Les Hérissons moving their clothing and personal possessions, while the Germans set up telephone

285

communications. They commandeered Rosie's study which became a map and operations room.

Madame was not giving an inch. To forestall any orders from the hated invader, she sent Henri to the general's room, asking if he and his A.D.C. would join them for dinner at seven thirty. Henri was also to announce that champagne would be served in the parlour at seven. An outraged Henri went reluctantly, grumbling to himself, even after Madame had explained her reasoning.

It was a strange meal. The general, who seemed a fairly cheerful old buffer and who had a naughty twinkle in his eye whenever he looked Rosie's way, seemed amused at Madame's tactics.

His A.D.C. was anything but amused, and barely spoke while the general, who explained he had spent some years in Britain, conducted the conversation in English.

"I trust you ladies aren't planning any mischief," he said as he cut into an excellent piece of chicken. "You haven't any menfolk hidden or guns, I hope."

Rosie laughed and opened her eyes very wide.

"If we had guns we wouldn't tell you," she said coquettishly, "but even if we did, I doubt if any of us could use them. And as for menfolk – there's Henri, of course, and a few of the field hands. All men who are too old to fight."

"My age, I suppose?" he said wryly.

"Surely older," she smiled.

"It would be foolish to cause us any problems," he said, still smiling. "Today we crossed the Marne, and it looks, my dear, as if the fall of Paris is now inevitable."

Suddenly the lieutenant spoke. "Where is your daughter?" he asked, an unpleasant smile on his face. "We would have enjoyed her company."

"Allie always eats in the kitchen when we have guests," Rosie informed him, and turning back to the general asked: "Do you know the Rheingau? My father talked of it so often. One day I must visit there."

It was strange how people accepted situations, Rosie thought. After four days she felt as if the Germans had always been there. She resented them no less, but they had become familiar. Sleeping on the floor and dining each night with these intruders had become almost normal.

She even enjoyed the meals they shared. The general was a soldier of the old school, and there were times when he reminded her of André. He liked to talk about old battles and army life, and he enjoyed using his English. Enemy or not, she found it easy to respond to him and was amused by his conversation.

Leiutenant Schmidt was a different kettle of fish. Marie, who had to clean his room, reported indignantly that he had pictures which she could not possibly describe all over his room. "All of little girls," she said, "and he makes no effort to hide them. He is disgusting."

He also crept about the estate. No one knew where he would suddenly appear, and he constantly gave the staff contradictory orders until they did not know if they were coming or going. He had attempted to coerce a child from the village into his car and back to Les Hérissons. Her mother, made bold by the danger to her ten-year-old daughter, had snatched her into the house. The entire neighbourhood had been warned to watch for him, and to keep their children indoors when he was around.

The lieutenant rarely drank, but the four N.C.O.s had not drawn a sober breath since they settled into Les Hérissons and discovered the wine cellar. They ate at night in the kitchen, and Cook, to her chagrin, was forced to prepare their meals. They were greedy, ignorant, arrogant and complained constantly about the food, while demanding more champagne.

The general seemed to have little control over any of them, and with a contemptuous shrug described them as wartime soldiers.

One saving grace was that a few of the sunnier fields were ready for the gathering, and the entire family and staff were able to escape the house for most of the day, working high on the hillside where the vineyards met the woodlands. The refugees had moved on, but Miss brought along her English class to help. Many of the villagers also joined in.

It looked like being a fine harvest, though some of the fields had been ruined by the fighting, and many grapes were lost and vines destroyed. As Rosie laboured on the crush in the sheds after the gathering was done each day, she was reminded of her youth back in California; the work then had been hard and demanding because there were so few hands to do it – just as it was now.

Madame Dupuis, who worked as hard as anyone, said quietly to Rosie when they had gone back to the vats after dinner on the fourth night: "Henri saw his cousin today."

Henri's cousin was a printer on the Reims newspaper and therefore a mine of information though the Germans were censoring all war news.

"And?"

"The counter-offensive has begun. Our boys are pushing the Germans back. The Moroccans have stopped them at the marshes of St Gond, and they're regaining ground. Tomorrow French troops should recross the Marne. Paris is safe."

"Thank God," Rosie said. She stood for a moment, one hand on her aching back, thinking of Sebastian. She had told no one of his arrival, but her thoughts constantly went to him, praying for his safety.

As for what had happened between them, she knew that her instinct at the time – that it did not matter – had been right. She had given him love, comfort and sleep. He desperately needed all three. There was nothing else she could give him.

"Maybe it will be over soon," Madame said, her hands and face stained with grape juice. "I shall fumigate the house when those pigs are gone."

By the tenth of September, Rosie could sense the uneasiness in her 'guests'. The general spent much time in her office, on the telephone. The sunlit fields, many with still ripening grapes, were ominously quiet, but Rosie sometimes thought she saw a high cloud of battle dust in the sky. And at night she believed she could hear gunfire.

By the eleventh, the general was definitely worried and the sound of gunfire was not anyone's imagination. It rumbled like giant drums. He was silent over dinner, and there was no more talk of the fall of Paris. His A.D.C. became more sullen, his little eyes darting, his wet mouth pursed and angry. He had continued to leer at Allie, and Rosie never let the child out of her sight.

They were washing barrels together in one of the sheds on the morning of the twelfth when Madame called her. She went back into the house where, amazingly, one of her agents from Reims was waiting to see her.

"I have a message from Monsieur Brunel," he explained. "He says he has arranged transport for five hundred cases to go to the United States – if you can get them to Paris in three weeks' time. If you have the stock, I will try to think of a way of delivering them."

"And I will find the stock," she said.

She saw him to the door, where he wobbled off on his old bicycle, and she was hurrying back to the worksheds when she heard Allie scream.

Madame had heard it too and was hurrying through the kitchen door. Together they ran to the shed. The door was open, and on the floor was Allie. On top of her was the lieutenant, his trousers down round his ankles, his obscene white bottom riding in the dim light, while the girl shrieked and cried.

He had not heard them and Rosie, without hesitating, snatched a pitchfork from where it leaned against the wooden wall. She ran with it towards where they lay. Without pity, without thought, she plunged the fork into his back with all the force her anger could find.

His cry at the climax of the last sex act he would ever know mingled horribly with the scream of his dying. Blood spurted from four wounds in his back as he lay collapsed on Rosie's daughter.

"Get him off her," Madame said, "quickly."

It was easier said than done. He was a dead weight, and in sudden death, his erection had not subsided.

"Mama, help me, help me," Allie sobbed. "Oh, God, please help me."

Somehow the women managed to separate the bodies, while Allie moaned with pain and fear. Rosie pulled the child to her feet and held her tight. Her clothing was torn; her face and legs bloodied.

"He hit me, Mama. He made me," she sobbed. "It was horrible. Horrible."

"Darling, darling, don't cry, be brave just for a little longer. Let Grandma take you indoors and clean you up." She knew that somehow she must get rid of the body or the German reprisals on them all would be savage. Her only hope was that the general was not looking for his A.D.C. "Mama, get her into a bath if you can, and get me some help here. Send someone out. Henri, Marie, it doesn't matter."

It was Cook and Miss who came in the end, both strolling nonchalantly across the courtyard and into the shed as if arriving to inspect the barrels.

"Oh, my God," Miss said, retching, when she saw the sprawled body, the pitchfork still sticking from his back.

Cook, however, was made of sterner stuff. She calmly pulled the pitchfork out, showing surprising strength.

"No point wasting a good pitchfork," she said, "I'll clean that up quick enough with earth. Now what are we going to do with him, the filthy pig?"

Miss, still white-faced, had recovered and was looking at the body with loathing. "We could put him in a barrel for now," she suggested, "and bury him when it's dark."

"They'll find him with dogs if we bury him," Rosie said.

"Cut him up in pieces," Cook said grimly. "You leave that to me. It'll be a pleasure. I'll get rid of his head so no one will ever know it was him."

Reaction was setting in. Rosie thought she was going to be sick, and her hands were shaking uncontrollably. But if an English miss could be calm, so could she.

"A barrel's a good idea," she said. "It's quick and easy, but we can't leave him there long. They'll find him when they start looking."

"Get the barrel into my pantry, that's all you have to do," Cook said. "Raped our little Allie, didn't he? Well, he may be dead, but as far as I'm concerned he's not finished paying for it yet."

Somehow, shuddering, they folded his dead, bloodied body into one of the barrels.

"Don't waste a clean one on him," Cook advised. "I'll help you roll him across the courtyard and into the kitchen. Marie'll give us a hand there."

She seemed to have taken over, and Rosie could only feel relief.

"I'll get the blood off this floor," Miss said in English. "It's a dead giveaway. Oh, dear." Her hand flew to cover her mouth. "No pun intended."

Rosie and Cook pushed the barrel over the cobbles of the courtyard. It seemed to make a terrible noise, and Rosie prayed that no German would appear. The only one that would have been likely to was Lieutenant Schmidt himself. She was beginning to relax a little, but as they reached the safety of the kitchen, Henri came from the back of the house. He was very pale.

"The general wants to see you, Madame," he said.

She felt as if her hands had turned to ice, and her stomach somersaulted.

"Give me a cognac," she said to Cook who obliged like lightning. She swallowed it in one.

"You forget all this now, Madame," Cook said soothingly. "You don't know anything about nothing, remember. I'll deal with him."

Holding herself together, Rosie hurried to her office where the general was sitting, his tunic unbuttoned, and his elbows on the desk. He looked tired and old.

"We may not be here much longer," he said without preamble, suddenly very much the soldier. "I am expecting orders to return to Reims. I would like to thank you for your courtesy to an invader, and to ask you to say that we have been correct in our treatment of you, should you ever be asked."

The relief was like a flood.

"I would most certainly say that of you, General, because it would be true." Rosie said quietly. "I am grateful, also, for your courtesy. Perhaps we might meet again in happier times."

"If you go to the Rheingau," he said, smiling. Then he wiped a hand over his face, and said: "Soon you will be able to put your house in order again. But not for long, I fear. This war will not end quickly."

"I know," she said.

He rose to his feet, and held out his hand.

"Goodbye, Madame Rosie."

She gave him her hand, and he bent to kiss it.

"Adieu, General." She turned to leave.

"Rosie – " he called.

She turned back.

"My name is Max."

Somehow she managed a smile.

"Goodbye, Max," she said.

Taking Cook at her word, she rushed upstairs. Mama was sitting by the side of the bathrub, and Allie lay in the warm water, her eyes closed.

"Darling," Rosie asked. "Are you all right?"

"I hurt, but I think I'm all right, Mama," Allie said.

"Then I want you to be very brave and get dressed, and act normally, as if nothing had happened."

"Is he dead?"

"Yes."

"You killed him?"

"Yes."

"Good," Allie said. "I'm glad. And I'll do as you say."

"Thank you, darling." Rosie turned to Madame Dupuis. "The general says that they are leaving soon. They'll be looking for the A.D.C. any minute now."

"Leaving? Thank God!" Madame sank onto the side of the bathtub. "If we can just get through."

"We must get through," Rosie said. "Just act normally. I'm going back to washing barrels."

It was unfortunate that the general met Allie in the passage on his way from Rosie's study, and wanted to know what she had done to damage her face.

Allie said she had fallen from her swing, playing.

"Looks nasty," he said. "Be sure you keep it clean. That was you screaming, I suppose."

"Mama said I made a terrible fuss over nothing," Allie said solemnly. "But it did hurt."

"It must have done," he said, patting her gently on the head.

The rest of the day passed without incident until dinner time when there was one empty place at the table.

"Where is Karl?" the general asked.

"I have not seen him all day," Madame said, serenely forking up her egg mayonnaise.

"Nor I, " said Rosie.

The general looked thoughtful and then rang the bell. Henri came into the room.

"Give Lieutenant Schmidt my compliments and ask him to attend at table," he instructed.

Madame went on eating.

Seconds later, Henri was back.

"He is not in his room, sir. There is no sign of him, and it seems he has taken his clothing elsewhere."

Rosie closed her eyes. What had her staff been doing? she wondered.

Were they trying to give the impression that the lieutenant had deserted?

"I see," said the general. "Well, we shall search for him after we have eaten this excellent dish."

He finished the egg mayonnaise and begged to be excused for five minutes.

Madame and Rosie looked at each other without speaking. Henri sidled back into the room.

"He's asking the others in the kitchen if they've seen him," he whispered. "Miss got rid of the clothes, she burned all his dirty pictures, but she didn't have time to burn everything."

They could hear the general's footsteps and in a second he was returning to the table.

"May I serve now, sir?" Henri asked.

"Please do," said the general heartily. "And what are we having tonight?"

"*Feuilletée* of sweetbreads," Henri said, his face expressionless.

He returned a moment later, three plates on a silver tray. Each held a piece of puff pastry filled with meat in a creamy sauce that spilled down onto the plate. Henri placed a portion in front of each of them, serving the general last, before handing vegetables.

They ate in silence until the general had cleared his plate.

"That was delicious," he said.

"Thank you, sir," said Henri. "I will inform Cook."

"And now," said the general. "I must start the search for Karl."

"Is there anything we can do?" Rosie asked.

"I think not. Perhaps he has deserted."

His expression was quizzical.

"Surely not!" said Rosie.

"It would not be in character. But we shall see." He paused and looked at her consideringly. Switching to English, he said: "Or, we could make a small arrangement, you and I, Madame Rosie. You could return to your bedchamber tonight, and I could tell my men that the lieutenant must have deserted, and that I have been expecting him to do that very thing. But we both know he has not deserted, do we not?"

Rosie hesitated, her mind racing over the possibilities of Schmidt's body or his clothing being found. Her problem was that she was uncertain of exactly what Cook and the others had done.

The safe thing would be to agree, but what would it entail if she did? A night, maybe more, in the general's bed.

And if she did not agree – a firing squad for all of them.

As if he could read her thoughts, he said: "If anything has happened to him, I am afraid that the consequences for all in this household will be grave."

There was little time to think, but her survival instincts were alive and well.

"General, I am certain that nothing has happened. Perhaps he found a young girl of his fancy in the village. And if I were to return to my room while you occupy it, it would be because I wished to, and for no other reason."

"And do you wish to?"

"I had not thought about it before. I do not know the answer. I shall need time to think."

"My dear Madame Rosie," he said, pulling at his beard, "it has always been my experience that it is not a decision for which women need time. But I await you. And I shall postpone the search for the lieutenant until the dawn."

He bowed stiffly in the Prussian way and left the room.

"What was he saying?" Madame Dupuis hissed. "You went quite white."

Another secret to keep. Rosie knew she could not burden her mother-in-law with this dilemma.

"I think he knows," was all she said. "If he finds anything, there will be reprisals."

"Coffee, madame?" Henri was poised with the pot. "It is all taken care of," he said quietly. "Cook cut him up. We took him up to the top fields by the woods. The foxes and the wild dogs will have finished him off by morning. Cook wanted to give him to the pig farmer at Chigny. She said it would be appropriate, but the pig farmer said no."

He handed the sugar and milk.

"Oh, and by the way, mesdames, the general and his staffs' portions of the sweetbreads consisted of, if you'll pardon me," he coughed delicately, "the lieutenant's testicles. Cook thought that appropriate, too."

Miss had not been able to get rid of all the lieutenant's clothes. She tried to burn them in the kitchen stove, but they smelt too bad, particularly the leather bits, and the buttons wouldn't melt. So, for the time being, she had dunked everything, boots as well, in a small wine vat, where happily they had sunk to the bottom. But wine vats would be the first place that the Germans would look.

If the foxes and the wild dogs didn't do what Cook expected of them, the lieutenant's remains would soon be found at dawn. The general would call in their own dogs from the Chigny headquarters.

Sitting in the parlour, Rosie reasoned it out. She could take a chance and go to her little sitting room with Allie, or she could secure their safety by going to the general.

She was well aware that the 'guests' would line up the entire

293

household and shoot them all, Allie included, if they thought anything had happened to Schmidt. She was surprised that they had not done it already.

There wasn't any choice.

At ten o'clock she reluctantly climbed the stairs to her room, telling herself that it couldn't be any worse than making love with Clovis. Indeed, it might be better.

She tapped gently on the door, and it was immediately opened. The general was wearing a black velvet dressing gown and a nightcap with a tassel.

"I had decided you were not coming," he said.

"I had one or two things to finish," she told him. "I did not intend to keep you waiting."

"I am honoured to see you." He smiled, taking her hands, and pulled her into the room.

He had just put his arms round her and she was trying not to tense when there was a pounding of footsteps on the stairs. One of the N.C.O.s was calling for him in a crackle of urgent, shouting German.

Rosie went cold. They must have found something!

But the general merely listened and then pushed her gently away. He shook his head, and said ruefully: "I have to go to the telephone, my dear. Headquarters wants to speak to me."

He took off the nightcap and went out of the room. She stood irresolute, and then decided to follow him downstairs. She did not wish Henri or any of the staff to see her in this room.

She waited in the hall, and after about five minutes he came back from the office, shouting for his men. When he saw her he halted, almost as if he were on parade.

"My orders are to leave for Reims immediately," he told her abruptly. "We will be pulling out of here in the morning. I must rejoin the men. Get Henri to bring the cars round while we prepare to leave."

She could not believe that she had been saved so easily.

"Of course," she said. "Is there anything I can do?"

He stopped and smiled at her. It was a tired, sad smile and she could not help pitying him.

"Yes," he said. "You can tell me honestly why you came to my room tonight."

She did not even hesitate.

"Because I wanted to, Max," she told him.

Chapter Eighteen

The minute the Germans had disappeared down the drive, Rosie flew to find Allie. She was sitting in the parlour, her head drooping and her arms folded tightly against her body.

"Oh, Allie!" Rosie said.

The child looked up, and her face crumpled. Her lower lip trembled uncontrollably, and she began to sob.

Rosie sat down beside her and pulled the girl's head onto her shoulder.

"You are my brave wonderful girl," she said. "I am proud of you. You saved us all."

"Mama, I was so frightened," Allie sobbed. "Grandma said we would all be shot if they found out what had happened. The general wanted to know what I had done to my face, and I said I had fallen from my swing. He said that must be why I was screaming, and I told him you said I had made a fuss over nothing."

Rosie closed her eyes, trying to think what to say.

"You are the bravest girl in the world," she said, trying not to cry herself. "That was so clever and quick of you. Oh, my darling girl."

She hugged her daughter feverishly, not knowing how to begin to speak of what had happened in the shed.

"Mama," Allie said, still sobbing. "He ravished me, didn't he?"

Rosie felt her throat constrict.

"Yes, darling. He did."

"Grandma always said that was what the Boche did. But it wasn't my fault, Mama. He just suddenly appeared when you went, and he – " she hesitated.

"Do you want to talk about it?" Rosie asked gently.

"I don't know. It was all so horrible. Mama, is that what sex is?"

"No, darling," Rosie said. "That is not what sex is. It was what you said – ravishing someone. Ravishing is when you don't want it to happen. Sometimes it is called rape. That's what happened to you. But you musn't believe that is what sex is, because someday when you love someone, much the same thing will happen. The difference is that you will want it to, and you will be happy and ready to have a good, kind man so close to you. Sex is really only another word for love and two people loving each other. That man was not capable of love."

Allie thought about it for a moment, her head quiet on her mother's shoulder.

"I can't imagine that ever being nice." She was calmer now.

"One day you will."

Allie was quiet again and then said: "He is really dead?"

"Very dead," Rosie said, controlling a shudder as she remembered what had happened to him.

"I'm glad he's dead," Allie said simply, "because I won't have to be frightened of him coming back and doing it again. And if he's dead maybe I can forget it."

"You must forget it, if you can," Rosie said. "Tomorrow, when you've slept, we'll talk about it, every little bit of it, and when you've talked about it, it will all be washed away. I promise."

"It's hard to talk about," Allie said doubtfully.

"It won't be when you start."

The girl was silent again, and Rosie could feel that she was trembling slightly.

"Mama?"

"Umm?"

"Can I sleep in your bed with you tonight?"

"Of course. Every night for a week if you like."

Allie sighed a sigh of pure relief, and then said: "I wish Papa was here. He wouldn't have let that man do that to me."

"Your Papa would have killed him," Rosie said fiercely.

"But you did that, Mama," Allie reminded her.

The words stunned Rosie. She had not accepted, even to herself, that she had killed a man. The simple statement of fact from her daughter brought home the full horror of what had happened. Her daughter had been raped, and she, Rosie, who considered herself so civilised, had abruptly ended the rapist's life with a pitchfork, and permitted his body to be chopped into pieces and left for the foxes. He was not even to have a decent Christian burial.

And worse, in her anxiety to keep them all safe from the firing squad, she had not even reacted when she had been told that his most private parts had been served up as a meal for his fellow Germans.

She suddenly felt dreadfully sick, but fought the feeling so she could continue to comfort Allie.

"I think it would be a good idea if you had another lovely hot bath to wash him all away," she suggested. "And then we'll curl up together in bed. How about that?"

"Ummm. Yes, please," Allie said.

It took Allie a long time to sleep. Sometimes she whimpered as she half-dozed, and at times she cried. She complained of pain, and Rosie wondered if in the morning she should take her to the village doctor. The girl slept on in the morning, and Rosie rose earlier than normal. She wanted to talk to Madame. She was suddenly desperate to share her burden with someone.

"Should I take her to the doctor?" she asked.

Madame Dupuis shook her head. "Only if it is necessary," she advised. "The fewer people who know what happened, the better. Otherwise the village will whisper for ever of how she was raped. I have cautioned all the staff to silence, and under the circumstances it is unlikely that they will talk to anyone."

"I suppose you're right." Rosie was uncertain.

"Of course I'm right," Madame said. "Allie has to live her life in this community. We don't want her to be either a figure of fun or an object of pity. No one must know."

Rosie nodded.

"But if she is still in pain this afternoon I must take her to the doctor."

"Of course," Madame said, and added in her forthright manner. "I doubt she will be. She is near grown."

She saw Rosie's stricken face.

"My dear girl," she said gently. "At times like these there is nothing left but to be practical, sensible and deal in the best way we can with situations. Just as you did yesterday."

Rosie felt herself beginning to shake again, as she had found herself doing every time she thought of the pitchfork plunging into the lieutenant's back.

"Mama, I am not sure how I can cope with the idea of having killed a man," she said painfully. "And what happened afterwards does not bear thinking about. But everything went so fast. There was no time for niceties."

"Of course not." Madame was brisk, matter-of-fact. "You were surviving, like the rest of us. Niceties have no place in survival."

"I feel, somehow, that they should have."

"Go and talk to the priest, my dear girl," Madame suggested, taking Rosie's hand in hers. "Place your burdens on him. That is what he is there for."

"But, Mama, I so rarely go to Mass," Rosie protested. "You know I am not religious. How can I give him my burdens now when I disregard him in safer days?"

Madame's voice was patient, as if she was speaking to a child.

"Because that's what he is there for," she repeated.

When Allie was out of bed and had breakfasted, and seemed settled, Rosie left her with her grandmother and set off on Clovis's old bike to Chigny. She had decided to take Madame's advice, though she wasn't quite sure why.

As she cycled along roads where bloated horses lay, trees were split asunder, as if lightning had struck, and huge holes tore the roads apart, she thought of those she loved who were facing greater trials than she and her family were at Les Hérissons. Whatever had happened, they all had their lives. But Sebastian, Clovis – and her much loved Philippe, where were they? She looked up into the grey sky and sent a brief message to God to keep them safe, and then grimly cycled on.

The little church with its sturdy square tower looked deserted as she leaned the bicycle against the old walls. There were no worshippers inside the cosy exterior of the friendly little place of worship. The confessional, set close by the font where a stone angel led a little child by the hand, was empty. Christ on the Cross looked unexpectedly serene under the stained-glass window. A smell of dust, flowers and incense was in the air.

Rosie wandered out and towards the little graveyard on the Ludes road. And there she saw the priest. He was busy tidying the graves, the wind whipping his cassock around his cracked black boots, whistling tunelessly to himself as he placed dead chrysanthemums in a battered old bucket.

He straightened as he saw her coming towards him, the wind tormenting her long black skirt and ruffling her hair.

"Good morning," he said. "It's Madame Dupuis, is it not?"

She found herself suddenly uncertain, and just nodded.

"I was just having a little clear-up," he said. "I like to keep it all neat. Particularly Madame Pommery's resting place, there. She liked everything looking right and in order in her lifetime. The family normally tend her grave, of course, but these are troubled times."

"It's a peaceful place," she said, as indeed it was, with its sturdy walls and gentle views of the vineyards.

"Well, yes." His face, creased like an old forgotten apple, widened into a broad smile. "I like to come here myself when I have something on my mind. And I'm thinking that perhaps there is something on yours. Did you want to confess?"

"No." She realised that was not what she wanted. "But I would like to talk to you."

"And why not?" he said. "I've near enough finished here, and it's just about to drizzle. Why don't we go and sit in the church. It's warmer there, but peaceful too."

She followed him into the church and noticed that he walked as briskly as a much younger man. Inside, he settled himself at the end of a pew, beckoning her to sit on the one facing him. And then he nodded encouragingly.

"I have killed a man," she said baldly, and stopped.

He just nodded, expressionless, waiting for her to go on.

"He was a German soldier, a lieutenant living in my home with other Germans. They took over the house. He was a bad man. I found him raping my fourteen-year-old daughter, and without thinking, without caring and without conscience, I killed him."

He still did not speak.

"I killed him with a pitchfork while he was raping her," she said, her voice almost a whisper. "He died immediately."

"And where is his body?" the priest asked gently.

"Gone. It was," she hesitated, "disposed of, by others, but I did not stop them. If it had been found, all at Les Hérissons would have been shot."

"I see." He was silent for a moment. "And what do you want to do now?"

"Forget it, if I can. But I am not sure I can."

"Umm. The Germans have gone?"

"They left last night, before they had time to look properly for him." She paused, sighed, and said: "His commanding officer guessed what had happened. He said he would agree that his lieutenant had deserted on condition that I spent the night with him."

"And what did you do?"

"I agreed. But something saved me. He had to leave immediately for Reims. His headquarters telephoned. I was already in his room."

"God saved you," the priest said, his voice full of confidence.

"God? After I had murdered a man, Father?" That did not make sense.

The priest rose to his feet, and with his hands behind his back, wandered a few paces up and then a few paces down the aisle of his church.

"The Germans are leaving Reims today," he said, almost chattily. "They've asked for hostages, you know. Dr Langlet has been obliged to supply General von Bülow with a list of a hundred people who will be shot if the inhabitants of the town make any kind of hostile move towards the German troops. The Mayor has put his name at the head of the list, followed by Monseigneur Neveux, the Cardinal's coadjutor. The rest have been chosen from amongst the counsellors, members of the Chamber of Commerce – men of that ilk.

"They are having to leave with the German army, well guarded, of course. But no one doubts they will be shot if the general decides upon it. Remember what the German army did to the hostages in Belgium? They massacred one hundred people, civilians, children, old folk. That was at Dinant, in August. Not long ago really.

"And how many more dead since? I seem to have attended a great many burials of men who were not of my flock lately, my dear."

Somewhere in what he was saying there was a message for her. She waited.

"But whoso shall offend one of these little ones which believe in me, it were better for him that a millstone were hanged about his neck, and that he were drowned in the depth of the sea," he said, nodding. "The scriptures are very clear on that." He stood thinking for a long moment before turning abruptly, his cassock flaring. "Your daughter? Is she all right?"

"She is glad the man is dead, and it cannot be right for a child to rejoice at death. But she says if he is dead she will not be frightened and perhaps she can forget what happened."

"She sees with a child's unclouded eyes but children do not understand that vengeance is the Lord's." He took another turn, and looked thoughtfully at the little altar dedicated to the Virgin. "These times are perhaps more suited to the teachings of the Old Testament. An eye for an eye ..." He had begun to smile. "You should, of course, report the matter to the police. The problem is that they might give you a medal."

"Father, are you telling me that what I did was not wrong?"

He puffed out his cheeks like a bullfrog. "I am saying nothing of the kind. Of course it is wrong to kill, even a man such as this. But shall we say that there were extenuating circumstances? Circumstances beyond your control. And though I doubt that he was a Catholic, I shall pray for him and for his soul. And you must do the same. We will now pray together that he may repent, that his sins are washed away and that he finds heavenly peace."

The old priest dropped painfully to his knees on the flagstones of the aisle, and Rosie followed suit. He muttered Latin prayers she did not understand, and with her eyes screwed shut and the cold of the floor striking up through her knees, she found that it was simply not possible for her to pray for the soul of Lieutenant Schmidt. All she wished was for him to rot in hell. Why then, when she felt like that, was she leading this sincere, kind old man through a charade? Hypocrite, she told herself. You are a hypocrite, wanting someone to tell you it was fine and dandy to kill the man. When the truth is that you are glad, glad, glad you did.

She got to her feet.

"Father," she said. "I cannot pray for him. The truth is that I am glad I killed him. I am glad he is dead. And why should he live when so many good, true men are dying? You have been very kind, but I was wrong to trouble you. I am not ready to forgive. And vengeance, in this case, was mine. The Lord might have taken far too long."

His russet face was calm.

"You have not troubled me, my dear," he said. "These are times that place an intolerable burden on the conscience of all of us. Go with God, and remember I am always here."

She went home, downhill, with her knees up and the pedals spinning on their own and then uphill again, peddling with vigour, the wind in her face. She felt restored. She felt like the Lord of Hosts. The lieutenant had deserved to die. And die he had. That was the end of it.

She was about to wheel the bicycle round the back of the house when she saw Madame Dupuis beckoning her from the window of the parlour. The old lady pushed up the casement and called: "You have a guest."

Sebastian, was her first thought, and she dropped the bicycle by the steps and hurried in the front door. But it was not Sebastian.

It was Philippe.

He stood in the parlour, ill at ease, wearing black polished boots, red trousers and a blue belted and buckled tunic with fringed epaulettes on the shoulders. There was a revolver on his right hip.

"Good morning, Rosie," he said quietly.

There had been only a business arrangement between them for more than two years now. She had hardly seen him, and finding him at Les Hérissons made her throat close and her cheeks flush.

"I'll be off," Madame said quickly. "I was just keeping Philippe company. I have a million things to do. Do say goodbye before you go, won't you, Philippe."

She left, quietly closing the door behind her.

For a moment they stood, looking at each other. He looked older and tired. His face was grey. Then he said: "I can only stay a very short while. But I had to see you before . . ." he hesitated. "Madame Dupuis tells me you have had a difficult time here. Are you all right?"

She nodded, uncertain of how much Madame had said.

"I came for two reasons. The first, I have something to tell you. Bad news I am afraid."

She still had not spoken. She knew what he was going to say.

"Sebastian is dead."

She stood immobile, her eyes closed against tears, her heart a clenched fist of sorrow.

"I don't think I can bear it," she said. "I loved him so."

"We both loved him." His voice was sombre. "And I cannot believe that he has gone."

He moved towards her and took her hands.

301

"You must be brave. He would not want you to grieve."

"I saw him only a week ago," she said, full of sorrow. "He came in the night, when the army was retreating. He was muddy, tired and, Philippe, he was frightened. He described what he had seen. It was a glimpse of hell. He slept. He said I always saved him when he was lost and crying."

More than that she could not tell him, but remembering that night, she felt an overwhelming wave of relief that she had loved Sebastian and not sent him away. She began to shed big, slow tears, and with the sadness was anger at the terrible, terrible waste.

"He loved you more than anyone else in the world," Philippe said. "I am glad that you saw him again. He wanted you to see him in his uniform. He was so proud to be a soldier. It was what he chose to do."

"He died in battle?" She made herself ask the question.

"Yes. Leading his men. Running into the fire and the bayonets. He seemed so confident of his safety, but he was so young. If he had been older, wiser ..."

"Death is no respector of age," she said dully.

"I know. So, Rosie, please do not think that I am being melo-dramatic, but I may not return from this war either. Few will. I could not let any more time pass without telling you that I love you, that I have always loved you and always will. Sebastian's death has made me realise how easily it could be too late to tell you how I feel. I have your letter ending our love with me. I have always carried it. I respected your wishes, but for me these last two years have been meaningless. I have missed you more than any words can say. Not a day goes past when I do not think of you. This war means little to me, for having lost you, and now having lost Sebastian, I have little else to lose."

He stopped, and stood, his head bowed.

"It would help," he added quietly, "if I could go away believing you have some feeling for me."

Their hands were still clasped and he was cold in spite of the warmth of the day. She felt as if she were suffused with light, and as if some unbearable burden had suddenly been taken away. But the thought of Sebastian laid the burden back. Sadness and joy were combined. She took one hand from his and tenderly stroked his face.

"You look tired, my darling," she said. "As I am tired of missing and wanting you. It has been so long ..."

He sighed, and his arms closed round her, and he was kissing her eyes, her mouth, her cheeks, her hair, muttering broken endearments, murmuring of love.

Then he drew back.

"Rosie, Rosie, why did you do it?" he asked. "Why did you send me away?"

"I thought it was right," she said simply. "With your new wife and your new daughter, it seemed best to stop cluttering your life. I was selfish in one way – I did not think I could bear to come second to your child. It was painful enough that we could not be together always without that. And I was hurt. I could reason that Lorraine would make you a father again. I knew that might happen. But the shock of finding out as I did ..."

His arms tightened round her again.

"I simply couldn't tell you," he said. "I just didn't know how to begin. I wrote several times, and tore the letters up. I rehearsed the words a thousand times and never found the courage to say them. I think I knew you would do what you finally did.

"Of course, I would have told you myself eventually. I would have had to. Sebastian just did it first. But how could he know what damage he was doing? And so we have lost two long years of our lives. And we have lost Sebastian. His death has shown us how short life can be. We must not waste any more of it. Will you love me again? Please, Rosie, let me back into your life."

"The truth is you were never really out of it," she said.

They were standing apart, but they looked at each other and smiled, and the smiles were like caresses.

"I wish I could stay," he said. "But the Germans are pulling out of Reims and we are going in. My commanding officer gave me permission to ride to tell you about Sebastian since it was so near."

"We still have our apartment there," she said, thinking of happier days.

"If it has not been shelled."

"Maybe we can meet there, soon."

"Maybe." He leaned forward and kissed her gently on the mouth. "Until we meet again. And whatever happens, remember I love you."

He half-saluted and was gone.

Madame Dupuis was as good as her word. After the Germans had left, she was determined that with Marie's help every room in the house that their presence had polluted must be scrubbed, washed, polished, and dusted.

While Rosie talked with Philippe, she bustled upstairs, Marie puffing behind, laden with pails, brooms and dusters. The two women worked together, Marie doing the harder work, and Madame polishing and dusting until Rosie's bedroom shone.

"Right," said Madame, "and now we shall do Miss's room."

Since Allie was sleeping with Rosie, she left the child's bedroom until the next day.

"We shall spend the entire morning on Allie's room," she informed

Marie, "so that not the slightest trace of that swine remains. Then gradually we shall go right through the house."

They worked on Allie's room on the morning of the fourteenth, even hanging the feather mattress out of the window to air, when Marie, who had been washing the polished wood surround of the floor, stood up, straightening her back.

"Listen, Madame," she said, "it's the guns again."

Madame, who was getting a little deaf, cocked her head, good ear to the window

"You're right, Marie," she said. "Are they coming back, do you think?"

"They drove the Germans out of Chigny last night. Every one of them has gone," Marie said. "And that general spoke true when he said they were pulling out of Reims. Word is they went."

"But they're up to mischief somewhere," said Madame, her listening ear still alert. "Well, we can do nothing. Let's get this room clean."

When Marie had finished scrubbing, Madame sent her off to start on the servants' rooms while she tidied and straightened her grandchild's little treasures. She was checking that the drawers in Allie's desk had not been disturbed when she spotted an exercise book underneath a pile of school manuals. Written on the front in careful, ornate script was MY DIARY, by Mademoiselle Rosalie Marie Dupuis, Les Hérissons, Chigny les Roses, Champagne, France, the World, the Universe.

Madame smiled, and picked up the book, idly turning back the cover to the first page.

"Today has been the very best day of the trip so far," she read in Allie's sprawling, careless handwriting, "though it did not start out well and I thought something dreadful might have happened."

One of her fantasies again, Madame thought fondly, as she read on to find out what it was that might have been dreadful.

She discovered how Allie had decided to watch the sunrise all on her own at five o'clock in the morning, and thinking how well the child wrote, was just about to put the book back when she saw the words about a man creeping from her mother's room, "all sly and furtive and looking as if he should not be there".

Aware then that this was a private diary she should not be reading, she hesitated, but curiosity won.

"Then to my dismay, I saw it was Monsieur Philippe," she read, "and because he looked so guilty I thought he must have done Mama a mischief so I rushed to save her.

"The worst thing was that when I went into her room Mama did not have any clothes on at all, and it was a shock because I have never seen a grown-up without clothes before. I could not help staring at her and seeing how shapely she was, and that she had hair on her body, down there. I wonder if this is normal."

By now it was too late to stop. Madame read on to where Allie had written of the ship's ball . . . "I saw Monsieur Philippe there. I suppose his headache had gone. He was dancing with Mama and looking into her eyes like on the cinema. I wish he was not here, and I wish Mama had had her clothes on this morning. It does not feel right to have seen her without them, even though she was only like a lady in a picture in the Louvre."

Madame put the exercise book back exactly where she had found it, and thoughtfully went downstairs.

She went to her own little sitting room and took out her tapestry to calm her while she mulled over what she had read. Madame Dupuis loved Rosie. She loved her for her strength and spirit and for her caring nature. She was aware that Rosie never had loved her son, Clovis, but she had always thought that they rubbed along well enough in their own way and that the marriage was a long way from being a disaster.

She had sometimes wondered about the friendship with Philippe Lefevre, but firmly put any suspicions out of her mind. Rosie had become the most important part of Les Hérissons. She had given them Allie, she had restored their prestige in Champagne, she had given Clovis a *raison d'être* with his work in the vineyards.

Madame Dupuis knew about Claudette and Madame Frédéric. She had always known. But it was one thing for Clovis to have his Claudette, and quite another for Rosie to have Philippe. Claudette was just a whore. Philippe was a lover. That could be dangerous and, in any case, infidelity was different for women. Madame did not approve of adulterous women, but was prepared to turn a blind eye to the behaviour of men.

She did not care to think of her son being cuckolded, but neither did she care to think of losing Rosie. And then she remembered that Philippe was married and a father again. Therefore the possibility was that nothing would change. Madame hated change.

She sighed, and thought how lucky she had been that she and her husband had loved each other so. Though she had not had him with her for anywhere near long enough before the good Lord had taken him away, she had been remarkably fortunate.

She decided to try to forget what she had read, or at least not let it influence her in any way.

A little knowledge was indeed a dangerous thing, but sometimes, she decided, as she went to see how Marie was getting on, a little knowledge could come in useful.

Chapter Nineteen

The guns that Madame and Marie heard were the Germans shelling Reims. But the true bombardment did not begin until the nineteenth of that black September.

At eight in the morning from the heights of the little towns of Brimont, Berru, Nogent-l'Abbesse and Cernay to the north and east, where the Germans were solidly entrenched, they fired on Reims: their target, the thirteenth-century cathedral. Their aim was precise. The first shells hit the North Tower.

All day the bombardment continued, systematic and implacable. The Remois either took shelter in the chalk caves where the champagne was stored, or they fled for the road westward to Paris or southward to Épernay. The shells hit the centre of the town again and again. The Place Royal was aflame, so was the Place Godinot and the most ancient quarters of the 'lanes' where it was impossible to halt the flames. The fire burned for four days, until the entire centre was blazing. The desperate and frightened Remois called for the firemen, but the fire station itself had burnt to the ground.

And at three o'clock in the afternoon, the cathedral roof was fired by a direct hit from these new vandals. The citizens who still had homes to come from or who sheltered in cellars crept out to stare in awe and anger at the sight of their cathedral, one of the most historic buildings in the world, blazing. There was nothing to be done. As they watched the huge wooden rafters groaned and collapsed in a shower of flame and sparks.

That night a red glow lit the sky and a pall of smoke hung high like a shroud where Reims lay. And it was while all the Dupuis family and their staff were out on the hillside at Les Hérissons, gazing, appalled, out across the Vesle River to where Reims lay beyond, that Clovis reluctantly came home.

He could not understand why Claudette was insisting on bringing him to this place. The turreted house, the drive and the steps to the front door meant nothing to him. He had tried to explain that he just wanted to stay in her room and listen to the clacking of her knitting needles, or see her nimble fingers crocheting lace. But she had insisted on coming here.

It irked him that he could not make her understand what he wanted. The difficulty was the noise of the guns thundering in his head. He wished that they would stop firing, just for a few moments at least, so that he could gather his wits. If it wasn't the guns, the flashing of the explosions worried his eyes so that nothing looked quite right, and all colours seemed to have become tinged with orange. When he tried to speak to explain something, it was almost as if the guns began again, quite deliberately stopping his thinking. What made it worse was that he had walked so far to get back to Claudette and he couldn't tell her how important and how difficult it had been.

In all the anxiety of finding his way he had forgotten that Madame Frédéric was dead. The establishment now belonged to Claudette, of course. That was good because she could now be solely his, though he had never really thought of her as being anyone else's.

He had been so pleased to find her, but she had looked quite frightened when he stumbled into the salon. She whisked him upstairs to her room away from the other girls. Then she asked if he had been home.

This was home, he explained, but she looked even more frightened and said that it was not.

That had made him cry, and she hugged and kissed him, crying herself, and saying over and over again, 'Oh, my poor Clovis,' until for a fraction of a moment, her voice and her arms silenced the roar of the guns.

She had let him sleep for a little while, and then made him bathe. She washed him just as his mother used to do when he was little. He liked that. She brushed all the mud and dust from his uniform and found him clean underthings. Then she insisted that her motor and her chauffeur drive him to this place, which she said was his home. He cried again and asked her to take him back to her room with the cuddly animals and the little boxes that he had given her.

He tried to stop crying, because every time he cried it made her cry, too. He did not want her to be sad, not now they were together again. But then when he stopped crying, the explosions started again and his head was full of yellow, red and orange lights. So he let her do what she wanted, thinking he would sort it all out when the guns went away.

They left the chauffeur at the main road, and she seemed quite distracted when she found the strange, isolated house empty. He explained to her at best he could that that was probably because the

Germans had been there and killed everyone. He had seen many, many houses like this, and sometimes whole villages, on his way to find her. When he told her this it made her cry again.

"I can't leave you here alone," she said.

"Why would you do that?" he asked her wonderingly.

"Oh, Clovis. I wouldn't. Of course I wouldn't," she said. "We shall sit here on the steps and wait until someone comes home. But you must not be upset if they send me away."

"I shall just come with you if they do." He was baffled as to why they would send her away. "I don't want to be here anyway."

But if she wanted to sit on the steps, that was what he would do. He settled himself beside her, taking her hand in his, yawning widely. He was very tired, and the noise of the guns was dreadful.

Time seemed to be meaningless to him at the moment, so he wasn't certain how long they were there on the steps before the people came walking up the path. There were quite a lot of people, and one of them, a young girl, detached herself and ran towards him.

She was calling "Papa, Papa." He looked around for the man she was calling to, and then realised she was running towards him.

Claudette was saying: "Clovis, please, please, embrace her. She is your daughter. Don't frighten her, embrace her."

He could not think why Claudette would believe he would want to frighten a young girl, nor could he understand why she should think he had a daughter, but the urgency in her voice momentarily quelled the guns.

When the young girl threw herself at him, he dutifully wrapped his arms round her. And then over her head as she clung to him, he said to Claudette: "What shall I do now?"

But Claudette was staring at the woman who seemed to be leading the group. She was no longer taking any notice of him.

With a strange young girl in his arms, and the guns thundering in his ears, and Claudette ignoring him, Clovis was suddenly very frightened. He wanted to hide. He disentangled himself from the child and ran up the steps to the shelter of the porch. There he lay down and curled himself into a ball as tight and as small as possible, his hands over his eyes, so that the shells would not find him and he would not see their livid flashes.

And just for a moment he felt safe again.

Rosie had not recognised Clovis at first as she and Madame Dupuis walked together up the drive of the house. Henri, Marie and Cook were behind, talking in hushed whispers about the dreadful bombardment. She noticed two people, a soldier and a woman, sitting on the steps, and said to Madame that it looked as if they had visitors, probably more refugees.

But then Allie who had been walking slightly ahead suddenly began to run.

"I do believe it's Clovis," Madame said.

Rosie felt a wave of relief that he was safe. She had not heard from him since that one letter, and though events had given her little time to worry about him, the sight of him meant that one more burden of anxiety was lifted.

The woman in bright pink sitting at his side she did not recognise. It was the woman who got up first and seemed to be pulling Clovis to his feet. As she and Madame increased their pace, she could see that the woman was small and plump, with a great many blonde curls under a small, saucy hat. It suddenly dawned on her who this must be.

Clovis seemed to run away as they neared, pushing Allie away from him, and inexplicably he lay down and curled up on the porch, like a frightened hedgehog.

"Mama, what's the matter with Papa?" Allie was calling.

The woman in pink was coming to meet them but she stopped, leaving a respectable distance that encouraged no handshakes between them.

"Forgive me, madame," she said to Rosie, twisting her hands. "I should not be here, but there was nothing else to do."

"You must be Claudette," Rosie said.

The woman flushed under the thick layer of powder she wore. She was embarrassed.

"Yes, madame," she almost whispered. "He came to me. I'm afraid he is shell-shocked. I brought him here, but he remembers nothing. I am so sorry, but he only seems to remember me. Please don't be upset if he does not recognise you."

Rosie knew that she should be affronted that Clovis's *poule* was standing outside the family front door, but she felt nothing of the kind. She could see that the woman's powder was streaked with tear tracks, and her expression was not so much anxious as heartbroken. Her mouth was trembling as she tried to control herself. This woman might be a whore, but she had feelings.

"I think we had better all go inside, don't you?" she said, and turning to where Madame Dupuis was standing, her back stiff with indignation, said: "Mama, may I present Madame Claudette. She has very kindly brought Clovis home to us, and she says he is shell-shocked."

Rosie was proud of the way her mother-in-law rose to the challenge. She extended her hand and Claudette timidly shook it. At that moment, Henri, who had gone into the house by the back, was just

309

opening the front door. Decencies over, Rosie ran up the steps and knelt down by her husband.

"Clovis," she said gently. "I am so pleased to see you. Please stand up and we will go indoors and be comfortable."

He jerked his body into an even tighter knot. He said nothing.

Allie's face was white; bewildered.

"Mama, is he ill?" she asked.

Rosie nodded, and Madame Dupuis came forward, peered down at him and said authoritatively: "Clovis, get up from there this minute."

He still did not move. Rosie looked up at her mother-in-law and shook her head. Then Claudette came to kneel on the other side of him. She gently took one hand from his eyes and held it.

"Clovis, please get up," she said softly. "For me. I'm cold. I want to go inside."

Immediately he clumsily unfolded himself, and with his hand in hers, permitted himself to be taken into the house. Awkwardly everyone filed indoors where Madame Dupuis ushered them into the parlour. Clovis hovered in the doorway, uneasily, looking around him as if to make sure there were no hidden traps.

"It's all right," Claudette said soothingly. "It's safe here."

"Sit on the sofa," Rosie suggested to her, "and then he can sit next to you."

When everyone was seated, an uncomfortable silence hovered, until Madame Dupuis said: "Tell us what happened, if you will, Madame Claudette."

"There is little to tell," the woman said. "Clovis arrived this morning, very dirty and very tired. He said he had walked to find . . ." she hesitated, and then said, her voice small, "me. I cleaned him up a little so that he wouldn't be such a shock to you, madame. But he cannot seem to remember anything at all about his home."

"You think he is shell-shocked?" Rosie asked.

Claudette nodded, biting her lip.

"You are sure?" asked Madame Dupuis. "You have experience of this?"

"In my work, in war, we have experience of many things that happen to men," Claudette said quietly. "Yes. I have seen shell-shock before. It is a terrible thing."

"But he is alive," said Rosie, thinking of Sebastian.

"Only half, for his mind is injured," Claudette said.

"And he remembers only you?"

"I think so. We have known each other for many, many years, madame," she added apologetically.

Rosie went and knelt in front of Clovis.

"Do you remember me, Clovis?" she asked.

310

He looked at her, his dark eyes dull, no expression on his face. Then gradually a faint look of puzzlement came.

"Should I know you?" he asked, each word produced separately.

"I am your wife, Clovis," she said gently.

He stared at her.

"Perhaps I may have seen you. But my wife? Can that be? I'm afraid I do not remember."

"And the lady there, sitting opposite, is your mother, and the little girl who is crying is your daughter."

His anxiety grew. He clutched at Claudette's arm.

"Is it true, Claudette?"

"Yes, Clovis, it is true. You have just lost your memory. It will come back in time," she soothed.

"It's the guns," he muttered. "Forgive me," he said to Rosie. "I cannot remember anything." He turned back to Claudette, like a child, asking: "Can we go home now, please?"

For once in her life, Rosie did not know what to do. The terrible troubles of the past few weeks had left her mentally exhausted. She looked at Claudette and said: "What do you think we should do?"

Claudette stood up and cleared her throat as if about to make a speech.

"If I may make a suggestion," she said. "If I take him back with me, just for a few days, and he has a lot of sleep and quiet, he should get a little better. Then I can explain everything to him and bring him home again. If he stays here now I think he will be very confused and frightened."

Rosie hesitated. It did not seem right to put the responsibility onto someone else. She turned to Madame.

"What do you think, Mama?" she asked.

"I think it is a very good idea, and most kind of Madame Claudette," her mother-in-law said firmly. "But if it is possible, it would be better if Clovis were to stay here, and Madame Claudette were to remain with him. Forgive my being blunt, madame, but I would prefer that it was not thought in the village that I had left my son in your establishment when he was sick."

Claudette went white and then pink.

"You are suggesting that I stay in your home?"

"Exactly," said Madame briskly. "That way he will become acclimatised again, with you to help him."

"But there is my business ..." Claudette was thinking out loud. "I have a duty to the girls. And to the customers, these days. We closed down while the Germans were here. I would not permit my girls to have anything to do with them. But now they have to live and earn again."

What Claudette said made sense. It would not be fair to expect her to neglect her livelihood.

"Could you spend part of the time here?" Rosie suggested. "I know it is a great deal to ask of you."

"And we would make it well worth your while," said Madame Dupuis.

Claudette drew herself up to her full five feet and said haughtily: "I should not require money for looking after Monsieur Clovis. I am very fond of him."

Rosie, who was horribly aware that they were all talking as if Clovis was not there, could have hit her mother-in-law.

"No, no," she said hastily. "Not money for you, madame, but for any extra expenses entailed at your establishment while you are absent. That's what was meant, was it not, Mama?"

Madame Dupuis caught Rosie's fierce look.

"Indeed," she said hastily, "that is exactly what I meant."

"In that case," said Claudette, relaxing a little, "I will do what I can to help."

Rosie could see that Allie was becoming frantic with curiosity, and said: "Madame Claudette, you have not met our daughter. This is Rosalie, who will help you as much as she can. Allie loves her father and will want to see him well again."

Allie came forward to drop the round little woman in pink a small curtsey.

"I would like to help, Madame Claudette," she said.

"It is very kind of madame to stay with us," Rosie explained to her daughter. "She has an establishment near to Épernay which it is difficult for her to leave. So we will have to get Papa well again quickly."

"What kind of establishment?" asked the ever-curious Allie.

"Dressmaking," said Rosie firmly.

It was an odd situation, having the local Madame to stay at the house. What made it more difficult was that Clovis could not sleep unless she was near, so a pallet was put up beside his bed. Claudette slept there when she could. Rosie moved to another room.

Rosie found herself liking the woman. She was silly in some ways, shrewd in others, but her devotion to Clovis was undeniable. She was able to get back to her establishment, as they all politely referred to the brothel, throughout most of the day. Without any problems, Clovis had slipped back into the work of the vineyard, and since the remainder of the vines were now ready for the gathering, he was content out in the fields, cutting, and gently piling grapes into the big straw baskets they used for the *vendange*. And he was as skilled as he had ever been.

The doctor from Rilly had confirmed Claudette's diagnosis. He said there was no cure other than time and patience. The memory would probably return one day. He could promise nothing more. But he undertook to make sure that Clovis had not been listed as a deserter.

"Though the way things are, he is probably posted as missing, maybe dead," he sighed.

Gradually, with Claudette's help, Clovis was settling down. It was peculiar that as he got to know his family again – though not to remember them – his attitudes towards them were unchanged.

Allie, he adored, and was more content with her than with anyone other than Claudette. Rosie he treated with veneration and a little awe. His mother was, as she had always been, the one who frightened him a little, and who made him do as he was told.

It was a bizarre time, Rosie thought, as she found herself taking tea in the parlour one day with Claudette, who had just hurried over to be sure that Clovis got to bed and to sleep early.

"You've been very kind," Rosie said, as the little woman, who was beginning to show signs of strain, sipped nervously at her tea.

"Clovis was always kind to me when I was young," she said. "It's not always like that with customers."

"I suppose not," Rosie said thoughtfully and on impulse added: "I was never jealous of you, you know. I used to think that he should have married you. It might have been better."

Claudette's hands began to tremble, and she put down the cup and saucer quickly but said nothing.

"Why do you think he remembers you and not the rest of us?" Rosie persisted, and catching Claudette's expression, said: "No, please tell me. I want to know."

The other woman began slowly, saying: "Perhaps because I am less complicated than you, madame. He adored you, but did not understand you, ever. He could always be himself with me because I am not clever either. Now with his poor fuddled brain ringing all the while with gunfire, someone simple like me would be easier for him to deal with. And I think he does have some affection for me, too," she added, a little defiantly.

"I'm certain he does," Rose said sincerely. "Poor Clovis. Life has not been very kind to him."

"I don't agree, madame," Claudette said firmly. "Before this dreadful war, he loved his daughter and he loved his work, and he could never believe his good fortune in having you for a wife. And he had me, for – other things. I believe Clovis was a happy man. Perhaps happier than any of us, because he expected so little. I know he wasn't very clever, but cleverness doesn't always bring happiness."

Rosie was not sure what to say.

"Forgive me, madame," Claudette then said. "I think I had better go and see if he is back from the fields."

And Rosie understood that she was escaping from a moment of intimacy that she found embarrassing.

In ten days Clovis was re-established in Les Hérissons and it was not necessary for Claudette to stay. The only problem was that some nights, after he had finished his work, he would wander off, taking one of the horses, to go and find her. The first few times he did this, the household panicked, searching for him high and low, until Claudette telephoned to say that he was safe with her. It became the pattern of his life. All day he worked, and some nights he went to the establishment, returning to his fields in the morning. Rosie did not mind. It was almost a relief.

Tha main bulk of their land was now inaccessible. The rich fields that Rosie had bought near to the Vesle and close to Reims were now no-man's land. Behind them (on more of Les Hérissons land) French gun emplacements were dug in. All down the north side of the Mountain of Reims trenches were dug and filled with troops. The Germans, entrenched on the other side of the Vesle and the Aisne Canal, constantly shelled the area. A stray shell had already wrecked one of the outhouses where they kept the first pressings. They were lucky that the house was untouched so far.

Clovis had always grumbled that, like the field at Ay, the Vesle vineyards were too far from the house. In the present circumstances, it looked as if he was right. Rosie knew that she could not depend on a harvest from these fields, and her output of champagne would be considerably lessened. But she was not prepared to worry about it.

Clovis still did not remember his family, but he was recalling more and more about the estate. His memory was curious. Sometimes Rose felt he remembered what he wanted to remember. And unfortunately he remembered the fields down near the Vesle Valley and fretted about them.

There was little Clovis could do about the fields where the French heavy artillery was dug in; the vines were already destroyed in a sea of chalky sludge. But on misty, foggy or hazy nights at the end of September he took himself off, wheeling an old bicycle, a basket behind and another in front, to pick the vines on both the strip of no-man's land and those just behind the French lines.

It was a hazardous operation, involving crawling along the rows flat on his stomach so as not to be spotted and fired upon by either the French or the German look-outs. If he did let himself be seen, the shells immediately rained down. He did not seem to understand the dangers, and had started taking Allie with him when he could sneak her past her mother and grandmother.

314

Allie connived to go with him, and when her mother shouted at her for frightening them all so, she said coolly that she didn't care what happened to her, and anyway, all the schoolchildren from the Champagne villages were doing the same thing.

"It's easier for us," she said. "We are small enough to hide. And the vines have to be tended, don't they?"

She was right, and ashamed to be shown the way by her daughter, Rosie also took to making the dangerous journey through the woods, and then down to the vineyards. She crept and crawled behind Clovis, wishing she was more agile as Allie wriggled ahead of them both like a caterpillar. Sometimes the shells exploded very near to them, and Rosie was frightened. But Clovis seemed to bear a charmed life and have no fear. While her ears rang with the shellfire and her eyes were dazzled by explosions, her husband never seemed to be aware of either.

But what they were doing was not exceptional. The Champenois, trapped in the battle area, were all equally courageous in their determination that their livelihood would not be ruined. And some afternoons Allie, who was now going to the little school at Chigny, would come home and say that one of the children had been killed tending the vines the night before. She spoke as if it were a fact of life that this should happen, and added that there had been extra prayers at assembly for the dead child.

And life went on. The *vendange* was completed with the help of the many German prisoners of war that had been taken at their retreat. And it was a fine harvest. But the profusion of fat, glossy deep red Pinot Noir grapes made Rosie shudder. She had the fancy that their bloom came from the blood of the men who had died on the fields of Champagne.

By November the fields had turned russet, glowing like new coins in the heavy mists and fogs. And as Christmas neared, Rosie noticed her string-bean daughter becoming more rounded. After a little questioning it became clear that Allie was pregnant.

Madame was distraught, much concerned with the disgrace. Rosie was less concerned with the disgrace, but anxious about the effect on her daughter's mental state. Remembering her own situation, her first instinct was to brazen it out, and to keep telling Allie how exciting it was to be having a baby.

"After all," she said, "we are not going to blame her or tell her never to darken our doors again. She has done nothing wrong."

But Madame would not have it.

"I don't like to bring up things past," she said, "but remember how you felt? Times have changed, but not that much in a small community like this. What chance will Allie have of finding a husband, and what chance will the child have if everyone knows it was fathered by

Lieutenant Schmidt? And if it was not fathered by Lieutenant Schmidt, who was it fathered by? Allie and her child cannot win, even though it is not their fault. They are not responsible, but we must be, and decide what is best."

Rosie listened rebelliously, her thoughts chaotic. It was so unfair. Finally she had to accept Madame's logic.

"The best thing would be if we could get rid of it," she said.

"If I thought it was safe, and I knew someone who would do it, I think it would be the best thing," Madame said. "But it is late in the day, and not safe. If it went wrong we could ruin her chances of motherhood for ever."

Rosie paced up and down the parlour, where they were talking. She stopped and stood with her back to the fire, thinking, and then said: "Then I shall have to have the baby, won't I?"

"I was thinking much the same thing," Madame murmured. "It's always been the best solution to such a problem. You go away with Allie and come back with a baby – yours. Is that what you had in mind?" she grimaced. "It's as well Clovis came home when he did, since you are to be a mother."

"And I register the baby as mine."

"Exactly," said Madame. "Many people will guess, of course, but they will never know for sure. It's the way these matters have always been handled in France. Many mothers are really the grandmother in country villages. It's easier, of course, to conceal the baby in a larger family, but we will manage."

"I shall have to start eating more or padding myself," said Rosie, her voice resigned. "How much longer do you think it will be before Allie really shows?"

"Another month, maybe. Perhaps you could plan a trip away about the middle of January."

Rosie took another turn round the room. "That means being away from here for nearly five months. What about the business?"

"Go somewhere you can still keep an eye on things. What about Paris?"

Rosie shook her head. "Paris wouldn't do. It's too far. I really need to be in Reims, but how can I take Allie there with all the bombardment going on? I don't even know if the apartment will be habitable."

"Then it has to be Paris."

"I don't want to go to Paris," Rosie said stubbornly. She could not explain to her mother-in-law that if she went to Paris, she would have to stay with André. Philippe had disposed of the apartment they had shared. And if she stayed with André, Lorraine would be on the scene, and she wanted nothing to do with Lorraine.

"Best find out what the situation is in Reims, then," Madame said.

Rosie waylaid Henri to ask if there was news from his cousin.

"I must go to Reims on business," she explained. "Does your cousin tell you how life there is now?"

Henri was not displeased to be asked for information.

"The bombardment ceases only at night, madame, as we can hear, and then not always," he told her, "but those who have stayed are snug and safe in the cellars of the town. My cousin tells me that even the police have their headquarters in the caves, and gradually the shopkeepers are moving below, too. Mumm, Pommery, Krug, Champion, they have all thrown open their cellars to the people. Above ground, it is frightful. There is little of the town left."

"But people survive?" Rosie asked.

"Indeed they survive."

"Then I shall survive," she said.

The decision made, her only problem was to explain everything to Allie.

Allie was caught in deep melancholy. She did not feel physically well. Worse, she could not escape the memory of the lieutenant. The moment when he had appeared like an apparition in the shed, his skinny white hands snatching at her, tearing her clothing, and his surprising strength as he hit her hard around the face, knocking her to the ground, would not leave her mind. She could still smell the damp, musky smell of him, and remember the shock of seeing this swollen red thing like a monstrous sausage as he dropped his trousers before her. The rest she would not permit herself to think about. But she had recorded every painful moment of it in her secret diary, and then carefully glued the edges of the pages together with flour and water paste. She wanted the facts there, but she did not want to look at them again.

She was also grieving for Sebastian, whom she had loved. She could not imagine life without his teasing presence, and wished with all her heart that they had been closer the last few times she had seen him. And then there was her father to grieve over, also. They were close again, and he was treating her as his daughter, but it hurt that he did not *recall* she was his daughter. She felt something must be lacking in her that he could only remember the flamboyant little woman from Épernay and not her, or even her mother.

Miss had opted to go home to England, and Allie missed her. Her mother seemed preoccupied and worried most of the time, and in the distance the sound of war rolled and thundered every day. She felt she might as well be dead, too.

317

She was in her room reading *The Three Musketeers*, one of her favourite books, when her mother put her head round the door.

"Darling," she said, "can we have a talk?"

"Of course, Mama." Reluctantly Allie put her bookmark at her place. She preferred the world of fiction to reality these days.

Her mother came in and sat on the bed. She seemed to take a deep breath.

"Allie, has it occurred to you to wonder why you haven't been unwell lately?"

There had already been some discussion about this and Allie found it embarrassing. No one talked of things like that.

"No, Mama," she said sulkily.

"Do you remember the first time it happened, I told you it meant that you were a woman, and that you could have a baby?"

Allie nodded, not liking the subject any better.

"Well, darling, I'm certain that you are having a baby. That's why nothing has happened these last two or three months. You are going to make me a grandmother. Imagine that."

Allie could not imagine it. She sat staring at her mother, appalled, and not understanding.

"But how could I be?" she said. "You said it had to be with a man you loved ..." The horrendous truth was dawning. "Oh, Mama! It couldn't be because of the Lieutenant, could it?"

Her mother shut her eyes and held her hands clasped tight together. She did not reply.

The weeks of pent-up misery exploded. Allie heard herself screaming: "No! No! No! I won't. It can't be true. I won't, I won't, I won't. What will everyone say?" She could not bear the thought of the awful shame of it. She flung herself into her mother's arms, sobbing, "Help me, Mama. Don't let it happen. Please don't let it happen."

Rosie rocked her, stroking her hair, hushing her like a baby, but Allie was not to be consoled. To her, it was the most dreadful thing in the world. The thought of it made her scream again. And then she heard her grandmother's voice saying: "Allie, control yourself."

The tone was so authoritative that she was reduced to a whimper. Her grandmother was standing in the doorway, shutting the door behind her.

"Your mother has told you?" she said, her expression stern.

Allie nodded.

"Listen, dear child, this is war." There was no softness in her Mimi's voice. The authoritarian note remained. "We are all victims. Sebastian is dead – worse off than any of us. Your papa's health is destroyed, but he will recover. The most dreadful thing that can happen to a woman has happened to you. But you will recover, too.

318

And by the time this senseless carnage is over, who knows what will have happened?"

Her mother's hand was still stroking her hair. Allie leaned against her and hiccupped back a sob, while she listened to her stern, unsentimental grandmother. She was not consoled, but she was no longer hysterical.

"Now, there is nothing to be done but to have the baby. But we will not let your life be ruined, nor shall we let you be shamed. We have a plan. Your mother will explain."

"We must go away from here until the baby is born, Allie," her mother said quietly. "Just you and I, and when it is born, we will come home again and I shall pretend the baby is mine and your father's, and it will be brought up as your little brother or sister."

Allie thought about it and said fiercely: "I don't want to go away from here, ever. And I don't care what happens to the baby. Not if it comes from that filthy man. I hope it dies."

Madame crossed herself, and contradictorily said: "We must not bank on that."

"And," her mother said, "you may feel quite differently when it is born."

"Never!" Allie said. "I shall always hate it."

She saw her mother and her grandmother exchange a look. Allie suddenly felt exhausted.

"I wish you'd both go away and leave me now," she said, with dignity. "I want to think." Neither of the women moved, their faces anxious. "Please," she said.

Her mother got to her feet. "I shall come back in a little while," she said, kissing her. "Is there anything you want?"

"Only to be alone." She felt very grown-up, as if she had aged many years in the last few minutes. "I'll call you when I am ready to talk."

They both left, closing the door carefully behind them. Allie then let the full horror of it all sweep over her. She reached in her bedside drawer, and from beneath a pile of school books produced her secret diary.

"Dear diary," she wrote, "the most unbelievably dreadful thing has happened. I am going to have a baby ..."

Chapter Twenty

It was nearly February when Rosie decided that she and Allie must leave Les Hérissons for Reims. The girl was so fretful and miserable that it was difficult to get her to eat. She had hardly changed shape at all and this worried Rosie, but Madame said it was not a bad thing. Babies had a habit of surviving in spite of their mothers, and anyway, perhaps it would be a small one. That would make the birth easier when the time came.

All the elaborate preparations for the deception were made by Madame Dupuis. It was she who announced quietly to the staff that Madame Rosie was to become a mother again, but cautioned them not to speak of it in case Madame were embarrassed. A story was concocted that it was necessary for Rosie to run the business from Reims. She was to take Allie with her both for company, and to stop the girl's dangerous sorties into the front-line area where she would persist in going with her father.

Rosie, who had been worried about taking her daughter to beleaguered Reims where the shelling never ceased, decided philosophically that perhaps the dangers were not any greater.

When they arrived, amazingly the small apartment on the Rue Cérès was still intact, though part of the roof of the apartment above had been blown off. The trees in front of the building were blackened and a pretty ornamental pond in the gardens that could be seen from the balcony had been destroyed.

Rosie could not believe what had happened to Reims. Huge gaps, like broken teeth, mutilated the streets. Piles of rubble lay everywhere; the cupola of the Grand Théâtre was ruined. The cathedral stood defiant, bloody but unbowed. Those buildings that were still standing were pitted with shrapnel holes, and more often than not had lost their windows.

And yet the milkmaids, wearing purloined German helmets as

protection against the shrapnel, still pushed their carts and cans of milk around to the remaining houses, the streets were cleared as best they could be, with old men and boys pulling the dustcarts since all horses had been requisitioned. The children still went in their pinafores to their classes at the École Ste-Anne. Somehow life went on, though many people were leaving the town during the day for the neighbouring fields, and returning only at night.

Allie was struck dumb by the devastation. She had come on the journey, by bicycle, unwilling and sulking. They had made up a bundle of a few clothes and necessities and Rosie had said they would buy anything else they needed. But Allie did not want to leave Les Hérissons, and she had made this perfectly clear.

Rosie's heart bled for her. Her sunny, talkative, inquisitive daughter had disappeared under a black cloud of misery that nothing could lift. Loving, cuddling, cajoling, sympathy; nothing got through to her. She was bitter and angry, and had retreated into some secret life of her own.

But the rape of Reims seemed to make her forget her own. As they pedalled through the destroyed streets and tottering buildings in pouring, chilly rain, she looked around, her eyes alert and interested again, her expression sad – but not for herself.

"Mama," she said. "So many people have lost their homes."

"And their lives. They say more than six hundred."

"It's terrible."

"War is terrible, darling, for everyone." Rosie put just the faintest tinge of meaning in her tone, hopeful that maybe her daughter's justifiable self-pity was receding.

Allie was silent as they let themselves into the apartment building and climbed the stairs to the third floor. Inside the rooms where Rosie and Philippe had been so happy, the dust lay thick. The ceiling had collapsed in the bedroom, and the bed was covered with plaster which had also nestled itself into the fabric of the curtains. Windows were cracked, and the apartment had a sad, unloved feeling.

"We're fortunate it's still here," Allie said, awed that the building had escaped.

"But whether it's safe to stay ..." Rosie said doubtfully. She could hear the crump of shells. "Let's leave everything and go and buy some food."

They had been installed for nearly a month and were getting the apartment into some sort of order when Allie begged to be allowed out to *do* something. She had been kept indoors as much as possible in case they met anyone that the Dupuis family knew. Reluctantly, Rosie took her daughter to meet one of her agents, Monsieur Marceaux, in his offices in the Rue Gambetta.

321

"We'll tell him that you are just here for the day," she said.

He was operating from his cellar, where he had set up an office surrounded by champagne bottles and stout stone walls.

"We are still exporting," he said cheerfully, after asking her to excuse his bowler hat set in place to keep the cold from his head. "Only half the amount of before the war, but considering the conditions that is admirable. Do you have anything for me, dear lady?"

"About half the usual amount," Rosie said. "We haven't had a bottle broken yet because of the war, but we don't have the labour. Nearly all our men were young and went immediately. We can't get chemicals and fertilisers either. And then we lost much of the *vendange* on the Vesle fields."

"Everyone tells the same story," he said, "but what champagne we have we can most certainly sell."

She promised to see that he received a new consignment, and said that she would be working from Reims most of the time now. Then she and Allie hurried back through the ruined streets. The bombardment had started again, but as all the Remois had learned to do, they tried to pretend nothing was happening. They had reached the Rue Chanzy when the noise and the danger became too much to ignore, and they took shelter in the doorway – about all that was left – of a ruined shop.

"They say lightning never strikes twice in the same place. Let's hope it's true," Rosie said as they stood waiting for the salvo to end.

"Mama." Allie had suddenly taken her mother's hand, and Rosie's heart lifted at this small show of affection. "Will the baby be like the lieutenant?"

The question took Rosie by surprise. Neither the baby nor the lieutenant had been mentioned since the day she had explained to Allie that she was pregnant.

"Not necessarily," she said slowly. "Your grandfather, my father, was not a very nice man. He was mean, unkind, a slave-driver and he could be brutal. Would you say I was like that?"

"Oh, no!" Allie sounded shocked at the thought.

"Would you say your father is like his mother?"

"Not in any way," said Allie, after a little consideration.

"I have a brother in America – your Uncle Peter – who is nothing like me, nothing like our father, and not even much like our mother. He's just Peter – his own person."

"Miss wasn't a bit like her parents," Allie added, as they both flinched at the whine and thud of another shell which sounded alarmingly near. "Nor was she like her brothers and sisters."

"Exactly. I suppose we're all made up of little bits and pieces of people going back generations, Allie. Perhaps our immediate parents don't have much to do with it. Nobody knows what any baby is going

322

to be like. I look like my mother, and you look like your father, but you're not like your father in intelligence or temperament. Anyone would know you're his daughter, but only because you look like him. That's the only clue."

"I hope it doesn't look like him," Allie muttered. "I could never love it if it did."

"What! If it looked like your father?" Rosie said, laughing.

"No, Mama," Allie said indignantly. "If it looked like the lieutenant."

"That's better," Rosie said, determined to lighten the mood. "But we'll just have to wait and see, won't we?"

As the barrage thundered on, she could not help thinking it was not the best time for such a serious discussion, but when the firing seemed to have ceased they walked on in silence for a while. They had just passed the side of the battered cathedral and were coming into the Rue Cérès when Allie gave a little cry.

"I think they've hit our apartment," she said, her voice excited.

She was right. There was a gaping hole in the front of the building where a shell, neat as could be, had gone straight through the window into Rosie's sitting room. Inside the building, the shell had torn a huge hole in the sitting room floor and formed a large crater in the floor below. The blast had sucked every bit of furniture from the two apartments into this hole. A grand piano from the ground floor flat reclined drunkenly at the top of the heap.

"Now can we go home?" said Allie smugly, and her mother could have smacked her.

"No, we cannot," she said. "We have to find somewhere else to go."

There were few homes left intact, and even the most stubborn of Remois were reluctantly beginning to accept that it was unwise to stay in their apartments and houses. God was not even looking after his own. The Mother Superior of a convent in Betheny had been killed by a direct hit on the convent buildings.

There was only one thing to do. Like the rest of the Remois, they would have to take to the cellars. It was unlikely that they would meet anyone there that they knew. The more affluent citizens of the town had long since left for Paris, or safer areas. Rosie decided they would become the Mesdames Dupont and Cremont, and that Madame Allie Cremont was a young bride whose husband had gone to war. She barely looked old enough to be married, but there was nothing to be done about that.

She found there was room at the Mumm cellars, and charmed two big lads who for a handsome tip took a bed, table, chairs, and a few other necessities from the ruined apartment and wheeled them on handcarts to the Rue du Champ de Mars where the cellars were. She

323

could go back for anything else they needed when they were settled.

Allie was enchanted once they had climbed down the steps into the cellars. And it was, indeed, a remarkable sight. In the chalk galleries of the caves, between the bottles of champagne, some piled, some in *pupitres,* the Remois had created homes, using piled packing cases to make partitions. Rosie and Allie first passed a group of chatting women, their outdoor clothes covered with thick heavy dressing gowns against the cold, knitting as they sat on kitchen chairs brought from homes above ground. Another woman in a long white apron cooked over a petrol stove in a snugly furnished kitchen-cum-dining room. The refugees had made themselves comfortable in well-furnished bedrooms where the beds were draped with curtains for privacy. Some people had managed to bring an entire sitting room with them, and a busy life was in progress.

"Mama." Allie whispered. "Isn't it exciting? Like cave dwellers."

Rosie and Allie set up home beside the other Remois families. It was tranquil enough, Rosie found, three floors below ground. People had hung their ornate oil lamps from the roof of the arches, though most lighting came from candles. Schools had been moved underground, and Rosie insisted that Allie attend Madame Cavarott's classes. There was a Catholic chapel (the Protestants held their services in the caves of Krug) where the devout went to Mass. Shops had been opened.

But above all, the spirit of the people was strong. They felt they had not deserted their town or their cathdral and that nothing would budge or defeat them. They believed they were the beating heart of France. And life would go on.

In the cellars people married and died. And only a few days after their arrival, a young woman gave birth to a bonny boy between the champagne bottles that served as the walls of her chamber.

Allie, who had begun to come alive in the austere but comradely existence of the cellars, so close to the front line, had refused to take any interest in this particular event. But that night when she and her mother had gone to bed, she suddenly said: "When did Sebastian die, Mama?"

"I don't know exactly when," Rosie said, "but it must have been somewhere around the end of August and the beginning of September."

"Do you think God might give his spirit to my baby?"

It was a curious thought from a fourteen-year-old.

"I don't see why not," Rosie said, hoping maybe the thought was comforting. "What made you think of that?"

"I sometimes feel very strongly that Sebastian is near us," Allie explained. "It makes me feel better. It makes me feel he won't let anything happen to us."

"I think he would try to keep us safe, if he could," Rosie said. "He did love us both."

"At the end he loved you more."

"Not really," Rosie said gently. "It would have been different if he had lived. When he was nineteen, you seemed like a little girl to him because he had grown-up. By the time you were seventeen everything would have changed again."

"And now it never will." Allie's voice was so tragic that Rosie gave a little half-laugh, half-sob, and hugged her near.

"Just go to sleep," she said.

Rosie made her last excursion from the cellars to see Monsieur Marceaux just about a month before Allie's baby was due. She had given up the idea of padding herself – it was too complicated. She just wore a huge cloak which she wrapped round herself in muddled folds when she went out. But now, in the middle of May, it was beginning to look a trifle odd.

She had informed Monsieur Marceaux that there was to be an addition to the family a full six weeks previously, and he had congratulated her and dear Monsieur Dupuis, but said he felt she might be safer at home in Les Hérissons.

"But we are constantly shelled there, also, monsieur," she said, exaggerating a little. "And at least in the cellars it is perfectly secure. One cannot even hear the bombardment."

"True, true," he sighed.

On this visit, which she had decided must be the last, and that from now on she must stay in the cellars with Rosie, he had two letters for her, sent on from Les Hérissons.

The postmark on one was from New York, and could only be from Lizzie. The other was in an official envelope and she recognised Philippe's handwriting. But it was the American stamp that had caught Monsieur Marceaux' eye, and he seemed quite pleased with the idea of presenting her with a letter from so far away.

"Of course," he said, as she took the envelopes from him, "our business is still doing well in America. All you can supply I can sell there. Do you know, madame, that we are still exporting almost as much as before the war. What an achievement! Something that we should all be very proud of."

"You are right, monsieur," she murmured, anxious to open her letters.

She went and sat in the small park opposite the station, savouring the early summer sun and the sight of the sky and daylight after the gloom of the caves. Which of her two letters should she read first? She decided to save the most precious – Philippe's – and read Lizzie's first.

Lizzie was anxious that all was well and that her dear Rosie was not being harmed by this terrible war. She wrote:

Your letter about Clovis and Sebastian made me cry. Of course, I did not know either of them well, but I know how dear young Sebastian was to you. What a terrible and tragic waste that one so young and alive, with so much to look forward to, should die. At least your poor Clovis will be cured one day.

I could hardly believe your account of the Germans in your home. It does not seem possible that such things could happen. And I am consumed with curiosity about the ending of it all. I suppose it is some war secret that you dare not put to paper, and you must tell me ALL when we meet again.

Rosie had not told Lizzie of the rape and the killing of Lieutenant Schmidt, mainly because she felt that Lizzie, away from the reality of war, would be appalled at what had happened. Also because what had happened to Allie was Allie's own secret, to tell only whom she chose.

Jim thinks we should join this dreadful war but I am afraid that I feel it would be better if we stayed neutral. Jim has all sorts of political reasons why we should not be separatist. I just think of the young men of this country going to their deaths as have so many in Europe, like poor Sebastian. I suppose I really think of Alexander.

And, of course, I really do not understand what it is all about, and I cannot help but agree with our President who says that Americans came here to get away from European wars. Though Jim is convinced we too will suffer in the end if we do not enter into conflict with Germany.

All goes well here. I am trying to persuade Jim to work less hard, but I fear it is an impossible task. He has entered upon a new venture. Alexander who now has a degree from Harvard has point-blank refused to go into the family business. I cannot tell you what dramas and trouble it has caused, Rosie. I have never seen Mr Webster so angry, and though I, too, am disappointed, I was quite proud of the way that Alexander stood up to his father.

Finally his father bellowed what did he want to do, and cool as a cucumber Alex said that he wanted to be a writer, and he wanted to start by being a journalist. Well, from Mr Webster's response you would have thought that the boy had said he wanted to be a murderer. Mr Webster said it was a dreadful life, full of dreadful people, and that under no circumstances would he permit it.

Alex then pointed out that he was over twenty-one, and therefore his father could not prevent him. So Jim said that he would not give him a cent. And Alex said that was perfectly all right, and that he did not want his father's money anyway.

Poor Jenny tried to intervene on her brother's behalf and was shouted at for her pains.

So Alex left home and started to try to get a job, but he had no luck at all. Jim then bought an enormous amount of shares in one of the smaller New York papers, and without telling Alex, of course, secured him a job as what is called a feature writer. So there he is, and I admit to being quite proud when I see his name in the paper, and I must allow that he writes very well.

I'm afraid though that all the joy of it would be lost for him if he knew his father had virtually bought him the job. I'm hopeful that soon he will go somewhere else in a position that he has gained through his own merit. Then I would feel easier in my mind about him altogether.

I'm afraid neither of the children are very popular with their father at the moment. Jenny says that she wants to work and is not prepared to sit at home, embroidering, waiting for someone to ask her to marry. She wants to be a nurse and had started her training at St Vincent's Hospital. She, too, thinks that it is dreadful that America is not in the war and talks of joining the Red Cross. I pray that she does not, I should be so frightened to think of her working at the front.

I am content at the moment, though worried about my parents. They are both getting old, and I wish I were nearer to them. But they will not leave Boston, nor their home, and I cannot insist. So instead I worry.

I pray for you and yours, my dear Rosie, and wish that you could come here, to safety. You know you are always welcome, but since the sinking of so many ships, I fear that crossing the Atlantic is as hazardous as being in your beleaguered Champagne.

Please write soonest to assure me you are safe and well.

All my love and prayers,

Lizzie

Rosie then carefully opened the other envelope, and drew out the sheets of paper inside. She did not start to read immediately, but held the letter in her hand, imagining him writing it, and praying that it contained only good news.

My dearest Rosie,

I am so happy that I was able to see you, even if only briefly,

327

and sad to be the bearer of such bad news. I still cannot believe that Sebastian has gone, and I am haunted by some terrible feeling of guilt that it should not have been him, but me. I find this hard to live with, though I know you will say it is irrational of me and wrong. But to lose a son in battle when one goes on living and breathing seems a terrible miscarriage of justice. But one that I can do nothing about.

As you can imagine, Father was most terribly distressed by the death of Sebastian, but old soldier that he is, he has accepted it, as so many have had to accept the loss of loved ones. But I fear it will have aged him. I doubt you will have the opportunity to visit Paris, but it would make him happy to see you.

I am comforted to have seen your dear face and held you in my arms again. You have given me hope for the future now I know that you still care for me. And I regret so much the time we have lost.

As guilty as I feel about Sebastian, I intend to live, if I can, to come back to you. I know we mean never to mention Lorraine, but I am assured by my father that she is content in Paris without me. She is working for the Red Cross, raising money, and my daughter, Françoise, is now being cared for by Nou-Nou. I hear from Lorraine rarely, but this causes me no pain. She explains that she finds writing letters difficult, and strangely Paris is still gay, even in these times, so I am sure she has better things to do with her time.

I cannot see an end to this war. Indeed we are stuck in a rut, with both sides in trenches, throwing explosive hot metal at each other. It seems to be stalemate, and when we do engage in battle, it is bloody, vicious and pointless. Many men die or are maimed to gain perhaps a few yards, or sometimes to lose a few yards. It is all senseless, and I will not burden you with it. I don't doubt that situated where you are, you have troubles of your own, and I beg you to be careful.

I think of you all the time, my darling one. It is sad that I do not have a photograph of you, but I have such a clear picture of you in my head that I only have to shut my eyes for your dear face to be before me. I can picture your dark lashes on your cheeks when you close your eyes as I kiss you. I remember how soft and pliant you are in my arms. I go over so many things in my memory. The sight of you the first time we made love, your hands offering me your white, full breasts. Other things, too, like your confidence and bravery. Remember how the Duke fell for you? How could he not!

Women can never truly know what memories such as these

mean to men, particularly men away from their homes and in deadly peril. We have our dreams of home, and love and comfort to sustain us. Sometimes in the trenches when the guns are quiet and we are all still, I see the men I serve with, men who curse and swear and think it manly to be crude, I see them slumped, tired and cold, but there is an expression on their faces that tells me that in their own private world they are transported to home and *their* Rosie. And their memories of things more gentle are giving them comfort.

I know that my expression must be the same, wistful and longing, wanting, as I think of you, and I think of you all the time.

Never leave me again, my darling one,
Your,
Philippe

Chapter Twenty-One

Allie's baby was born on the nineteenth of June, 1915 at 8.05 in the morning. It was an easy birth, and the baby was small – just 5lbs 3ozs – confirming Madame Dupuis' forecast. Allie started labour at around midnight, and at seven in the morning, when the birth looked imminent, Rosie ran for the midwife who had her 'apartment' on the level above.

Allie went through both the labour and the birth in frightening, writhing silence. She made no more than an occasional strangled groan as her body heaved against the pain, but her lips were bitten and bleeding from refusing to cry out.

"Scream," Rosie urged her. "No one will mind and it will help you."

Silent, hands clenched into fists, her face the colour of plaster, Allie shook her head.

It was all that the midwife could do to get her to push, and in the end she only received some co-operation by shouting at her patient.

"Do you want this baby born dead?" she demanded.

Rosie, who was sweating even in the cool of the cellar, held her breath. The midwife did not know how unfortunate her question was.

"It's not the baby's fault," Rosie whispered to her daughter, and reluctantly Allie began to push.

A small crowd of excited women had gathered outside, asking if there was anything they could do. The midwife co-opted some for boiling water, and another to make hot drinks.

"You stay with her," she ordered Rosie, and added with a sharp look: "She's very young, isn't she?"

"She's older than she looks," Rosie said calmly. "Her husband is away at the war."

The midwife, a stringy woman with a mass of wild grey hair, snorted. It was painfully obvious she didn't believe a word of it.

Rosanne Dupuis, named for her grandmother, made her début soon after, complete with a cap of black hair, a bright red face, and a lusty cry that had Allie's audience smiling in delight. "Small, but perfect," pronounced the midwife.

"It's a girl, Allie," Rosie said, tenderly wiping the sweat from her daughter's forehead and sponging the blood from her lips.

Allie was silent, and then she said, breathing heavily: "Then it can't be Sebastian."

"I don't see why not." It was difficult to sound convincing.

"Sebastian would never be a girl," said Allie scornfully.

"Well, she's a beautiful little girl," Rosie said, feeling desperate. "Would you like to hold her?"

"No, thanks."

And Allie turned onto her side to face the chalk wall of the cave.

Rosie had never felt so helpless in her life. She turned to the midwife, and grasping for comfort, asked: "Does this often happen?"

"Sometimes when they're that young. And often when they're not married," said the midwife. "But they come round. Don't worry. She's tired and so are you. It'll be better when you've both had some sleep."

Rosie looked at the tiny baby in her arms. Its perfect hands were closed, its small rosebud pink mouth puckered in little sucking movements. Then it opened milky blue eyes that seemed to look straight at her, and yawned a round toothless yawn.

Rosie laughed in delight.

"Please, Allie," she coaxed, "look at her. She's beautiful. She looks exactly like you did when you were born."

She seemed to have found the right thing to say, and reluctantly the weary girl heaved herself over and permitted Rosie and the midwife to sit her up.

With no great enthusiasm she took the baby, looked at it, and said: "Did I really look like this?"

"She could be your twin." Rosie put a positive emphasis on the word she. "And she ought to be fed."

Persuading Allie to put the baby to the breast was a performance. She insisted no one but Rosie and the midwife should be near or should see, tried to cover herself up, and grimaced at every pull of her daughter's small hungry mouth.

And when Rosanne fell asleep on her mother's breast, Allie announced that never, never, never would she do that again.

The midwife did not seem too surprised.

"We'll just have to find a wet nurse," she said.

There were plenty of offers from other women in the caves to feed the new-born baby. In time she was adopted as a little pet, and a diversion against the long, gloomy days. The only female who showed no interest in her whatsoever was her own mother. But Rosie found

331

herself besotted by her granddaughter. She was glad the baby was not a boy, and already she was firmly wiping the little thing's parentage out of her mind. Her only regret was that she couldn't feed the baby herself, and was sad, remembering the pleasure she had felt at nursing Allie, that her daughter was so adamant in her refusal to feed her baby. She feared they would never bond, and then thought perhaps it was as well if they did not.

They stayed in the Mumm cellars until a wet nurse could be found at one of the villages near Les Hérissons, and then they went home.

It was a triumphant return. Rosie was congratulated by all. Though he could not quite grasp who this baby belonged to, Clovis took to sitting by her cradle when he was indoors, and liked to hold her on his lap. A sight that made Allie's lips tighten.

Madame Dupuis, like Rosie, soon doted on the baby, who rarely cried, showed her gums in a funny little smile at the slightest bit of attention, and was always content. It was as if she was determined to be loved, in spite of her unfortunate start in life.

People came from the village especially to see the new baby. The christening took place at the little Chigny church on a shimmering July day, with the noise of the front-line artillery competing with the music of the organ. The church was packed, and there was a festival air about the day. Not many babies had been born since the men went away.

Allie had to be ordered to go to the christening. She was to be the baby's godmother, and the old priest was so gentle with her Rosie wondered if perhaps he had guessed the truth. Allie was forced to hold the baby, something usually she avoided. She never wanted to hold Rosanne, never wanted to talk about her, and acted as if she did not exist. When people said she must be thrilled to have a little sister, she either muttered a few unintelligible words or just scowled.

Marie said privately to Henri that the girl was jealous at no longer being the only child after so many years.

But Madame Dupuis had a different theory. One day when Allie was out with her father, Madame went to her granddaughter's bedroom and searched for the secret diary. She did not feel right about doing it, but it was the only way she could discover what was going on in Allie's head.

Aware that she was violating the girl's privacy, she hurriedly found the book in the same drawer as it had been before and turned immediately to the end.

Allie had described the pain and her feelings at the birth of the baby, but then she had written:

"Mama was right. She does look like me, and she is a very nice little baby. I have been thinking that perhaps I was wrong, and it is better

332

that she is a girl, then she will be more like me than him. I could not bear it if she was like him.

"They all think me callous and uncaring that I do not seem to love Rosanne, but Mama and Grandmama should understand better. She is my baby. I went through all those dreadful things to have her, but I can never claim her as mine. Mama has taken her away from me, as Mama takes many things. So it is better if I do not let myself love the baby, or become attached to her at all. For I am only to be her sister.

"What is so difficult is that I cannot help loving her. I want to hold her and cuddle her, and say: She's mine! particularly when everyone tells Mama what a lovely baby she is. But I mustn't. And I do so wish I didn't want to."

Madame's face was thoughtful as she carefully put the book back where she had found it.

She surprised Rosie playing with the baby one day, blowing kisses on the round pink tummy while its nappy was being changed. Allie, who was also in the room watching, suddenly got up and left, shutting the door behind her with exaggerated quietness.

"Perhaps it might be better if you were a little more casual with the baby when Allie is about," Madame suggested.

Rosie gave her a questioning look, was silent for a moment and then nodded.

"I expect you're right," she said ruefully. "I have been insensitive, haven't I?"

"A little."

"It was really just that it seemed so sad for her not to be loved by her mother. And the little thing is flesh of my flesh. I want her to be loved."

"Perhaps she is more loved than we think," Madame suggested.

One hurdle over, Madame bided her time, until she and Allie were alone in her little sitting room. Allie was reading one of her books, and Madame said thoughtfully: "I've been meaning to say, Allie, girls are allowed to show lots of love to little sisters and brothers, you know. Why, I know big sisters who act really more like mothers. Particularly when they are as old as you are." She put down her sewing. "It's difficult, I know, *chérie*, but don't hold back too much. One day we'll be able to tell Rosanne the truth, and she'll be hurt if she feels that you always resented her."

"I don't resent her . . ." Allie began passionately, and then stopped and stared at her book.

"I know you don't," Madame said. "I know how you feel, and so does your mother, but your baby deserves love from someone. All babies must have love, and so your mother is only doing what must be done. Don't resent her, either, will you? She is only trying to do the best for all of us."

She did not wait for an answer, but picked up her sewing and left the room, giving Allie a gentle pat on the head as she went.

Jean Paul lit himself another cigar with some care in the room of his suite at the Palace Hotel. He was just the slightest bit drunk, but then he had good reason to be. His wine had taken first prize for Californian Champagne at the Congress of Wine that was being held in San Francisco that July of 1915.

He stood puffing on his Havana, a handsome man of thirty-nine, grey wings at the sides of his curly black hair, satyr eyebrows turning grey, but with a remarkably unlined and youthful face. He had temporarily detached himself from his own party to look with satisfaction at the distinguished group of guests he had gathered around him to celebrate Champagne D'Or's win at the Wine Temple that afternoon. He wished that Peter and Pierre could be here to share his triumph, but Peter was in Philadelphia and Pierre at school in New England.

Among his guests was the short, stocky Henry Lachman, probably the finest taster in America and the greatest wine man in all California. He stood near the distinguished, white-haired and moustachioed French-born Charles Carpy, who had been chairman of the jury. Carpy was in earnest conversation with the Japanese American Kanaye Nagasawa, the man considered to be *the* authority on Californian wine.

There was Mosby from Australia, Quirago from the Argentine, Talocchini from Italy and LeClerc from New York. The most revered men in the wine world, all gathered in his suite to drink to the success of his champagne.

Monsieur Gendrot, the tall, thin Parisian member of the jury, came over to join him. His English was not good, and Jean Paul greeted him in French.

"I have to offer you my congratulations," the Parisian said. "It is very creditable wine that you make."

"Only creditable?" Jean Paul asked, smiling.

"Very fine," Gendrot said hastily, "but of course it is not champagne. I would describe it as champagne-type and an excellent wine."

Jean Paul felt himself begin to bristle.

"Monsieur," he said. "I am Champenois myself. My family are makers of champagne. Here I grow the correct varieties of grapes, I use the same methods as we do at home. Not by one step does the process vary."

"But you do not have the soil of Champagne, monsieur," the elderly Frenchman pointed out, "and therefore, I fear, never will champagne produced in California be anything but champagne-type."

The maddening thing was that the man was right. Jean Paul decided to capitulate.

"I would not say this to anyone but another Frenchman," he said, lowering his voice, "but you cannot imagine how frustrating it is not to be able to reach the finest peaks of taste and quality that are created so naturally in Ay or Reims. I thought at first it was perhaps a question of temperature, and I have spent a fortune digging caves into the rock." He grimaced. "How much simpler at home to dig into chalk. But to no avail. As you say, one does not have the soil."

"It is a fine wine, but different," Gendrot said soothingly. "You are a true maker of wine. Have you never thought of returning to the soil of your home?"

Had he? Jean Paul never looked back. Only forwards.

"There is no reason," he said. "My brother now has the business. We are no longer in touch."

"Your name is Dupuis, no?"

Jean Paul nodded.

"Ah, yes, the family Dupuis at Les Hérissons. They make a fine champagne which the young Madame markets under individual labels. They were having a grand success – and then came the war. Poor France. Poor Champagne, overrun once again by the Boche. I myself fought in the Franco-Prussian war on that very same soil."

"The war has helped business here a great deal," Jean Paul said unwisely, his mind on the information he had been given, "and delayed prohibition."

Gendrot looked as if he could not believe his ears. He took a pace backwards and bowed stiffly from the waist.

"I wish you good day, monsieur," he said coldly and moved away.

Well, it *had* helped business and it had delayed prohibition, Jean Paul thought, unmoved by the man's reaction. He agreed with President Wilson, who had said that it was courageous to remain neutral. Not only courageous, he thought, but extremely profitable if you were in the wine business.

He wandered over to join the group where Claus Schilling, a delegate to the conference who had not given a paper, was holding court. Schilling was as much a businessman as a brilliant producer of wine. He was also known for his sharp tongue and forthrightness.

He congratulated Jean Paul, sipped his champagne appreciatively, and asked brusquely: "Do you still have tenants on your land?"

Jean Paul felt the faint warning prickle that his spine always gave to remind him to be careful.

He nodded.

335

"Umm," said Schilling. "Have any of them managed to buy any land yet?"

"I really don't know," Jean Paul said. "I leave all that to my manager. I would imagine that some of them have."

"That's not my information," Schilling said, looking at Jean Paul hard from under bushy eyebrows. "You could give your wine a bad name with all that, you know." He sipped again, and added: "And it's good wine. Still, the word is that they're getting themselves unionised, so maybe you'd better have a word with your manager. See what's up. Or you may lose a harvest."

Jean Paul thanked him for the information, though he was not sure whether it had been given maliciously or helpfully. He was aware that none of these men really cared for him; he inspired some kind of instinctive dislike in them all, but his champagne had won fair and square because they were honourable. And also, he thought cynically, because there was no way to cheat on a tasting. Would they have let him win if they had known it was his wine? He reluctantly had to conclude that they would. Their love of wine would take precedence over their dislike of him.

But he would have to do something about the tenants. The unionisation worried him not a jot. But if his labour methods had at last been recognised and could harm his champagne, then he would have to change his ways.

The opportunity came sooner than he had imagined. As the last of his guests drifted off, he received an invitation to dine with Dino Angelino at the Palm Court dining room.

The invitation was delivered by the hotel pageboy, and Jean Paul whistled quietly to himself as he opened it. Gino Angelino was a man of great power and influence. He was also a mobster. He owned a chain of America's finest hotels, a whisky distilling company in the south, and a brewery company in the Midwest. Born and bred in New York to an Italian immigrant family, he had clawed his way to wealth by dubious means. Word was that he had come to the Congress to buy wine for his hotels.

"And why does he want to dine with me?" Jean Paul asked himself, debating whether to decline and see what happened, or accept and see what happened. Knowing he was playing with fire, but unable to resist, he accepted. There was no point in not. If Angelino really wanted to see him, one way or another Angelino would make sure he did.

It seemed reasonable to suppose that the mobster would want to buy Champagne D'Or for his hotels, but given the man's reputation it seemed unlikely to be quite so straightforward. Jean Paul took a cold shower to sober himself up. He also drank several cups of black coffee before leaving his suite for the restaurant. He decided to be ten minutes late.

Angelino was already at the table and the head waiter seemed flustered as he hurriedly led Jean Paul towards him. Angelino, a small fat man who looked as if he had been squashed into his well-cut dinner jacket, had a bottle of Dom Perignon and a lobster in front of him.

He bared tombstone teeth in a humourless smile as Jean Paul seated himself.

"Since you were discourteous enough to be late," he said, his tone jocular, "I have been discourteous enough to order. Will you take a lobster?"

"Thank you, no," said Jean Paul, smiling back without apologising. "With Dom Perignon I prefer a little caviare."

Angelino grunted and refilled his own glass before pouring champagne into Jean Paul's. The waiter tried to take the bottle and Angelino waved him away.

"Just get the caviare," he instructed, before turning to size up Jean Paul.

The two men brazenly stared at each other. Jean Paul took in the boot-button black eyes, and the seamed skin. His host had had a bad acne problem at some time in his seventy-odd years. Jean Paul, who had felt that twitch of the spine again, decided to concentrate on the thought of this man with his face covered in pustules. It made him less alarming.

For there was a growling menace about Angelino which, as Jean Paul stared, suddenly disappeared. He grinned. "Not afraid of me, eh?"

"I have never been afraid of anything or anybody in my life," Jean Paul said, while privately thinking that if he did decide to be afraid of anybody, this man would be a candidate.

Angelino nodded, a Buddha-like nod.

"I've heard about you," he said. "I like your style."

The waiter had returned and was spooning caviare from a silver bowl. Jean Paul did not stop him until there were six, round, glistening black mounds on his plate. As he generously spread one spoonful onto toast, he asked: "What have you heard?"

"Nothing but bad," Angelino said, laughing so that the seams on his face doubled. "But your champagne is good."

"It won the prize today."

"I'm told it was well deserved. I'm also told there's no racket involved. You couldn't have fixed it if you tried."

"But of course I would if I could have," Jean Paul said cheerfully.

The old man snorted with amusement.

"I was thinking of buying into your business," he announced.

337

"You were?" Jean Paul savoured another mouthful of caviare, and then pushed the plate away. "I prefer the beluga," he murmured before saying: "Unfortunately, my business is not on the market, and I have no need of either partners or finance."

Geniality vanished.

"I do not go into businesses that have need of either finance or partners, young man."

"Then you must find it difficult to find any to go into," Jean Paul said, a fraction too flippantly.

"Not at all," Angelino said softly. "Not at all. Most people come to see things my way."

There was the prickle again.

"I think I could quite easily see things your way, Mr Angelino," Jean Paul said, "on certain conditions, of course."

He took a long, appreciative sip of his champagne. "I hate to say it," he sighed, "but Dom Perignon is better than mine."

"Dom Perignon is better than anything, and call me Gino. All my business associates do." Again the tombstone smile. "What were the conditions that you had in mind?"

Just for the moment, thought Jean Paul, he was in the driving seat. And somehow he had to stay one jump ahead of the man facing him.

"How can I say until I know what you have in mind?"

He learned then that what his new friend Gino had in mind was to buy Champagne D'Or at rock bottom prices for his hotels, and to pay a lump sum for half of the business.

Jean Paul considered. More irritated than angered or alarmed, he knew that he was going to have to come to some deal with this man. If he did not, his vats would be smashed; Gino's mobsters would have him begging to let them in before he had no business left. But, on the other hand, the right deal with Gino could perhaps be valuable.

"Right," he said, speaking slowly and improvising fast. "It sounds good, but let me explain the position. I can't sell you half of the house and the winery, because it's not mine to sell. I have a partner and I also have a son. Some months ago, I legally put the original part of the business in trust for my son. It wouldn't be breakable now, and I wouldn't want to break it. You as a family man will understand that," he added, thinking he must see his lawyer right away, and wondering if a trust could be backdated. "I could sell you a share in half the actual output. But," he added still improvising, "what isn't in trust is all the land I bought myself years ago."

"The land on which you have your tenants?" Gino asked.

The man had been doing his homework.

"Right. The main bulk of my grapes comes from that land. They cost me very little. In fact, they cost me peanuts. I get them at a very advantageous price from my tenants, and if you were to buy that land and take over the tenancies, you would get them at a very advantageous price, too. You might even work out some way of getting them for nothing.

"I would expect a very good price for the land, I would expect to buy the grapes from you at a price advantageous to me, and I would expect you to pay nearly the right price for the champagne. What you get for it elsewhere is up to you. After all, if we are to be partners, we would only be robbing each other."

It was all off the top of his head, but he thought that even with what he had suggested he would still have room for manoeuvre, enough to win financially.

Gino Angelino threw back his head and laughed. It was not an attractive sight. But Jean Paul was already thinking about the huge parcel of land lower down the valley, where the ground was less rocky, that he could buy with Gino's money. Quietly, of course. Under a different name or company. That would have to be worked out later.

"You've got a nerve," Gino was saying, without rancour. "Why should I go along with that? I know you've got problems with your tenants."

"And who better to deal with them . . ." Jean Paul made a wide gesture that took in Angelino and his entire organisation. "It's time I became more respectable, but I think we are two of a kind. We should have met before."

"I said I liked your style," Angelino grunted. "We'll meet at my lawyers tomorrow."

"Correction," said Jean Paul briskly. "We'll meet at your lawyers this time next week. My lawyer is out of town and my partner is in Philadelphia. I'll want them both to be present."

The old man looked at him from under heavy lids, the black eyes flat and expressionless.

"Don't get too cocky, sonny boy," he said softly. "It might not be a good idea."

Chapter Twenty-Two

Philippe, sitting with his back to the chalk wall of the trench in the north-east of Champagne, reflected that a man with stamina and a taste for discomfort could, if he wished, in this September of 1915, walk in a continuous trench all the way from the North Sea to the Alps.

It was four o'clock on a misty, damp Saturday morning. Philippe was in one of the two trenches that contained the frontline troops of the opposing armies, waiting with his men for the offensive to begin. The enemy's trench at this point was no more than about a hundred yards away.

Very shortly, when the general gave the order, Major Philippe Lefevre and his men, plus thousands more, would go over the top. Their object, to drive a wedge into the German defences and cut them from the railheads that ran north-east from Reims to Mézières and Luxembourg, and the railway line from Mézières west to Hirson.

If the enemy could be separated from these railheads, he would lose his supply route from the central Rhine Valley. All his supplies would be forced to travel through one route, and the congestion caused could be disaster for the German army.

But would it work? Philippe wondered.

Every morning there were dogfights in the air. Men in flying machines battled with guns high above the trenches and over the strange, bare, rolling chalk downs and shallow valleys, split by the waters of muddy little streams, that formed the scenery in this part of Champagne. The weather had been perfect since the beginning of the month. An east wind had brought clear, cool days. But the wind had changed to the south-west on the day before, bringing a damp and chill that shrouded the bleak countryside in mist.

It was the same unlovely terrain where the French had beaten back Attila the Hun centuries before and the soldiers, still optimistic in spite of defeats, believed it was lucky terrain for France.

340

At the beginning of the month a bombardment had begun along the full length of the front, that ditch that ran from the North Sea to the Alps. The firing was more for show than anything else, intended to confuse the enemy as to which part of the line the French would choose to attack. The Germans had bombarded in retaliation, but that, too, was a demonstration of power rather than an attack, though much damage was done.

Behind the French lines, new trenches had been dug, new telephone wires laid and bomb stores constructed. All civilians between Chalons-Sur-Marne and Bar-le-Duc had been evacuated, and the area had been declared a military zone. Troops and guns were in constant movement.

Philippe, who until a week ago had been billeted a mile behind the front line in a comfortable bunker cut from chalk and even furnished with a bed, knew only the orders for his own men. But the men themselves, crawling along the maze of narrow trenches that led to the front line, sensed battle ahead. The tension that heralds some momentous event had made them quiet and dogged as they made their way forward. The Allies, for the first time, were taking the offensive and they could hope again that the war might be over soon.

The main bombardment had begun on the day before, the 23rd. The German front line was methodically destroyed by a hailstorm of shells, while random fire from howitzers battered their second line. It was midnight when the bombardment reached crescendo. Every gun was barking and whining, balls of fire lighting the sky above the ditches in which the men of both sides hid. The noise was indescribable, and Philippe, waiting in the fetid odour of the trench, tried to convince himself that the worst of war was this terrible, unbearable noise. It stopped him thinking of the battle to come.

It began to rain on the night of the twenty-fourth, and the men were issued an extra ration of wine, and a trench knife for the hand-to-hand fighting that awaited them in the morning. Philippe, in the new battledress of pale blue-grey, carried the letters that Rosie had written him under his tunic and close to his heart. Thinking of her, he waited, and the men grumbled and waited, crowded into the depths of the trench. Machine-guns were set in concrete and steel, and narrower trenches had been dug out towards the German front line so that the troops could spring, like lethal jack-in-the-boxes, from the earth.

As the dawn struggled up, the guns ceased. The sudden silence was as frightening as the dreadful thunder had been. An uneasy murmur ran along the walls.

"It's all right, lads," Philippe said to the men clustered around him. "The gunners are shifting ranges and lengthening their fuses to give us cover. It's nearly time."

"When do we go, sir?" asked a soldier who could not have been

341

more than nineteen, his trench knife in his belt, his rifle in his hand and his gasmask on his shoulder.

"Quarter past five," Philippe said.

"Five minutes," the soldier said, his voice awed. "Just five minutes left."

Philippe found himself praying as the minutes ticked by. He had no expectation of living through what was to follow. He knew the German strength and that their trenches were fortified encampments, armed with every modern device and weapon. He feared for his men, he feared for himself and he feared for France.

As the moment came, the guns began to fire a barrier of shells between the French and their enemy, and wave upon blue-grey wave of men swept from the cover of the trenches into the rain from heaven and the rain of fire from the German guns.

Philippe found himself blindly running through the drizzle that turned the torn, chalk ground into slime, blood-stained slime, already piled with blue-grey dead. Running that hundred yards until he and his men fell into the German front-line trench seemed to take for ever. And once in the trench they were confronted by a machine-gun that some poor heroic German soldier was desperately trying to reload. The French lad who had asked how long, coolly shot him dead.

Philippe's orders were to 'clear up' once in the trench — take prisoners and capture machine-guns, bigger guns, and any other weapons. And he was to leave men to man the captured fortifications and then move on to the Lübeck line, the second German trench.

It was blind, confused fighting. He was leading his own men as well as soldiers from other battalions whose leader had been killed or who had somehow become separated from their own officers.

He found himself calm as they fought on, mostly crawling flat in an effort to evade the machine-gun fire, searching out every blasted tree and hillock that might give shelter, killing every German they could, as his own men fell about him. But he kept going forward, slipping in the bloody mire, and telling himself that all he had to do was get to the Lübeck line and then they would all be safe. Just two and a half miles, that was all.

It was midday when he and the men who had survived stumbled upon the huge fortification.

"Forward," he called. He covered the last desperate few yards on his feet before kicking aside barbed wire and poising himself on the brink of the second German line.

He jumped down. And as his booted feet found the ground, he called out in triumph before he felt a sudden searing pain, saw a blinding flash ... and then nothing.

*   *   *

Rosie's December birthday came and went without word from Philippe. She was thirty-four and some days felt that. She feared for Philippe and yearned for him. She yearned for love. There were days when she was so hungry for the kisses and caresses of a man that she felt she would almost welcome Clovis in her bed. But Clovis, still in his twilight world, spent many of his nights at the brothel on the Épernay road. When he was at home, all pretence of their marriage had ended. Madame and Rosie had made him a room of his own, next door to the marital bedchamber. Even Madame had agreed that there was nothing else to be done. Neither mentioned it. They were not certain if Clovis still slept with Claudette, but tacitly agreed that if he did, and so openly, it would not be *comme il faut* for him to share Rosie's bed.

Philippe's safety nagged at her all the time. So many had died — and for what? The war rumbled on just a few miles away beyond the Vesle Valley. The sounds of warfare had become the background to their lives. Occasionally there was the odd skirmish and the enemy gained five hundred yards. The French would regain them a few days later. And for every yard there were heaps of bloodied dead and scores of wounded men, their lives blighted.

Secretly she found her greatest comfort in little Rosanne. Sometimes she would put the baby to her barren breast and its contented suck soothed her. She had no milk to give, but the babe seemed happy to lie in her arms, nestled into her. Feeling guilty and that she must be perverted, she could not help sometimes wishing that it was Philippe's mouth encircling her hard nipple.

Allie seemed to have gratefully reverted to childhood and her normal happy self. She had gone back to the village school where she found herself something of a heroine for the time she had spent in Reims. But she would not go near the young German prisoners of war who had been sent to work at Les Hérissons.

She did now play occasionally with the baby, and seemed to have come to terms with the situation. But Madame and Rosie both watched her anxiously and showered her with affection until, if she had been that kind of child, she would have been spoilt. Sometimes, as she watched her daughter playing games and reading books that were now too young for a fifteen-year-old, Rosie wondered if her reversion to childhood was perhaps more of a retreat.

Somehow they had managed to keep the business going, though more of the Vesle fields were destroyed and it was impossible to look after the grapes at Épernay. They barely had the labour to deal with even the vineyards around the house, and without the prisoners of war, the harvest would have been lost. Everyone, including the house servants, did their best to help, but there was no way that pre-war production could be kept up. And the picking had been early this year

343

– the grapes were ready from the sixth of September. The *vendange* was safely in, with the help of soldiers who were home on leave.

Rosie hated the war but had learned to tolerate it. Madame grew angrier by the day. She had lost weight and was all beaked nose and wild grey hair. She could hardly bring herself to be civil to the German soldiers who worked for Les Hérissons. She said that now she had no sons left, for the Boche had taken Clovis from them. And her granddaughter had been sullied, her life ruined by them.

Rosie watched the young fresh-faced Germans working with a will for no return, relieved and grateful to be away from the front line, the war behind them. They certainly made no attempt to escape, and she could not equate them with the carnage. They were young human beings, dragged into the horror of war by their politicians and elders. And their presence hardened in her the conviction that any war must be madness.

But she did not say so to Madame, who would have accused her of an 'American mentality', for America still refused to be brought into the fray. It was perhaps the only thing they had ever come near to quarrelling about.

Christmas had come and gone and snow cossetted the vines from the late January cold when the letter came from André.

Rosie held the envelope in her hand, afraid to open it. She stood, in the hallway of the house, her eyes closed, silently praying: "Please God, let him be safe." Then she went up to her little sitting room and opened it.

> My dear, dear Rosie, I have good news and bad. At long last I have heard from Philippe's commanding officer, and I am grateful to be able to tell you that he is alive. Though not, I fear, well. But he is not going to die.
>
> He was grievously wounded in the September push. Why we have not heard before is because he was not conscious for some time and the authorities could not discover who he was in all the confusion after the battle.
>
> Apparently he is to be given a medal for exceptional courage under fire, but the medal will not give him back his sight.
>
> Our Philippe has been blinded.
>
> He is in a military hospital somewhere secret where his head injuries are being attended, but I am told that very soon he will be well enough to convalesce. For the time being only Lorraine is permitted to be in touch with him, though this will change.
>
> I am hoping for more news soon, and I am hoping, too, that I can impose on you to visit me here in Paris. I know that travelling is hazardous and difficult, but I feel a great need to see you. I must

now admit to myself that I am growing old, and the death of my dear Sebastian and then this have left me broken. The sight of your sweet face would restore me.

I write to you in sorrow, but all is not lost. He lives. Be of good heart,

André

She sat crouched in her chair, her arms across her chest, rocking backwards and forwards, the letter crumpled in her hand. He was alive. Relief flooded her, almost negating the shock of the news. The blindness hardly mattered if he lived and breathed. She had been so sure that the letter would tell her he, too, was dead. She could rejoice in the blindness. She could still love him. They could still hold each other and touch each other. He could still do the thing he was best at – taste wine – and if Lorraine would not be his eyes, she would be. Her own eyes felt as if they had been filled with scalding water; her heart beat at twice its normal pace, and she felt dizzy, but above all he was alive, and would not have to go back into the war again. What use was a blind soldier? But a blind man could do many things. And then she cried. When her tears had dried she thought again about the blindness.

Not to be able to see. How dreadful was it? She closed her eyes tight shut and walked about her room. That was easy enough. She knew where everything was. With her eyes still shut, she went to her wardrobe. Touch and recognition of the feel of the fabrics told her which clothes were which. She had no problem either with the items on her dressing table, though she sent a hairbrush flying to the floor and then could not find it.

She was thoughtful when she had finished her experiment. To be blind was just possible when all was familiar and in place. But what about the world outside? she wondered as she went to tell the sad news to Madame Dupuis and Allie.

She left for Paris the following morning. The journey was tedious more than anything else. The train went from Épernay through Château Thierry, and was crowded with troops going on leave or back to their units on the Somme. Tired men slept on their kitbags in the corridors and it was bitterly cold. But they stopped as ever at the Gare deL'Est, and taxis still waited outside for fares – some of those same taxis, maybe, that had transported the French troops to the victory of the battle of the Marne just fifteen months before.

Driving through the boulevards to the house in the Île de la Cité, she was shocked by the numbers of men who walked with crutches, an empty trouser leg below, or with an empty sleeve pinned beneath the cross of war. But they walked with heads high, stiffly erect, still soldiers, and home again.

345

She was also shocked by the sight of André. He, like Madame, had become feverishly thin, and he seemed to have lost inches in height. His hair was now in thin strands over his skull, his moustache snowy white. But he was still a handsome and distinguished man.

He held her very tight when they were alone, and said into her hair: "It was good of you to leave your baby and come."

"I should have come before," she said.

"Wartime is no time to travel." He stood back and looked at her. "Are you all right?" he asked tenderly.

"André, I am just relieved he is alive. I was so sure that he would die. And now he will not have to die. He is free of the war."

"It is a sort of death." he said, his voice sombre. "I grieve for him. Perpetual darkness. Never to see Paris, her bridges, her boulevards again. Never to see you. What can he do with his life, and not yet thirty-eight? Robbed of his independence. Lorraine says he is in a state of despair. She has spoken to his commanding officer and apparently Philippe did not want us to know what had happened to him. He felt that he could only be a burden from now on." Shaking his head, he moved to sit, patting the sofa beside him for her to join him. "It is a dreadful tragedy."

She did not sit, and stifling her fears that he might be right, said crisply: "That is nonsense."

He looked up at her and half smiled, as if he had been expecting such a response.

"Why should he be a burden?" she demanded passionately, angry with the defeatism of the conversation. "His career has always depended on his sense of taste and smell, not his eyes. He won't be able to judge the colour of a wine again, but blindfolded he was a superb taster. He still has his livelihood. And more important, he still has his life."

"You make it all sound very easy, my dear," he said gently.

"Of course it's not easy. But if he believes his life is over and that he is nothing but a burden, he needs to be made to see this is not so. He loves literature — he can be read to. He can learn Braille. He loves to walk – he needs an arm to hold. He loves good food and wine – he still has that. He enjoys his job – he needs a pair of eyes to travel with him. André, he's alive. Can't you see? Only death is the end."

She was pacing up and down the room, her colour high.

"But he is as you say yourself, dependent, and no man cares for that. And who is going to provide these arms and eyes?"

"It is Lorraine's right. I wish it were mine." She stopped pacing, sighed and asked: "How has she taken the news?"

"She is appalled at the thought of having a blind husband. She tries not to show it, and is enjoying the drama of telling her friends

346

about poor Philippe, but at heart she is truly appalled. But then, she is only twenty-two. I should feel a great deal more content if you were his wife."

"So should I. And I too am appalled that she should feel that way," Rosie said fiercely. "I want so much to see him. Or at least write to him. How can I, André? How can I?"

"For the moment, you cannot," he said. "But I have been making enquiries since I wrote to you. Many blinded officers have committed suicide, I am afraid, so now an organisation exists to help them. At the moment the headquarters are at the Crillon Hôtel here in Paris. The proprietor has lent them the space. The intention is to re-educate the men, teach them Braille and so on. It is run by a countrywoman of yours, a Miss Winifred Holt, who worked with the blind in New York. I have made arrangements for Philippe to go there eventually. I am making my own enquiries, but Lorraine has promised me that she will tell me when and where he goes to convalesce. She thinks that I will visit him for her. I thought you might go in my place."

Rosie could not believe her ears.

"She is not even going to visit him?"

"She is very busy with her work. She seems to be secretary to some young man called Didier who is a captain in General Gallieni's Paris defence regiment. I met him once at a perfectly dreadful party she gave. She says her work is of vital importance."

"I see," said Rosie.

"But it did occur to me that a visit from you would do him a great deal more good than one from me." He was beginning to be more cheerful, and there was a faint sparkle in his eye. "My own enquiries will soon bear fruit. There are some advantages to being an old soldier. I am to be told where Philippe has been sent in two or three days. Perhaps before Lorraine knows – just in case she should change her mind about performing her wifely duty – though my old comrade could not promise that."

"So it may not be too long?" Rosie said eagerly.

"It may be quite soon. After all, it is four months since he was wounded. I thought we might not mention you were planning to visit him, just in case he refuses to see you. He is, apparently, very depressed."

"He won't be once we are together again." Rosie said confidently.

André pursed his lips and nodded, his eyes smiling.

"You Americans!" he said.

But her confidence was not as high on the train going back to Épernay later that day. She and André had lunched together at La Tour d'Argent on the Quai de la Tournelle. They ate pressed duck and drank

347

André's Laurent Perrier champagne. The food was as good as it had ever been, for fortunately, M. Delair, the proprietor, still had his duck farms in spite of the war.

They were given a table overlooking the Seine and Notre Dame, for Rosie was one of the most elegant women in the restaurant. She had deliberately dressed her best, with her sable coat over a fashionable coat-frock that buttoned from neck to hem. With it she wore a shallow-crowned hat with a large brim. She appreciated that though André might be old he still found pleasure in being seen with an elegant woman.

André was tired after lunch and Marius took her to the train. In these less formal times of war, he ventured to remember the afternoon, so many years before, when he had taken her first to the Gare de L'Est and then to Chigny les Roses.

"It all worked out very well, madame," he said. "Why, you have become quite famous in the champagne world."

On the train, where a young soldier slept opposite her, his mouth open, a huge bandage round his head, her euphoria and joy that Philippe had survived began to fade a little.

André was right. It was a terrible thing to be blind, but she told herself that she was not allowed to think that way. She must think positively and persuade Philippe of all that there was to live for. She remembered with a chill André speaking of the men who had committed suicide, and that Philippe was deeply depressed. She was instantly in an agony of impatience to see him. And once home she spent more time practising being blind, sometimes even blindfolding her eyes when no one was about. She had some falls and stumbles, and when out of doors became so lost and disoriented that she had to tear the blindfold off. But she believed that to try to experience his calamity could only help her to help him.

The second letter arrived four days later on a wet February morning. It was brief. Philippe had been sent to a small hotel in Cannes in the south of France. She sighed with relief while worrying that it was a long way away. What could she tell Madame Dupuis?

She broached the subject over lunch.

"I heard from André this morning," she said, trying to be casual. "Philippe has been sent to convalesce in Cannes. André is most upset because Lorraine does not wish to travel so far to see him, and the journey would be too much for him at his age."

She was aware of sounding stilted.

"So you are going to see him instead?" Madame said, helping herself to more soup.

It was not the response Rosie had expected, and for a moment she was lost for words.

348

"Seeing you will be the best thing in the world for him," Madame said calmly, "though of course he will not be able to *see* you now. When were you thinking of leaving?"

Rosie was nonplussed. "Well," she said lamely, "I thought fairly soon. Philippe is apparently very depressed."

"He is a brave soldier who has given his sight for France," Madame said in ringing tones. "You must go at once. He needs you."

Was Madame carried away by patriotism, or had she guessed the truth? Rosie asked herself. And if she had guessed, had she come to terms with the fact that her daughter-in-law had been unfaithful to her son?

It was all very puzzling, but a relief that there were to be no problems about getting away.

The war followed Rosie south. There were no guns as background chorus, but the windows of the wagon-lit were plastered with warnings not to speak to strangers, the enemy was listening, and again there were many wounded men on the train.

Rosie had left Paris around ten o'clock, and when the woman attendant woke her at eight the next morning she could see the blue of the Mediterranean outside her window. It was warmer, and the sun shone as bright as a spring day in Paris. She had left winter behind. Her sable coat would be too much, but then she had another purpose in mind for that. She was excited, she had not seen countryside like this since she left California. But this was so much more mature than the California she had left, with charming terracotta houses and, again, endless vines. She thought she would feel at home here. And then there would be Philippe.

Her stomach turned over at the thought of him. She felt desire welling back from the deep dark place where she had buried it. But she would have to be slow and careful with him. He could not be rushed.

The train pulled into Cannes station after spectacularly beautiful coastal views. A taxi took her the short journey to the small hotel on the harbour, and she drank in the sunshine, the sparkling sea and the flowers already blooming in the gardens around the big solid building the taxi driver said was the winter casino. The harbour was full of little boats, and on the hill above an old church with a square clock tower looked down on the tranquil scene. It was just ten thirty.

Outside the hotel, two young men, well wrapped in greatcoats, sat in the sunshine, watching her with curiosity. Inside the small entrance hall another soldier, with a bandage round his head, sat looking out of the window towards the harbour. He wished her good day and pointed out the desk where she rang the bell for the concierge. A woman appeared in a white apron, wiping her hands on a towel. She had a round, rosy, pleasant face and must have been in her late forties, but was still attractive.

"Good morning," she said. "Can I help you?"

"Please," said Rosie. "I have come from Paris to see Major Lefevre. Is that possible?"

The woman put her elbows on the desk and leaned forward confidingly. "Indeed," she said. "The poor man is in need of some company. So unhappy. Are you his wife?"

Rosie hesitated. The honest eyes of the woman were scrutinising her.

"No," she said. "But I think he will be pleased I am here."

The woman laughed.

"I would think he might be," she said. "Shall I take you up?"

"No." Rosie put out her hand. "Please. Could I go up alone, because – well – I'd like to surprise him. You see, it's important." She was stammering, uncertain how to put her case.

The woman nodded, her eyes knowing. "I see," she said. "Well then, here's a key. He's in room five on the first floor."

"Thank you," Rosie said gratefully. "May I leave my things here?"

"Of course. But you can't stay, I'm afraid. We've only convalescent soldiers at the moment. Shall I book you in somewhere else?" She looked at the sable coat. "Perhaps the Carlton?"

"Wherever you think," Rosie said, in a fever to be off to the first floor. "And thank you."

She ran up the stairs, and at the first landing hesitated before walking more slowly towards room five. She quietly put the key in the lock without knocking and turned it. The door opened and she stepped into a small, austere room with wooden floors, a large bed covered with a white lace bedspread and a few pieces of wooden furniture. The long windows to the balcony were open, letting the sun stream through, and she could see that Philippe, wearing a dressing gown, was sitting quietly, dark glasses over his eyes, staring out at the sea.

She shut the door with a positive click, and he lifted his head and listened.

"Elisabeth?" he asked.

"No."

"Who is it?"

Suddenly short of breath, she began to walk across the room.

"Rosie?" he asked, his voice puzzled. "Is that you?"

"Yes," she said. "It's me. How did you guess?"

"Your footsteps... I recognised ... What ..."

She was standing by him now on the small balcony, and gently she leaned forward to take off the black, blind glasses.

"Rosie, don't!" he said, anguished.

"Why not?" Somehow she was making her voice normal. "How can I kiss you with those in the way?"

His eyes were shut, and there was heavy scarring on his temples and forehead. He looked much older, with heavy carved lines at the sides of his mouth, and he had the drawn look that pain brings.

"Oh, darling," she said. "My beautiful darling. Let me look at you."

She took his face in her hands, and he sat still, his mouth trembling.

"I cannot look at you," he said.

"There's no need," she said laughing. "I assure you I am as beautiful as ever." She bent and kissed him gently on both closed eyes. "And if you would get to your feet we could go inside and you could kiss me properly. Come, give me your hand."

She understood that he was anxious about moving, for his hand groped for the rail of the balcony. She took his hand in hers and then slid it along her arm, and firmly pulled him up and back into the room.

"There were men on boats in the harbour watching us," she said, wrapping her arms round him and laying her head on his shoulder as she had always done. And instinctively, as he had always done, he began to rock her.

"That's better," she sighed. "You're back. Oh, Philippe, I feared you were dead, it had been so long. Why didn't you write to me?"

"Like once before, I didn't know what to say," he said, his voice so low she had to strain to hear it.

"All you had to say was I'm alive. I am blinded, and I love you," she told him.

"I am blinded," he repeated bitterly.

"You are *alive*," she said violently. "You are still a man. My man, and I cannot bear you to believe anything different."

She put up her face to kiss him, and he clung to her convulsively, kissing her wildly. She could feel he was crying and so was she, but they held on tightly to each other, each in their own darkness.

When he had calmed, she wiped their faces, and as he stood, wooden, she again took his hand and led him to the bed so he could sit.

"I want to talk to you," she said. "There's so much to say. Can we go out? We could walk, have coffee and then walk some more and have some lunch."

He looked agitated.

"I don't know," he said. "I've not really been out since I've been here. I don't know where we'd go."

"It doesn't matter where we go as long as we're together. It's a beautiful day. Did you feel the sun on your face? It was raining in Champagne. Philippe, it's so strange not to hear the guns. It must be even more so for you. I feel we've come into peace, into a new start. We both have to learn different things."

351

"I have to learn to live," he said. "What do you have to learn?"

"How to help you, of course, as you have always helped me," she said, with a little chuckle. "And my first lesson is to prove that your legs still work. Later we might prove something else works, if, of course, you still care for me."

A very small smile curved his mouth.

"Rosie, you are no lady."

"Never was," she said cheerfully. "In spite of trying. Now, do we walk?"

"All right," he said. "We'll walk."

"Then get dressed." she ordered him.

She deliberately did not help him to dress. He found his clothes at the side of the bed, and managed to put them on correctly. This was something he had obviously mastered and if he could master one thing, he could master many.

She debated whether to walk him down the stairs, and decided to take one thing at a time. They went down in the creaking lift which jerked and bumped to a standstill. He held her arm very tightly all the way.

As they came into the foyer, he lifted his head and listened.

"Elisabeth?" he called.

The woman who had greeted Rosie appeared again.

"Yes, Major?" she said.

"We are going for a walk. I will not be in for lunch."

Elisabeth's face lit up in a delighted smile and she nodded approvingly at Rosie.

"Yes, Major," she said. "I have booked madame into the Carlton Hotel, and sent her things there. Is that correct?"

He turned to Rosie.

"You are staying?"

"As long as you'll have me," she said. "Thank you, Elisabeth. Major Lefevre tells me he has not been out. Could you recommend somewhere that we can eat?"

"The Carlton itself is very good, madame. Or the Belle Époque in the market. But all the restaurants in Cannes are good. You will have no difficulty."

"And where is the Carlton?" Rosie asked.

"On the seafront. It is quite a long walk. It will do monsieur good. I was told that he must have exercise. But until now ..." she threw up her hands and laughed, creating a feminine conspiracy.

They walked along the edge of the harbour, and Rosie described the boats to Philippe, who held tightly to her arm. But by the time they had passed the casino and were walking past the ferry port he was gaining confidence and stepping out more easily. She guided him as unobtrusively as possible over steps and obstacles, and as they walked she told him how life in Les Hérissons had been. He was shaken from his own despair to hear how Allie had found herself pregnant.

"And so, by proxy, I have become a mother again," Rosie said. "You are the only person in the world who knows the truth, other than Madame. I have lied to my dear Lizzie who is enchanted with the news, and even to your father who, I suspect, secretly believes the baby is yours. And now I find I adore the little thing. She is such a charmer. Just as your Françoise must be."

"Ah, yes," Philippe smiled. "But I have not seen her for so long." His face saddened. "And now I shall never see my daughter turn from child to woman."

"You will hear her, and hold her and love her," Rosie said briskly, determined to stamp out any gloom. "It will be sad not to see her, but I shall describe her to you."

"Oh, Rosie, how I have needed you!" he said. "At first I wanted to die. I considered taking my pistol and killing myself. I did not do it because of the disgrace it would cause my father, and the pain he would feel in losing me as he has lost Sebastian. But I saw no reason to live."

"But didn't you think of me?" Rosie asked, her voice full of pain.

"No, I did not. I know your strength. I knew you would survive. And what I needed was to lean on your strength as I am now."

She squeezed his arm against her side.

"Sometimes, Philippe, strength is nothing more than a determination not to be beaten or bowed. That is the strength you need now. The strength never to give in. Not mine."

"And that is the strength I may be able to find, now you are here," he said.

They took coffee on the terrace of the hotel, and she described the view to him. Then they walked further along the seafront until the grand buildings ran out and there were only simple homes and hotels. All the time they talked. He told her of life in the trenches and she described how they had managed to harvest the grapes from the Vesle Valley. She deliberately told him of the children who had died. She wanted him to realise that even blindness was preferable to death.

Then they walked back to the hotel and had lunch in the restaurant. He managed to eat without making too much mess, and she realised that he must have been practising, just as he had been practising dressing himself.

"I presume everyone is staring at the blind soldier, spilling his food," he said, angry when he found his fork empty as it reached his mouth.

"We are in a corner, your back is to the restaurant, as a gentleman's should be," she told him tartly, "and everyone else here is too busy

353

eating their own food to worry about how you are eating yours. More important, is it good?"

"Very good," he assured her.

After they had eaten, she took him across the road from the hotel and down onto the beach. They crunched across the pebbles until the water was near, and then she made him bend to put his hand into the first little wave that lapped up.

"Taste it," she said. "It's so salty. I have never tasted seawater before."

He tasted, his brow furrowed in concentration.

"And I know now why they call it Mediterranean blue," she told him.

"The blue of Allie's eyes."

"Exactly."

They wandered hand in hand back to the hotel. She asked if he could smell flowers, she described what she saw, she made him feel the smooth curve of a pebble, the roughness of a shell. She told him their colours.

And in the hotel, she left him sitting in a deep leather armchair while she asked for the key to her room. Then she took him straight up with her.

The concierge looked askance for one moment, and then, realising that the man on Rosie's arm was blind, took no more notice.

The hotel was new, furnished in the latest mode and with considerable luxury. Hers was a huge suite with sitting room, bedroom and bathroom with a large stone balcony that overlooked the sea. She took Philippe into the bedroom, and said: "I think you should rest a while now. Have you walked so far since it happened?"

He shook his head.

"But I'm not tired," he said.

"A rest after lunch is civilised," she told him. "And I must unpack."

She led him to the bed, and sat him down, kneeling to take off his boots. Then she went to close the shutters, making the room dimly lit.

"Just take your jacket off, and lie down and rest," she said firmly. "I'll be back in a little while."

Protesting, he did as she said, but she noticed that there was a sigh of relief as he swung his legs onto the bed and settled down, his head on the large pillows.

"I shall only be emptying my suitcases," she said. "You will be able to hear me if you want anything."

But he was asleep within minutes as she moved quietly about the room. She let him sleep for an hour, by which time she had changed her clothes and put on a heavy silk robe. She took her sable coat and carefully laid it on the other side of the large bed from where he was sleeping.

Then she sat beside him and very gently began to stroke his hair with a feather-light touch.

He moaned a little, and then made a little sigh of pleasure. His eyes remained closed, so she was not certain as to whether he had woken. But a nerve jumped at the corner of his mouth.

She continued to stroke his fair hair, now touched with grey, and he lay calm, occasionally making a contented murmur. Then he groped for her other hand, and for a while they sat in silence, his hand in hers, while she continued to stroke him.

"I had not noticed how my head hurts," he said, "until you began to stroke it."

"Does it still hurt?"

"No, the pain has gone."

He raised himself from the pillows and his free hand found her arm.

"Silk," he said.

"Oyster silk. It's the gown from the Paris apartment."

"I remember it. It opened with a sash." He ran his hand down over her shoulder to her waist where he found the bow that held the garment together. His fingers pulled it loose.

"Lie down beside me," he whispered.

Without speaking, she rose and went round to the other side of the bed, and lay down on the sables.

"Come towards me," she told him.

He rolled over, and his hands found the fur.

"Fur," he said.

"Sable. For us to lie on. Smooth, soft fur, good to touch."

"Umm." He was pushing aside her gown, and searching for her breast. His questing fingers traced the pattern of lace, and hesitated as they encountered something hard and diamond shaped.

"Remember?" she whispered in his ear, making her breath warm.

"Is it the corselet? The one you wore our very first time?"

She was learning it was not enough to nod.

"It is. Can you picture it? You remember?"

"I have pictured it a million times. Oh, Rosie!" He groaned, but his fingers were releasing the hooks that ran down between her breasts. "And I can still take it from you even without eyes."

"I have closed the shutters," she told him. "We are both making love in the dark."

She threw the corselet onto the floor, sent the silk gown after it, and began undressing him. He helped her without difficulty and then he sat up, and his fingers found her head on the pillow and combed through her hair.

"It feels longer," he said.

"It is, a little."

He took one long tress and pressed it to his face, inhaling deeply.

"It smells so clean. And feels like a different kind of silk."

He found her eyes and kissed them, then traced the line of her jaw, explored her ears, before touching her mouth. She let her tongue dampen the tips of his fingers, and then, with a quick little movement, took his index finger into her mouth and sucked on it deeply.

"Wait," he said.

His hand ran down the line of her throat and felt for her shoulders, and stroked her back.

"The hollow in your throat is still there," he whispered. "I remember it so well."

She lay passive, letting him explore her. He slid his hands down the length of her arms, stroking her fingers one by one. Then he returned to her throat before his hands ran down over her breasts, finding the nipples. They were standing proud. He gently twisted them, before cupping the soft weight of her breasts in his hands. She was beginning to moan a little and her hips were rising, wanting him.

"Wait," he said again.

One finger had discovered her navel and was searching there, and then he used both hands to feel the soft swell of her belly before slipping lower. He scratched gently at her public hair en route to finding that she was wet and open, hungry for him.

"The creamy rose of Rosie," he murmured, "wanting me."

It was the turn of her thighs. He stroked them, one by one, moving on to feel behind her knees and down to her feet.

"Such little feet," he told her. "I have thought of them too. Many times. Now my hands have learned all of you again, it is my mouth's turn."

Swiftly he slid down until he was lying beside her, and he kissed first her forehead, and then her ears, his tongue exploring each curve and curl. And then he found her mouth, and they clung together, in an embrace that seemed endless, with only the sound of their breathing in the room. His tongue tasted her as hers tasted him. He sucked gently at her lips, nibbling at the soft red flesh inside. She could remain passive no longer, and her own hands began to stroke him, over his chest, down the flat stomach to find that he was rampantly ready for her.

"Now! Please now!" she begged. "It has been so long."

"Wait," was all he said, as his mouth left hers and found her nipples, biting and teasing, sucking and rolling with his tongue. She was in an agony of need, but he continued to kiss her — soft kisses around the indent of her waist, his tongue in her navel, and licking her belly. And then he twisted to push his head between her thighs, and the wetness of

356

his mouth mingled with the wetness of her body.

It was almost as good as having him in her, and she twisted to take him in her mouth, until he gently pushed her away.

"Oh, the scents of you! The softness of you!" he groaned and let her guide him into the depth of her. He rode her frantically, and her response was equally wild. It did not last long before they both came to a shuddering, musky, exhausted finale, collapsed in each other's arms on the soft sable skins.

"Well, we proved it works," she said drowsily after a few minutes, and was overjoyed to hear him chuckle. "It works very well," she added. "But then, it always did."

"It might well work again if you let me get some sleep," he said.

She stayed with him for the whole week of convalescence, and Elisabeth turned a blind eye of her own to the fact that Philippe was rarely at the small hotel. His confidence grew with Rosie's arm to hold, and they discussed the future. She could not see why he could not continue his work, as long as he had an arm to lean on.

"There's Lorraine's, mine, your Georges', Henri's, your father's — we would all consider it a privilege," she told him, though she had her doubts about Lorraine. Lorraine had written to say that she was so happy that Philippe was improving, but she could not come to Cannes to see him because of her war work. However, she could hardly wait to see him in Paris again.

He was to go back to Paris from Cannes to join other blinded men at Winifred Holt's classes at the Crillon. Rosie said she saw no reason why she should not come to Paris one day a week. She would look for an apartment that they could use as an office, and start again in their pre-war routine.

"But you mustn't be too optimistic about me, Rosie," he said. "Without you I shall stumble a lot."

"Of course you will stumble," she said. "I only wish I could always be with you to pick you up."

"You are probably the only person in the world that I would not mind picking me up," he told her sadly.

Throwing caution to the winds, they travelled back on the train together, and made love in the *wagon-lit* in rhythm with the rocking of the wheels. And at the Gare de Lyon, Rosie held back so as not to be seen while Georges collected his master to take him back to the apartment at Neuilly.

Then, with a heavy heart, she crossed Paris to the Gare de l'Est and home that would never be home without him there.

Chapter Twenty-Three

Champagne, May 1917

Alexander was alone in Paris in a car with a chauffeur and a slip of blue paper that permitted him to remain at 'a certain place' inside the war zone for ten days. He was a guest of the French war department, and sent by his new employer, the *New York Times*. America had been in the war for less than a month and his brief as a war correspondent was to witness the devastation of Reims and to get as close to the front line as possible.

He was trying to look as if he was an old hand at war, but excitement and trepidation were mixed in equal parts. He was uncomfortable in the staff officer's khaki uniform and forage cap with which he had been issued. But still he was proud to wear it. And not against wearing it, either, since his foreign editor had explained it would prevent him being shot as a spy should he fall into enemy hands.

The chauffeur, a friendly fellow called Jacques, picked him up from the Roblin Hôtel where he had been staying. It was Jacques who dealt with the gendarmes who halted them for their passes, and Jacques who pointed out landmarks as they drove east from Paris. There were some signs of warfare, but the chauffeur explained that his countrymen had cleared up most of the mess that the battles of 1914 had caused.

"There's not much left of Reims," he told Alexander. "The Germans bombard it daily. They're mad, those Remois," he said admiringly. "They refuse to go. They live in the champagne cellars like rats, while above them the town collapses under the shells."

"What about the surrounding countryside?" Alexander asked. "I have friends nearby I would like to visit when I've finished my work."

"Depends where they are," Jacques said. "Which village?"

"Chigny les Roses."

Jacques thought. Then said: "I'm pretty sure that's behind the front line, but near enough to make life unpleasant. I can take you there, though. It's out of the military zone."

As they neared Reims, Alexander heard the guns for the first time, ominous, threatening, booming in the distance. The twin towers of the cathedral appeared on the horizon, and around them a pall of heavy, black smoke.

"The bastards have hit something," Jacques said. "Sure you want to go in?"

"Positive," said Alexander.

What the bastards had hit was the Hôtel de Ville. Alexander watched while it blazed, the *pompiers* fighting in vain. Men ran in and out of the burning building carrying paintings, pieces of furniture, anything that could be saved. French soldiers were helping to fight the fire, but it was obvious that there was no hope for the fine old building.

Alexander could not believe the devastation. The Place Royale was but a shell, with nothing intact but the proud statue of the "well loved King, Louis XV", which still stood in the centre. The cathedral, its irreplaceable stained glass gone for ever, was boarded up and covered in sandbags. The archbishop's palace was in ruins. The Place des Marches no longer existed. The town could not boast a pane of glass, and the buildings that were standing were no more than tottering walls. Yet Jeanne D'Arc's statue stood unscathed in the Cathedral Square. Alexander doffed his cap to her.

His chauffeur had delivered him to a young lieutenant, who politely acted as his guide through the mutilated streets. He took Alexander into the ruined, naked cathedral, where all the paintings, tapestries and carvings had been removed. A sacristan spoke a set piece, telling of burning rafters, of the dead and wounded German prisoners who had been inside the building at the first bombardment. He told, too, how those same prisoners had tried to help save the treasures that their compatriots were at pains to destroy.

And all the while the shells whistled overhead. The lieutenant seemed to ignore them. Alexander tried to do the same, but he could not help flinching when the sound seemed to be in the next street.

Back in the car, he scribbled notes as Jacques drove him further east towards the trenches. There he was delivered to yet another young lieutenant, who, for a man who lived in a trench, seemed remarkably cheerful.

The lieutenant described his trench as the deck of a battleship, sunk underground. He pointed out his conning tower — a telescope set into a steel plate, with which he could scan the surrounding countryside. In the trench were offices, a wardroom, a cook's galley, telephones, running water and electric lights. In his own quarters there was a carpet on the floor, a four-poster bed and photographs on his dressing table.

"You'd never believe we were underground, would you?" he said, obviously delighted with his own domestic arrangements. "Things aren't so organised and comfortable nearer the battle lines, though. And that's where you want to go, isn't it?"

"Please," said Alexander. "As near to the front line as possible."

The lieutenant looked dubious.

"I don't know about that," he said. "Let's see how you hold up on the walk. "

It was a long walk; at least two miles, beginning in a ditch carved out with hard labour through the chalk soil.

"Mind your head," the lieutenant said, pointing out the lethal balls of barbed wire which swung above their heads, snatching at Alexander's forage cap. "If, God forbid, we had to retreat, we'd drop those into the trenches. Tricky for the Boche, that would be."

Alexander was beginning to feel claustrophobic when abruptly the trench came to an end in the centre of a sunlit, but totally wrecked, small town. The place was a pile of rubble; not one wall remained standing and even the trees had been blown away.

"Makes Reims look untouched, doesn't it?" the lieutenant said, leading the way through shell craters down what had been the main street. "Now watch out here. This bit is tricky."

They had come to a huge barricade of timbers and steel doors, with apparently no way through. But the officer slid through a gap in the steel, and Alexander followed to find himself climbing down a well. It was damp, dank and dark. The wooden crosspieces that offered footing were slippery and hard to find. Alexander was sweating when they finally reached the bottom where they turned into a tunnel and began to climb upwards again. A square of sunshine appeared, and then they were walking in a cemetery with yew trees, hedges, and carefully tended paths and gravestones.

He looked around him bewildered. War had not been here. A blackbird chattered a warning in the yew, and the sun smiled on the artificial flowers that decked the tombs of long dead French men and women.

"All right?" asked the lieutenant, striding down the gravel path.

"Fine," said Alexander as they plunged into another trench. It twisted and turned, with steel doors at every bend, taking them through a ruined house, someone's neglected garden, beneath railroad tracks where the sleepers rested crazily across the divide, and through the cellar walls of abandoned houses. The journey was like some strange, surrealistic dream. Little seemed real, except the gas extinguishers, ammunition, casks of food and water, and dressing stations for the injured. All underground.

"We'll have to wait until nightfall to do the last bit," Alexander's guide said. "There's a full moon, so it won't be too bad. You ought to have a steel helmet, you know."

"How close to the German lines will we be?" Alexander asked.

"We'll see how it goes," the lieutenant said. "But the front line itself is about fifty yards from the bastards. It's not a good idea to put your head up there. You can get it blown off."

Alexander resolved to keep his head down.

The last part of the journey was the most unpleasant. The air in the much narrower trench that connected to the front was foul, and most of the time they had to crawl. Ghostly voices from either side warned them of obstacles. In about twenty minutes they were at the first trench, gasping for breath and fresh air.

"This is it," said the lieutenant. "The front line. The Boche are within throwing distance now."

Alexander was awed by the sights he was seeing. Men stood guard, silent in the darkness of the trench, the stray beams from the moon turning their helmets into silver, their uniforms white. Above, guns barked. Rats scrambled in the darkness across the men's feet, scurrying in the open places. Alexander, repressing a shudder, kicked one away.

"No good doing that," whispered his guide. "They're persistent little buggers. And they bite."

The silence was eerie. No one spoke, but occasionally a soldier, believing he had seen movement, would take his rifle and fire into barbed wire beyond. An explosion, a flare and a flash of red and then silence again.

"Right," his guide whispered after about ten minutes. "You've seen the front line. I think it's time to go back, before we get you killed."

"Can't we stay for a while?" Alexander whispered.

"More than my life's worth. Could be more than your life's worth. I shouldn't have brought you this far as it is. We've never let a war correspondent see this last trench. It's that damn smile of yours that did it. So think yourself lucky, and don't argue."

Meekly, aware he'd been given something of a scoop, Alexander followed him back.

Allie had just finished her breakfast when Marie came into the room, looking quite flustered.

"Where is your mother?" she asked. "Or Madame Dupuis? I can't find them anywhere."

"Mama went down to the cellars to taste the reserve. I don't know where Grandmother is," she said. "Why?"

"There's a young gentleman. The young American, Monsieur Webster. So smart and handsome, all in uniform. He's just arrived with a car and a chauffeur. He wants to see your mother."

"Alexander? Is it Alexander?" Allie shouted.

"The very same," said Marie with a broad smile.

Allie left the table and rushed down the hall to the parlour, and there, indeed, was Alexander.

"I can't believe it," she said, flinging herself into his arms. "Alex, how lovely. What are you doing here? And all in uniform! Have you come with the American forces?"

"Hang on!" he said, pushing her back to get a look at her. "Gosh, you've grown."

"You too," she said. "But what are you doing here?"

"I'm a war correspondent," he said.

Allie was impressed.

"A real war correspondent," she said, her voice awed. "*Formidable!*"

"Father doesn't think so," Alex said, "and Mother's worried sick. I happen to think it's pretty good myself."

Allie was scrutinising him from head to toe.

"And they give you a uniform?"

"It's so you don't get shot as a spy if you get caught by the enemy."

"*Zut!*" Allie said.

He smiled his wonderful and surprising smile.

"It's good to see you again, Allie."

"It's good to see you. Would you like some breakfast?"

"Love some. Could the guy who's driving me have some too?"

"Of course," she said. "I'll get Marie to take him to the kitchen."

She went back to the breakfast room with him, and talked excitedly. She wanted to know every single thing about New York.

"You know," she told him, "I'll be seventeen in June. Do you think your mama would have me to stay as soon as the war is over? I've thought about it so much. I loved it when I was there with Mama and Monsieur Philippe. I'd love to live in America. I want to get away from here, you see."

He looked surprised.

"Why do you want to get away from here?" he asked.

Her eyes fixed on the red checked tablecloth, she crumbled a piece of bread, thinking what to say.

"I don't know really. I suppose I'd rather live in a town and have fun when I'm young. Mama's very occupied with my little sister these days, and Papa's never been the same since he was shell-shocked. Did you know about that?"

"Yes, your mother wrote mine about it. Mama was thrilled to hear you had a new little sister."

"Well, yes, but she's too young to be much fun yet. You'll see."

"And you want to live in New York?"

"I'd really like that."

"I would, too," he said.

There was something odd about his voice that made her look at him quickly, but he was only drinking his coffee. He put down the cup and said: "Now tell me about what happened when the German came."

She felt herself freeze and hurriedly rose to her feet.

"Mama will tell you all about that. I'll go and find her. I'll be right back."

She was aware of his surprise as she sped from the room, but she did not want to talk about what had happened when the Germans came. It was bad enough having Rosanne to remind her of it every day.

Alexander had said he could only stay for two days, but the morning after he arrived, a telegraph message came for him from New York.

Henri brought it in on a silver tray as he was taking coffee with Rosie, Madame Dupuis and Allie in the parlour. He opened it, and Allie saw that he flushed with pleasure.

"Good news?" her mother asked.

"Well, yes," he said. "It's from my editor, congratulating me on my piece about the front line. He says I can take a brief holiday and then go on and join up with the first American troops to arrive here."

"That *is* good news," Rosie said. "This must be your first big assignment for the *New York Times*."

He nodded. "I've only been there for three months. I was surprised they chose me to come. It might have been because I speak reasonable French."

"I'm not surprised," Allie said stoutly. "I bet you're the best writer they've got. But does it mean you can stay here longer?"

"Well, if your mother will have me."

Rosie laughed.

"I think we might put up with you for a while."

"Hurray!" Allie jumped to her feet and ran to give Alex a great hug and a smack of a kiss on his cheek. "That's lovely," she said.

As she let him go, she noticed that he looked rather pink, but her mind was on other things. She said: "Shall we get your chauffeur to take us into Épernay this afternoon? We never get the chance to go anywhere these days. We don't get any petrol, and it's such a long way by bike."

Alex agreed to take her to Épernay and wandered with her around the shops and up the Avenue de Champagne. Then Allie insisted on driving to Ay so she could show Alexander where their vines were.

He was enchanted by the scene, the gentle field running down to the river, and the vines showing green. There was a light fragrance to the air that Allie said came from the grape flowers.

363

"You'd never guess that this was all destroyed and beaten down by the war when the Germans came through, would you?" she said, pleased at his reaction to the peaceful Marne and the abundant vines. She could talk about the Germans here, because here they had not touched her. "It was terrible after they were driven back, but everyone worked to make things right again," she told him. "Papa says we should all be very proud. But our fields near the Vesle are quite ruined. Papa says he doubts if grapes will ever grow there again. I could take you and show you if you like, but we have to wait for a misty night so that the Boche can't see us."

Driving back in the car, more content that she had been for months, she curled up against him and put her head on his shoulder. Sighing she said: "It's so lovely to have a friend again. I've been lonely since Miss went."

"Yes, I expect so," he said, and his voice sounded a little strangled.

"Is anything the matter?" she asked, sitting up.

"No, nothing," he said. "Just a frog in my throat."

That night her mother came to her room and sat on her bed. Allie put down the book she had been reading and waited to see what her mother wanted.

"You're very fond of Alexander, aren't you?" her mother asked.,

"I *love* him! I wish he hadn't got to go away. It's terrific having him here."

"Yes, well, of course, he is a man now, you know. Not a boy any more. He's twenty-two." Her mother cleared her throat and seemed to be choosing her words with care. "It's difficult for him to have a pretty young girl clinging to him. He's not like one of your girlfriends, Allie. He's a man, darling."

Allie wasn't sure what her mother was on about.

"Why should it be difficult for him to be friends with me? I don't understand what that's got to do with anything. I've known him for ever."

Her mother looked uncomfortable.

"Well, he might perhaps prefer to spend some time with older people."

Allie was outraged.

"I'm not a child," she said. "And I suppose you mean you want him to spend more time with you."

"That's not what I meant." Her mother sounded defensive.

"You always get in the way," Allie told her, still angry, defensive herself and still not sure what all this was about.

Her mother sighed.

"I don't mean to darling," she said. "Forget it. Go back to your book, and sleep tight. God bless."

She planted a kiss firmly on Allie's forehead and went, closing the door behind her quietly.

Resentfully, Allie watched her go. Her mother was too bad, always spoiling things and taking things. But she wasn't going to take her friend Alex. Most certainly not! Full of righteous indignation, Allie settled back to her book. The world in books was better. It was horrible having to get older.

The night before Alexander was leaving, Rosie insisted that they have as near a banquet as was possible with the wartime shortages. Cook killed two fine capons and cooked them in champagne, stuffed with chicken livers and truffles.

Rosie produced some of their 1906 vintage, and Allie was allowed to take a glass with them. Alexander said it all reminded him of the very first night that he came to Les Hérissons.

"When you saved us from the mob," he said to Rosie.

Allie felt herself bristle. A little tipsy, she knew she was laughing too loudly, and she kept leaning her head on Alexander's shoulder. Her mother gave her a warning look. Allie glared back defiantly and decided that she would really annoy her mother.

"Alexander says that he thinks his mother will let me come and stay with them in New York," she announced rudely. "I shall do that when this war is over. I don't want to be stuck here all my life."

There was a sudden appalled silence.

"Yes, well, that depends on whether your mother will let you go, doesn't it?" her grandmother said coldly. "You will have to be more grown-up and more of a lady before we can permit you to go anywhere."

Allie felt her cheeks flame and tears tremble.

"Tell you what, Allie," Alexander said easily, putting his napkin on the table. "I think I need a bit of fresh air. Will you walk around the courtyard with me? Do you mind, Madame?"

Madame Dupuis inclined her head in agreement.

Her mouth tight shut, Allie got to her feet.

"You are excused," said her grandmother, reminding her of her manners again.

"Thank you, Grandmama," she managed.

Outside in the cool of the mid-May evening, Alexander said gently: "What's the matter?"

"I don't know. I feel so peculiar all the time. Restless, miserable. I feel I hate everyone and want to be anywhere in the world except here. No one understands except you. If you hadn't come, I don't know what I would have done. Killed myself maybe," she said darkly.

"I used to feel a bit like that at sixteen," he said.

"But I'm almost seventeen," she wailed.

"Yes, you are, aren't you, and a very beautiful seventeen." His voice sounded funny again, but then he laughed awkwardly and wrapped one arm round her waist. She turned to him, putting her head on his shoulder.

"You will ask your mama if I can come to New York, won't you?" she said, her voice muffled, and then she lifted her head to look into his eyes. "Please," she said, making her expression as appealing as she could and her eyes as wide as they would go.

His arms had joined round her back, and his expression was so odd. It reminded her of something she could not quite place as he looked down at her. Then his arms tightened and he began to lower his head, and the look in his eyes intensified. To her horror she realised that he was going to kiss her. Properly kiss her, like grown-ups did.

"Don't!" she hissed. "Don't touch me. Don't ever touch me." And wriggling from his grasp, she ran across the courtyard, and into the house.

She could hear him calling her name, but she took no notice. How could he? How could he? she was asking herself as she fled, trembling, to her bedroom. Her mother was right, after all. You couldn't just be friends with men. They always wanted something, and what they wanted no man was ever going to have from her again.

Chapter Twenty-Four

Paris, April 1918

Nineteen-eighteen had brought a small quantity of fragrant wines to Champagne, but looking at ravaged fields from the window of the train that was taking her to Paris it was obvious to Rosie that there would be precious little wine this year.

Europe was not to be permitted to return to normal yet. Though people predicted that this would be the year that saw the end of the conflict, the end was not yet in sight. They said that war brought plague and pestilence, and the plague of 1918 was influenza. It was killing people faster that the war had been doing. Germany had suffered greatly, losing many of her troops. But every European country, town, village and family was slowly being blighted by what would become a pandemic, though Les Hérissons, perhaps because of its remoteness, had not yet suffered.

Paris had. And one of the victims was dear André.

Early that morning the boy from the Chigny post office had cycled up to Les Hérissons bringing an urgent telegram for her. The lines had been damaged in the fighting, and their telephone was out of order. The message, from Philippe, asked her to go to the house on the Île de la Cité if she possibly could. André was dying and wished to see her.

The family had not wanted her to go. Madame was anxious that it was unsafe, and little Rosanne had cried because her mother was going away. Allie, still introvert but darkly beautiful at eighteen, had asked if she could come too. But Rosie thought it was better for her to stay away from the risk of infection.

Philippe was waiting for her at the Gare de l'Est, Georges at his side, as Georges had been since his master came home from the war. Philippe's head lifted questioningly as his heightened hearing picked out her footsteps hurrying across the forecourt. She called his name as she neared, and he nodded, satisfield.

"Don't kiss me," he said when he sensed her closeness. "It's not wise. Are you free from this dreadful infection at Les Hérissons?"

"So far," she told him, taking his hand.

"Then you mustn't take it back if we can avoid it," he said. "I didn't feel we should ask you to come here, but then I knew you would never forgive me if I didn't."

"How is he?" she asked. "The train took so long I was afraid I would be too late."

"Not good, I'm afraid. It won't be long. But he is a very old man, Rosie. You mustn't be too distressed."

She felt a stab of pain at the thought of André's passing, but trying to be controlled said: "I've never known how old he is."

"I've never really known, either. But his doctor tells me that he is nearly seventy-nine. He has had his span."

Georges had gone ahead to get the automobile and, without speaking, she took Philippe's arm and led him towards the station exit.

"And you, my darling, are you all right?" he asked her. "Has the fighting in Champagne affected you? I worry about you all the time."

"It's not been good, but we've all survived," Rosie said. "The worst has been not being able to see you. I worry about you all the time, too. And with more reason," she added, squeezing his arm.

She took him to where Georges waited with the car. The valet helped them both in and then drove off through the surprisingly heavy traffic. Paris had an almost festive air about her, as well she might, Rosie thought, having been spared both bombardment and occupation. The Germans never reached here and if the predictions were to be believed, now never would.

They said little on the journey. Rosie, her head full of memories of André, just held Philippe's hand until they arrived. As they went through the front door where the maid waited, her smile absent, Rosie whispered: "How is he?"

"He is old and tired," the maid told her.

Philippe waited downstairs while she was taken straight to André's bedroom and a strange nurse nodded her in. In all the years she had known André she had never before seen this big, sombre room with its four-poster bed and dark velvet hangings. André was in the bed, his head propped up by high pillows. He appeared to be dozing as she crept on tiptoe towards him.

His fine face had not really changed though there was a hectic red flush on his thin cheeks. The slender, high-bridged nose looked thinner, but his hair and moustache were neatly combed. The sight of him made her throat close and her eyes fill with tears.

"Rosie?" he asked, his voice thin and breathless.

"Yes, it's me, André."

"Don't come too near," he whispered. "Sit on that chair I've had them place ready for you." He had to pause for breath, and his lungs rasped as he lay there, his eyes closed. His bony hands clenched on the embroidery of the linen sheets, and she realised that it pained him to breathe.

Trying not to cry, she settled herself on a chair which had been placed just near enough for her to be able to hear his voice.

"Are we alone?" he asked.

She tried to say yes, but a sob came out instead.

"You're not to be upset," he said, sounding stronger. "I'm an old man. I've had my time. I'm not afraid of death. There are many I loved gone before me. But you, Rosie, I loved you the best. And I wanted to tell you. I loved you as a woman, a daughter and a friend. These last eighteen years I've treasured the memory of those two nights we spent together. I wanted to thank you for them." He had to stop to catch breath again, and she gave up any attempt not to cry, but sat, letting the tears run unchecked down her face. "But you did more. You gave Sebastian the love he lost, and now it is you who keeps my son sane. I don't know why, but I feel strongly that one day you and he will find happiness together. God could not be so unkind as to keep you apart for ever." He waited again to recover strength. "But Lorraine is so young, and how could you abandon your poor, shell-shocked Clovis? Clovis is a good man, Rosie. Lorraine, I fear, as you so forcefully said, is a stupid woman."

He lay quiet for a moment and then he said: "I have left all my property to Philippe, but I have also left you a good sum of money that should ensure that you are never poor. Whatever happens. You were always so afraid of being poor, my Rosie. Lorraine may try to fight this, but Philippe will discourage her. There is plenty for little Fran-çoise." He was silent again. She could not speak. Her throat had closed up and she did not want him to realise how distressed she was.

"I have left the money to you on the pretext that it is to expand your business so that my blinded son will always have a livelihood and something to do."

"But you know that I will always be his eyes when I can," she managed to say.

"Of course, I know. I leave him in your care, my beautiful Rosie, so beautiful in her white gown. The lady she wanted to be. My lady." His voice was so quiet and rambling she could hardly understand. She thought perhaps he was delirious. "So proud I was that night. The most beautiful woman in Paris, and mine for a little while. But I never lost you, Rosie. You've been mine for always in my heart. Your love was so rare, so perfect, but I kept the best of you. I had your true, pure love, and you needed me. It was me you came to when you needed help.

369

But you'll survive, Rosie. You've grown strong and straight enough for others to lean on, and the last thing you will do for me is to save my son."

His voice trailed away. "So tired," he sighed, "so tired . . ." She crept forward to take his hand in hers. He was quiet, his breath coming harshly, and then suddenly he opened his eyes, and their feverish blue, bright as those of a young man, burned a smile at her. The years were wiped away, and his voice came clear and true.

"Goodbye, my Rosie," he said.

Philippe was shocked by the violence of Rosie's grief. She wept until he could even feel how swollen her face was, and she would not be consoled. He held her, soothing her, forgetting his own sorrow in his attempt to assuage hers.

André had died holding her hand.

"He said goodbye, and he died," she sobbed when she could finally speak. "But you should have been there, too. It was all wrong. But, Philippe, I loved him so. I shall miss him dreadfully. He said I was strong, but I'm not. Not really. Not always. If I was strong, it was because he showed me how. What will we do without him?"

"Go on living, as he would have wanted us to do," he said quietly, thinking how much of his own strength had come from his father.

"He said he thought we would be together one day," she told him. "He said God couldn't be so cruel as to keep us apart for ever."

"He said the same to me," Philippe told her. "We said our goodbyes this morning, before I came to meet you. He was afraid he wouldn't last until you came."

"And now what?" she said dismally.

"Now I will have to go home to tell Lorraine what has happened. I haven't seen her for two days. And you must rest. Your room is ready for you."

"You're going home?" she sounded stricken.

"I must. I don't want to, but at times like this one must do the right thing."

"Yes, I see. But I think I'd rather go home to Les Hérissons, if it's possible."

She was standing stiffly in the circle of his arms, her voice miserable. He could feel her distress.

"I can be with you later," he told her. "Please, darling, understand. I must just tell her, and then I'll come back. In fact, I should come back. There's so much to deal with here, and I could use your help."

He had struck the right note. He felt her relax in his arms.

"Very well," she said.

Georges drove him back to the apartment at Neuilly and took him through the front door and into the lift. He left him at the door of the apartment. Philippe had not entirely come to terms with his blindness, but he would not let it beat him. He could let himself into his apartment, he could manoeuvre his way around the furniture; once inside his own home, he was independent. He had to be, with Lorraine so rarely there.

Françoise would be in the nursery having her tea with Nou-Nou. He had not been entirely happy at the thought of taking Nou-Nou into his home, aware that Sebastian had never liked the woman, but she was so much part of the Lefevre family that tradition decreed she continue to bring up the next generation. And, besides, both he and his father had debts there.

Lorraine, he thought, should be home. She was generally in by four o'clock, though these days she frequently went out again in the evenings.

He called her name as he carefully placed his hat on the hallstand.

"Here," she called back, her voice coming from the salon. Cautiously – whenever he was alone he was cautious – he went along the parquet-floored passage that led down to the salon. The doors were open, and noting just the faintest change of light behind the blackness that shrouded his eyes, he entered the room with its long windows that overlooked the parkland below.

He had taken two careful steps into the room when his foot landed on something that moved. It moved rapidly, taking him with it, so that he was flying across the polished floor until he landed heavily and untidily in an undignified heap.

"Oh, my God!" he heard Lorraine's voice say in tones of deep disgust. Lorraine had most certainly not come to terms with his blindness.

Dizzy, he sat up. His hand and arm hurt where he had hit them on something. He had no idea where in the room he was, and he hesitated to get to his feet.

"What the hell was that?" he asked angrily

"That," said Lorraine's cool voice, "was Françoise's little horse on wheels. She had been playing with it before she went for her tea."

"For God's sake," he said, "couldn't you have moved it?"

"I hadn't even noticed it was there until you fell over it," she told him coolly. "You can't expect me to see everything as if the whole world were blind."

"No, but it is only me who is blind in this household," he said. He wanted to get up but was afraid, not knowing where he was. "I wouldn't have thought it would have been too much of a chore to watch out for obstacles for just one person. And would you mind helping me up? I've no idea where I am."

371

She heaved a theatrical sigh and he heard her footsteps clack across the polished floor, smelt the Guerlain perfume she wore, then her hand descended onto his arm, helping to pull him to his feet.

"I'll put you in your armchair," she said.

"Thank you." He knew his voice was sarcastic, but he was furious with the loss of dignity, and his hand and arm were painful.

"Did you hurt yourself?" she asked perfunctorily

"I'm all right." She had parked him in front of the armchair he always used and as he sat down a sense of security was coming back.

Her heels were clicking away back to her usual chair.

"And I don't know why you have to be bad-tempered with me, just because you fall," she said frostily. "It's not my fault you're blind."

"It's your fault if you leave children's toys where I can fall over them," he said. "You can see the damn things. I can't."

"There's no need to swear. I've said I'm sorry."

"Did you? I didn't hear."

"Well, if you're deaf as well ..."

Had she said sorry? Of course she hadn't said sorry. It was not Lorraine's style to say sorry these days. Rage was blazing in him.

"I am not deaf, and you did not apologise."

"Well, I'm sorry. Will that do?"

"Not in that tone of voice."

"What tone of voice would you prefer?"

Suddenly his anger evaporated. What was the point of this idiotic, silly quarrel when he was losing more dignity by taking part in it than he had by falling. His father was dead. Rosie was waiting for him. His own grief had been allowed no outlet, and he was letting his flibbertigibbet wife rile him. He settled back in his armchair and decided to make peace. He would tell her now that his father had gone. She liked his father. It would end the quarrel.

But before he could speak, he heard her get to her feet and take a step towards him.

"We have to talk," she said.

"What about?" he asked cautiously.

"Us."

"Oh, yes?"

"Philippe, I'm sorry but I can't stay married to you." The words came out in a rush. "You see, I know."

"You know what?" Her words were a shock and he did not know what to feel. Dismay? Relief? Or anger that she should choose a time like this for what she had to say?

"About you and Rosie Dupuis."

"And what do you know about me and Rosie Dupuis."

"That you are lovers. Have been for years, before and after me."

"Why should you believe that?" he asked, playing for time. His mind was racing. What would this mean? If Lorraine left he wouldn't give a damn, but there was Françoise, cuddly and chubby, who sat on his knee and young as she was described things to him. He loved his daughter. He had lost Sebastian; he did not want to lose her.

"I believe it because Nou-Nou told me. You've not been very discreet since you came back from the war. All those days you spend with her in Paris. All this pretence about business."

"It is business," he said, his mind registering Nou-Nou's final treachery.

"Business? And a great deal more. How dare you! How dare you make such a fool of me with a woman almost old enough to be my mother and who had an affair with your father? If it comes out, I shall be the laughing stock of Paris. You had no right to marry me if you intended to carry on your affair with her. In fact, I don't understand why you ever did marry me. You never loved me. I soon realised that. But I loved you, until I saw that you never cared a sou for me. You made it plain enough without meaning to."

He was silent, knowing there was truth in what she said, but thinking more that Nou-Nou continued the *canard* that Rosie had slept with his father. Rosie had said it was not true, and Rosie did not lie. Or did she?

"But I've had enough," his wife was saying passionately. "You can go to your common, money-grabbing American mistress. A woman of no class. I don't know what you see in her."

"She is not stupid," he said, stung.

"I suppose I am."

"Yes. And you are having an affair with a man almost young enough to be my son. Should that not make me the laughing stock of Paris? I may be blind, but I am not a fool. I have understood about you and your boring Didier for a long time."

He heard her sigh.

"But you don't care," she said, her voice low. "That is the difference."

There was a long, long silence, and then her crisp footsteps clicked towards the entrance to the salon. Neither of them spoke, but as she reached the doorway, she asked: "How is your father?"

"He is dead."

This time the silence was oppressive, and then she said heavily: "I'm sorry. But he was always on Rosie's side."

He sat and listened to her footsteps receding down the hallway. His marriage was over, she was going out to meet Didier, her lover, and all he felt was relief.

The sun shone patchily in the summer of 1918 and the grapes ripened

373

unevenly in a climate in which the war had regained its ferocity. Since the start of June it was as if both sides, equally weary of combat, were making one last desperate attempt to win and have it over with.

At first the Germans held the advantage. Reims had finally been evacuated of all civilians. The town's champagne cellars were left to the French troops who repulsed an attempt by the German army to re-occupy the town. But by July the Germans were sweeping through Champagne again, pressing on down to the Marne and establishing themselves to the west of Épernay and at Château-Thierry. As the fighting raged along the Reims-Épernay road, Rosie and Madame Dupuis had climbed their hillside to see the deadly parade below. They stood appalled, watching useless gun carriages dragged by frightened horses and exhausted men retreating on stumbling feet. The Germans were hard on their heels.

"It is 1914 all over again," sighed Madame, "and what progress have we made?"

"A little," Rosie said, sardonically. "The French soldiers no longer wear red and America is with us."

The Les Hérissons vineyards had suffered. The ripening grapes were trampled under military boots, neat rows of vines dug up as improvised scratch trenches. The juice of the trampled Pinot Noir grapes mixed with the blood of the men, both French and German. Each night, when the guns ceased, Rosie, with Madame and Allie, had searched their fields for wounded. They brought those they found back to the house on a farm wagon, doing their best to ease dreadful wounds, woefully aware of their lack of medical knowledge. In that bloody July every bedroom and barn had been filled while they waited anxiously for the men to be taken to hospital to be cared for by those who knew what to do.

And then, by the middle of August, the push came from the south, with the Germans in retreat. The French and the British, their confidence restored by the smell of victory, struck and struck again from behind, chasing their enemy all the way back to Belgium, Luxembourg and Germany itself.

Now, in October with the invader's boots banished from her soil and the Kaiser calling for peace, France was beginning to breathe and hope again. It was nearly all over.

On the eleventh of November, 1918, at eleven o'clock, peace was declared. The war was over. The Allies had won. Madame Dupuis sent for the 1906 vintage from the cellars and the entire household assembled to drink it.

The champagne was a little caramelised and a trifle flat – like the celebration. Clovis seemed uncertain of what the excitement was about, Allie was withdrawn and silent, and Marie, whose Robert had come home without his left arm, burst into tears and rushed from the room. Even little Rosanne, who grew to look more like Allie every day, sensing hidden sadness, cried without knowing why.

Rosie tried to make the occasion a happy one for Madame's sake, but the grief caused by the war could not be wiped out simply by its ending. With an attempt at enthusiasm they drank to the British and to the Americans who had fought on the soil of France. They drank to General Foch, the man who had never lost heart, and they drank to all those who had perished in the four years of conflict.

Then, curiously subdued, they all went about their business.

Rosie slipped out of the house and walked up the hill to where she could see both the land and the house. The land had long since lost its customary trimness, the house below looked shabby and unloved. The barn that the German shell had found had not yet been repaired, and the gravel paths were unkempt, the grass surrounding them too long. The reserve stocks of wine in the cellars were depleted.

The Vesle fields would have to be completely replanted, as well as many of those nearer home. The Ay field would be overgrown. There was much to be done.

But sitting on a tree stump, shivering as she stared over the russet and grey landscape, Rosie thought of the other, worse havoc that the war had wrought. Sebastian dead, Philippe blinded, Allie with her life perhaps ruined, poor Clovis still confused and not right in the head. André gone, and Lorraine rejecting her blind husband. Philippe now lived alone in the house on the Île de la Cité, missing his child.

There was as much to be mended in life as in the fields, Rosie thought.

She sat for another ten minutes or so, mourning her dead until the damp cold began to bite. She sighed, stood and looked around her. A sliver of sun pierced the grey sky, and this small tinge of brightness lifted her spirits. With a stern self-lecture she shook off her sadness. Today was brand new, tomorrow would be different. She shut her eyes tight and remembered this view as it had been, ordered and fecund. With the feeling that the cold was stinging her to action, she made a vow. Les Hérissons and life would soon be back to normal. But even better. More fertile. More beautiful. She would do the things she had always wanted to do to the house and the winery. They would start the business all over again.

She would permit Allie to go to America and stay with Lizzie if that was what her daughter wanted. Little could be done about Clovis. The doctors had assured her that only time could help him. But at least he was content, working on the land, and entirely enchanted by Rosanne who did not confuse him and whom he had accepted as his daughter. Madame was growing old. For now, peace would satisfy her.

375

France had not been beaten and neither had she. Starting again would be the challenge she needed and she had André's extraordinarily generous bequest to help her. The memory of André also raised her spirits. André had said he believed that somehow she and Philippe would be together. She could not abandon Clovis, but she could share herself between him and Philippe – for he needed her as well. She would spend half her time in Paris with Philippe, running the business end of Les Hérissons, and half her time in Champagne with Clovis, Madame and Rosanne. Now the war was over, anything was possible.

Her natural optimism restored, she strode down the hillside, whistling like an errand boy, her head full of plans as the sun began to break through even more strongly.

The war was over, peace declared, and everything was going to be all right.

Chapter Twenty-Five

Allie had been in New York for five months, and her intention had been to stay for six. But as sunny May warmed the windy corridors of New York she began to think that it was nearly her birthday — her nineteenth birthday — and, more important, Rosanne's. Rosanne would be four, and already she had missed five months of her growing. And a lot could happen to a little child in five months.

So one morning over breakfast at the Park Avenue house she asked Mrs Webster if it would be all right if she went home in time for her sister's birthday.

"Of course, my dear," Mrs Webster had said. "But we shall be so sad to see you go. Mr Webster and I have been delighted with your company. And if you go, Alexander will be devastated."

It was patently obvious that the smiling, sentimental Mrs Webster was hoping and praying for a union between Allie and her only son. It was equally obvious that Alexander was hoping for the same thing. Which was another reason why Allie felt it was time she went home.

The whole question of Alexander was vexed, and one she did not know exactly how to deal with. In her handkerchief sachet she still had the letter, now dog-eared and splitting at the folds, that he had written her after that dreadful time in the courtyard at Les Hérissons when he had tried to kiss her:

Dearest Allie,
    Forgive me for frightening you so. I had not intended it, but I had mistaken your kindness and affection for something different.
    In that moment when you let me put my arm around you, and your face looked into mine, I forgot that you are still so young. It was wrong of me to have approached you. But you must believe that I did so only out of the most sincere regard, indeed love, for

you. I was not trifling with your affections, nor my own.

I pray that this untoward incident will not make you change your mind about visiting my family in New York when the war is over. Please come and stay with us.

But I cannot promise that my feelings for you will change, or that one day I shall not hold you in my arms again. But only when you are ready for me to do so.

Forgive me, I beg you,
Your servant,
Alexander

The letter had both alarmed and thrilled her, and his presence in New York had produced the same effect. It was exciting to think that someone loved her, but she felt it was all too soon. Nevertheless she found herself flirting with him, leading him on, playing the coquette. At the first sign of response from him, she would turn cold, or flee, or repulse him.

She managed to make him as thoroughly miserable as she often was herself. She knew it, yet she could not seem to help her behaviour.

His sister, Jenny, a practical, no-nonsense nurse, watched this treatment of her brother with mounting exasperation.

"Don't you like my brother?" she demanded one Sunday afternoon when the young people of the family had gone for a walk in Central Park to feed the squirrels.

Alexander was walking ahead.

"I like him very much," Allie said.

"Is it a French thing to treat people you like so badly, then?"

"Do I really treat him badly?" Allie knew perfectly well that she did, but was not going to admit it.

"You treat him abominably!" Jenny said. "He adores you, and you walk all over him. If you can't be kind to him, and if you don't love him, you should stop leading him on. And if you can't stop leading him on, perhaps you ought to go back to France where people will understand that sort of behaviour."

Allie looked at the girl in amazement. She was not used to such frankness. For a moment she was tempted to pour out her complicated feelings about Alexander. But Jenny's face was set and scarlet with the embarrassment of having said what she thought, so Allie ended the conversation by muttering: "I really don't know what you mean." At which Jenny snorted in a way that declared her disbelief.

Thinking about it in her room that night before she went to sleep, Allie realised that her uncomfortable, confused feelings about Alexander had made New York as bewildering a place to be as Les Hérissons. The difference was that at Les Hérissons when one of her 'moods' came on, everyone understood. New York was good for her in a way. With comparative strangers she could not let anyone see when she was feeling difficult, scratchy and down-at-heart. She had made an effort to hide her depression. And poor Alex bore the brunt of these hidden moods when she was so miserable she could have cheerfully thrown herself off the tallest building on Wall Street.

And added to all that, her mother had written saying that everyone missed her very much, especially her father, who seemed lost and worried that she was not there.

"Of course," her mother wrote, "he adores little Rosanne, because she is so like you when you were little, and perhaps that somehow triggers something in his mind. For he is certainly most distressed that you are not here. I wonder perhaps if he is beginning to remember exactly who you are? Alas, he still cannot grasp that Madame is his mother or that I am his wife.

"Rosanne also cries for you. I have to spend so much time in Paris at the moment that she feels the loss of her 'big sister'. I worry that she is sometimes insecure, as competent and loving as her nanny is. Madame, who is old, is the only stable person in her life.

"Reading this over, it sounds as if I am trying to persuade you to come home. Not so. We all want you to stay away for as long as you wish, if you are happy, well and enjoying yourself. But perhaps it won't hurt to let you know how much we all love and miss you."

The letter and the approach of June were what decided her. And the night after her conversation with Mrs Webster, Alex took her to dinner at the Plaza.

"Mama says you are going home," he said suddenly as they were both inspecting the menu.

"Yes. For Rosanne's birthday. I'm not going to tell them. I'm just going to arrive as a surprise."

"Will you come back?"

She thought about it.

"Probably," she said. "I like it here. I think I'm just not quite ready to leave home for a long time. My family need me."

"I need you!" he burst out.

Her decision to go home had left her calmer than she had been for a long time.

"I don't think I'm quite ready for anything, Alex," she said gently. "I'm really a very confused person."

He leaned across the table, taking her hands in his, imprisoning them, and a faint feeling of panic began in her.

"Allie," he said, his thin face alight with feeling. "I don't think you understand. I love you. I want to marry you. I decided that when you were ten years old."

379

She snatched her hands back and stared at him appalled. Marriage! He wanted to marry her.

"But Alexander, I can't get married," she blurted out. "I can't marry anyone."

"Why not?"

There was no way of explaining. How could she say to this elegant and charming young man that she had been raped, had had a child by the rapist, a perverted German lieutenant, and that the child was known as her little sister. How could she tell him! She knew she could never, never tell anyone.

But how could she not tell him if there was to be anything serious between them?

She took a deep breath.

"Because a lot of things have happened since I was ten, because I'm still too young to think about anything so serious, and because I'm going home to France," she said coldly. "Now, can we order supper?"

And as she busied herself with the menu, trying to ignore his stricken face, her mind was full of the bleak future where there could be no love, no marriage for her. Because if the truth were told, and the truth must be told, who would want her?

California, June 1919.

"So what is the position?" Jean Paul asked, banging his fist on the antique surface of his oversized desk.

His lawyer, a man with greased-back black hair and narrow beady eyes in a narrow bony face, jumped and looked aggrieved.

"The position is not good. This time next month you will be out of business."

"What about the injunction against the Act those southern wine-makers applied for?"

"The government has turned them down. And now it seems certain that Congress will not exempt the wine industry from Prohibition."

"But haven't we got until January?" asked Peter from where he was sitting anxiously on the edge of a leather sofa.

"The situation is," said Al Friedman, attorney-at-law, patiently, "that as from the first of July it will be illegal to manufacture alcoholic beverages from foodstuffs. Grapes, of course, are foodstuffs. Once the Volstead Act is passed by Congress and becomes law next year, it will also be illegal to manufacture, sell or transport intoxicating beverages. This means that the wine industry in this country is dead. They do say that licences will be given for the making of sacramental wine or alcohol for medicinal purposes, but champagne hardly falls into either category. And there's talk of permitting the head of any household to make two hundred gallons of non-intoxicating fruit juice or cider for home use. Other than that, nothing."

"That must be why those men were about in Calistoga offering thirty dollars a ton for this season's grapes," Peter said.

"How much?" Jean Paul could not believe his ears. The going rate last season had been ten dollars a ton. He had paid Gino $7.50, for Gino had frightened the tenants into accepting an even lower price than Jean Paul had given them.

"Thirty dollars," Peter said, "but some of the growers are holding back. They reckon the price will get higher."

Jean Paul thought about it. The whole of the United States was going to be as dry as a bone, with nothing but sarsparilla to wet its whistle. A lot of people in the States where vines did not grow were going to be buying grapes to make wine in their backyards and bathtubs. And there were a lot of States where vines did not grow.

"Of course, they'll get higher," the lawyer said tetchily. "Nothing is going to stop people drinking. All that these new laws will do is create a field day for people like your friend Gino. In fact, I happen to know that some of those men offering thirty dollars a ton actually work for Gino."

"And I sold him all my vines, and left myself the winery," Jean Paul said softly. "I guess he knew what was coming and I walked straight into it."

"The grapes he can sell. The winery you can do nothing with. Nothing at all," the lawyer said.

"We have the new fields up the valley," Peter said eagerly. These days Peter had absolutely nothing to do with the manufacture of the champagne. He was the dude in white shoes who sold it. Peter was not going to have anything to sell. Peter was out of a job. And Peter had conveniently forgotten all he ever knew about growing grapes.

"Correction. We *will* have the new fields," Jean Paul said. "They're not producing. There's another year to go. It takes four years, remember?"

"You're rich enough to hold out for a year, and you'd better sell what champagne you've got in stock as quickly as you can," his lawyer advised. "In six months, selling it will be illegal. But at least you should get a really high price for what you've got. Everyone will be hoarding booze in every nook and cranny."

Jean Paul's mind was already working to find a way out of this disaster. He had about 500,000 bottles of champagne at various stages in his cellars, plus his vats of reserve wine for blending. He was filled with a futile anger against a puritanical, idiotic government that made wine, which had been the comfort of man through all generations, illegal, and destroyed people's livelihoods while doing it.

"I can't believe it," he muttered. "It's madness."

"I agree," said Al, packing up his papers and putting them in his attaché case. "But it's also going to be law."

Later that afternoon Gino called him from New York.

"Heard the news?" he asked.

"I've heard," Jean Paul told him.

"Not good, eh. Listen, I want every bottle of champagne you got."

"It'll cost you, Gino. I've heard about the price of grapes per ton. And you won't be needing to sell them to me at our agreed figure, will you? I'm not going to have any use for them."

There was a silence that went on long enough to be menacing.

"How much champagne you got?" Gino wanted to know.

"About four thousand cases ready to drink," Jean Paul said, roughly halving the true figure.

"Don't sell 'em. We'll discuss price later. I'll see you, OK? And, Jean Paul ..."

He seemed to require an answer.

"Yes?"

"If I find you got more, I shall personally twist your balls off."

Jean Paul laughed.

"Listen, at this moment I feel like twisting them off myself."

"We'll talk," Gino said, and hung up.

Jean Paul spent the rest of the afternoon trying to decide what to do. What to do with the wine that was still in its first fermentation, unless he sold it as still wine. What to do with the blending wine in the huge vats, vats that were far too big to move. What to do with the wine that was going through the second fermentation and aging process. Much of it still had three years to go. What did the government expect him to do? Destroy it all? Pour it into the ground? Drink the lot in a month?

Most of the second-fermentation bottles were in the new cellars he had built into rock. He could hide them by sealing those cellars off and then leave the wine there to mature. He'd worry about what to do about the final stages later. He could also hide much of his finished product in those cellars. He and Peter would gradually have to move them by night. The fewer people who knew about it the better. But four thousand odd cases! He groaned at the thought.

Gino did talk later that week. He wanted to know if Jean Paul thought there was any way he could keep the winery going.

"I'm still gonna need champagne for my hotels and clubs," he said. "The brewery and the distillery are too big and obvious for even me to get away with. I'll have to close them down, but I'll find other sources for the hard stuff. You're stuck in the backwoods there. Could you get away with going on? Anyone you could bribe?"

Jean Paul had been thinking along the same lines himself and said so, adding that he was thinking about it very hard indeed.

For the moment Gino needed him, and anyway, Gino had shares. It was as much his business that was going bust as Jean Paul's. And when Gino settled on $2.50 a bottle, a dollar a bottle more than Jean Paul expected, he found him three thousand cases – but still stashed away the remainder for a rainy day.

He sold a lot in small amounts locally. People were panicked by the news, and many of his neighbours and folk from Calistoga approached him to buy. He put the price up to $3.50 a bottle – what his champagne would cost in an expensive restaurant – and was amazed at how much he shifted. Peter's customers from all over were begging to buy, but he was anxious about shipping too much out of the state in case the eyes and ears of Gino's empire found out what he was up to. But, for the moment, it was not illegal to sell, and cases were walking out of his cellars. He reckoned that come Christmas he'd get five dollars a bottle.

He was coining money, but it wasn't going to last.

Pierre came home from the East early in July for the summer vacation. He had been at Harvard for a year and had grown tall, taller than his father. He had Jean Paul's neat handsome features but there was a softness about his face that his father had never possessed. Sometimes he reminded Jean Paul of Clovis. But the East had changed the boy. He was cool, composed and he said very little. But Jean Paul felt dizzy with emotion at the sight of him after so long.

"It's not good news, son," Jean Paul said over a candlelit dinner the first night Pierre came home. The three men of the house, Peter, Pierre and Jean Paul, were at the table, all in dress suits, with a butler serving. There were no women present.

"Prohibition?" Pierre suggested, picking up his glass as if the thought made him thirsty.

"Prohibition," Jean Paul said. "My life's work destroyed. They say now that we have to pour away every drop of wine on the premises. I can, of course, apply for a permit to make two hundred gallons for us to drink ourselves." His voice was sardonic. "But to pour all that wine away! It's like murder. Champagne is a living thing. I can't bring myself to do it. It's not even the money," he said pleadingly, "it's the wine and the way I feel about it. There are only two things in life I care about – you and my champagne."

"Thank you very much," Peter said waspishly.

"OK, three," Jean Paul said impatiently. "But it's the blinding stupidity, the waste, the *sacrilege* that gets me."

Pierre rarely expressed an opinion. All he said now was: "So what will you do?"

"Break the law. Go on. Hide what I can of the stock. Keep going for as long as I can. What else can I do? When they catch me, the enforcement officers will break it all up. So be it. I couldn't do it myself."

Pierre just nodded and tackled his steak.

"But the empire that I built up for you – with Peter's help," Jean Paul added hastily, "will be gone."

"That's all right, Father," his son said pleasantly. "I never wanted to make champagne anyway."

Jean Paul felt his mouth fall open.

"What do you mean you never wanted to make champagne?" he roared.

"Under the circumstances it's just as well, wouldn't you say?" Pierre said, picking up his glass again. "I like drinking it, mind. That will be a loss. But I certainly don't want to make it."

Peter seemed faintly amused by the turn the conversation had taken, and Jean Paul glared at him.

"What do you want to do?" Peter asked.

"I'm going to be an entomologist," Pierre said calmly.

"A what?"

"An entomologist. It's someone who studies insects."

"Insects?"

"That's right. Things like the phylloxera bug."

"And how do you propose to earn a living doing that?"

"Well, until Prohibition it wasn't going to be too necessary for me to earn a fortune, was it? You are very rich, Father, and I guess you always will be. I'm not that interested in money."

"Only because you've always had it, perhaps," Peter suggested gently.

Pierre looked at him with interest.

"Were you poor once, Peter?"

"Very."

Pierre half-smiled and shook his head.

"You give the impression of having been born to money."

"Your father taught me that."

Pierre looked from one to the other and there was something knowing in his look that alarmed Jean Paul. Had he guessed the relationship that he and Peter shared? One thing was sure, his good obedient little boy had disappeared. In his place was a mature, independent man. Jean Paul was not certain whether to be proud – or angry that he had sent his son away for the kind of education that had divorced them.

"Well, maybe I would dislike being poor," the boy was saying. "And I suppose if I did dislike it, I'd do something about it, like you did."

"Not studying insects, you won't," Jean Paul said.

"We'll have to see, won't we?"

Baffled, Jean Paul let the conversation drop.

Over the two months that Pierre was at home, Jean Paul had the definite impression that his son did not like him very much. There was no warmth; certainly no respect from the boy. He was always exquisitely polite, while doing exactly what he wanted. And he showed no interest whatsoever in the vineyard and its problems. He talked more to Peter than his father, but that, Jean Paul recalled, was nothing new.

One morning before lunch they were sitting in the courtyard of the house with a bottle of forbidden champagne. After he had drunk two glasses, Pierre asked suddenly and disturbingly: "Are there any pictures of my mother?"

One thing that Jean Paul was certain of was that there were no pictures of the slut Sarah. But an unbidden picture of her, spread-eagled on a bed, taunting him with hot eyes, her legs apart to receive him, assaulted his memory. He had not thought of her for a long, long time.

"I don't believe we do have any pictures of her," he said. "Like Peter said, there wasn't much money in those days for things like that."

"What was she like?"

Jean Paul remembered again the woman who fought him tooth and nail, her divine cooking, her insatiability in bed, the way she could throw a plate and hit him at forty yards, her foul mouth and how she had to be bullied into washing herself.

"An angel," he said solemnly. "A beautiful, gentle woman, loving, kind and dead, alas, too soon."

"What were her parents?"

What the hell were her parents? he wondered. Irish, probably, at a guess. Tinkers maybe. She certainly had an Irish temper.

"English," he said. "Gentlefolk. Both schoolteachers in Philadelphia."

"What was her maiden name?"

Jean Paul couldn't remember. He seemed to recall it began with an s. "Smith," he said.

"I always got the feeling that Peter didn't like her."

He would have to have a word with Peter.

"Nonsense," he said stoutly. "Everybody loved your mother."

"And do you have any family, Father?"

Jean Paul understood the boy was wondering about his roots. It was the great American preoccupation.

"Maybe," he said. "Back in Champagne. We've lost touch. I had a twin brother and a mother. My father was already dead when I came here." It was a relief not to have to lie.

"Why did you lose touch?"

Why indeed?

"Just one of those things," he said with a shrug.

"Didn't you worry about them in the war?"

They had never crossed his mind.

"All the time, son, all the time," he said heavily. "One day you and I will go back there and find them, shall we?"

Pierre did not answer, but he did say thoughtfully, leaving little for Jean Paul's comfort: "I think I might take French next term."

It was February when the enforcement officers came. Jean Paul recognised one as an old adversary from the days when the tenants had used their children for the picking. The man had tried to prosecute him for under-aged labour, but he had been able to point out – quite accurately – that the tenants were picking on what would one day be their own land. And since their children were receiving no pay, how could he be employing them?

In the small group of men who came withe the officers, he noticed the broad, middle-European face of one of the Yugoslav tenants that Gino had thrown out when he bought the land. The man was grinning.

It did not take them long. They informed him they knew that he had been breaking the law. He was manufacturing intoxicating beverages from grapes, and he was selling and transporting the said intoxicating beverages.

They smashed his vats so that the floors of the winery were swimming in wine; beautiful, carefully blended wine. The Yugoslav triumphantly showed them where Jean Paul's hidden cellar entrances were, and they smashed every bottle of champagne in the caves, leaving broken glass and pools of champagne, still gently fizzing, on the rock. When they had finished wielding their pickaxes and sledgehammers they told him that this time they would not prosecute him. But if he did it again ...

Then they went.

Did it again? There was not enough left to create so much as a thimbleful of wine. Everything had gone. His life's work, his life's ambition, left swirling, bubbling, draining into the greedy ground in a mess of broken glass and equipment.

Even though he had been expecting them and preparing himself for the end, when it came to the point he could not bear to look at the devastation. He went back into the house, shutting the terrace door that led down to the winery with a firm and final click. He found Peter in the living room, sobbing his heart out. Jean Paul ignored him and went to the ice-box that looked like a walnut cabinet where the last few bottles of champagne they had were hidden. As he chose a vintage Krug, Peter cried out: "What shall we do, Jean Paul? What shall we do?"

Jean Paul, grimly taking the cork from the Krug, cage and all, with one vicious pull, had already decided what they should do. The thought had been in his mind for some time, and it was Pierre who had put it there. What he was not going to do was stay surrounded by the wreckage of his dreams, nor would he cry over spilt champagne. Champagne could be made again.

"For God's sake stop crying," he said irritably, thrusting a full glass at his long-time partner and lover. "What we shall do right now, this minute, is drink to the future. And then we're going on a trip. A very long trip. So when we've finished this bottle, you can stop weeping and wailing and do something practical. Like getting me Gino on the blower and then packing."

Chapter Twenty-Six

Les Hérissons, March 1920.

Clovis was enjoying his supper. It was rabbit cooked in a mustard sauce, a dish to which he was partial and which Cook prepared extremely well.

It was one of his better days, and therefore he had automatically joined the rest of the family at table. On his bad days he usually ate in the kitchen, sitting by the range on a small wooden chair away from everyone. There Cook would hand him a plate of food. She then left him to get on with eating it while the gunfire in his head deafened him and took away his appetite. The war still raged in Clovis's head.

But lately the gunfire had been less obtrusive. In his better moments he was not sure whether he was now so used to the noise that it did not disturb him, or if indeed it was gradually disappearing.

He ate hungrily, not listening to the conversation around the table. Allie, the one they puzzlingly said was his daughter, was describing some tall building in America. He decided that she must be exaggerating. He liked her very much, but it seemed to him that she had a tendency to over-dramatise things. It was possible that she was his daughter because she looked so remarkably like him, but somehow he couldn't make himself feel that she was.

Then there were the ones who called themselves his mother and his wife. He was inclined to believe that the fine-boned, grey-haired fierce older woman might be his mother, because she bossed and bullied him so. He felt she would not do that unless she had some right.

But Rosie, who called herself his wife, he simply could not believe, even though Claudette assured him it was true. He wanted to marry Claudette, but she said it wasn't possible. And that was because he was already married to this incredibly good-looking, dark-haired, amber-eyed vivacious woman who seemed to be entirely in charge of Les

388

Hérissons. He could not credit that such a woman would ever marry him.

Whenever he ate with the family he wondered and worried about the blanks and the mysteries in his life. They had told him that he had lost his memory, but it didn't seem to make sense to have a whole chunk of his life just disappear like that. How could you mislay the memory of a wife and child? He hadn't mislaid Rosanne, though. He accepted that she was his. Rosie had gone away like women sometimes did when they had babies, and when he came back from Claudette's one night, there was this little thing who also looked exactly like him. He reasoned that they often didn't tell him the truth. So he preferred to eat in the kitchen on his bad days. Then there was no reason to think about anything at all. Certainly not anything that was confusing.

His mind was so fixed on the pleasure of the rabbit on his plate that the knock on the front door made him jump and spill a spoonful of the sauce. As he spooned it up again, Madame Dupuis asked tetchily: "Who can that be, arriving in the middle of dinner?"

He went on eating, but everyone else stopped until Marie came in, looking flushed, agitated and excited all at the same time. Pondering what could be the matter with her, he carefully eased a piece of meat off a nasty little spiky bone.

"Madame," the maid said, her voice almost a squeak. "There's someone to see you."

"Well, who is it, Marie?" Madame Dupuis asked impatiently.

"He says he knows you, madame, and oh, madame, he does!"

She flung back the dining room door. A sudden silence was followed by a concerted gasp and a crash. It was the crash which finally took Clovis's mind off his supper.

He looked up to see that Madame Dupuis had fainted dead away, falling off her chair in doing so. Allie had leapt to her feet and was kneeling by her grandmother. Rosie was sitting, like a petrified tree, her face dead white. And standing in the doorway, Marie to the side of them, were two men, one fair and one dark.

Clovis peered, blinked and peered again. The dark man was surely him, Clovis. But how could Clovis be sitting eating at the table, and standing in the doorway, smiling, both at the same time? It wasn't possible. He pursed his lips and thought about it, staring at the version of himself who stood there in a black overcoat, holding a homburg hat. He didn't own a black overcoat and a homburg hat. And though he hadn't deliberately looked in a mirror for a long time, glimpses of himself in the many mirrors at Madame Frédéric's told him that he looked not so much older, but more worn, than this man.

And then it suddenly dawned on him who this was, and he felt such rage blazing in his head that the guns were frightened into silence by it.

389

He put down his spoon and fork with a clatter. "So you're back, are you, Jean Paul?" he said, not getting to his feet, his voice hostile. "As usual, you've managed to give Mama an awful shock. And what do you want here, anyway?"

"Clovis!" his twin said mockingly. "What a welcome, and after all this time. Here, Marie, take our coats," he was stripping off the black overcoat, and motioning his silent companion to do the same. "We've been travelling all day. Get Henri, or whoever is about, to lay a couple more places and bring us some supper."

He loaded Marie's arms with their coats, and then looked around the room.

"Nothing has changed," he said with satisfaction, and moved forward to pick up their mother bodily from the floor. She seemed to be coming round as Clovis watched, impotent and furious.

His brother looked prosperous. His clothes were expensive and he had an air of authority about him. He set Madame Dupuis back in her chair, and kissed her soundly on both cheeks.

"Mama, behold," he said. "Your prodigal son has returned."

No doubt, Clovis thought sourly, wanting the fatted calf. And his mother would kill it. She would do whatever Jean Paul wanted.

Indeed, their mother, still white and dizzy, was beginning to smile. She held out her hands to her long lost son. "My dear Jean Paul – I can't believe you are home again. How happy this makes me."

Clovis could see that if Jean Paul's dramatic reappearance was making her happy, it was not exactly delighting his wife. Rosie still sat as if frozen, staring at the two men. From the look on her face, it occurred to Clovis that she also knew the blond stranger.

Jean Paul had turned from Clovis's mother to Clovis's wife. He bent to take Rosie's face in his hands and kiss her on the forehead.

"Ah, *ma petite* Rosie." His voice was tender. "I have brought you back your brother."

Clovis saw how Rosie flushed crimson before turning white again. She shut her eyes tight.

"You are twenty years too late, Jean Paul," she said, her voice flat.

He clicked his tongue against the roof of his mouth.

"Punctuality was never my strong point," he said lightly. "And besides, I had to wait for Peter."

Rosie seemed to recover herself.

"Mama, Clovis," she said, "this is my brother, Peter. The one I told you I met in New York." She looked directly at the fair man who moved uncomfortably under her stare. "Why didn't you wait to talk to me that night?" she asked in English.

The man almost wriggled with embarrassment.

"I had an urgent message," he said. "I had to catch a train. I couldn't find you to tell you."

"What you mean," she said evenly, but speaking fast, "is that you didn't want to tell me you were still with Jean Paul." She turned her back on him and put her arm round Allie who was standing, holding her grandmother's hand, her face bewildered.

"Allie," she said still in English, "this is my brother, your Uncle Peter, and this is your father's twin brother, Jean Paul. You have suddenly acquired two uncles." She then pushed the girl gently towards where the men stood. "This is Clovis's and my daughter, Rosalie," she said. "Our other daughter is in bed and asleep."

"You're married to Clovis?" Jean Paul asked, the satyr eyebrows winging upwards.

"She is my wife," Clovis said belligerently.

Jean Paul threw back his head and laughed out loud.

"Who would have believed it! My, we have a lot of catching up to do." He turned to Allie and said: "You're a real Dupuis, my dear. You look just like your father – and me, come to that. How old are you?"

"Nearly twenty," Allie told him, her face bright with curiosity.

"Don't exaggerate," Rosie said sharply. "You are nineteen and three-quarters."

The girl looked surprised and Clovis caught a well remembered, considering look crossing his brother's face, and fury possessed him again.

There was a confused five minutes while Henri brought in more knives and forks and glasses, before resetting the table. Madame sent for champagne. Clovis stolidly resumed his meal, realising with wonder that all the gaps and mysteries had abruptly gone from his life. It *had* been true that he had lost his memory, and now, quite unexpectedly, it had returned. The details were still not clear, but he felt that soon everything would come back.

As more food was served, Jean Paul began to talk. He told how he and Peter had built up Rosie's father's winery, and how now it had been destroyed. His business, it seemed, had been ruined by some new American law.

Rosie and her brother listened, silent, he looking totally uncomprehending and as if he wished he were back in California. Allie's face was agog and Madame clucked sympathetically, unable to believe that anyone could wantonly pour away so much champagne.

"Never mind, eh, Mama," Jean Paul said when he had finished his tale of triumph and disaster. "Not all is lost. Not while we still have Les Hérissons and I have all of you."

He looked around the table and smiled that smile that was only a baring of the gums. And with a cold, sinking feeling, Clovis realised

391

that his brother had come back to stay. He would without any doubt reclaim his portion of the family estate and business. And it was something he was legally entitled to do.

But Clovis knew that a share would not be enough for Jean Paul. His brother would be searching for a way to take everything from all of them, the running, the product, the business. Nothing would be safe and nothing would be the same any more.

Somehow he, Clovis, would have to make sure that Jean Paul did not succeed in stealing all they had achieved. Jean Paul would win only over his dead body, he told himself grimly. And if necessary, the dead body would be Jean Paul's.

The shock of seeing Jean Paul standing in the doorway of the dining room with her brother had completely unnerved Rosie. She had not known what to say or do. Her breath had deserted her at the sight of the man who had caused her so much misery all those years ago, standing there in the company of her brother. And so she had sat silent through the tale that Jean Paul had to tell. A tale she suspected was full of convenient gaps.

Now, aged thirty-nine, she could see exactly why the eighteen-year-old backwood's child she had once been had fallen in love with him. But she had learned a great deal since she was eighteen. He was handsome, true. But so were many men. It was his magnetism, that sense that the sun shone only on him, that made him so compellingly plausible – and totally untrustworthy.

She saw how Allie watched him, fascinated, and prayed that neither would guess their real relationship. But she had little hope that Jean Paul would not ferret out the truth and somehow use the knowledge. She had once believed him to be a gentleman. Now it was all too clear that he was a liar and a confidence trickster.

And yet to her dismay she still felt the old attraction for him. She watched him talk, filling the room full of sparkle, and blatantly flirting with her as he had flirted over her father's table so long ago, and was angry with herself that she felt some response. For even though she saw with her clear adult eyes that the Emperor had no clothes, he was still remarkably attractive without them. And she could see her mother-in-law blossoming at the return of her favourite son.

Rosie sat, saying little, ignoring her brother, though there were a million things she wanted to ask him. It would have been kind to speak to him in English. He obviously had no idea of what was being said, nor could he contribute to the conversation. He sat there, mute. She would have felt sorry for him if he had not been part of that past betrayal that had led her here to Les Hérissons. And watching him and Jean Paul, so slick in their smart suits and waistcoats, she clung to the thought of Philippe. Gentle, true and loving Philippe. At least all that had happened had led her to him.

She was beginning to sense that Clovis had regained his memory. And from the expression on her husband's face, he was not relishing this sudden cure. He must be thinking that Allie's real father is here, she thought miserably, just as I am. But it was not so bad for her. She was still the girl's mother, whatever Jean Paul did.

Madame Dupuis could not hear enough of her son's adventures, and when coffee was finally served, Rosie made her excuses and said she was going to bed. Clovis had already left some time before without speaking to anyone.

Jean Paul leapt to his feet and came to kiss her on both cheeks. "We will talk tomorrow, *ma petite* Rosie," he promised, speaking in English. "You are more beautiful than ever, you know."

They were the first words that Peter had understood, and Rosie saw him bristle. He was still jealous of her and she felt a glimmer of satisfaction in it.

The dining room door closed, she hurried to her office where there was a private telephone. Even though it was late she intended to speak to Philippe. She would not disturb him too much; because of his blindness he had the luxury of a telephone beside his bed and he would probably be reading one of his Braille books.

He answered almost immediately.

"Did I wake you?" she asked.

"No," He reassured her, "I was reading."

"Something quite extraordinary has happened," she told him, speaking low and hurriedly. "Clovis's twin brother appeared here tonight, with my brother, Peter. You remember we met him in New York and he disappeared."

"I do indeed. And he was with Clovis's twin? The man that you – "

"Yes, that one," she interrupted, not wanting him to say more on the telephone. There was no need to say more. Philippe knew everything about her, with the exception of her brief relationships with his father and his son. "The complications are going to be dreadful. It seems they've been running my father's old winery, making champagne, and had a great success. Because of the new Prohibition laws, everything, equipment, stock, has been wrecked, and they have nothing left. Imagine, they actually smashed the vats, and broke every bottle. I think the American government must have gone completely mad."

"But what does he want?" Philippe asked.

"I don't know. He said all was not lost while there was Les Hérissons and all of us."

"He wants his inheritance," Philippe said. "He'll have come back for that."

393

"His inheritance?"

"In French law, children cannot easily be disinherited. He legitimately owns half of Les Hérissons. The other half is Clovis's. You are entitled to live off it, but it must eventually go to Allie and Rosanne."

"He mentioned tonight he has a son."

"Then the son will be entitled to share it."

Rosie was thinking about the implications.

"So, he could really take it over and run it with Clovis."

"I'm afraid so."

"Clovis would never be able to oppose him in anything?"

"I wouldn't have thought so."

"Oh, my God," she said softly.

"Rosie," his voice was urgent. "You can't stay there with him. I wasn't going to tell you until it was all settled, but Lorraine is talking about getting our marriage annulled."

"No!"

"Yes, it seems she wants to marry Didier. Didier's parents are a great deal richer than I am, but they are also practising Catholics, so it has to be an annulment for her to be acceptable to them. The family is friendly with some priest who has pull in Rome, and it seems to be going through."

"So you would be free?"

"Rosie, you could do the same with Clovis. He wouldn't even know if you were there or not. And the situation with Claudette should make everyone sympathetic to you."

Her heart had temporarily lifted. Now it plummeted again.

"But I think the sight of his brother tonight brought his memory back," Rosie told him, her voice bleak.

He was silent.

"Should that make any difference?" he asked finally.

"Not to wanting to be with you," she said, "but I can't leave him to the mercy of his brother. It would be like putting a lamb in the same cage as a tiger."

"Rosie?"

"Yes?"

"You don't want to stay because he has come back?"

"Oh, Philippe, how could you think such a thing!" she said passionately, even while fearing there could be truth in it. "Listen, I'll talk to you sometime tomorrow when I see more clearly what is happening here. And I'll come to Paris at the first possible opportunity. Thank God I have you. Don't doubt me, Philippe, please."

"I love you," he said.

"And I love you."

She sped upstairs to her room on tiptoe, wondering where Marie had housed Jean Paul and her brother. Her room door was ajar. She pushed it gently open, and peered in. A fire burned in the grate, throwing warm red dancing shadows across the furniture and the bed. And someone was lying on her bed. She drew in her breath, and whoever it was sat up.

"Quickly, come in, Rosie," Clovis said. "We have to talk."

What Clovis wanted to say was much what Philippe had already told her, though Clovis's fears were greater. He was afraid that Rosie would fall in love again with his twin, and he dreaded the possibility that it would come out that Allie was Jean Paul's child.

"He could steal you both from me," he said fearfully.

Rosie did her best to reassure him on both counts, and hugged him and said how happy she was that his memory had returned.

"It might have been better if it hadn't," he said gloomily.

She slept badly. She was no longer used to sharing her bed and she had such a weight on her mind. She thought how much labour, love – and, indeed, money – she had put into building and then rebuilding Les Hérissons; how important the business was to her and to Philippe. Why should Jean Paul simply claim it from them? Madame would be no ally, that was certain. Madame was back under her favourite son's spell. Long after Clovis had begun contentedly snoring beside her, Rosie slept.

She was up early in the morning and came downstairs to find her brother standing, purposeless and dismal, in the hall.

"Good morning, Peter," she said, "are you lost?"

"You could say that," he said angrily. "I don't know what I'm doing here."

"Come and have some coffee," she said. A glimpse of the bewildered little boy from all those years ago softened her. He had really aged very well, she thought. He had filled out and become quite cinema star handsome in a blond, boyish manner. But there was something soft and weak about him. She felt if she prodded him, the dent of her finger would remain.

She led him through to the breakfast room, and rang for breakfast.

"Now you'd better tell me all those things you avoided telling me in New York," she said firmly.

"There isn't really much to say." His tone was defensive. "About a month after you left, Jean Paul came back. Pa was dying from pneumonia and after he'd passed away, Jean Paul found some money under the floorboards. He thought that's where you found the money to get away."

She nodded.

"I did. I took a third of it. My share. Did Pa ever get a letter from me, explaining everything?"

"Not that I know of."

She sighed. "So he died not knowing what had happened to me."

"I guess so."

"And then what happened?"

"Well, we used the money to buy new cuttings and start making champagne. Jean Paul brought some woman in to look after us, and she had a kid by him. She died, too. The rest you heard last night. But the kid turned out great. He's at Harvard now. Jean Paul's going to bring him over for the summer vacation."

"So you're planning on staying?"

"Looks like it." His pretty-boy face was set in lines of gloom. "Don't know how I'll stand it, not speaking the language and all that. He hadn't even told me that you'd be here. I hadn't made the connection between you and this place. I thought that guy you were with that night in New York was your husband. Jean Paul only told me coming up the drive that you had something to do with Les Hérissons' champagne. I don't know how he knew. It's good stuff you make, Rosie, and Jean Paul's got a great market for it lined up. I'm hoping I'll have to go back to the States and deal with that end of it. I shall be selling it, you see."

"We already have our own markets for our champagne," she said sharply.

"Reckon Jean Paul's got other ideas." His voice had toughened. "I reckon he'll do what he wants. He always does. And anyway, he's explained to me that this place is his, Rosie."

"This place is half his," she told him, getting to her feet. "Your coffee won't be long. Enjoy it."

She strode out of the breakfast room, her back rigid with rage. In the corridor, she stood irresolute for a moment. She would calm herself by going to the tasting room and working on the assembling of this year's *cuvée*. She had already been working for some weeks, and believed she was near to deciding on the blend.

She turned and went to what she called her little laboratory. Her anger had not subsided as she banged the door open. Then she stopped in her tracks.

Jean Paul was at her tasting table. He was wearing her white overall, and holding a glass of champagne to the light.

"What are you doing here?" she hissed at him.

"Trying out your blends, Rosie," he said, smiling. "Not at all bad. Who is our *chef de cuvée* these days? The one we used to have, I've long forgotten his name, must be dead."

"I am the *chef de cuvée*," she said, through gritted teeth.

"Indeed, I am impressed, *ma petite* Rosie."

"And don't call me that. I am not your little Rosie."

"Ah," he said reproachfully, "you are angry with me. I had thought you would be so happy to see me. After all, you came here to find me, no? And here I am." He held his arms open wide.

"How did you know I was here?"

"A compatriot of yours told me. He said you made fine champagne, and indeed you do. But I shall make it better."

Controlling herself with a great deal of effort, Rosie crossed the room to sit on a hard-backed chair by the tasting table.

"Jean Paul, what do you want?"

The blue eyes sparkled at her. "Want?" His voice was the cooing of a dove. "Want? Why nothing. I have just come home to my mother, my brother and my inheritance, dear Rosie. And to find I have you as a sister-in-law and also a charming, grown-up niece," he raised his voice to a question mark as he said niece, "is a delightful surprise. I have great plans for Les Hérissons, Rosie. It was too modest of you to sell our champagne under other labels. Believe me, in three years' time we shall be ranking with Rodier, Crystal, Krug, the best that Bollinger can produce." He was now confiding in her. "To be truthful, I am not too sad to lose Champagne D'Or. You cannot imagine the frustration of attempting to make truly fine champagne away from the soil of France. I could never reach the heights I dreamed of. Here, it will be different. And with Peter to sell for us, Les Hérissons will become famous – and rich. Your brother is a persuasive salesman, I can tell you."

"But we already have our own selling organisation which is perfectly successful," she burst out, her calm gone now Philippe was affected. "And how can Peter sell? He doesn't even speak French."

"Our sales will be mostly in the United States from now on."

"With Prohibition operating?" she said, her voice scornful.

"Think what certain people will pay for it," he reminded her gently.

"And if Clovis does not agree?"

"Clovis? Disagree! Come, come, Rosie, can you imagine Clovis disagreeing with me, and with his mother?" He saw her startled look. "Yes, Mama is most excited by the idea. We talked long into the night after you left us. Mama just wants me to be happy again."

She rose to her feet.

"I suppose you own all the property back in California," she said bitterly.

"Peter sold it to me long ago. You are thinking of your share? Your father willed it to Peter."

"I don't believe you," she said flatly.

"Of course he did. You had run away, taking his money, looking for me." He was advancing on her, and he took her arms firmly in his grip and looked down at her. She found herself mesmerised by the velvet blue eyes with the flecks of sunlight in them. "Why did you come here, Rosie?"

"Because you left a note saying you were returning home. Remember?"

"I did?" His expression was meant to convey doubt.

"Yes, you did. I have the note still. I brought it here with me. So don't lie to me."

He laughed. "Maybe I did then. But why did you follow me?"

"I was foolish enough to think that I loved you."

"And no other reason."

"No other reason."

"You, too, might lie to others, Rosie, but you can never lie to me. Remember, it was I who made you a woman. Remember?" One hand still held her arm, while the other riffled tresses of her hair. "Do you still have the appetite, Rosie? Such a greedy girl, such an appetite. I cannot believe it no longer exists."

Somehow she dragged herself back from the drowning depths of his eyes.

"I have an extreme appetite for my breakfast," she said, briskly. "If you would just let go of my arm ..."

He released her, but one gentle hand stroked her cheek.

"Don't hate me, Rosie," he wheedled, the blue eyes open wide, seeming so honest. "Why do you think I went back to your father's winery? I went back because I could not live without you. I came back only to find you gone. If you had waited, everything would have been so different. I loved you, Rosie. I went away for us, and I came back for you. That you must believe. Can we begin again where we left off? I have always loved you, *ma petite* Rosie."

Without replying she darted round him and sped out through the door, back towards the breakfast room. She was trembling, and worse, his touch, his eyes, his words had aroused her. Could he have been telling the truth? All her instincts told her he was lying. She groaned, cursing laws made three thousand miles away that had sent him back here.

Peter had vanished from the breakfast room, but Madame Dupuis was there, looking tired but happy.

"Oh, Rosie," she said, as her daughter-in-law came into the room. "Isn't it wonderful? Aren't you thrilled? I've barely slept. To have him back, and so well and successful. I was thinking that maybe we should tell Jean Paul the truth about Allie. After all, since he was shell-shocked, Clovis doesn't even know that she is his daughter so what harm would there be?"

Rosie's anger erupted on a legitimate target.

"Mama," she said, keeping her voice low with difficulty. "If you do any such thing, I shall kill you and him, I swear it."

Her mother-in-law looked at her open-mouthed.

"Don't look at me like that! How do you think Allie would feel? She loves Clovis. But you, you were so pleased to see your erring son return that you didn't even notice that poor Clovis's memory came back last night. And at what a time! When his brother returns to snatch all your love and affection again, and with every intention of taking over this place and everything that we have worked and slaved for over the years. And you're going to let him do it, aren't you?"

"He has every right to do it," Madame Dupuis said frostily.

"He has no moral right to do it. I've laboured over this place, and every bit of money I had has gone into it. It was André's money that got us in such good shape again after the war. I never begrudged using it because this place was my future and my home. Allie's too. But what now? Doesn't poor Clovis have any say? You do have two sons, you know."

Madame's hands were trembling. "I find all this concern for Clovis most touching," her voice caustic. "You only married him because there was nothing else to be done. You've been a good daughter-in-law, Rosie, I must give you that. And I have great affection for you. But you have not been a good wife. I know that you and Philippe Lefevre have been lovers for years. And if Jean Paul's homecoming does anything, it might at least end that when your brother becomes our salesman. Unless, of course, you decide to leave us and go off with him. I suspect you've wanted to do that for years."

Rosie sank into the nearest chair. Her legs had given way. She poured herself an unsteady cup of coffee, and looked distractedly for the milk, which Madame pushed towards her. They were both silent for a long time.

"Why didn't you say something if you knew?" Rosie finally managed to ask.

"Because I understood," Madame said quietly. "Clovis isn't easy to love. I could never love him myself, and we had both lost Jean Paul."

"But I do love Clovis," Rosie said, realising that it was true. "You said a long time ago that he was good, and he is. He has been good to all of us, and I am sorry, Mama, but I won't have him hurt. He's terrified that Jean Paul will find out about Allie, and I don't want her to know either. I know you're happy to have Jean Paul back, but the truth is he is bad. I can see it so clearly now, and you know it yourself. You said it a hundred times when I first came here and you thought I should marry Clovis. It's just that Jean Paul weaves a spell of lies, charm – all sorts of things. I feel it myself, even now. You're his mother so you can't help but love him. Do what you like about the estate, but don't let him hurt Allie and Clovis. I won't let him hurt me. I'm staying, and I'll fight him tooth and nail."

"What for?" Madame asked.

The question made Rosie pause.

"I don't really know," she said. "But I'll fight him."

"Until he doesn't attract you any more?" suggested Madame.

Rosie paused again.

"Maybe," she said. "Maybe."

Chapter Twenty-Seven

Rosie tried to be reasonable. She tried to tell herself that half Les Hérissons was Jean Paul's. She did her best to accept that he had every legal right to be there, and that she had no real say in the matter at all. But one thing she was sure of, and that was that the estate had been well run under her guidance. Nothing had ever been left undone that could improve the quality of their grapes and their wine. Jean Paul had the same ambitions to produce fine champagne, but he was not averse to a little cutting of corners when it came to saving a few francs here and there.

The Ay field was now producing the finest grapes possible, but he decreed it was too far away, and therefore too expensive to maintain. He sold it for a hefty profit. To her dismay, the small walled field near to the house that had been planted with the cuttings she had brought from America, was to be torn up. The vines, for sentimental reasons, had been allowed to grow *en foule*, uncut, but Jean Paul decided that the field should be replanted and used for proper production.

One of his earliest grumbles was that they employed too many men at too high wages. Some would have to go, and the others would have to work harder to earn their corn. One of those fired was Marie's Robert. Jean Paul did not think that a one-armed man was much use to anyone, despite the fact that Robert, with his one arm, was faster at the *remuage* than many men who still had both their arms. Even Madame was shocked by this decision, for Marie promptly gave in her notice, saying she had found a better job with the Pommery family. And they were happy to employ her Robert with her for he had a reputation as a good, loyal worker.

Jean Paul also decreed that a blind man was not a fit salesman for their product. Rosie tried to explain that Philippe was more than someone who merely sold their wine. He was and had been part of the business from the beginning. It was his taste and his contacts that had built the business to the success it was.

"If you can call it a success," Jean Paul said. "Who in the world has heard of Les Hérissons champagne? You might have made a lot of money, but you haven't got a cat in hell's prestige."

Rosie was in despair. Philippe would not starve. He was a wealthy man and he represented some of the finest Bordeaux châteaux who made him more money than her champagne ever had. But if he were not selling her wine, what excuse would she have to see him?

She had to allow that Jean Paul had prodigious energy. He took over the handling of the workmen, attended to everything himself, leaving Clovis with no authority, or even much to do except the labouring work. He said that in future he would be handling the business end, and requested the books and accounts from Rosie. He took over her little office, changing the lock so that she could not get in. All she did now was physically to keep the books and write letters to his dictation. And there were few of those. Jean Paul preferred the telephone where no records existed. She was no more than a clerical worker, knowing little of what was going on.

He was making vast shipments of their stock to South America at the expense of their regular customers, and he was secretive about the buyers. Peter seemed to be in Paris much of the time, but within six weeks the pair of them were entirely in control.

Rosie had said she would fight him tooth and nail, but it was like fighting jelly. There was nothing there to fight. He just did what he wanted without reference to anyone, and the truth was that he had the right. And he knew it.

Madame was rather quiet after Marie had gone, and complained that she was too old to break in a new maid. The new maid, one whom Jean Paul chose, was young and pert and made eyes at him. He and Peter quarrelled about it.

Life was not made any easier by Jean Paul's constant pursuit of Rosie herself. He had told her bluntly that he intended to have her again; that they had unfinished business. And he made no attempt to hide his intentions. Clovis watched smouldering as his brother flirted with his wife. He never spoke, but his watchful eyes registered that Jean Paul was ever touching Rosie, her face, her hands, her neck. Sometimes he would slip his arm round her waist, but a little too high up for comfort. And Rosie knew that he was merely tormenting her and Clovis and also tormenting Peter, who watched jealously. There was no love or affection in any of it. She had no doubt that he wanted to make love to her again, but only as a conquest. André and Philippe had taught her what love was, and it was something that Jean Paul did not understand.

Her problem was that he aroused something in her that had long

402

been buried. Maybe it was what he called the appetite, but his hands and eyes made her hot with what was nothing more than lust. And she knew that if she gave in, she was lost. She had to do something to get away from him.

"Mama," she said one morning when they were both in Madame's little sitting room, embroidering. Rosie had taken up embroidery for something to do since Jean Paul had taken over all her duties. "I think I shall go to Paris for Easter and take the children. Would you mind?"

The shrewd old eyes regarded her.

"You're not happy, are you?"

"No." There seemed no point in lying.

"Are you going to see Philippe Lefevre?"

"I hope so."

Madame sighed, and put down her work.

"Rosie," she said. "I have made a bitter mistake."

Rosie remained silent.

"But you see, I was so pleased to see him again. Euphoria, that's what it was, euphoria. He is my son, and therefore I must always love and forgive him. But you were right to remind me that he is bad. He is bad, and I fear what I have brought upon us all." She seemed almost to be speaking to herself. "But what could I have done? He belongs here. This is his home. But he has done you a grave injustice; his treatment of you is wrong. He is humiliating his brother, and he seems to enjoy humiliating yours. And when he told Robert to go . . . After so long . . . I miss Marie. I'm old. She is part of my life. What more damage will he do? How can we stop him?"

"We can't," Rosie said sadly. "There is nothing we can do."

"You could leave it all. You could go to Paris and stay."

"I can't abandon Clovis, and I can't take the children away from him. He loves them too much. My situation was workable before, but now . . . Now it seems hopeless."

"I'm sorry," Madame said.

"There is nothing to be sorry for," Rosie said. "None of us could have prevented it." And wanting to help Madame's guilt, she smiled and said: "Only perhaps the American government, but they wouldn't have listened to us, would they?"

Allie was relieved when her mother suggested going to Paris for Easter. With the arrival of her two strange uncles the atmosphere at Les Hérissons had subtly changed. She knew her father was right when he said that she over-dramatised things, but there was an air of menace about the place. And so much secrecy with Uncle Jean Paul locking himself in rooms, and Uncle Peter sulking about the place, refusing to

403

learn French, and always trying to get her to talk to him.

She actually didn't really mind talking to him. He was peculiar and she couldn't quite pigeon-hole him, but he was quite a soft old thing, really. He just liked to chat and gossip, and he had travelled so far over the United States that he could tell her all sorts of things that interested her.

She had confided in him her wish to go back to New York again and live there for a while, but not yet. She felt she had to give her father a little of her time while he settled down after recovering his memory.

The thing about Peter was that she never felt threatened by him. Maybe it was because he was so much older than she was, or maybe he just saw her as a kid. Whatever the reason, she had struck up an awkward kind of friendship with him, one that gave them both a little companionship and pleasure. But he, it seemed, wasn't to be permanently about the place. Ten days ago he had gone away for a month on a selling trip to Chicago. He'd been excited about it, saying he was going back to a civilised place where they spoke a civilised language.

Uncle Jean Paul was different. All her highly developed antennae when it came to men told her that this one was dangerous. She watched his overtly sexual behaviour with her mother, and saw how her mother tried to deflect and ignore it. She registered how it distressed her father. Once when she herself had been in the room alone with him, he had begun the same flirting, suggestive approaches to her. She had got up and left.

She disliked him very much. She could see that he had destroyed her father's happiness in Les Hérissons, and excluded her mother from all that she had built up over the years. Her parents were both wretched, and it seemed to Allie that he had walked in and stolen their lives. Yet no one talked about exactly why he had gone away from here in the first place.

She knew there was some secret because she had overheard Marie complaining to Cook, just before she left. Marie had been saying something about the nerve of the man coming back here after what had happened. But Cook had said it was all a long time ago and no one was going to do anything about it now.

But what had happened? If she could find out, maybe the knowledge would help to get rid of him. Who else would know?

She asked Henri first. He looked extremely uncomfortable and (obviously lying) said he really had no idea and why didn't she ask Marie.

Marie, still smarting at the treatment of her Robert, was only too pleased to tell her.

That Sunday afternoon in the Pommery's cosy kitchen, the

Dupuis' ex-maid unfolded a tale of the village schoolmaster who had been entrusted with the local children, and who had betrayed that trust.

"Disgusting, it was. He was interfering with them all, Miss Allie, particularly the little boys, and he threatened them with dreadful things if they ever told on him. But then he went too far. He really hurt Madame Dupré's little boy, young Michel – well, he's not young any more, of course. The lad came home and cried, and then it all came out. All the children told on him, and the parents would have killed him if they'd got their hands on him. But he left, and fast. Ahead of both the police and the parents, he was. But I tell you, it wasn't until your mother came here and won 'em over that anyone would have anything to do with the Dupuis family again. And they'd been that respected in the area before."

Allie listened, agog.

"He's causing dreadful trouble at Les Hérissons again, Marie," she said. "Not as wicked as that, but making everyone unhappy."

"He would," Marie said, viciously poking at the range. "He'd better keep away from the village; there's folk there with something to say to him. He's a bad lot, that one. He'll come to a sticky end one of these days, you mark my words."

Allie was thoughtful as she cycled home again. It was an incredible piece of knowledge, but she wasn't sure how best to use it. Marie's revelations hadn't particularly surprised her. She'd already had her Uncle Jean Paul marked down as another filthy man. She only hoped the maid was right with her prediction about him coming to a sticky end.

That April Sunday afternoon, Clovis, too, felt the need to get away from Les Hérissons, and while Allie was chatting with Marie in the Pommery kitchens, he took his bicycle and set off down the Épernay road to see Claudette. She was rarely busy on a Sunday afternoon.

She greeted him a little coolly at first; he had not been there since Jean Paul had arrived home. Nevertheless, she put her assistant in charge of the salon and led him upstairs to her room.

"My memory's back, Claudette," was the first thing he said to her. "I had a shock, and it came back."

"Well I never!" she said, as if she knew already as she fussed him into an armchair. "What sort of shock?"

"Jean Paul came back."

"I know. The cheek of him."

"You'd heard?"

"A lot of my clients were his pupils in those days. And when he sacked Robert, word soon got round. Marie saw to that. And some

405

clients of mine wouldn't mind having a little chat with him, I can tell you. What's he like now?"

"Smooth, charming when he wants to be. Just like he always was, I suppose," he said gloomily. "Always smiling without meaning it. He's upset things at Les Hérissons."

"How?" Claudette was making Clovis the little hot toddy he liked to sip while they talked.

"Taken over everything. I'm only allowed to do manual work now. He deals with everything. I hate him," he added, almost conversationally. "I know Rosie always ran things before, but I had my place and my areas where she let me get on with it. I did all the things I like doing and the bits I'm good at. I realise now that I was pretty happy. I suppose that's why I only remembered my work and you all that time. The two things that made me happy."

She flushed with pleasure.

"I love Rosie," he went on thoughtfully, "and I'd do anything for her. But I couldn't say she'd ever made me happy. Allie did, but I didn't even remember her when I was ill. Rosanne makes me happy now, too. Funny how they both look like me."

"Why shouldn't they?" Claudette said casually, handing him his drink.

"Because neither of them is mine."

"What!" Claudette almost dropped her own drink.

"No, it's true. Allie is really Jean Paul's child. That's what's so difficult about him turning up now. Rosie met him in America, fell in love with him and came here to find him. It was quite an achievement when you think about it; getting all that way on her own. I fell for her hook, line and sinker. She was exotic, somehow. I married her to give the baby a name. That's what I said, anyway. The truth was I wanted her. But it was a mistake really. I should have married you. I'd have been happy with you."

He paused to sip his drink, blowing on it to cool it.

"These are secrets I'm telling you, you know, Claudette. I'm trusting you to keep them. But you're used to keeping secrets, aren't you?"

She nodded dumbly.

"Rosanne is Allie's really. She was raped by a German soldier, and Rosie passed the baby off as hers. I was out of my mind with shell-shock at the time, but I can see it all clearly now. Not that anyone's actually told me she isn't my daughter. They probably think I'd be upset. I don't mind pretending the children are mine. They believe I'm their father and I love them. Particularly Rosanne now, but that's maybe only because she's nothing to do with Jean Paul. But I've never really had anything of my own, you know, not ever. Never will, now Jean Paul's back. And I've always had to share you."

Tears were furrowing through the powder on Claudette's face.

"Why are you telling me all this?" she asked.

"I don't know really. I suppose I was wondering if there was any way of getting out of the whole damn mess. If you'd have me, I'd like to marry you. But I asked you that when my mind had gone and you said it wasn't possible. If it was possible, would you?"

"Oh, Clovis," she said, "how could we? Me a brothel keeper and you totally dependent on your brother. What would we live on? Why can't we just go on as we are?"

He swallowed his drink and grimaced as the hot liquid hit his throat.

"I suppose I thought you'd say that," he said. "Can I have another one of these? A bit stronger this time though. Then we'll go to bed if you like."

He was rather drunk when he left Claudette, as much from emotion as from the alcohol. He wobbled off down the path while she watched him from the upstairs windows. He attempted a backward wave but nearly fell off his bike, so contented himself with a sharp ring-a-ling on the bicycle bell as, by a small miracle, he missed the gatepost.

No one appeared to be in at Les Hérissons. His mother would be either sleeping or already off on her Sunday afternoon outing. Rosie and Allie would be out walking while Rosanne had her nap in the nursery. He had the place to himself, and having got the taste, he settled himself in the dining room with a bottle of Marc de Champagne. He knew his mother would kill him if she caught him, but he didn't intend to be caught.

He sat drinking and brooding on the unfairness of life, his gloom increasing. After the third Marc, he made the decision that the time had come to have things out with his brother. He had just had what he thought was a brilliant idea. He could threaten to bring up the old story of why Jean Paul had left so precipitately all those years ago. He could pretend that the charges were still on the books against him – for all he knew they might be – and see if that might make him go, or at least be more reasonable.

Staggering slightly he carefully put the Marc back in the sideboard and hid his glass before going to look for Jean Paul.

He did not appear to be in the house so Clovis headed for the winery buildings. The yellow Hispano-Suiza car with the flying silver stork on the bonnet that Jean Paul had bought was gleaming in the drive. He must be somewhere.

The first building yielded nothing, but he could hear noises coming from the structure that housed the biggest of their blending vats. He lurched across and as he reached the door, he heard Rosie's voice saying desperately: "For God's sake leave me alone."

"Rosie, why are you so cruel to me?" His twin's voice was mockingly reproachful.

"Because I want nothing to do with you."

"I could always tell Allie the truth," he heard his brother say. "She should know the truth."

Clovis felt as if a volcano was erupting inside him. He pushed the wooden door. It swung open silently, letting an oblong of light fall into the interior. Caught in it, as if in a spotlight, but unaware of it, were Rosie and his brother. Rosie with her back to the wall, his brother pinning her with one hand each side of her body, pressing her flat against the wall. She looked like a rabbit cornered by a fox. He was leaning forward, forward until his mouth found hers. Clovis stood boiling, but transfixed, watching for a brief moment while she turned and twisted, wriggling like a butterfly on a pin to get away, and then suddenly slumped, her arms coming round his brother's back, her mouth joining his in the kiss.

He heard his own roar of rage, heard his feet thunder across the cobbles of the barn until his brother, startled, spun round. Jean Paul had no chance. Clovis's big workman's hands came out and grasped him round the throat above his red silk cravat. With the strength of years of heavy work, fuelled by buried anger, he swung his brother off the ground, both hands squeezing as tight as they could. His twin's neatly trousered legs dangled, the polished boots tried to kick. Then Jean Paul's blue eyes began to bulge and turn red, and his tongue shot, bleeding, from his mouth. Clovis squeezed harder. Manicured hands clawed frantically at him, scratching his face. Clovis felt no pain. His grip tightened until the writhing body in his grasp jerked and then slackened. Clovis gave one more squeeze to be certain, and flung his twin's mortal remains on the floor where they lay like a broken doll.

"And as for you!" he shouted, advancing to where Rosie stood cowering against the wall.

"Papa, what's happening?"

Allie was standing silhouetted in the doorway with her bicycle, her hand over her eyes, peering into the gloom. Clovis froze where he was standing, and Rosie moved away from the wall, carefully walking round the body.

"Don't come in, Allie," she called.

But Allie was already in, advancing purposefully towards them, still wheeling her bicycle.

"What's the matter?" she demanded. "What's happening?" She caught sight of the body grotesquely limp on the cobbles.

"Oh," she said, her hand flying to cover her mouth. "Oh."

Intuition was telling Clovis this was not the first dead body she had seen.

"Did you kill him?" she asked calmly, nudging her uncle's ribs with the point of her shoe. "I suppose he was trying to ravish Mama."

Clovis managed to croak something. He had abruptly sobered and the terrible realisation of what he had done was filtering through to his consciousness.

"This afternoon Marie was telling me about him and what he did to the schoolchildren. You were right to kill him, Papa. It's the best way to deal with people like that. Where shall we hide his body?"

She smiled brightly at them both.

Her mother was staring at her, appalled.

"Oh, Allie," she whispered. "What have we done to you?"

And Clovis sank down onto the cold stone floor, his head in his arms, and howled like the animal that he knew he was.

Chapter Twenty-Eight

The terrible sounds that Clovis was uttering made Rosie pull herself together.

She knelt beside him and with calculated force slapped his face hard.

"Be quiet," she hissed. "For God's sake, be quiet."

He whimpered into silence, but the dreadful, high-pitched howling had not gone unnoticed. In seconds Madame Dupuis in her motoring clothes, her old-fashioned hat tied on by a chiffon scarf, was coming through the open door into the barn. Hard on her heels was Henri, holding his chauffeur's cap.

"What on earth . . ." Madame began, and then gave an uncharacteristic small, sharp scream. "Rosie! Allie!" she said. "What has happened?"

"I killed him, Mama," Clovis said, looking up at her. "I did it. He was . . ." a terrible sob shook him, and he began to moan again, quietly rocking himself backwards and forwards.

"He was trying to ravish Mama," Allie explained with an unattractive touch of self-importance. "Papa had no choice."

Madame Dupuis ignored her, and bending her stiff, old knees to the stone floor, knelt beside the body of her son. She touched his face, and then placed her hand over his heart.

"He is dead," she whispered, and crossed herself.

There was a grey silence, which Rosie broke. She said reluctantly: "I think we should call the police."

The words hung, ominous, in the air.

"And if we do that, what shall we tell them?" Madame demanded fiercely.

"The truth." Even to her own ears Rosie felt her voice lacked conviction.

"Then they will lock Papa away," Allie said fiercely. "Papa has suffered enough."

It was true. Silenced, Rosie looked around at the scene. Her mother-in-law was still kneeling by the crumpled body. Clovis had curled into a ball, just as he had when he came home from the front. Allie was standing imperious, more in control and less distressed than anyone. Henri, a few paces behind them all, was wooden-faced, no doubt aware that this was no time for him to be present.

But it was Henri who spoke. He gave his gentle butler's cough and said: "Forgive me for speaking, madame, but if we were to move the body out of here – well away from here, and leave it, I think the police would believe that someone in the village had killed monsieur. He was not popular. People were outraged that he had come home. Threats had been made against his life."

Madame was climbing painfully to her feet.

"Henri, old friend," she said, emotionally. "We cannot permit anyone else to take the blame. And we cannot afford to invite the police to ask question. Clovis would never stand up under questioning. But the shame. My son has always brought us shame."

"We have to pretend he has gone away," Rosie said slowly. "We must try to make it look as if he has gone back to California. And maybe, by the time it is discovered that he has not done that, the trail will be sufficiently muddied for no one to care."

"Mama's right. We should bury his body somewhere," Allie said. "In a place where no one will think of looking."

"But where?" asked Madame.

Again the gentle cough from Henri. Rosie looked at him, a small, thin, unobtrusive but tough man, who had spent his life in the service of the Dupuis family. Now he was so much older, greyer and nut-like than when she had arrived all those years ago. Henri had no reason to care for Jean Paul. He missed Marie and the old routine and could not bear the pert new maid. Henri would be loyal to them as he had been loyal once before over the killing of the German lieutenant.

"If I may suggest," he was saying in his diffident manner, "only on Friday Monsieur Jean Paul had Monsieur Clovis start to dig up the vines in Madame Rosie's little vineyard where the vines from California are. One corner of the ground is already turned over and soft. It would be easy to dig deeper. And, if I may say so, it would be an appropriate place for monsieur. One might say poetic."

Madame Dupuis looked at her manservant, and her face crumpled.

"Henri," she said, "was he really hated so much?"

"I'm afraid so, madame," he said gently, hesitated and added: "Cook will help us bury him, and Cook will never speak."

"But I must be punished!" Clovis said suddenly. "It will be wrong if I am not punished."

"Papa," Allie said, sitting on the ground next to him. "You must not

411

be punished. You did the right thing."

Rosie could not bear to hear her daughter condone murder, but she knew that it was she who had sewn the seeds of the girl's state of mind. She herself had not cared when she killed the lieutenant, and now it seemed that no one cared that Clovis had killed Jean Paul. Pushing scruples away, she turned her mind to deal with the problem.

"Clovis," she said gently. "You will have to help bury him. You are the only one with the strength to do it. We have to dig deep into that soil, and it's hard work. If you can't bear it, just make the grave, and we will do the rest. But Clovis, you must help us. We need your strength."

"Look what my strength has done," he said bitterly.

"Your strength, Papa, has rid the world of a bad man," Allie said in ringing tones, and Rosie could have slapped her.

A farm cart took Jean Paul's body to the small walled vineyard where Clovis set to work digging. He seemed to have become calmer with something positive to do. He said he would not need Cook's assistance, and Rosie suggested to Henri that perhaps the fewer people who knew, the better.

"Then should anything go wrong, fewer of us will have to lie," she said.

She took Allie to Jean Paul's bedroom where they carefully repacked the trunk he had brought with him with as many clothes as they thought he would need for a month's travel. Rosie intended to ship this trunk back to California. She had thought of dropping it into the chalk cave, but she reasoned that the less there was to find of him, the better. She put aside all his travel documents, and other personal papers. There were surprisingly few of them but later she would burn them in the grate in her room. She and Allie worked, almost in silence, until the room held little trace of his occupancy.

"But what are we going to tell Uncle Peter when he comes back?" Allie asked when they had finished.

"We are going to be as baffled as he is at Jean Paul's sudden departure," Rosie told her.

"Suppose he goes to the police."

Allie was right. That was exactly what he might do after a few telephone calls to the States.

"We'll have to give him some proof that Uncle Jean Paul has gone," Allie said. "Could we get someone in the States to send a telegram, or something? I bet Alexander would."

"But who would it come from?" Rose said.

"His business partner's name was Dino or Gino. Gino, I think."

"Are you sure?"

"Uncle Peter talked about him. He didn't seem to like him. He said he was a crook."

"Not really surprising," Rosie said dryly.

"Shall I ring Alexander and ask him? What should we say?"

Rosie was thinking.

"When is Peter back?" she asked.

"In about two weeks' time."

"Then we have time. No. For all we know, Peter is meeting with this Gino. It might not be safe. But we must get the trunk shipped off. He wouldn't have left here empty-handed." She was thinking out loud. "Philippe's Georges could deal with that for us once we get it to Paris. He's dark-haired and about Jean Paul's height and build. If anyone were asking questions as to who sent the trunk, the description could almost be Jean Paul himself. And it will take a long time to arrive, thank God. Nothing can happen while it is en route." She was trying to cover all eventualities.

"But he wouldn't just go without leaving a letter for Uncle Peter, would he?" Allie asked

"Unlikely," Rose conceded.

Both women thought.

"Do we have any samples of his handwriting?" Allie asked.

Rosie shook her head.

"He didn't believe in committing things to paper," she said, and then gave a little whoop of excitement.

"I know," she said, "I still have a note he wrote from years ago. It just says 'I am returning home'." Her face then dropped. "But will Peter remember it? He saw it at the same time." She measured the odds. "No," she decided, "he couldn't possibly."

"Why did you keep it, Mama? And where was he going home from?" Allie was intrigued and curious.

"I don't really remember," Rosie said, making her voice deliberately vague. This was dangerous ground. "But thank God I did keep it. If we could just trace the handwriting onto newer paper, or copy it ..."

"I know how to trace it," Allie said full of confidence.

By the morning, before the workmen returned after their Sunday off, Jean Paul's body was under the American vines. Rosie had rung Philippe and asked if Georges could meet her at the Gare de l'Est on Monday morning. She, Allie and Clovis manhandled the trunk into the car, and Henri drove her to Épernay station in the morning, where porters took over. She was aware that all this was too open and unwise, but what else could they do?

At the Gare de l'Est, the waiting Georges took her burden to the shipping office where he would despatch it to the United States. She then went on to the house on the Île de la Cité where she saw Philippe and explained what had happened.

"Would it not have been better to go to the police?" he asked when

413

she had told the story. "Clovis is hardly in his right mind. They surely would not have punished him severely."

"It would have been better. But Madame would not hear of it. And perhaps this way will work in the long run. If we get away with it."

"Rosie, my darling, your only hope of getting away with it is if the police are never involved." He sounded truly concerned. "I'm afraid that all you have done will be dreadfully easily discovered if ever there is any investigation. And you, having organised all this, will be in as much trouble as Clovis. If not more, since there is nothing wrong with *your* mind. It will look as if he has been killed for his share of the inheritance. I beg you to tell the police."

"It's too late now," Rosie said, trying to sound cheerful. "Oh, Philippe. I know it's wicked, but in a way I am glad he is dead. He was such a bad man. And then I think that he wasn't bad enough to die so young. And if I'm truthful, I'm terrified that the truth will come out. What would they do to us? I'm very confused, just like I was when I killed . . ."

His fingers found her lips and silenced them.

"Shush!" he said. "Don't talk about that."

She was lying with her head in his lap along the length of a long settee, and they remained quiet for a few moments while he stroked her hair.

Then he said abruptly: "Perhaps this is not the time to mention it, but I shall soon be free. Lorraine believes she will have her annulment in the next few weeks. She is hoping to marry Didier in June and they are to go to Italy for their honeymoon."

Rosie sat up.

"But she married you in June and went on honeymoon to Italy."

He laughed with genuine mirth.

"She's either forgotten, or she wants me to be aware that this time she's going to get it right."

"Really!"

He laughed again, and said: "Darling, it doesn't matter. What does matter is you. When are *you* going to be free?"

She shook her head.

"I don't know. Maybe never. Everything that happens seems to make it more impossible to leave Clovis. I couldn't leave Rosanne behind and I couldn't take her from him. But since Sunday, he's been acting very strangely. I'm wondering if his memory will go again. He walks around muttering to himself and never seems to hear anything that anyone says to him. Poor thing, Madame can hardly bring herself to speak to him. I know he's a murderer, but that fragile mind of his has borne all the brunt of this horror. We shouldn't have asked him to bury Jean Paul, but there was no one else strong enough. Philippe darling, I'll have to stay with them all until this is resolved and God knows how long that will take. Les Hérissons is becoming a house of secrets."

"One day, one day," he sighed. "Oh, Rosie, my poor Rosie. So many people needing you, including me. How is Allie taking it?"

"Still refusing to grow up, acting like a little girl most of the time. And yet so tough. I almost think she enjoyed that terrible scene in the barn. Death does not soften her. She has no compassion. I suppose one day she'll solve her problems, but Rosanne is a living reminder of what caused them."

He bent to find her mouth and kissed her.

"Do you know what I'd like to do?" he said.

"What?"

"I'd like to take you back to Cannes, where we were so happy. Just for a week, maybe, but while we were there we would make love, eat wonderful food and never mention your house of secrets and its inhabitants once. Shall we do that?"

She sighed.

"Please, please, please. The minute it looks as if everything is safe again." And she gave a little shiver as she turned to be kissed.

Peter arrived back in Paris on a soft balmy June day. He did a little shopping for himself in the Rue Faubourg St Honoré and then telephoned Les Hérissons from the bar at the Ritz to ask if he could be met at the station at Rilly. Henri, who answered the telephone, immediately passed him over to Allie. Feeling inadequate, Peter wished he had more proficiency with the language. He was beginning to understand a little of what was said, but talking on the telephone he found impossible.

"Of course, Uncle Peter." Allie said. "I'll be sure Henri's there."

"While I'm on, can I speak to Jean Paul?" Peter asked.

There was a brief pause.

"But he's not here," the girl said.

Peter was about to ask where Jean Paul was, but then thought it wasn't worth the trouble.

"Then just tell him what time I'm arriving."

"I can't," Allie said. "He's not here. He's gone away."

"Gone away?"

"Yes."

"Where to?"

"I really couldn't say exactly, but I believe somewhere in America."

"America!"

"Yes, that's right."

"But he can't have."

415

"But he has," Allie said, rather cheekily he thought.

Baffled, Peter hung up the telephone. If Jean Paul wasn't at Les Hérissons it would explain why he himself had received no phone calls from France while he had been away. But why on earth would he have suddenly left for the States? It didn't make sense. He shrugged. For the moment there was nothing to be done but get himself back to Les Hérissons.

Henri was waiting in the family saloon outside the station, and he hurried to help the porter with the many pieces of baggage. Peter climbed onto the back seat while it was all stowed away.

Once Henri was at the wheel, Peter asked in his halting French when Monsieur Jean Paul had gone away.

"I do not know exactly, monsieur," Henri said, woodenly, and further conversation was not possible.

Peter settled into an uneasy silence as the car drove through the village and along the Épernay road before turning onto the rough lane that led to the estate. He decided perhaps it was as well he couldn't ask any more questions. After all, the staff would expect him to know where Jean Paul was and what he was doing.

At Les Hérissons, he received a surprisingly warm kiss and hug from Allie, who was waiting on the doorstep.

"Do you know," she said, clinging to his arm, "I've missed you." And he felt quite charmed.

Rosie was as cool as ever, but did at least tell him that dinner would be served in an hour. There was no sign of anyone else.

"Where's Jean Paul?" he asked abruptly after the new maid had vanished with his hat and light coat.

Rosie looked surprised.

"Don't *you* know?"

"I wouldn't be asking if I did," he said scratchily.

"Well, we don't know. We thought you'd tell us."

"I've no idea where he is. You tell me."

Rosie shrugged.

"He went one morning, about ten days ago. He suddenly announced he had to go back to the States. We assumed he'd had a telephone call from you. Or a telegraph, or something. It was all so sudden. Allie wondered if he'd gone to see that Dino or Gino man you told her about as he did seem to be a little agitated. But he packed his trunk in a great hurry and went. It was a Sunday evening. He's left a lot of things here, and his Hispano-Suiza is still in the garage, so he must be coming back soon."

"Are you saying that he just went without telling anyone where he was going?"

"Yes. We did notice that the trunk was addressed to California."

416

He stood in the hallway, indecisive. He simply could not think of a reason why Jean Paul would have left.

"I think he's gone to see Dino," Allie chipped in.

"Gino," Peter corrected. "He shouldn't have. I was with Gino in Chicago a fortnight ago. If he had wanted to see Jean Paul, he would have mentioned it."

Or would he? he wondered. Could they be cooking up some deal and intending to cut him out?

"I must make some telephone calls," he said abruptly.

Not caring about the hour, he rang Gino in Chicago first. It took for ever to get through, and battling against what sounded like Atlantic waves Peter learned that Gino had no idea of Jean Paul's whereabouts. He sounded genuinely puzzled at being asked.

"I hope he's shipped that consignment to the Bahamas, that's all I can say," he said, his voice full of menace.

Peter then got Tony out of bed at the winery back in California. Their manager had not heard from Jean Paul for some weeks. The new vineyards were all doing well, but what was he to do if Gino started asking questions?

"How the hell should I know!" Peter screamed into the mouthpiece.

He was walking, dejected, down the hall, all his instincts telling him there was something seriously wrong, when Allie popped her head round the dining room door.

"We forgot to tell you that there's a letter for you in your room, Uncle Peter," she said.

Why couldn't they have mentioned it before! He hurried upstairs, and there on his dressing table was a thick, white sealed envelope with a P scrawled on the front.

He picked it up and thoughtfully weighed it in his hand before opening it.

On a flimsy piece of paper were written the words: "I am returning home. Jean Paul." And nothing else at all.

The few words created such a terrible pain in him that he felt as if he'd been punched. He thought he must be having a heart attack. He had to sit down heavily on the dressing table chair, gasping. As the pain subsided, he stared at the paper in his hand, and began to sob and cry, his head in his hands.

It had all happened before. The sense of *déjà vu* was overpowering. The memories flooded back, clear as if it had happened yesterday instead of all those years ago. He could see himself reading the note in the attic room that dreadful morning after Rosie had found him in bed with Jean Paul. He could feel again the terrible shock; remember himself at sixteen years old, half-running, half-falling down the ladder

417

in the winery, and rushing to the house to fling the piece of paper down on the breakfast table.

And then Rosie's quavering voice, reading it out loud: "I am returning home."

And then he had sobbed, and his father's contempt had been tangible.

"Guess I'll never make a man of you, son," he had said. "You're the man of this family, Rosie."

It was all so obvious. The man of the family, Rosie, had somehow got rid of Jean Paul. She wanted the inheritance for herself. She had resented Jean Paul and him; hated them from the moment they had arrived. Now, while he had been out of the way, she had done something to Jean Paul. Because it was the same note Jean Paul had written years ago. She had kept it, and copied it. He *knew* it was the same note; the one that had caused him so much distress that a facsimile of it had stayed in his head for twenty years.

Almost hysterical he ran down the hall and stairs and into the dining room.

"What have you done to him?" he screamed, waving the note. "I know, it's the same note. You've done something to him, I know it."

The past hour had probably been the longest in Rosie's life. She had heard the frantic telephone calls and her brother's shouts of anger, but after Allie told him about the letter, the silence had been even more nerve wracking.

She, Madame and Allie had decided to seat themselves at table and wait for him in their usual places. They had told Clovis that he must act naturally, but since there could be no conversation between the two men, Rosie was not worried that her husband might say or do the wrong thing.

A place had been set for Peter, and they waited in silence until his angry footsteps pounded down the stairs, and they heard the hysterical cries of 'What have you done to him?'

And Rosie knew it had all gone wrong.

"Courage!" she whispered – to herself as much as to everyone else.

He burst through the door waving the note. They all stared at him without speaking and he stopped shouting and waited, panting, for an answer. Only Clovis, obeying his instructions, ignored his presence.

Rosie broke the silence.

"What are you talking about, Peter?" she asked calmly.

"This." He flung the note on the table, just as he had once before. "I know it's the same one. I remember it. I've never forgotten it, so you can't fool me. Where is Jean Paul?"

Rosie picked up the flimsy piece of paper, read it, and shook her head.

"I don't understand."

"Oh yes you do. What did you do? Keep the note? You loved him enough to keep the note all those years. Well, I loved him enough to have it engraved on my heart. I didn't need the piece of paper."

Rosie sighed, aware that Allie's expression was one big question mark.

"Hasn't it occurred to you that to write the same words is just the kind of cruel, evil thing that Jean Paul would do?"

"His writing isn't like that any more. Don't lie to me, Rosie. You always wanted him, and because you couldn't have him, and because he took this place away from you, you've done something to him. But you won't get away with it. I'm going to the police."

He turned to slam out of the room, but Rosie drew in her breath as his way was barred by Clovis. The word police must have registered, for Clovis's eyes were bulging in his head.

"Police? No police," he said.

She could see that Peter was instantly terrified. He backed round the table keeping the bigger man at bay, one hand held out to ward him off.

Clovis lurched forward. Peter cringed backwards, but Clovis was not trying to reach him. Bizarrely, her husband thrust his index finger into a silver dish of redcurrant jelly that sat in the centre of the table. He then slashed the finger across his forehead, leaving a thin shiny stain of bright red. And then he advanced on Peter.

"See that?" he hissed as Peter backed until the wall prevented him going further. "That is the mark of Cain. I killed my brother. Like this." He gently put his hands round Peter's throat, and lifted him from the ground. But the hands, Rosie saw, were not squeezing. Peter had shut his eyes and appeared to be praying.

"Your precious, Jean Paul, my evil brother, was trying to seduce my wife." Clovis was explaining in a monotone. "He wanted to tell things that should never be told. He had to die. I killed many men for nothing in the war. I killed him for something. I killed him because he was bad and cruel and wicked and he always was. I am his Nemesis, but Nemesis come too late. Ask Mama to tell you what he did to the children. I could not bring myself to speak of it."

He paused in the tirade and let go of Peter's throat. Coughing, Peter staggered to sit down.

"What is he saying? He's mad! He's dangerous! He should be locked up," he babbled. Clovis took no notice and went on relentlessly with what he had to say.

"But from henceforth," he intoned, staring up at the ceiling, as if he was addressing God, "I shall bear the mark of Cain, and I must be punished. But not by you!" He swung round to point at Peter.

"Vengeance will be my own ..."

The last words were shouted, and, the light gleaming on the red stain on his forehead, Clovis strode from the room in long, measured steps.

"Oh, my God!" Peter was clutching his throat. "He could have killed me. I thought he was going to kill me. What was it all about?"

"He didn't want you to go to the police," Allie said.

"Why not?" Rosie could see that her brother was beginning to think again. "If no one has anything to hide, why shouldn't I go to the police?"

Madame was shaking Rosie's arm and asking what Peter was saying. Rosie rapidly translated. She could see her brother's anger swelling at the interruption.

"Don't talk in that frog language," he shouted. "I want to know what's going on here. What was that business with the jam on his forehead? What was he saying when he half-killed me? Something about Nemesis. He was talking about Jean Paul, wasn't he? It's him! He's killed his brother. That's it, isn't it?"

To tell the truth or not? That was the question. Rosie decided on one last desperate lie.

"No one has killed Jean Paul," Rosie said. "He undoubtedly went because he was afraid."

"Afraid of what?" Peter asked belligerently.

"Afraid for his life."

"And why should he be afraid for his life here?" Peter sneered. She could see his throat was hurting. He took a sip of water from the carafe on the table.

"Because of what he did, long ago."

"What could he have done that would make him afraid for his life?"

She was framing her words, when Allie began to speak.

"Uncle Peter," she said, "please don't go to the police. What good would it do? Anyone round here might have killed him if they had the opportunity, and he must have known it. You see, he did dreadful things to the village children when he was the schoolmaster here. That's why he had to run away to America."

"How did you know that?" Rosie asked, startled.

"Everyone in the village is talking about it. They said they wanted to 'have a word with him', but they wanted to do more than that."

Rosie would have preferred that Allie had not known the old story, but her intervention could not have been more timely or helpful.

"Those children that Jean Paul abused are grown-up now, Peter," she said gently. "And they have not forgotten. Neither have their parents." She came and put her hand on his shoulder as he put his head down on the tablecloth. She stroked him as she turned to Allie and said: "Allie, please go and find your father. Try to calm him if you

420

can and bring him back to the house."

Allie hesitated, her gaze darting from Peter to her mother, then she nodded reluctantly and hurried from the room.

"We must go to the police," Peter said, almost pleadingly. "You don't understand. I love him." His control had run out. He was crying. "I don't care what he did. I have always loved him. Where has he gone? I must follow him."

Watching his distress, Rosie felt her heart contract. He was the little boy lost again, the brother she had protected and loved after their mother's death. She could not bear to see his misery. She moved to sit by him. She took his hand in hers and placed her arm around his shoulders, pulling him close to her so that he could cry on her shoulder. She tried to soothe him and dry his tears, whispering encouragement until he was able to control himself again. Then she handed him a white linen napkin from the table to wipe his face and eyes.

"I must go to the police," he said stubbornly. "What else can I do?"

"Stay here with me and wait and see what happens," Rosie said. "He separated us. Now we have time to learn to be brother and sister again."

He was looking at her, and she hoped that perhaps he, too, was remembering their childhood. He had loved her before Jean Paul had come between them.

But Madam Dupuis, at the sound of the word police, had drawn in her breath with a hiss.

"Tell him that I shall tell the police that they were lovers," she said.

Rosie quickly obliged.

"It's not true," he cried.

"Of course it's true," Rosie said calmly. "Madame may be old, but she is not a fool. We have all heard you creeping along the corridors in the night."

"Even if it were true, it wouldn't change anything," he said defiantly. "I shall go to the police."

Madame Dupuis began to stand threateningly, and he cowered back in his chair, no braver than he had ever been. But the sound of a terrible scream diverted everyone's attention.

As one, Madame and Rosie leapt to their feet, listening. Rosie said: "It's Allie. In the kitchen, come quickly, something dreadful must have happened."

She flung down the napkin she had been holding, and ran for the door, Madame close behind her. They burst into the kitchen to find Allie there, half-fainting, while Cook supported her and fanned her face.

"Oh, Mesdames," Henri said, his face the colour of flour. "It is too horrible. Monsieur Clovis has fallen."

"Fallen? Where?" Rosie said frantically. "Why are we standing here. Why is nothing being done?"

"It's no good, Mama." Allie had begun to sob hysterically. "He fell into the Roman chalk pit. I tried to stop him, but I never could have, he was so far ahead of me, striding up the hillside, not looking back. I called and called but he took no notice. It was as if he was deaf and blind and he just walked on, not running. He wasn't even hurrying. He just went on, straight to where the pit opening is. He took no notice of the fencing, he sort of brushed it aside, and then he plunged through, and he – he was gone. He wasn't there any more. He fell all that way down." She ran from Cook and into her mother's arms. "Please tell me he didn't do it deliberately, Mama. He wouldn't do it deliberately, would he? It was just that he couldn't see, that was all. He just didn't know where he was going. Please, Mama, tell me he didn't do it deliberately."

Rosie rocked her child backwards and forwards in her arms.

"It was a terrible accident, my darling," she said firmly. "A terrible, terrible accident."

And prayed, as she spoke, that it was.

Two of Clovis's field hands brought his broken body up from the white depths of the cave. They carried him back to daylight on a rough stretcher of planks through the tunnels he had built that connected to the cave. It was Cook who laid him out on his own bed, put a pillow under his head, a blanket over his injuries. She then made sure that his eyes were decently shut, and his face wiped clean of the mark of Cain.

Rosie and Madame, themselves in a state of shock, had watched, holding their breath, as Allie knelt by her father. She leaned to kiss him gently on the forehead, and then flung herself across his body, where she sobbed uncontrollably.

Trying not to break down herself, Rosie let her cry for a few minutes, and then gently pulled the girl to her feet. Allie clung to her mother frenziedly.

"Oh, Mama," she said, "he is dead. It is terrible! Wicked. Poor Papa gone. And I loved him so. Death is the cruellest thing of all, Mama. The cruellest thing that can happen. I understand that now. Poor Papa. Poor Mimi. Poor you and me. Oh, and Mama, poor Peter, too. We have all lost someone we love."

Rosie let her cry the healing tears, but as she stood holding her daughter in her arms, she saw Peter standing in the doorway, his face pale.

"He did mean it as the mark of Cain, didn't he?" he said. "He killed Jean Paul."

Chapter Twenty-Nine

Henri, on his own initiative, had called for the doctor, and now there was no argument. The doctor called the police.

Within the half-hour, Les Hérissons was buzzing with official people, asking questions, taking measurements and offering condolences. The gendarme from Chigny reprimanded them for removing the body, but Cook stood, arms akimbo, and asked if he really thought that they were going to leave the poor man in the cold and dark until his lot arrived

The gendarme, a sergeant who knew Cook of old, left it at that and the doctor, after his examination, sighed as he pulled the blanket over Clovis's face.

"He is yet another casualty of the war," he said, his voice sombre. "As much a casualty as if he had died on the field of battle."

He prescribed sedatives for them all, and said he would deal with all the formalities. Now they must get some rest. He insisted that Madame Dupuis, who was dry-eyed with shock, and Allie, still weeping uncontrollably, went to their rooms immediately.

After he had left, the gendarme lingered. Uneasy in his uniform, standing in the drawing room where only Peter and Rosie were left, he seemed to want to say something. He accepted a glass of Marc and the alcohol gave him the courage to speak.

"Madame," he finally said. "Monsieur Jean Paul has returned to Les Hérissons, no?"

"He *had* returned," Rosie told him. "But he left two weeks ago for the United States."

"I see." The sergeant looked relieved. "Are you expecting him to return?"

"No," Rosie said firmly. "Why do you ask?"

"It is nothing really. There has been a complaint laid against him in the village. Something from a long time ago. I am glad that we do not have to proceed and distress Madame Dupuis again." He nodded ponderously. "You are certain that he is not returning?"

"I am certain." But she turned to Peter who was standing looking lost near the window. "Peter," she said in English. "The sergeant would like to know if Jean Paul is returning. There is a matter they wish to discuss with him. I have said that we are not expecting him back. Is that correct?"

She waited, watching him, willing him not to betray her. Time stood still before he replied.

"No," he said, shaking his head. "Jean Paul will not return, ever."

Rosie turned back to the sergeant.

"My brother is Jean Paul's business partner. He says he will not return."

"Probably got wind of the complaint," said the sergeant.

"Yes, it was a nasty business," she said, grimacing.

Again he looked relieved.

"Ah, you knew about it?"

"Yes. I thought it unwise of him to return."

"The complaint would never have stood up after all this time. But poor Madame Dupuis has enough to concern her without that. Poor woman, husband and both sons gone. Life is hard."

And he downed his Marc and left, shouting goodbyes to Henri and shaking his head at life's misfortunes.

Alone with Peter, Rosie turned to him.

"Thank you," she said simply.

"For what?" he said roughly. "He wouldn't have understood what I said. You could have lied. What was it he wanted?"

"Allie was telling you the truth. Jean Paul had to leave all those years ago because he had been abusing the children in his care."

He shrugged his shoulders with a fatalistic calm.

"I'm not surprised. I suppose I was little more than a child. But it was what I wanted. I encouraged him. I've never been interested in women."

"Please don't be hurt," she said, "but I find that so hard to understand."

"So do most people," he said shortly. "That's why it's a difficult way to live. But now I want the truth, Rosie. What happened to Jean Paul? Clovis did kill him, I suppose."

"Yes."

"Why?"

She hesitated. "He was trying to make love to me. Trying to force me. Clovis caught him."

He clenched his jaw tight.

"He was different from me," he said. "He had many women.

Always when I wasn't there. I pretended not to know. I presume you buried him. Where?"

"In the little vineyard, under the vines I brought from California."

He nodded.

"I suppose I'd better go back to California," he said. "Though how we'll sort out this mess ... What am I going to say to Pierre?"

"Will it all belong to his son?" she asked.

He shook his head.

"Only part of it. Years ago I signed fifty per cent of the property over to Jean Paul. I'd have given him the lot to stay then. It was just after Pa died and I was desperate. You'd gone. There was only him. But some instinct of self-preservation told me to make it half. And that's how it remains to this day. I own half the house and half the wine business and a lot of the land. He sold some of the vineyards to Gino, as well as fifty per cent of the wine business. But that's worth nothing now."

"He told me you had signed everything over to him."

He puffed out his breath.

"I suppose he was afraid you'd ask for your half. Pa never left a will."

"He told me Pa had left everything to you because I had run away."

"Oh, God." Peter's voice was despairing. "He was so cunning, so quick, so dishonest. He'd never tell the truth if a lie would do, but I loved him. Now what am I going to do?"

"Stay here," urged Rosie. "There's work for you. You could help Philippe. We need someone who speaks English. Peter, we were close once. Couldn't we be again? It was only Jean Paul who divided us."

He was thinking.

"It's all very well, Rosie," he said. "But the complications are frightening. Where is he supposed to have vanished to? What am I going to tell Pierre? How do we sort out all the legal aspects? It would be better to go to the police."

"And what about the complications of that?" she said. "With Clovis dead, all the old scandals being raked over, this whole household probably being arrested for trying to hush it up. Then what would you tell his son? Better that Jean Paul has disappeared. And besides, half of Les Hérissons will become Pierre's once we can establish that his father is missing, presumed dead."

"You're probably right," Peter said heavily, his eyes filling with tears. "I don't seem to be able to think straight. I suppose none of us can afford any scandal."

The maid had not closed the curtains and he walked across the room and looked out at the soft starlit night outside.

"I shall go back to the States and tell Pierre that his father has disappeared," he said. "I shall give him the impression that Jean Paul offended Gino. Many people who are involved with Gino disappear. Then I shall go back to California and see if I can bear to be in the house without Jean Paul. I shall have to work out what to do with the vineyards we have left. Which, incidentally, are half yours. And then I may come back and take up your offer."

"I wish you would," she said.

"And now I'm going to my room to mourn my dead."

"And I shall do the same," she said quietly.

Dear Philippe,

I have much to tell you, but I cannot tell it on the telephone, or even in this letter. I want us to be completely alone, away from anyone we know. You see, your father was right. We can, at last, be together. But our happiness has come through so much pain for others that I shall find it almost unbearably difficult to recount it all.

If you will send Georges to Thomas Cook's at the Madeleine, he will find that there are two tickets, one for him and one for you, to Cannes. They are booked for the twentieth of June, just a week from today.

I shall be waiting for you at Cannes Station when you arrive, and we shall then send Georges back to Paris. You will not need him. You will have me, as you will have me for ever, if you still want me.

I love you and always will,
Rosie.